Unexpected Entrapment

Alissia Roswell: Book Two

Tianna Holley

Unexpected Entrapment

Copyright © 2014 by Tianna Holley

ISBN 978-0-9894908-2-5

Published by:
Canton Walk Publishing

*There is only one man capable of taming my wild-spirited heart.
He is patient, understanding, and extremely intelligent,
but most importantly, he has never tried to hold me back or
change me. He brings out my best and supports me in everything I do
—no matter how crazy it is.*

*To my dear husband, Daryl: You are my one true love, and I am very
blessed to have you at my side.*

Chapter 1

Alissia Roswell stood on the porch of the cabin and stared at the large group of men before her. She quickly estimated there to be about twenty of them sitting on horses in perfect form. Almost all of them were wearing maroon uniforms trimmed with gold, and they each wore a sword at their side. Some also carried bows and arrows. They were sitting straight in their saddles, at attention. Two men wearing black were at the back of the line, and she guessed them to be the two members of the league.

Her first instinct was to stand tall and stare back at them defiantly, but she immediately remembered what Luke had just told her. She was to act shy and timid, which was the complete opposite of how she felt now—cornered and forced to go somewhere against her will.

If she could not fight her way out of the situation, she should at least be able to get some gratification by causing trouble.

She then noticed Grady and another man in uniform walking towards her, and she quickly looked down, cringing to herself. As her thoughts went to what had just happened in the cabin, blood rushed to her face. Not only had she betrayed Grady by giving in to Luke's advances, but she had also told Luke she did not want him to leave her alone.

"Lady Alissia, this is Captain Bayard. He will be leading your escort today to the castle," Grady said.

She looked up and politely nodded as the captain gave a short bow. "It is an honor to meet you, Lady Alissia. Are you ready to begin the short journey?"

"I am," she answered softly, with a smile.

She followed the captain to a horse in the middle of the group, and then she smiled at the young, uniformed man holding his hands together for her to step onto. Once on the horse, she watched Luke and Grady follow the captain to the front of the procession.

She looked down and closed her eyes as she began to search for Fang with her mind, and she was surprised when she found him frantically pacing near the edge of the tree line. He was confused, panting wildly, and did not know what he should do to protect her. She felt his urge to bellow a long, deep howl, but she immediately began to soothe him.

As her horse began to move, she completely focused on soothing the agitated wolf with her mind, and it was not long before he stopped pacing. She continued to comfort him as he secretly began to follow the group of horses.

After a while, her mind drifted to what all she had learned from Grady and Luke that morning. Her fix-it personality continuously tried to think of a solution to their situation, but her frustration quickly grew strong as she realized there was nothing she could do. She would have to rely upon Grady and Luke, and Grady seemed powerless at this point. Luke would have to find a way for them to get out of the city, but how could he save them all?

She could not help but feel responsible for Grady, Anika, and Langley. If they had never met her and tried to help her, their lives would not be in danger. In a way, this was her fault. They were in Pallen because of her.

Guilt consumed her as she thought over what had happened back at the cabin. Although she had kissed men before, she had never gone further with them, except for the night she had been raped while on what seemed at first like a teenage date. This morning she had passionately kissed two men within the same hour. Although she had heard stories from her friends and had never judged them, her actions went beyond who she was.

She had never really believed in love or getting close to anyone, yet she had been drawn to both Grady and Luke back at the cabin. It frustrated her how she had completely lost herself in Luke's kiss, as if he were an intoxicating drug she was addicted to.

Once she could see the massive gates to the city of Pallen, her focus went back to Fang. Although he was much calmer than before, his fur was still standing straight up on his massive, tense body. She hated what she was about to do. Wolves were pack animals, and he had left the safety of his pack to be with her.

She scanned the area with her mind to check for other wolves and was relieved at the lack of their presence. She had already learned what a pack of wolves would do to a lone wolf found in their territory, and the idea of Fang being killed because of her filled her with fear.

She looked down and closed her eyes again, in an attempt to hide her own emotions.

"Fang, my dear protector, you cannot follow me once I get to the city. I want you to follow the wall of the city, and it will lead you towards the mountains." A sudden thought came to mind, and she added, hopefully, *"I have friends in the mountains, similar to me. If you find them, they will give you rest and shelter until I can meet you there."*

She felt his emotions surge, and she immediately began to soothe him. As the trail left the thick forest, she warned Fang to stop at the tree line. She had to push aside her own feelings of loss, as she commanded with authority, *"Stop, Fang! Follow the wall and go to the mountains."* In an attempt to soothe his pain, she added, *"You are my protector, Fang. Be strong for me."*

The large wolf sat down at the edge of the forest and began to whimper. Once again, she reminded him to be strong, and he sat up tall and proud for her. Although she soon lost her mental connection with him, she knew the wolf's eyes were staring directly at her, and they would continue to do so until she was no longer in sight.

Her group stopped at the gates to the city, and she watched as the captain handed something to one of the guards before they continued. As she passed through the gates, she noticed the same guard handling a bird and guessed he was sending a message to someone at the castle about her arrival. She took a deep breath and tried to calm herself.

Her anxiety grew even more as everyone around them turned to stare at her, the lone woman surrounded by guards traveling through the city. She pulled the hood of her cape lower over her head and was thankful for her dark glasses.

After traveling through the city, they moved along a private path surrounded by bright and bushy evergreen trees. The procession stopped near the edge of the trees, and Alissia heard the captain give orders before the men in front of her moved aside and motioned her forward.

She gave a confused look to the captain, Luke, and Grady as they smiled back at her. She then nudged her horse to move on and soon caught her breath as the castle came into her line of vision.

"Lady Alissia, welcome to your new home," Grady said as she stopped between him and the captain.

Alissia was speechless as she stared out in front of her. Her new home was a massive castle that circled endless gardens filled with gazebos, paths, statues, small ponds, and fountains. The garden alone was big enough that she could get lost in it for days, but the castle itself was something she could see herself never finding her way out of.

The castle was made of stone, and she guessed it to be bella flowers that covered most of the walls, even at the top. She immediately thought of how cold it had to be and wondered how hardy the bella flowers were to survive such frosty weather.

After a moment, Grady asked, "Is it as beautiful as I described?"

An ache caught in her throat as she realized he was putting on a show for the captain. "Yes, you were right. I will love it here," she responded politely.

He grinned and replied, "Welcome to the Eldership, Lady Alissia. I'm sure you will love it here."

So this is how it was to be? Yes, she had known how they would act towards each other while at the Eldership, but she had not anticipated the ache in her heart she would experience by acting so distant towards someone she loved.

As they began to move again, she looked down and thought about how hard this truly had to be for Grady. She knew he had been a wreck while she was missing; yet he had acted professional and personally uncommitted the entire time, even with his own life in danger. A new sense of respect filled her as she realized how strong Grady truly was.

The sound of horses' hooves on stone made her look up, and once again, she found herself in awe of her surroundings. They were now traveling on a stone path surrounded by an arched-canopy, covered in white bella flowers.

She stared at the backs of the three men traveling in front of her. Both Luke and Grady sat straight in their saddles, so unlike the casual way she was used to seeing them.

When she glanced at the soldier riding on her right side, he acknowledged her with a smile, and she looked down at her saddle.

It was not long before the covered path ended, and they were in a clearing near one of the entrances of the castle. They rode around a large, three-tiered fountain before stopping, and the two soldiers that had been riding at each of her sides dismounted. One of the men took the reins from her, while the other lifted her from the horse and set her down.

She then followed Captain Bayard, Grady, and Luke to a group of older men standing on the stairs to the castle entrance. The moment she recognized Alrik Durst as one of the men in the group, she had to look down to gather her emotions. She was thankful for her dark glasses, because she knew her anger would easily show through her glaring eyes.

Grady introduced Alissia to the five assembly members, but she quickly lost track of their names. She did not pay much attention to their polite welcome speeches either. She did, however, study Alrik's every word.

"My dear girl, we have been worried about you, and I am told we can thank Luke for your rescue and safety."

His overly kind tone with the same accent as Luke made her cringe, but she forced a polite smile onto her face and answered, "Yes, I am most grateful to him for bringing me back to Pallen, and I'm sorry to have caused everyone so much worry."

He picked up her hand and hooked it onto one of his arms as he began to lead her up the stairs. "You have nothing to apologize for," he said, patting her hand. "We're all glad you are safe, and everyone is excited to have you here as an ambassador for the Lamians. I do hope you can join my wife and me for dinner once you are settled in. I would love to hear more and want to help you in any way I can. Grady tells us you have suffered some memory loss."

If she had actually had memory loss and did not know he had put a bounty on her, she would have thought he was the kindest man she had ever met. His smile, touch, and voice truly appeared genuine. However, Alissia knew the truth—that he had slithered into Pallen, wrapped his coils around the city, and was constricting it to do his bidding—and she saw him for the foul and evil snake that he was.

At that moment, she was grateful she had been instructed to act shy and timid. She kept her head down as she forced a smile onto her face and answered, "Yes, I have lost a lot of my memories. As for dinner, maybe later." She looked up at him and added, "I am quite weary from all the traveling I've done. Although I am very grateful to Luke for his rescue, he was extremely determined to get me back to Pallen in a timely manner. He woke me before dawn each morning, and we traveled our entire days on horseback. I look forward to a comfortable bed, warmth on my skin, and some real food."

She hoped her words would buy her a few days of solitude.

He stopped walking and took her hand from his arm as he turned to face her. "Of course, you need plenty of rest. I can only imagine how difficult things have been for you." He squeezed her hand and added, "Say no more. I will let the assembly know you need rest. Do you require the service of one of our fine doctors?"

"No, thank you."

"Then I will leave you now in the hands of Odell. She is to be your lady's maid and will show you to your chambers. She will provide you with all your needs, and all you have to do is ask. Remember, this is your home now, and you are safe." He motioned towards the two guards standing off to the side and added, "The assembly has appointed guards to stand watch at all times over you. They will be posted outside your door, and the Eldership guarantees your safety. We will try our best to provide you with anything you require, so please don't be afraid to ask. We all want to help you."

Alissia nodded as he let go of her hand, and then she turned to face the long, grey-haired woman. Odell bowed her head politely, and the sound of Alrik's footsteps as he walked away helped to ease some of the tension Alissia had felt during his presence.

"Lady Alissia, it is an honor to meet you and be in your service. Shall I take you to your chambers now?"

"Yes, please."

Alissia followed the woman through the massive doors of the castle and stepped into a large foyer with a high, floral-painted ceiling. Bright sunlight came down from the large windows situated above the entrance doors. Thick, burgundy curtains hung down at each side of the windows, and a beautiful, enormous chandelier with polished glow stones hung in the center of the room. The floor was shiny and resembled white marble and had variously-colored glow stones assembled in place like tiles. The glow stones were arranged so that their natural light made an intricate floral pattern. Each of the walls held paintings and was decorated with detailed carvings. Large, handcrafted chairs, benches, and tables were positioned throughout the room with fresh flowers situated in various places.

Alissia did not realize she had stopped following Odell until the woman got her attention by saying, "It's amazing, isn't it?"

"Very," Alissia answered, in awe.

"Although the castle was originally built well over a thousand years ago, it is always under reconstruction, but the Eldership tries to keep things as they were."

Alissia nodded and started walking, but as soon as they went through another door, she became distracted again. Every room and hallway they entered while on the way to her chambers was filled with intricate designs and amazing art like nothing she had ever seen before.

Although she knew Pallen was a place known for its art and had seen a lot while walking through the city, nothing had compared to what she now saw in the castle. She imagined someone could spend years in the massive, city-like structure and still find new and amazing things to look at every day.

As they took an elegant elevator up to the third floor, she silently wondered what was the source of its power without electricity. In the end, she gave up on her curious thoughts and reminded herself she did not think like an engineer. She was sure she would still not understand, even if someone texplained it to her, but this was a feeling she had grown quite accustomed to since being torn from her reality and dropped into this one.

Chapter 2

"Oh, my goodness, Alissia! You're here."

Alissia had barely stepped out of the elevator before she found herself in a tight embrace with her arms stuck by her sides. She heard Anika's sob before she felt the tears hit the side of her face, and she closed her eyes and smiled.

"Anika, I think you're smothering me. I can't breathe," she said teasingly.

Anika released her and began to wipe the tears from her eyes while gathering herself. She grinned and said, "We didn't know if you were dead or alive. I thought I'd never see you again, and now you're here." Her voice cracked as she added, "Oh, Alissia, I've missed you!"

Anika took her by the hand and tugged for her to follow. "Let's go to your rooms, and we can spend the rest of the day together. You're going to love your rooms. I helped prepare them for you, and you're going to be very surprised."

Alissia could not help but smile at Anika's temporary excitement. Even as she reminded herself of how bad the situation truly was, she told herself she would not think about it today. Instead, she would make her friend happy. Grady had said Anika had been miserable, and Alissia had the power to bring a smile to her face. Today, that was what was important.

The two women and guards followed Odell along various hallways lit by sculptured sconces that held removable glow stones. Just as Alissia began to think she would never be able to find her way back to the elevator, they arrived at a set of thick, wooden doors covered in detailed carvings. The trim that surrounded the doors held even more detail, and two guards stood at the side of each door.

Once they saw Alissia, the guards opened the doors and silently watched as she and Anika followed Odell through the doors.

Alissia did not notice the doors close behind her. She was too busy staring in amazement at her surroundings. Surely, this was not to be considered her rooms.

Anika laughed and began to give Alissia a detailed tour of her new living quarters. Her suite consisted of a large, main room with a crème-colored sofa and two chairs off to the right of the room. They were placed in front of a stone fireplace set into the wall. A large, marble table with claw feet was situated in the center of the room, holding a fresh-floral arrangement.

A small bathroom with only a toilet and sink was in the left corner of the room, with a beautiful, elegant mirror on the wall. Matching glow-stone sconces gave out enough light for the small bathroom.

In the back, left corner of the main room was a round dining table with four chairs, made of heavy, dark wood and trimmed in detailed, floral carvings. A door on the right wall of the room led into the bedroom, and Alissia stood in wonder at the massive canopy bed with pink bella flowers wrapped around the large, four-poster beams. A pink curtain made of a thin, shimmery material surrounded each side of the bed and covered the top. Pink bella flowers were arranged on top of the bed, and they sparkled through the sheer material.

Alissia touched the thick, pink bedding and could not help but smile at the thought of sleeping in such a soft bed that night. Anika delighted in the look on Alissia's face and grabbed her by the hand to continue the tour.

The fireplace in the main room was double sided and added warmth to the bedroom. A large bookcase covered a portion of the wall, and it was filled with books that looked enticing to Alissia.

A matching pink curtain made of a thick, velvety material separated the sleeping area from the bathroom, and Alissia gasped when Odell pulled back the curtain to reveal the bathing pool surrounded by stones and more pink bella flowers.

A door in the sleeping area led into a walk-in closet with more drawers and compartments than Alissia thought a person could ever use for clothing and jewelry. A large crème-colored ottoman was placed in front of a hand-carved, standing mirror, and although Anika had brought Alissia's clothes from the townhouse, the closet still looked bare.

The entire suite was filled with fresh flowers and scented candles, which added a pleasant fragrance to the old castle chambers.

"What do you think?" asked Anika, excitedly.

"Wow!"

Anika laughed and gave Alissia another hug before saying, "Oh, I've missed you so much. I knew you'd love this, but I've saved the best for last." She gave a mysterious smile before adding, "I'll show you after everyone leaves, and we're alone."

Alissia followed Anika's gaze and realized Odell and three other women were watching her. The older woman stepped forward and said, "My Lady, I should introduce you to your chambermaids and handmaid."

Although Alissia wondered why she needed so many maids, she smiled and nodded politely before Odell motioned towards two women and said, "This is Belinda and Ima, your two chambermaids. They will be responsible for all the housekeeping in your rooms, so please don't be alarmed by their occasional presence."

The two women stepped forward and bowed politely before stepping back into their original positions. Odell then motioned towards a younger woman, looking to be in her twenties. She wore her dark-brown hair in a simple braid down her back and had a pleasant smile on her face.

"And this is Nadia. She is to be your handmaiden and will assist you with everything you need. If you want or need anything at all, be sure to let her know, and she will take care of it. In fact, she will be delivering your meal shortly." Odell turned to Anika and asked, "Miss Anika, will you be joining Lady Alissia for lunch?"

Alissia could not help but wonder why she was a lady and Anika was a miss, and she made a mental note to add it to the list of things to ask Anika once they were alone.

"Yes, I will be joining Lady Alissia for most of the day."

"Very well. Would you prefer the same meal that has been prepared for Lady Alissia, or would you prefer something with meat?"

"I have already made arrangements with Nadia. Thank you."

The older woman turned her attention back to Alissia and said, "Do you have any questions for me?"

Alissia shook her head, and Odell said, "Then I shall leave you to get some rest. If you should find any of your arrangements unsatisfactory, please ask for me, and I will see to it that all is resolved."

The four women walked out of the bedroom, and as soon as Alissia heard the door to the main entrance close, Anika ran to the bedroom door and looked out.

"We're finally alone! I've got so much to tell you, and I want to hear everything." She grinned slyly and added, "But first, I have a surprise I know you'll love."

Alissia followed Anika out of the bedroom to a set of French doors at the back of the main room. As Anika put her hands on the handles of both doors, she turned back around and asked, "Ready?"

Alissia laughed at Anika's excitement, and she nodded.

Once the doors opened, Alissia stared out in front of her in disbelief. Anika waited patiently for a moment before walking through the doors and flopping down onto a chaise covered in pillows and a blanket.

"Well, what do you think?"

The large veranda they stood on held a crème-colored chaise and sofa, both of which were covered in pink, floral pillows. A stone table was centered in front of them with a large, glowing heat stone on top of it. Light-blue bella flowers covered the ceiling, walls, and iron railing that surrounded the outside edge of the partially enclosed veranda.

Alissia walked to the railing and looked over the edge before backing away in surprise at how high she was from the ground. She sat down on the sofa and looked at Anika.

"Is this what your rooms look like?"

Anika frowned playfully and answered, "No, we don't get the special treatment. You're Lady Alissia, remember?"

"Yeah, and why am I a lady but you're a miss? What's the difference?"

"Only the elders and assembly members are called lords, and their wives are called ladies. You're considered an ambassador of the Lamians, and it's the Eldership's way of saying you hold power, even though you're not an elder."

"Yeah, if I'm so powerful, how come I'm forced to be here?" Then a thought came to mind, and Alissia asked, cautiously, "Can anyone hear us or be recording us?"

"No, we're safe."

"Are you sure?"

"Alissia, we don't have anything like that in our reality."

"Then how come Watchers were able to record me from my reality?"

"That's completely different and consumes a lot of power from a jade. We're safe. I promise. So tell me what happened to you. You do realize you didn't even say goodbye."

The playful jab felt like a knockout punch, and Alissia paused before responding, "I'm sorry." The words sounded unemotional, even to her, and she silently chided herself for not knowing how to be softer. She stammered as she tried again with more meaning, "Anika, I'm really sorry. I had no idea Grady had been set up. They made it look like he was using me. When I walked in and saw him with that woman, I freaked out and ran. I hate myself for it, and I was wrong."

She wished she could show more emotion. Anika deserved it, but she did not know how. Gentleness and true emotions were not something she knew how to give, even if she wanted to. She had killed that part of herself years ago as a child, and it was too foreign to her. She hoped Anika could see through her emotionless tone and realize she meant every word she said.

Her friend said, "I want to hear everything that happened and don't leave anything out."

Alissia found relief in the change of subject and began to relax in her seat. She pulled off her headscarf and tossed it to the other side of the sofa. As she was taking off her boots, Anika asked curiously, "Did the Eldership buy you new clothes already?"

Alissia cringed as she turned the mouth of her boots towards the sofa and covered them with the edge of a blanket, concealing the knives Luke had given her. As she pulled the blanket over her body, she told herself she would have to find a suitable hiding place for them.

Once settled, she grinned at Anika and tried to change the subject so she would not have to talk about Luke buying her new clothing. "I don't think I ever want to ride a horse again. I am *so* tired of traveling."

Anika did not seem to notice the unanswered question and said, "Well, you look great. I see nothing else . . . has . . . uh . . . changed."

"Thank heavens for that!" Alissia replied. "Although I guess having your hair, eyes, and nails turn purple is not something to be thankful for."

"Alissia, after being sucked into another reality, spat out half-dead, and revived by an apparently ancient race—who were thought to be pure mythology until now, I might add—it seems you have much to be thankful for."

Alissia spent the next few hours telling Anika most of what had happened on her journey. They were served lunch on the veranda, and Alissia greatly enjoyed a large, hot meal. She indulged in a warm dessert and told her handmaid she never wanted to see cheese, nuts, dried fruit, murdock root, or any other traveling food again.

Anika and Alissia both laughed hard when Alissia described the night she had distracted Luke by screaming over a small animal. However, Anika spent most of the afternoon with a look of disbelief on her face as Alissia recounted what all had happened.

When Alissia told about the death of her two attackers, she remained unemotional, and she shrugged off her friend's attempt at comforting her.

She did not mention having nightmares since the two men's death, and when she got to the last part of the journey where she found herself in the cabin with Luke, she stopped. Although she did not want to go into much detail about what all had happened between them, she thought it would be wrong to hide the truth from Anika.

Somewhat hesitantly, she finished with, "Luke and I kissed a few times when we got back to the cabin."

Anika shook her head in disbelief.

"No. No. No. Alissia, you can't do that to Grady."

Alissia responded by biting on her lower lip.

Anika continued with, "He loves you. I've never seen him like this with anyone, and he'll do anything for you. You know that, right?"

Alissia's chest tightened, and she felt herself swallow.

"I know, and I told him what happened, too. I didn't lie, and I won't lie to him, Anika."

"Do you love him?"

Alissia wanted to run from the question.

"You mean Grady?"

"Yes, Alissia. Do you love him?"

"I've never told him I loved him."

"So you don't?" Anika asked, somewhat accusingly.

"I didn't say that. Anika, I've never said those words to anyone before." She thought for a moment before adding, "Yes, I love him, but right now we can't focus on any of that. We have to find a way out of here, and from what I've been told, I have to stay away from him for his own safety. It's too complicated right now."

"Alissia, when you disappeared, it devastated my cousin. He didn't know if you were dead or alive, and . . ." Anika let out a shaky breath. Her voice was thick with emotion when she continued. "He had to act brave and go to the Eldership in Pallen. Then he realized the Eldership here is corrupt, and all our lives are in danger. He's doing everything he can to save us, yet he's never been this powerless." A tear rolled down her cheek as she added, "He needs you, Alissia, not physically, but he needs to know you're there for him emotionally. That's what's keeping him together. He's holding onto you."

Alissia felt the heat rise within her body as she struggled to appear calm in front of Anika. She had already known all that her friend was telling her, and she had already been full of guilt for all the pain she had caused Grady. The last thing she wanted to do was hurt him, Anika, or Langley even more.

At that moment, Nadia opened the doors and walked onto the veranda, giving Alissia an escape from the conversation.

"Excuse me, Lady Alissia, but I thought I should let you know you have received some gifts and should probably expect more."

Alissia looked at Anika questioningly, and they both got to their feet. She made sure her boots were still covered before following the two women into the main room.

Chapter 3

lissia spent the rest of the afternoon opening extravagant gifts and writing thank you cards with the help of Anika. Some of the gifts included luxurious oils, expensive jewelry, and even beautiful sunglasses carved out of rare materials. Her favorite, however, was a music box with a large variety of crystals that had recorded music on each of them.

She was glad to hear that all guests were being turned away, and her handmaiden could only deliver the gifts. At Alrik's request, the Eldership had promised her a week of rest before meeting anyone or making any public appearances. As she was finding out, however, nothing was as it seemed when it came to Alrik Durst. This could just be the first of countless gestures, which on the surface seemed kind, but essentially, fit into his selfish, seditious plans. She clenched her jaw at the thought of being manipulated and pushed it from her mind.

The gifts were expensive tokens of friendship from people within the Eldership. Anika explained everyone would want to befriend her now that she was in a high position, even those who had tried to intimidate her at the ball.

The idea of everyone wanting to be near her because of who she was did not please Alissia. She had never been one to care about being popular, or even about what people thought of her. Just the thought of having to be polite to such shallow women disgusted her. She knew she would have a problem acting the part of a shy, little Lamian around them.

Langley joined them that evening, and she enjoyed the bear hug he gave her. They had dinner at the table in her main room. Unlike Anika, he kept the conversation light and did not talk about her relationship with Grady or ask about Luke. He listened to her stories of adventure and teased her on occasion.

Alissia greatly enjoyed the food and their company, and she spent the evening laughing. After her friends left, she watched as Nadia oversaw the nightly duties of her chambers. Fresh glow and heat stones were brought in by two men to replace the used ones, and her fireplace was given extra wood.

Once finished, Alissia dismissed Nadia and told her she did not want to be bothered until late morning. She wanted to sleep in.

When she was finally alone, Alissia searched her chambers for places to hide her knives before settling down for the night. It took a while, but she finally decided upon wedging the knives in various stones around her bath. She did not trust that her room would not be searched, and she had to be certain they were in a secure location.

She then picked out a book titled *Her Heart's Betrayal* to read before covering most of the glow stones in her bedroom. After crawling into bed, she sprawled across it and smiled to herself at how soft and comfortable it was.

It had been a long day, and the events of that morning seemed as if they had happened on another day. Thoughts of Grady saddened her as she remembered all that Anika had said. Alissia had nearly broken him, yet he loved her more than anyone ever had, even Luke. Grady was committed to her and ready to give up everything for her. Now he was even in danger because of her. Her feelings for Luke were wrong, and she should never have kissed him.

Yet, when Luke came to mind, excitement filled her, and she could not stop thinking about the way he kissed her. Unlike Grady, something within his eyes demanded a response from her. Not only his eyes, she remembered how he had gotten her to reveal she did not want him to stop pursuing her. Instead of pushing him away, she had basically told him she wanted him.

She closed her eyes and groaned at her lack of self-control with Luke. Not only did he now consider her as his, something within her had been thrilled when he had claimed her.

And what did he really mean when he had said she would be his one day? Did he mean sexually, or did he mean his woman to control all the time? During their travels, he spent most of his time telling her what to do.

Grady treated her as his equal, yet Luke tried to dominate her. The logical response would be for her to choose Grady; however, there was nothing logical, except for the physical attraction, when it came to Luke. They would never work, and their future would be filled with fighting.

In the end, she decided it was foolish to think about a future with either one of them while they were trapped at the Eldership. She would not allow herself to ponder over things that would probably never even come true. She would rather have no dreams at all than live her life yearning for something that would never happen.

She needed to stop thinking about love and men, which were foolish thoughts in the first place, and start thinking about Alrik Durst and the Eldership. She had bought herself a week of rest and solitude, and she planned to enjoy it before having to make an appearance in front of everyone. Some of the gifts she had received also had invitations to private dinners, and Anika made it sound as if Alissia was the most popular person in the castle. Everyone wanted her attention, and she would soon have to be social.

Alissia picked up the book next to her and began to read, and it did not take long before her surroundings lulled her into a peaceful sleep. Although she felt well rested when she woke the next morning, she stayed in bed, not wanting to get up.

Once she did crawl out of the bed, she chose to stay in her pajamas when she walked into the main room. She found her breakfast on a warming tray near the freshly kindled fireplace, and she put on a pair of serving gloves before picking up the hot tray and carrying it to the table.

After savoring the large breakfast, she opened the latest gifts she had received, and then she took a bath and put on some clean clothes she found in the closet.

She was tempted to spend the day reading out on the veranda, but she knew Anika was waiting for her. Although she highly enjoyed her friend's company, she worried their conversation would turn to Grady again. She did not want to think about either Luke or Grady and only wanted to focus on her current situation.

It did not help that she continuously had to force herself to stop thinking about what had happened yesterday morning. Her body had enjoyed Luke's touch more than she wanted to admit, and she still found herself excited by the memories of his lips on her neck.

She needed a distraction, and she needed Anika to be that distraction. With that thought, she went to the thick, pink chord hanging down by her bed and pulled on it. Shortly thereafter, Nadia entered her chambers with a smile.

"Good morning, Nadia. Could you please let Anika know I'm awake?"

"Yes, Madam. She has come to visit more than once this morning and will be pleased to see you."

Alissia could not help but smile as she imagined her friend's frustration at her for sleeping in, and when Anika arrived, she laughed at her verbal complaints.

They spent another day relaxing in the privacy of her chambers. Each time Grady's name was mentioned, Alissia would remind her friend that she needed to stay focused on their current situation.

She received more gifts and invitations, and Anika helped her write the thank you notes. Langley joined them for dinner that evening, and Alissia went to bed smiling that night.

This routine continued the following day, but on the third day, she received an unexpected visitor. Alissia and Anika were resting outside on the veranda when Nadia came to them. A young, black woman with beautiful natural curls held back by a sparkling headband was with her. The young woman wore a long, somewhat fitted dress with bangle bracelets on both arms and dangling earrings hanging down from her ears. Nadia introduced her as Mela, a clothing designer.

There was a hint of excitement in Mela's voice when she talked. "Hello, Lady Alissia. The Eldership has sent me here to consult with you on the design of your wardrobe. I brought many sketches and fabric samples for you to look at so I can get an idea of what you prefer."

Alissia tried not to look confused as she turned her attention to Anika, who was now staring at her with a large grin across her face. Alissia's confusion quickly turned into a laugh as she remembered how much Anika loved shopping for new clothing.

They followed Mela into the main room and watched as she pulled out her sketches and fabric samples from a large, rolling suitcase. As the woman set everything on the dining table, Alissia noticed Nadia's interest and asked her to join them.

In the end, the four women sat around the table looking at sketches and rubbing their fingers against various fabric samples.

The first thing Alissia noticed about the styles being presented was that the women at the Eldership loved to wear dresses that were long and sleek. Alissia planned to wear as many knives on her body as possible, even if it only meant one. That meant she would need to wear dresses with a lot of layering to hide them.

As the other women sat and talked about the possibilities and colors that would best work for her, she began to get an idea. Her rebellious spirit eventually turned her small idea into a full act of subtle rebellion.

If the people at the Eldership wanted a Lamian, she would give them a Lamian, hair and clothing. She began to think of pixies and fairies and what she had seen of them in pictures, and she smiled to herself. She was petite and could pull the look off perfectly.

She cleared her throat to get the women's attention before saying, "I don't really like how long and constricting these look, and I have a different idea in mind. Is that all right?"

All the women looked surprised, and Mela responded, "Yes, My Lady. It would be an honor to make anything you desire. That is why I am here. If you tell me what it is you would have me design, I will begin immediately."

Describing what was in her head was much harder than Alissia had expected. It would have been so much easier if she could just say the word "pixie," but that would have gotten her nowhere with the women. Luckily, Mela was talented with drawing detailed sketches as she listened, and it did not take long before Alissia was pleased with what she saw.

Once they were finished, Mela had a stack of sketches and was eager to get started on the work. Alissia told her she wanted to practice sewing and would like some materials of her own. Her plan was to make straps to hold the knives, but she feared that asking for leather would be too obvious.

The next day the Eldership sent over a hair stylist to trim Alissia's hair. That evening a private masseuse came, and Alissia made sure her stomach would not be touched or seen. It was one thing to cover the small scar—a memento of her father's abuse—with a carefully placed tattoo by her navel. However, the handprints on either side of her stomach—marks left by a being that could apparently use his or her hands as a defibrillator—were providing more difficult.

Although she greatly enjoyed her first week at the castle, Alissia was abruptly brought back to reality on the seventh day. Nadia came to her chambers to discuss her schedule, and Alissia knew everything was about to change. The time had come for her to leave her rooms and make public appearances. The first thing on the list was a meeting with the assembly. Although she had met each of them at the stairs of the castle, this was to be an official meeting.

That evening as she, Anika, and Langley dined privately in her suite, they discussed what all she was to say. Langley had talked to Grady, and even Luke had found a reason to go to the stables that week.

Langley said, "The assembly will want to know everything about you. You need to tell them you don't remember anything before waking up alone outside of Auntaire. That's a small village south of Allure. You had a little money on you, but you didn't remember your name or anything else. You were found by an old merchant couple on their way to Allure. Their names were Hoyt and Larsina. You don't remember their last names.

"After many days of travel, you all made it to Allure, and Hoyt found Grady and told him about you. When Grady met you, you were scared and confused, and the only name you could remember was Pallen. He wanted to take you to the Eldership in Allure, but you were too frightened and refused to go. In the end, you agreed to going to his cousin's cottage outside the city."

Langley added firmly, "Alissia, Grady has told the assembly you were very frightened and fragile when he met you. You were greatly confused. Anika felt sorry for you and talked him and me into taking you to Pallen in search of answers."

He paused and Alissia nodded in understanding before he continued. "As for Luke's story, he was traveling home when he noticed you with two men at an inn. He immediately recognized you from the ball, and he noticed how scared you seemed. In the end, he killed both men in front of you, and you spent most of the journey back to Pallen scared of him. The men's names were Nolan and Slade. Luke gave the Eldership their identity cards as proof of their death, and he told the Eldership you refused to talk about what happened during your kidnapping. Asking you about it only makes you upset."

Langley paused before asking, "Any questions?"

Alissia frowned and responded in frustration, "So I'm supposed to pretend I don't remember anything, I'm scared, confused, and fragile?"

"Yes," responded Anika and Langley, simultaneously.

Anika added, "Alissia, it's the only way."

Alissia gave a reassuring smile and replied, "I can act like a fragile Lamian." Deep down she knew how hard that truly would be. There had been nothing fragile about her since childhood. Everything within her screamed strong and defiant. She swore she would never be a victim again, and now she had to act scared and weak.

She reminded herself that the lives of her friends and Grady and Luke, whatever they were, depended on it. She would do this for them, no matter what her pride demanded of her.

"There's also another thing," Langley said. "Morton is the Eldership's representative from Allure. Grady said that although Morton has remained somewhat passive about Alrik's illegal interactions with the assembly, he is furious over being left out of meeting you upon your arrival.

"Grady says that Morton has told him he will not allow Alrik to use you against Allure. It is his belief that you belong at the Eldership in Allure, and since you have arrived at the castle, he has become more vocal with the assembly."

"Won't that get him into trouble?" Alissia asked. "I thought Grady and Luke agreed Grady needed to remain in the background and not cause trouble for Alrik and the assembly, at least for now."

Langley nodded. "Exactly. Grady has warned Morton that the assembly is corrupt and controlled by Alrik. Just because Morton has the power on paper, doesn't mean they are abiding by the laws. However, I think Morton's anger and pride are starting to get in the way. I've warned Grady that he needs to distance himself from Morton before the assembly starts to think he's causing trouble."

"Will he listen?" Alissia asked.

Anika answered, "He's not senseless, and he knows how to control his temper, unlike Morton. Grady knows how to get things done subtly, and I think he'll try to avoid trouble, especially with Langley and me here. He feels responsible for us, along with you. Morton can be arrogant at times, and that's not a problem for Grady."

"There's already some strife between Grady and Morton," Langley added. "He's not happy with Grady for bringing you to Pallen when he should have taken you to the Elders the moment he met you."

A troubling thought entered Alissia's mind. "Will he be in trouble with the Elders if he ever returns to Allure?"

Anika gave her a firm look and said, "He defied the Eldership in Allure the moment he lied to them and traveled with you to Pallen."

Although she and Grady had had more than one conversation about his future within the Eldership, that had been when he was set on having a future with her. It had also been when no one had known about her.

Now, she was not certain about their future, and the Elders would eventually learn about Grady's actions.

Alissia ended her night in a restless sleep, knowing she had possibly ruined the one thing Grady had spent his entire life working for, becoming an Elder himself.

Chapter 4

Nadia woke Alissia up the next morning, and shortly after breakfast and getting dressed, Mela stopped by with two finished dresses. She was filled with excitement over the work her people had done on the new designs, and Alissia was more than pleased by the quality of the work.

Mela and Nadia were eager to see them on her, and Alissia was glad to have something new to wear for the meeting with the assembly. One was sleeveless, long, and black with streaks of purple that matched her hair. It was fitted at the waist and hung down to her feet in shimmery layers.

The other dress was sleeveless and fitted at the top. It was a deep blue color, and it hung down in layers a few inches past her knees. Purple, silk-like flowers were woven into it.

Both dresses had matching arm warmers with a hole for her thumbs, and both dresses could easily conceal a few daggers if she had the proper sheaths. Mela had even thought to bring two pair of sunglasses made of fine ivory and tortoise shell. She had also brought matching jewelry, and Alissia could not help but wonder how much each outfit was costing the Eldership.

The effect of the dresses was exactly what Alissia wanted. As she tried on the second dress, she stared at her reflection in the mirror and could not help but compare herself to a magical being from a Hollywood movie.

The black dress gave her an edgy and rebellious look, and she chose it for the meeting. She was already nervous and filled with anxiety. The dress helped to ease her nerves, and it helped with her confidence. Surely, none of her friends expected her to go into battle, which is what this meeting felt like, without something to ease her nerves.

Mela stayed and watched as Nadia pulled Alissia's hair into a beautiful up-do before adding shimmer powder to it. The handmaiden then applied subtle makeup to Alissia's face, and Alissia learned it was Nadia's duty to get her ready each day. She had to be a master with hair just to be considered a handmaiden within the Eldership.

Once finished, Alissia stood in front of the mirror in amazement at herself. She wished she had a camera to capture her new look. If she were in her reality, she would be considered beautiful and magical, especially with her purple eyes. However, in this reality, Alissia did not know if people would think of her as beautiful or freaky. She was definitely different, although Mela and Nadia both assured her they loved the new style.

She refused the shoes Mela had brought with her and went for her new riding boots instead. They were hidden by the long dress, but if she did pull up the dress, it gave her an edgy look that made her smile.

She gave the excuse of having to relieve herself so the women would leave the room. She then retrieved two knives and hid them in her boots. She took one last look at herself in the mirror and took a deep breath.

Two guards accompanied her and Nadia as they walked to the meeting, and everyone they passed along the way stared at her. She noticed a lot of hushed conversations, and the attention made her even more uncomfortable. She instinctively lifted her head and set her jaw defiantly. She then remembered she was supposed to appear shy and meek, and she immediately directed her eyes towards the ground.

During the rest of the walk, she continuously reminded herself to be timid, which turned out to be a fierce internal struggle. However, once she saw the closed doors of the meeting room, she no longer had to keep reminding herself. She began to feel lightheaded, and she had to clasp her hands together in an attempt to hide their shaking.

She only had a short wait before she was called into the meeting room. The assembly members and Alrik Durst were seated along one side of a long, elegant table made of thick wood. A man she did not recognize was seated in the middle, while Luke and Grady were seated on the opposite side. All the men in the room stood to their feet when Alissia walked in.

Unexpected emotions filled her as she saw Luke and Grady standing in front of her, and she quickly reminded herself to remain focused on the meeting.

Although all the men were smiling at her, Luke's dark, penetrating eyes caught her attention, and she had to look down for a moment. Alrik made his way across the room and politely took her by the hand. "Lady Alissia, you look very lovely, as usual. I take it you've had a pleasant and restful week?"

She noticed his eyes scanning her outfit, and it was at that very moment she remembered her choice in clothing was exactly the opposite of what Luke and Grady had told her to do. Instead of trying to blend, her whimsical clothing set her apart. It had been a bold thing to do, and she was not supposed to be acting bold.

Although she had known that from the moment she had made the choice to design her own clothing, she had reassured herself that no one would notice it as an act of rebellion. However, standing in a room full of older, royal men, she now began to second guess that decision.

Forcing those thoughts aside, she answered, "Yes, thank you."

"Good. We've all been worried about you. I'm sorry you've had to go through so much over the past few months. I do hope you can find peace and refuge here within the Eldership."

The man she did not recognize stepped up and said, "Lady Alissia, my name is Morton Gelling, and I am from the Eldership in Allure. I apologize that I was not able to meet you on the day of your arrival, as there was a miscommunication.

"I believe Grady has informed you that our main offices are in Allure, and that is where our true power lies within this land. I do hope you will consider traveling there this spring to meet our Elders."

Alissia was momentarily caught off guard, and she gave a silent nod.

Alrik cleared his throat before he pulled out a chair and motioned for her to sit down. As she went to sit down, she deliberately lifted her dress slightly and was rewarded with knowing Luke had gotten a quick glimpse of the boots she was wearing. As their eyes met for an instant, she mentally smiled, thinking he would be pleased she had chosen to wear them.

Alrik pushed her chair forward before walking back to his seat. Luke and Grady sat down on each side of her, and as everyone else in the room sat down, she glanced over her shoulder and realized there were no guards in the room. This conversation would be completely private.

She placed her hands in her lap and stared back at the two men sitting across from her. Although she was certain it was proper procedure for Morton to be seated directly in front of her, she was also certain it was not proper procedure for Alrik to be sitting beside him. He was not even supposed to be in the room.

Morton placed his hands on the table and clasped them together, and Alissia immediately began to wonder if he was using one of her subtle tricks to conceal anxiety. His tight grip assured her that he was.

In an assertive voice, he said, "Lady Alissia, Grady and Luke have told us a lot about you, but we would now like to hear what you have to say. Could you please tell us all that has happened to you within the past year? How did you meet Mr. Bolair?"

Alissia cleared her throat nervously. She then reminded herself not to feign confidence, as was her first instinct. She looked down at her fingertips and allowed herself to sound small and fragile as she said, "I don't remember much before meeting him. It seems I have somehow lost my memories, and I was blessed to have been found by a very nice couple on their way to Allure. The man found Grady and told me he would help me."

She looked up and continued, "Grady tried to talk me into going to the Eldership when we first met, but I was too scared and thought that I would find answers in Pallen. Luckily, Anika was able to talk him and Langley into bringing me to Pallen, but after searching, we didn't find anything in the library."

"What were you searching for in the library?" asked Alrik.

Alissia noticed Morton's jaw twitch before she answered, "I was hoping it would give some answers as to who or what I am."

"What do you mean, what you are?" asked Morton.

"I . . . um . . . don't exactly fit in with the rest of the people around me. I'm somewhat different."

Alrik asked, "How are you different, Lady Alissia?"

Crap! How am I going to answer this one? she thought. She felt Grady's leg rub against hers reassuringly, and she answered, "I don't look like anyone else, and my eyes hurt in sunlight. I also found that I get sick if I eat meat."

"Any other differences?" Alrik asked.

Alissia searched her mind for anything else they may know about her before replying, "No, I don't believe so."

"Could you tell us what happened the night you were kidnapped?" asked Morton.

Luke's boot struck hers lightly, and out of the corner of her eye, she could see him playing with a coin in his hands, as if he had not a care in the world.

She looked down for a moment before answering, "I don't want to talk about it." She then cleared her throat as she looked back up and added, with a shake of her head, "I don't ever want to talk about those two men, and although I'm very grateful to Luke for rescuing me and bringing me back, I don't want to think about any of it. They weren't very kind, and I hope you can understand. I'm sorry."

Alrik said in a voice filled with both reassurance and authority, "No need to apologize, Lady Alissia. You should not ever have to ponder such things again. What matters is you are safe, and you can trust the Eldership here in Pallen to take care of you. Nothing will happen to you again, and I've been told by the assembly you are welcome to live in this castle as an ambassador for your people for the rest of your life. You are guaranteed the protection of the Eldership in Pallen."

Morton abruptly added, "However, the true power of the Eldership lies within the city of Allure, Lady Alissia, and the Elders are the ones that can truly guarantee your safety, as they hold higher authority and rank than the assembly here in Pallen. That is why I urge you to consider going back to Allure."

Alissia glanced around the room to consider everyone's reaction to Morton's words. While two of the assembly members seemed to be staring ahead, deep in thought, she could see hostility in the eyes of the other three.

Alrik leaned back in his chair and gave Morton a calculating stare.

She decided against risking a glance at the two men sitting next to her. Desperate to end the thick silence in the room, she stammered,

"I . . . um . . . am grateful to the Eldership, but how will I be able to repay such kindness?"

Alrik coolly replied, "My dear, no need to worry about repaying the Eldership. That is what we are here for. We are here to serve, and it would be an honor if you would allow us to serve you. You have a home here in Pallen, and I hope it is pleasing to you. Do you like your accommodations, or is there anything else we can do for you?"

Hoping to end the uncomfortable conversation, she said, "No, nothing else. I am more than pleased with all you have given me." She was about to add she was in their debt but stopped herself before going that far.

"Then we are done here." Turning his attention to Luke, Morton added, "Luke, how soon before you leave?"

"As soon as I can get the clearance. I believe Reece and Jerrell can take my place here," Luke answered, leaning back in his chair.

"We've heard you have a reason to return home," replied one of the assembly members.

Luke grinned and said, "I see my men love to talk."

The man chuckled before replying, "She must be special to get your attention. Congratulations, and I wish you the best."

Luke nodded his head. "Thank you, but nothing is ever certain."

The man laughed as he said stood to his feet, "Always in doubt, Luke?"

All the men got up from their seats, and as Grady began to pull her chair back, she heard Luke answer, matter-of-factly, "Always."

Alrik walked over to her and said, "Lady Alissia, my wife and I are about to eat, and it would be an honor if you would join us."

Alissia's thoughts were on Luke as he quickly walked out of the room, without a glance back. She reminded herself of what he had said back at the cabin about having to appear cold and unemotional, but he had never mentioned anything about leaving or another woman.

Alrik misunderstood her delayed answer for shyness, and he took her by the hand and said, "Come, Dear. You must eat. I can only imagine what a member of the league fed you during your travels. You need more weight on you, and my wife truly wants to meet you."

Alissia followed in silence as Alrik led her out of the room, where a woman almost immediately came up to them.

"Lady Alissia, this is my lovely wife, Beula. Beula, please meet Lady Alissia."

Alrik released her hand as the woman gave Alissia a warm hug. When Beula pulled away, she said, "Oh, you poor child. Alrik has told me of your misfortune, and I can't imagine all that you've been through. You must still be exhausted. How are your rooms? Do you need anything?"

The older woman had an olive-skin tone, as did Luke and Alrik, and she talked in the same northern accent. Her black hair was mixed with grey, and it was long and sleek. Unlike her husband, she was not overweight and was not much taller than Alissia. Her nails were perfectly manicured, and she was dressed in fine clothing and jewelry.

Alissia said, "My rooms are very nice. Thank you."

Beula took her by the hand and began to lead her away from the meeting room when Alissia realized Nadia was following along behind the guards. She stopped abruptly and said, "I should tell Nadia she doesn't have to wait for me."

The older woman chuckled lightly. "Oh, don't worry about your handmaiden. Her job is to serve you. Come child. She will be fine."

The couple led Alissia through a part of the castle she had not yet been. Just as before, everyone seemed to be staring at her. Although she told herself it was because of her different clothing, she knew it was because she was the freaky Lamian.

Beula gave compliments on Alissia's beauty and choice of clothing, and what Alissia had first seen as politeness from Alrik, now bothered her. She now thought he and his wife were being overly nice.

The couple took Alissia to a fine restaurant in the castle, and they were seated at a table near the back corner of the room. Nadia and the two guards stood against a wall not too far away. Alissia really wanted to dismiss her handmaiden, but she did not want to go against Beula's words. She reminded herself that a shy, little Lamian would not stand up for what she believed in. Instead, she would nod her head and go along with whatever she was told.

Alrik and Beula both seemed good at leading, as they even chose her food. Alissia spent most of the meal nodding her head and smiling. Part of her was happy to play the part of being shy, for she knew if she spoke too much her words would get her into trouble.

"I received a message this morning from Ian and Emera," Beula said, as they were eating.

"And?" Alrik asked.

Beula smiled and answered, "They should arrive within the next two days."

This news seemed to make Alrik very happy, and he turned to Alissia with a grin. "Ian is our second eldest son, and Emera is our only daughter. She's the baby in the family, although she's now in her mid-twenties. She looks to be only a few years younger than you. How old are you?"

"I don't really know."

"Oh, I forgot. I'm sorry. Must be frustrating not having memories or knowing who you are."

Alissia nodded her head but remained silent, and he continued. "Ian is my only unmarried son. Although his older and younger brothers have both found wives and have started families of their own, Ian is more interested in the family business, and his mother here believes he works too much."

"He does," Beula confirmed.

"It has been over a year since we've seen Ian, longer for Emera, and they are traveling this way now." He paused before adding, "In fact, we should plan a small celebration for after they arrive. Beula, will you take care of the details?"

His wife answered, "Oh, it will be fun." To Alissia, she said, "We would love for you to join us. It should be three nights from now. That way the kids will have a night of rest before the celebration." Before Alissia could respond, she added, "I'll get the details to your handmaiden so she can put it on your calendar." She then put her hand on Alissia's shoulder and stressed, "It would be an honor for you to join us, Lady Alissia."

Alissia smiled back at the woman and politely thanked her for the invitation.

After the meal, Alrik left to attend to business, and Alissia found herself being led around a portion of the castle by Beula. As the older woman showed her various pieces of art and described the inspiration behind them, Alissia could only think of Nadia having not eaten.

It was late afternoon by the time Beula walked Alissia to her door and said goodbye. At first Alissia thought the woman would follow her into her suite, but she surprisingly gave Alissia a hug and told her she would be back the following day to take Alissia to lunch.

Once inside her suite, Alissia immediately dismissed Nadia, and then she flopped onto the sofa in front of the fireplace. Her mind went to the meeting with the assembly, and it warmed her heart at how Grady had tried to comfort her, just as he had often done in the past. If he could have held her hand, he would have, while rubbing his thumb inside her palm.

When she began to think about Luke, she tried to fight the sadness she felt at hearing about another woman. The thought of him leaving confused her and made her mad at the same time. She told herself there was no other woman, but then she remembered she really did not know anything about his personal life. They had never talked about it. All she knew was that he was an orphan, he had been raised by the Eldership, and he was an assassin. He was also controlling and egotistical. Yet, his touch sent involuntary shivers throughout her entire body.

She groaned out loud, closing her eyes, when she realized where her thoughts seemed to be taking her.

An unexpected knock on the door pulled her back to reality, and she hoped it was Anika. She needed a distraction at that moment.

When she opened the door, Anika stared at her outfit for a moment before walking into the room. Once the door was closed behind them, she turned and said, "Wow!"

"Is that a good wow or a bad wow?" Alissia asked.

Anika scrunched her face in thought before answering, "It's a good wow. Very different. Pretty, but very different."

Alissia went back to the sofa and sat down before responding, "I have purple hair and freaky eyes. I'm already different. The dress didn't make that happen, Anika."

Anika sat down in one of the chairs across from her, "True. I guess you really don't have to try. You do look very nice though. I guess you can wear anything you want. You're going to stand out either way."

"My thoughts exactly. Besides, in my reality, I look like I should be in a movie. Put wings on me, and I could be a fairy, well, except for the boots. I'm more of a rogue fairy princess. I can also wear this dress in the spring without the arm warmers."

"What's a fairy and movie?"

Chapter 5

The next three days were busy for Alissia, and she did not get to see Anika much. She had a formal lunch with the wives of the assembly members. Morton's wife was also there, and Alissia found herself feeling somewhat sorry for the older woman. The high-ranking wife from Allure did not seem popular among the other women, and Alissia noticed the tension, along with some cutting remarks directed towards the lone woman.

Alissia remembered the night she had first met women associated with the Eldership. It had been the night of the ball, and many of the women had angered Alissia with their pretentious attitudes. Anika had explained how power hungry most of them were and how they were raised to be that way. Although they never talked about politics, they seemed to have their own social structure, slightly different from their husbands.

Under normal circumstances, Morton's wife would be considered a high-ranking woman, deserving a lot of respect. However, with the corruption in Pallen's Eldership, she was no longer considered influential.

All the women at the luncheon invited Alissia to private meals or socials, and when she was not meeting with one of them, Beula and Alrik made sure to have her attention.

Nadia continued to fix Alissia's hair each morning, and Mela brought her more custom-made dresses that resembled the clothing of a pixie and fairy. Most of the dresses were made in deep colors with fine materials, and they all highly exceeded Alissia's expectations.

She enjoyed dressing differently than the other women at the Eldership, as she felt she could never be like any of them. Without her glasses, she did not even look human. Her eyes and hair were just too different.

Alissia took the shoulder strap Luke had given to her, and she rigged it to be a thigh sheath. Although some of the dresses were long enough that she was able to wear the boots with the hidden knives in them, she took more comfort in the feel of the knife concealed against her upper leg.

She did not talk much around people, and she was more than happy to act shy around the women at the Eldership. They seemed to enjoy talking mostly about themselves, and Alissia smiled a lot and pretended to like the conversations.

Because she was considered high on the social scale, every female Alissia met fawned over her somewhat, which made it easy for her to act meek, as she never had a reason for her pride to want to lash out. She mostly found herself bored around the other women.

When it came time for the celebration party, Alrik arrived at her suite to be her escort, along with her guards that never strayed. He hooked her hand into his arm and kept his hand on hers as they walked. He was the perfect gentleman, and Alissia was amazed by his acting skills. Part of her was tempted to ask about the bounty he had put on her, just to hear his response, but she knew that would be a big mistake. Both Luke and Grady had told her to feign ignorance when it came to his plans.

"Alissia, so glad you're here to join us," Beula said as she gave Alissia a hug. The older woman had stopped with the formalities of calling her Lady Alissia within the second day of their meeting. She took Alissia by the hand and led her through the main room of their suite.

A man Alissia had not seen before was sitting on a sofa in front of the fireplace, and he stood to his feet and studied Alissia for a moment. He looked to be in his thirties, and his black hair was pulled back into a short ponytail. He was dressed in a black suit with a gold vest, and a grey ascot was tucked in over his white shirt. His eyes were dark and penetrating as he took in her appearance, and although he was much taller and broad shouldered, Alissia could see the resemblance to his somewhat petite mother.

"Ian, this is Lady Alissia, and, Alissia, this is our son Ian."

Ian took her hand from his mother and brushed it against his lips. He looked into her eyes, and the right side of his mouth curled into a smile.

"Although my parents spoke of your great beauty, I find myself at a loss for words." He let go of her hand and added, "It is an honor to meet you, Lady Alissia. I have heard much about you. It seems you have won the hearts of both of my parents."

Alissia had to force a polite smile onto her face. She did not know why, but she had been expecting something much different than the man standing before her. He was handsome, wealthy, and confident, too confident.

She had come expecting a party, but after seeing the plates on the table and empty room, she now realized she had been invited to a private family event. She knew she would be the center of attention, and she now realized there was a reason they wanted her to meet Ian. He was not an old workaholic, as she had imagined. He was a highly eligible bachelor, and she was a highly sought out Lamian woman.

Alrik had a reason for her to meet his son, and she was certain there was a plan behind the façade.

Beula said, "Although I had hoped for you to meet Emera tonight, she is not feeling well after the long journey and needs rest."

Alissia had to stop herself from asking why Emera and Ian had traveled such a long distance in the cold, knowing spring would soon be upon them. She felt the heat rush to her face and her pulse quicken as she quickly came to the conclusion they most likely traveled to Pallen during the winter because of her.

She knew her silence would easily be mistaken for her shy personality, so she took advantage of what they thought of her, as she did not trust herself to speak at that moment.

Her quiet persona did not bother them, and they continued to talk to her as if she were a cherished guest. Throughout dinner, Beula and Alrik bragged on Ian's many accomplishments as he laughed at the stories and dismissed his parents' boasting.

He was extremely charming and well mannered, and Alissia's dislike of him began to grow even stronger.

She had met plenty of men just like him in her reality, and she had even dated some of them. Her friends were always amazed at how she could easily find fault in what they saw as perfection. Money had never won her over, and neither had looks. She often saw too much confidence as a big ego. Some men knew they could charm women, and those were the type she disliked the most.

She knew the mirror could easily be turned on her. She had never been an easy woman for a man to approach or get to know, and she had been mistaken for a snob more than once. She was nearing her thirties and still happily single, but she knew her problem and could live with it. She did not trust men, or even women, and she was fine with that realization.

The fact that Ian was the son of Alrik was not the only reason she would never like him. He and his parents thought of her as a pitiful young woman, naïve and needy. They saw her as an opportunity they could take advantage of, and her strong pride lashed out within her while she was around them.

By the end of the gathering, she had spent most of the night in silence, nodding and trying to fake a laugh when needed. It was when Beula was hugging her goodnight that she realized Ian would be the one to walk her back to her chambers, which was about a fifteen-minute stroll away. She was tempted to tell them she could just follow her guards home, but she knew it would not get her anywhere.

Luckily, he did not try to take her by the hand as they walked, but he did occasionally hold her elbow to pull her in closer as someone passed by. He did not talk much, and Alissia was surprised when they stopped in front of a small pub built inside the castle.

He said, "I hope you don't mind, but I was hoping you would join me for a drink before we part ways tonight. Please?"

As she scanned the open-walled room, Alissia's heart skipped a beat when she noticed Grady sitting at a table with two other men. Their eyes met for a quick moment before they both looked away.

She wanted to say no to the drink, as she had already had a glass of wine at dinner, but the idea of being in the same room as Grady was too enticing, even if they could not talk to each other. Then she began to mentally question why they could not speak to each other. They had spent time together traveling, and obviously, they knew each other. It was not as if they were strangers.

"Is that a yes?" he asked.

Her attention went back to Ian, and she smiled.

"Yes, one drink will be fine."

He led her to a small table in the back corner of the room, where it was more private. She sat down as he pulled a seat out for her, and then he sat down across for Tier. Grady's table was across the room, and she would have to turn her head slightly if she wanted to see him.

She instantly reminded herself to stay focused on the man in front of her. She knew this was the part of the night he would want to learn more about her. She always hated this part of a date, if that was what this was to be considered.

Ian touched her right arm warmer and said, "This is different. I like it. Is this how your people dress where you're from?"

Let's get this over with now, she thought. "I really don't remember anything about where I come from."

"That's what I heard. What happened?"

"I don't know, can't remember."

He said, "Does it hurt? I mean, did you wake up in pain?"

That was a good question, and Alissia did not want to commit to an answer. "Somewhat . . . a little."

"It must be scary, not knowing where you're from or what happened."

A waitress came to the table, and Ian ordered a wine for Alissia and something stronger for himself. After she left, he leaned back in his chair and gave a smile that would have made many women weak in the knees. However, it had no affect on Alissia.

That realization lifted her mood somewhat. Since being in this reality, she unwillingly has fallen for two men. Ian's affect on her was more suitable to her character. She was not desperate, and no matter how charming and enticing a man appeared, she was the type of woman that would see right through it, just as she always had.

After countless nights of pondering over her strong emotions towards Luke and Grady, she was beginning to think she had become weak since entering this reality. She now realized she was still the same Alissia, which meant she had no idea why Grady and Luke had such a strong affect on her.

"What are you thinking so hard about?" Ian asked.

Alissia turned her attention back to the man sitting across from her. He leaned in closer and put his elbows on the table. "You're thinking about something, yet you're so quiet. Although, after all you've been through, I imagine you have a lot to think about."

As he studied her face, she smiled back at him innocently while trying to think of a proper response. "I was just thinking of how nice your parents have been to me."

"They think very highly of you, especially my mother. My sister is not very close to my parents, and I know my mother hurts over their relationship. You have made her very happy, and it's been a while since I've seen her smile as much as she did tonight. Thank you for that."

The waitress brought their drinks, and Alissia took a few sips.

"Do your eyes hurt much?" he asked.

"Mainly when I'm in the sun."

"Can I see them?" At her hesitation, he reached out and took her by the hand, as if to reassure her. "Please, I want to know what you look like."

Just for the sake of removing her hand from his, she pulled her hand away and lifted her glasses. Without hesitating, he smiled.

"Beautiful. Why do you hide them?"

She lowered her glasses back down and turned her head towards Grady, as if responding shyly to Ian's compliment. Her heart immediately flew to her throat as she looked into Grady's eyes and realized he had witnessed what she had just done.

Although she turned her attention back to Ian, she could not help but remember all the times Grady had told her how much he loved her eyes. He used to remove her glasses, just so he could see them. She then remembered what she used to tell Grady, and she got an idea.

"They don't look human," she said.

"And that bothers you?"

She did not want to act as if she was special because she was a Lamian, but at the same time, she did not want him to think she was a human. Maybe then he would never want to cross any lines with her, and she could shut the door on the idea of them becoming a couple. It would be like her wanting to date an alien. It was just wrong and should never happen.

She said, "They remind me that I'm different." She wished this reality used the word freak, because that was the closest word that came to mind. "I'm strange," she added.

He unexpectedly leaned in closer and took both of her hands in his. His eyes bore hard into hers as he said firmly, "Being different is not always a bad thing, Lady Alissia. You are a beautiful woman, and you should never believe otherwise."

She had not been expecting such a strong response from him. She then decided she would need to try again.

"Ian, I don't think I'm human."

"You're a Lamian, and that's nothing to be ashamed of. I've heard stories about your people, and they are honorable. Just because you are a Lamian doesn't mean you're that different from us. I've heard that there were even marriages among our people. Even if your family is never found, you do not ever have to worry about being alone." He searched her face as he added, "Does that worry you now?"

Oh, he was good, real good, and Alissia was certain he could easily make a woman swoon over him. She quickly made a mental note to never take him as a fool. He was too accustomed to being a player. But, she reminded herself, she was not a fool either, and if he wanted to play this game, she would play.

Some of the anger she had felt towards him began to fade, and she started smiling and talking more. Her confidence around him grew as she told herself she would win, and she would beat him and his father at their own game.

Chapter 6

Grady had already left the pub by the time she and Ian got up from their seats. Ian walked her to her rooms and told her he would like to see her again the following day. She then told him she was already committed for most of the day, and she said goodnight.

Although she desperately wanted to talk to Anika now that she knew more about Alrik's plan, it was too late in the evening. She scowled to herself as frustration set in over the lack of a telephone in this reality.

When Nadia came into her room to help her undo the pins from her hair, Alissia told her to try to move things around on her schedule to fit Anika in the next day. She also told Nadia that nothing else was to go on her calendar without checking with her first. She had met all the wives of the assembly, and she had been social enough over the past few days. She needed a break from people.

The next day Nadia came in and helped Alissia dress for another day of social meetings. Alissia then met a group of women for something similar to hot tea, yet called chet, while being entertained by a small group of musicians. She then ate lunch with the wives of the assembly members. Morton's wife was excluded from the small gathering, and at the end of the meal, she was surprised when Ian walked up to the table.

He knew all the older women's names, and he made a point to compliment each one of them before telling a small joke. The women laughed and seemed to love Ian, and Alissia could not believe he could be that charming, even to older married women.

He looked over at Alissia with a grin and gave a wink before saying, "I beg your pardon, ladies, but I come to you with a request. You see, I met a beautiful young woman last night, and I do believe I have become smitten with her. I have been told she has a busy schedule, and she has no time for me. I implore each of you to help me with this dilemma. I would like to spend some time with her to prove my worth, and I can assure you all that my intentions are honorable when it comes to Lady Alissia."

All the women smiled, and they all looked at Alissia as if she was the luckiest woman alive. Within minutes, Alissia found herself being led toward one of the gardens, while Nadia ran back to her chambers to retrieve her cloak and alert two more guards. While inside the castle, she only needed two guards, but four of them were required for her to walk outside.

This time he held her hand as they walked.

"You don't mind, do you?"

Alissia returned his playful smile and answered, "Hmm . . . That you charmed those little old ladies?"

He chuckled and said, "It was you I was hoping it would work on."

"Ah, but now I know how crafty of a tongue you have."

"But my tongue only spoke the truth, my dear Alissia."

"I thought you would have to work today with your father."

"I can spare time for you. The business won't suffer. Besides, that's not where my mind is today."

"Where is it?"

He gave a light squeeze to her hand and said, "On you, my dear."

Alissia spent the rest of the afternoon in one of the gardens near the castle, where she learned that Ian was not only a master of words, but he was also smooth with his hands. When he was not holding one of her hands, he seemed to find a reason to touch another part of her body, such as her hair or her arm.

He then took her to a restaurant inside the castle for an early dinner, and unlike his parents, he did not order her food for her. Instead, he described the vegetable dishes on the menu, and she made the final selection.

During dinner, he told her of a ball that was coming up in three weeks, and he asked if she would be his date. Her first thought was to tell him she could not dance, but she then remembered how she had danced with Grady at the last ball. Ian would easily know the truth. She then tried to explain to him how uncomfortable she felt around so many people, but that did not work. He took that opportunity to tell her he would be at her side, and he would help her with her fears. In the end, he was persistent, and she could not say no without being too assertive.

It was not late when they walked out of the restaurant, and Alissia was glad to hear he would be taking her back to her suite. It seemed he did have some work he needed to take care of.

As they were walking through a well-traveled corridor, Alissia noticed Luke walking towards them with two other men by his side. The men had the same skin tone as Luke and Ian, and Alissia assumed they were also from the North. Her eyes met his, and he smiled. She was surprised when he and the other two men walked up to Ian and her.

"Good evening, Lady Alissia. Ian, I had heard you were in Pallen. Any problems along your journey?" Luke asked, casually.

"None that I couldn't take care of. It seems the roads are busier than normal for this time of year," Ian said, as if there was a hidden message behind his words.

"And so I've heard. I tend to stay away from the main roads, but I would not advise that to most others," Luke replied. He looked at Alissia and added, "I don't think Lady Alissia enjoyed the way I travel."

She smiled up at everyone but remained silent. It took all her will-power to look calm and unemotional with Luke standing so close. Unlike when they were traveling, he was wearing much finer cloth-ing, and memories of what had happened between them at the cabin began to flash through her mind. It had been over a week since he had held her in his arms and claimed her as his. Until this moment, she did not know how much she missed being around him.

Ian was holding her hand, and she began to fear that he could feel her body become tense.

"I was wondering if we could meet tonight to discuss a few things. Do you have a moment?" Luke said.

Ian answered, "I'm walking Lady Alissia back to her rooms now, but I can spare some time after that. Shall we meet at Jiliano's for a drink?"

"That will be fine, and we'll go there now." Luke turned to Alissia and said, "Lady Alissia, it was a pleasure to see you again. I do hope you are happy and settling into your new home. Good-night."

She nodded back but did not respond. If ever there was a time to act shy, it was at that moment.

As Ian walked her to her door, she began to wonder if he would try to kiss her goodnight. She reminded herself they had only met the night before, and there would be a set of guards as an audience. Surely, in this reality, those were reasons to wait until another time.

She was filled with relief when he placed a kiss on the top of her hand before saying goodnight, and she was surprised at how short the goodbye was. Maybe it was his way of making a woman want more: Spend the entire day in heavy flirtation, only to leave her with a swift goodbye.

Once inside her suite, she sent for Anika before she began to pace the floor of her main room. Nadia came back saying she could not locate Anika, and then Alissia dismissed her for the night. She did some yoga and then took a long bath, hoping to settle her mind, but nothing worked.

She was worried about how fast Ian seemed to be moving with her. She would soon have to find a way to turn him away. She also knew this was Alrik's way of winning her trust. What would he do when he realized she would not be falling for his son?

After her bath, she lay in bed holding one of the knives Luke had given her. Being so close to him that night had brought a longing deep within her she was not prepared for. Was it lust that made her want to be back in his arms? All she knew was that she missed him tonight. She also knew she did not really know anything about him. They had wasted all their time traveling together in silence. She should have asked questions, because now she seemed to be filled with them.

What if he really was leaving her? She then reminded herself that even if he did not care for her, he would never leave her in the hands of the southern Eldership.

That night she went to sleep with the knife strapped to her leg, hidden beneath her gown.

Chapter 7

She was surprised the next morning when she woke up on her own instead of being awakened by Nadia. She found her breakfast near the fireplace, and she ate it at her dining table. Afterwards, she called for Nadia, because her curiosity had gotten the best of her.

"Nadia, why didn't you wake me this morning? Don't I have to be somewhere today?"

"My Lady, it was determined by the assembly early this morning that you have been overcommitted, and I have been told to reschedule everything on your calendar, to space everything out so that you will have more time for yourself."

"I don't understand, Nadia. Why would the assembly care so much about my time, and why would they have a meeting about this so early in the morning? Were they already at a meeting and it was casually mentioned?"

The young woman looked uncomfortable for a moment before answering, "I don't truly know the answer to that question, but it is rumored that Mr. Durst made it a priority last night."

The thought of Alrik going to the assembly over her schedule worried her. Was it so she could spend more time with his son, which worried her even more?

"Will you please go find Anika for me?"

"Yes, My Lady. Shall I pull up your hair now or when I return?"

"If there is nothing on my schedule today, I would like to not have to dress up. I can take care of my own hair," Alissia responded.

"Then I shall go find Miss Anika."

After Nadia left, Alissia went to her closet and found a pair of leggings and a long shirt that she and Anika had bought together. She then cleaned her teeth and pulled her hair into a ponytail. She chose a pair of thick socks, no shoes, and she hid the knife she had slept with.

She and Anika spent the morning together in private, and Alissia told her everything about Ian. She finished with, "Anika, he's not stupid, and he's moving fast. Have you heard anything from Luke? Does he have a plan?"

"All I know is that Langley hired a new stable boy that lives with the horses, because Luke told him to. He's an orphan boy around twelve years old that was living on the streets in Pallen.

"Langley has not seen much of Luke, but he says Luke has told him he's working on something. Two other members of his league are with him now. They actually got here before you and Luke did."

Alissia responded, "Yeah, Luke contacted his people when he first saw me at the ball."

"Well, Langley says more people are arriving at the castle than usual. It's obvious something is going on, and I'm worried there will be a war. There hasn't been a civil war among our people since the

Eldership was created, and I can only imagine what that will do to our land."

Alissia said, "I know, but Luke told me it's been coming. The North is not happy with all the control being in the South. He said the South seems to be getting wealthier, and it's the opposite for the North. Alrik is just taking advantage of the situation." She paused for a moment before asking, "Have you seen Grady, and did he tell you he saw me the other night with Ian?"

Tears came to Anika's eyes as she nodded, "I've seen him, and he told me about seeing you with Ian. He knows what the Dursts are doing."

Anika's sudden emotion worried Alissia, and she asked, "Anika, what's wrong?"

Her friend blinked her eyes a few times in an attempt to regain control of her emotions before answering, "Alissia, Grady is a good man. I mean, he's honorable, loyal, and so much more. I can't stand to see him like this."

"Like what? How bad is he?"

Anika wiped the first tear away and said in a trembling voice, "Oh, he's acting strong, but I can tell it's killing him inside. Did you know the assembly has now excluded him from all the meetings? He has no power. He's just here. He's keeping himself busy by working in other departments within the Eldership, but he's been stripped of everything. The assembly isn't even trying to hide what they're doing anymore. Alrik Durst attends their meetings, and that isn't even legal. He's blatantly stepping into power here." She paused before adding, "And now Grady feels even more powerless, because he can't protect you from Ian. We're all at the mercy of Luke, and Grady already knows you care for Luke. He's losing everything he loves, yet he's doing everything to protect Langley and me. I hate this. I hate seeing him like this."

Guilt and hurt filled Alissia.

"I wish y'all had never come to Pallen with me. I'm sorry, Anika."

Anika shook her head and responded, "It's not your fault. None of this is. It's just a bad situation, and we're stuck in it."

"How about Morton? I noticed his wife wasn't at lunch yesterday."

"Grady says Morton's pride is going to get him killed if he doesn't stop, and Grady has had to distance himself from him. He also said Morton threatened him."

"Physically?"

"No, not physically. Morton says when he gets back to Allure, he's going to make sure the Elders know of his treason."

"Treason?" Alissia asked, angrily.

"That's how he sees it. Grady found you in Allure, yet he delivered you to the Eldership in Pallen, especially at a time like this. Morton is threatening to say Grady planned this and is working with Alrik."

Alissia said, "Why would he believe that?"

"He doesn't. He's mad at Grady for not standing with him and fighting the assembly here in Pallen, yet Grady says that would do nothing but get me or Langley killed. He and Luke both believe that.

"The best thing they can do is wait until more representatives from other cities arrive and that could possibly mean more allies. They also believe one of the assembly members might be swayed into turning against Alrik, possibly two. The other three, however, are set on a resistance from Allure, and Alrik has been pouring money into Pallen's military for a while. They have more power than they are legally supposed to."

Alissia nodded, remembering what all she had been told back at the cabin.

Anika continued with, "Luke says that private bodyguards in regular clothing protect Alrik. He doesn't know how many yet, but he believes if someone made an attempt on Alrik's life, they would swiftly be killed. Morton can't use his position at the Eldership to fight a rogue army, league members, and private bodyguards."

A knock at the door got their attention, and Alissia got up to answer it.

A delivery boy stood on the other side of the door with a large bouquet of flowers. Alissia took the bouquet from him and set it on the dining table before reading the note. A few seconds later she turned to Anika and said, "It's from Ian. It seems I will be having dinner tonight with him and his parents." She let out a small, sarcastic laugh and added, "Well, I guess there's nothing else on my calendar."

Alissia spent the rest of her time with Anika trying to cheer up her friend. However, she could feel Anika's frustration with her over Grady. His life was falling apart, and Alissia knew it was her fault. To break off their romantic relationship could possibly destroy him, especially now that his future at the Eldership was in question.

By the time Anika left, Alissia had made the decision that she needed to forget her feelings for Luke. She owed it to Grady.

That afternoon Nadia returned to help Alissia get dressed for dinner. Alissia wore another of her pixie-type dresses and arm warmers, and she hid a knife against her leg.

Ian came to escort her to the restaurant, where his parents were already seated. His sister was not mentioned or anywhere around, and Alissia could not help but wonder why she had not yet met Emera.

As Ian walked her back to her suite, he held her hand.

"Did you like the flowers?"

"I did, thank you."

"And what did you think about not having to spend your day with a group of assembly wives?"

"I was surprised. Did you have anything to do with that?"

He squeezed her hand and grinned. "I did. It's not your place to entertain them, although they believe it is. I just think you have better ways to spend your time."

"Like what?"

"I don't know." He stopped walking and looked down at her. "You tell me what you want to do, and I can make it happen."

His sudden attention made her nervous, and it was hard to think of an answer. "I enjoy being able to sleep in, and I love to exercise in the morning," she said.

He raised his left eyebrow and grinned. "So Lady Alissia likes to exercise? What do you do for exercise?"

Alissia immediately realized her mistake. They did not use the word "Pilates" or "yoga" in this reality, and although the women played many sports similar to tennis and other things in her reality, she did not know the rules. What exercise could she say she did?

She tried to give him a shy look as she answered, "I don't know. I do some stretches when I'm alone, and I try to build my muscles."

He took that opportunity to let go of her hand, and he began to feel her upper arm.

"Aw, I see. You surprise me, Lady Alissia. I had not imagined so much strength hidden beneath all your fine clothing." He grinned flirtatiously and added, "Gives me something to think about, and I can't wait to see you in the warm weather."

He took her by the hand and started walking again. "I shall have to consider a different way to court you, and I think I have the perfect idea for tomorrow."

"Is that what you're doing, courting me?" she asked.

He laughed. "Yes, my dear. I have never been this enthralled before. It seems I am already under your spell."

She bit her bottom lip before responding, "Ian, you do realize I'm a Lamian, and you're a human. We are different."

"Yes, but we are not that different."

She tried again to put some distance between them. "It's just that I need to try to figure out who or what I am before I begin to think of any of those possibilities with a man."

They arrived at her door, and he lifted her hand to his lips and kissed it. "Yes, but I'm here to help you with all that. You are not alone, Lady Alissia. Now goodnight. I have some work to do, but I plan to see you tomorrow."

He opened her door, and she walked into her chambers without glancing back.

Chapter 8

"Ugh! I can't get rid of him, Anika." Alissia motioned to a new bouquet of flowers placed on the table behind the sofa. "And you want to know what today's plans are? Swimming! He sent over a stack of bathing suits for me to choose from, and I'm supposed to go swimming with him this afternoon." She plopped down on the sofa before adding, "And it's all my fault. I just had to tell him I like to exercise last night. That was a big mistake! What am I supposed to do with him in a swimming pool? Do you know what happens in swimming pools? I've seen the movies, and it's not going to happen! I swear! I'm going to swim a hundred laps or more if I have to, but I'm not getting near him in a pool. And what about chaperones? Don't we have to have a double date?"

Anika had just walked in, and she sat down in one of the chairs across from Alissia in the sitting area. Alissia was surprised when her friend chuckled and said, "You know, when you get like this, I can barely understand you. You talk too fast in your old accent. It's cute."

Alissia rolled her eyes and groaned. "I don't want to be cute. I say we chop off my hair, and I start dressing horribly. Maybe I should start skipping baths. What else can I do to turn someone off?"

Anika said, "Your guards will be there and will serve as your chaperones." She reached down and pulled something from her bra and held it out. "Maybe this will cheer you up."

When Alissia took the small notes from her friend's hand, she grinned, and her eyes widened.

"Two of them?" she asked.

"When we told Grady that Luke was sending you a letter, he took that as a sign he could send one too. The only reason he hasn't been writing you already is because Luke was adamant that we not write anything down that could be read. In fact, you have to read them, and then give them back to me. He doesn't even want you to burn them in your fireplace, because that could leave a trace. He also says you can't write on any of the paper from your suite to send him a message. Your rooms are not private, and you are to remember not to trust anyone."

"You've seen him?"

"Not me. He came to the stables yesterday and gave it to Langley."

Alissia opened the first letter and immediately recognized Grady's handwriting.

My dearest Alissia,

I cling to the hope that we will overcome what is set before us, and I strongly hold onto the memories I have with you. I am sorry that I cannot take you away from this, and I hope you'll forgive me for bringing you here.

You carry my heart with you daily so you are never alone. For now, I can only be with you in spirit. One day this will only be a memory that we'll talk about as I hold you in my arms. You will be safe again, and I stand by my words of love for you.

I know about Ian, and I know how he must upset you. Your inner beauty and strength has always amazed me, and I am confident you will overcome this.

I have been told there is a plan, but it's not easy or simple. We must wait, and that is the hope I cling to. One day we will be together again.

Love always,
Grady

She read the letter twice and had to force herself to appear calm in front of Anika as she looked up.

"Have you read it?" she asked, forcing herself to sound unemotional.

"No."

"While I'm reading, why don't you go look at the bathing suits I'm supposed to choose from? They're over on the table."

Anika got up, and Alissia lifted the second letter. It was sealed with wax but not stamped.

When the bell strikes six times, leave the garden and go to the first ladies' room you see. It will be on the left side, as soon as you walk in. Be alone.

Alissia read the note twice before she turned to Anika. She did not try to conceal her confusion as she said, "Um, is there anything else besides a note? It's short and cryptic."

Anika was holding up a bathing suit, as if it was the one.

"Langley said I'm to take you to the Darell Garden tonight. It's a summer garden, so no one goes there now. I'm supposed to say in front of the guards that I wanted to teach you about certain summer flowers. It seems you and I love to talk about gardening."

Alissia could barely breathe as she realized what the short note might be saying. Either they were about to escape, or she would be able to see Luke.

She quickly got up from the sofa and said, excitedly, "I'll go swimming with the player this afternoon, and then we'll go to the garden tonight."

Anika's eyes narrowed.

"What did the note say?"

"It said we need to leave the garden at the sixth bell."

"What else did it say?"

Alissia frowned and walked over to Anika. She exchanged the bathing suit for the note, and then she went to the bedroom and shut the door. When she came out with the new suit on, Anika was staring at her with her arms crossed.

"What does he mean?" Anika asked.

"I don't know. Either there's an escape plan for tonight, or he needs to tell me about an escape plan. It's cryptic. He didn't even sign his name or put my name on it." In an attempt to change the subject, she added, "I'm not wearing this bathing suit."

"Why? It's cute."

"That's why! I don't want to look cute. Did he send anything homely or motherly?"

Anika laughed and shook her head. "Alissia, Ian will not try anything physical with you. He's courting you, and that means a lot. We do things differently in this reality. Remember? The two of you will never be alone, as it goes against our customs, and it is more formal now that we are at the castle. He must follow certain rules when it comes to you."

"So he won't try to kiss me?"

Her friend hesitated before answering, "Well, he can kiss you, but that is all he can do."

Alissia scowled back at Anika before gathering the rest of the bathing suits and cover-ups. She did not say a word as she took them to her bedroom and closed the door behind her. Half of the suits were too big on her chest, so her choices were limited. Luckily, this reality was more conservative than where she came from, and none of them were bikinis. In the end, she chose a deep blue top that fit like a dress. It was tight but hung down loosely around her hips. It tied behind her neck and had matching bottoms. As with most of her clothing, it shimmered in the light. She chose a matching, long dress for the cover-up.

Mostly to avoid Anika's interrogation over Luke and the garden, Alissia locked herself in her bedroom for a quick bath. She needed to prepare for the swim before Nadia offered to help. However, she allowed the handmaiden to pull her hair back into something resembling a French braid, but more complicated.

Anika was still there when the knock came at the door, and Nadia quickly finished fastening a thin, gold necklace she had chosen for Alissia. She then took one more appraising look at her mistress before running nervously to the door, as if Alissia's date was something to be excited about.

Alissia's last thought before the door opened was regret over not being able to carry a knife that day.

Chapter 9

Alissia stared wide-eyed at Ian as he stepped into the room. Since being in this reality, she had not seen a man dressed in clothing so similar to what she was used to seeing from home. His clothing resembled a male yoga instructor's.

He wore a black pair of loose pants, sandals, and a tight, olive-colored shirt with long sleeves. With his broad shoulders, Alissia could easily see him as one of the men she had often seen at the gym.

Noticing her eyes on him, he grinned, and she immediately turned her attention towards Anika, chiding herself for giving Ian the satisfaction of thinking she was checking him out.

"Ah, you must be Anika," he said walking towards her friend. He swiftly picked up Anika's hand and bowed. "It is an honor to meet you. Talk of your beauty has preceded our meeting, and I can easily see why."

Anika looked back at Ian, unamused. "And you must be Ian. I see you're not shy around women, just as Alissia had warned."

Alissia nearly choked on Anika's disapproving tone. Noticing Ian's smile falter for a moment surprised her even more.

However, he quickly recovered and released Anika's hand. "Ah, I fear the custom of my people has been misunderstood, as I have been taught to only show respect when I am in the presence of a beautiful woman." With a perfect smile, he skillfully acknowledged all three of the women with his eyes as he added, "And at this moment I seem to only be surrounded by them."

Nadia blushed as she smiled nervously and looked down.

"I'm ready," Alissia said, briskly. Eager to get the date over with, she began to walk towards the door.

The pool was about a twenty minute walk through the castle, and Ian was all smiles and flirtatious the entire time. Alissia's nerves grew with each step, and she greatly hoped the pool would be crowded.

Since she was not wearing her arm warmers, the star-shaped scar she had received in the forest was now visible, and he asked about it. She told him it had been there for as long as she could remember, which was not that far back in time.

The pool was in a glass dome outside the castle, and the first thing Alissia noticed when they got there was how empty it was. They would be swimming alone in a beautiful swimming pool made of large stones and surrounded by a garden. It made her think of what the Garden of Eden could have looked like. Exotic flowers seemed to be everywhere.

There were two levels of the pool, hand the top one flowed down as a waterfall into the bottom one. It resembled a natural, clear stream without fish or other aquatic wildlife.

He watched her as she stared at the pool for a moment, and then she said, "What's making the water flow? Where does it get its power?"

He glanced around before answering, "It's either solar or jade powered."

She remembered Grady had said he had used a jade on the window when she had crossed into this reality. They were highly illegal to have, yet Agro had sent him one.

Wanting to know more, she asked, "What's a jade?"

"It's a power stone. The Eldership uses them for various things. Have you never heard of them, or do you know them by another name?"

"I don't know anything about a power stone."

He pulled off his shirt before removing his loose pants, and once again, Alissia was taken aback by his choice of clothing. His bathing suit resembled a miniskirt with a split along one side. It was made of a shimmery material in a deep olive-green color that was a perfect choice for his naturally tan skin.

Not only was he wealthy and charming, he was also physically fit. His broad shoulders and stomach, along with the rest of his body, were ripped in muscles, and she could not help but wonder what he did to stay in such great shape. His parents had not done him justice when they had described him as older and a workaholic. She had imagined him to be completely the opposite of what he was. With his dark hair pulled back into a ponytail, his muscles, tiny skirt and sandals, he now resembled a fierce gladiator standing before her, and she could easily see why he was so bold when it came to women. She imagined he was used to having his way with many of them.

When she realized he had caught her staring at him, she awkwardly turned away. She told herself she had to be more careful. The last thing she wanted him to believe was that she had checked him out twice in one morning, when it was actually his choice in clothing that had drawn her attention.

"Your turn," he said. When she hesitated, he laughed and walked over. Reaching down, he took hold of her dress and began to lift it over her head.

Although she knew all four of the guards were watching them, they were too far away to hear Ian and her converse. The setting was too private, and she did not consider her bathing suit enough clothing in front of the overly confident man standing before her.

Even Anika's reassuring words that Ian had to follow certain courting rules did not help to ease the wild spasms in her stomach. It's not that she thought he would try to go too far with her; it was that she did not want to go anywhere physical with him, not even a kiss.

After setting her dress on a lounge chair, he turned his full attention back to her. He lifted his hand to her upper arm and gave it a light squeeze.

"Ah, you do have a lot of muscle for such a tiny woman," he said, playfully. She then noticed his eyes subtly scan her body, and she stiffened.

Images of Luke brutally beating Ian flashed through her mind before she quickly pushed those thoughts aside. She reminded herself that Luke was not there. This was her problem, and she would have to deal with it.

"Are you ready to swim?" he asked.

"Yes, I could use the exercise." She did not wait for him to respond before she stepped out of her sandals and rushed towards the pool. She set her sunglasses down at the edge of the pool and jumped in. When she came up for air, he was still standing where she had left him, and he was grinning. She waved, and then she began to swim laps.

She lost count of how many laps she swam, and she did not stop until it became too much for her body. When she finally stood to her feet at the shallow end, she found Ian still swimming laps on the other side of the pool. She put her glasses on and began to watch him, hoping he would continue for a while.

That thought did not last long, and he soon swam over and circled her. He touched her leg playfully before standing up behind her, and she turned to look at him.

"You really do love to exercise, don't you?" he said, taking her by the hand.

Dread filled her as he led her to the stairs of the pool, and they sat down. The stairs immediately began to glow brighter, and she realized she was sitting on a large glow stone. Although the sky was filled with clouds, she hoped it was sunny enough that Ian had not noticed what had just happened.

"That's interesting," he said.

Alissia's heart stopped, and she tried to sound calm. "What?"

He stood to his feet and walked over to a corner of the pool. When he came back, he was holding a glow stone in both of his hands. He sat down beside her and put the stone in his lap.

"Let's see what happens when you touch this." He took her by the hand, and she instinctively tried to pull it away. "It's only a glow stone. It won't harm you," he said, holding her hand firmly, yet gently.

As soon as her palm touched the stone, it brightened.

Alissia stared down at the stone, and her mind began to race with excuses.

"Did you know you could do this?" he asked.

She wanted to run, and it took every bit of her willpower to appear calm and unemotional.

There were only two answers to his question. She could act as if she had not known, but that was not realistic. Glow stones were everywhere, and he would easily know she was lying.

She had no other choice but to admit she had been keeping a secret, and she would have to give him a good reason for keeping that secret.

"I did," she answered, pulling her hand away from the stone. "Ian, please don't tell anyone. No one knows about this, not even Anika and the others."

"Luke and Grady don't know about this?"

"No, I wore gloves the entire time I traveled with Luke, and I had no reason to touch a glow stone around Grady. No one knows, and they mustn't find out."

He set the stone on the edge of the pool and stood to his feet before bending down so his face was level to hers. "Alissia, why haven't you told anyone?" he asked, softly, while studying her face.

She tried to appear sad and defeated as she answered, "I don't know who to trust. I read what the books said about my people. Humans killed them, and then those awful men kidnapped me. Who would you trust if you were me?"

"Oh, Alissia." He pulled her into his arms and held her tight. As she was forced to rest the side of her face against his bare chest, her body stiffened, and she cringed. Although she was happy he was no longer staring into her eyes, she hated being so close to him. Being held by him was the last thing she had wanted to happen. She had only met him a few days ago, and he was moving way too fast.

Stroking her hair, he said, gently, "You've been through a lot. I won't pretend to understand all that you're going through, but I can promise you I will be here for you. I only ask that you let me take care of you. Will you do that? Will you let me try to make you happy?"

She did not dare look up with his face so close to hers. Although everything within her wanted to push him away and tell him she did not need a man to make her happy, she told herself to go along with him, especially now that he knew about her power. She did not need to make an enemy of Ian, and she needed him to keep her secret, even from his own father.

She closed her eyes in defeat and tried to sound fragile as she said, "I'll try, but please go slow. I just met you, and you scare me."

Her words went against everything she stood for, as did playing the part of a helpless woman. Her pride raged within her, and with her eyes still closed, she began to focus on her breathing in an attempt to calm down.

She forced her pride aside and determinedly told herself she would pretend to be the most delicate woman he had ever met if that would help to get him to slow down and keep her secret. She only needed time. What if Luke had a plan and was ready for them to leave that very night?

Ian remained silent for a moment before he carried her to a ledge and set her down. "I'm sorry I've scared you, Alissia. That's the last thing I ever wanted to do. I admit that I'm not used to the feelings you bring out in me, and I don't know what to do about them." He kissed the inside of her hand and added, "The truth is you scare me. I know we just recently met, but I fear I'm losing my heart to you. I have never met a woman so intriguing and beautiful as you."

He smiled and gave her hand a gentle squeeze. "I will slow down, and I will prove myself to you."

She nodded, and in an attempt to change the subject, she said, somewhat pleadingly, "Please promise me you won't tell anyone, not even your parents."

He gazed hard into her eyes and said, "I promise I won't tell anyone, not even my parents. It will be our secret. The guards could not even see what happened. Is there anything else you can do that you've not told anyone about?"

She scrunched up her face, as if in thought, and he said, "You wouldn't tell me if there was, would you?" He added, as if to himself, "You don't trust me yet."

"I'm sorry, Ian."

He shook his head and smiled as he lifted her hand. "I understand, and you are more than worth the wait, Lady Alissia." After placing a soft kiss on her hand, he looked at her with eyes that would have made most women melt.

She gave a weak smile and said, "Thank you."

"Are you ready to leave now, or do you want to swim some more?" he asked.

"I'm ready. In fact, I think I swam too much, and I'm going to be sore later," she lied. She could not help but think she was doing a lot of lying lately, and she hated it.

Chapter 10

When Alissia got back to her chambers, she got dressed quickly for her walk to the summer garden. Eager to talk to Anika about all that had happened at the pool, she tried to dismiss Nadia early. However, her handmaiden insisted Odell would reprimand her if she did not do something with Alissia's hair. Alissia had to force herself to feign patience as Nadia worked her magic on her wild, natural curls.

She was dressed in the most rebellious and even somewhat Gothic dress she owned, and she wore the boots Luke had given her with the two knives hidden in them. She hoped tonight would be their escape, and she was ready for it.

The moment Nadia walked out of the suite Alissia ran up to Anika and hissed, "He knows! He knows I'm a power source!"

"What? How did that happen?"

Alissia quickly told her friend all that had happened with Ian at the pool, and then the two of them put on their cloaks and began their walk to the garden.

At the summer garden, she pretended to be interested in Anika's discussion of the various summer flowers. Her friend's knowledge of gardening surprised her, and she wondered if everyone in this natural reality had a green thumb.

The garden was still pretty, even without most of the flowers in bloom, but it was void of people. Everyone seemed to prefer other gardens at this time of the year.

When the bell began to toll, Alissia could barely conceal the excitement from her voice as they began to walk back to the castle. She had already seen the bathroom on the way to the garden, and without asking the guards, she entered it as they passed by.

The moment the door was closed behind her, Luke's hands grabbed her, and she was shoved against the stone wall. As his mouth covered hers, she heard him close the latch on the lock, and then his hand went to her back, pulling her in closer. Without taking his lips from hers, he picked her up and into his arms, and her hands made their way to his unruly hair.

He pulled away and whispered in a shaky voice, "We don't have much time."

The room was completely in darkness until he lifted the cover from a sconce at her head. He set her down, and then she remembered what had been said about him. She pulled away and whispered accusingly, "You didn't tell me there was another woman, and you're leaving."

He grinned smugly and said, "You're jealous."

"I'm not jealous. I'm mad. There's a difference."

His grin got bigger. "You stay mad at me. Have I ever told you how beautiful you are when you're mad? I wish you'd take your glasses off so I can see the full scowl. I've been missing it."

"Luke, it's not funny!"

He laughed and grabbed her by the wrist before pulling her back into his arms. With his lips at her ear, he whispered, "There is no other woman, Alissia, and I've already told you I'm not leaving here without you." He began to kiss her neck, and shivers went throughout her entire body.

When he lifted his head, he gave her a hard look and added, "I also told you not to believe anything you heard about me. I have to distance myself, remember? My men knew to spread that rumor the moment they arrived, which was before we even got here. And as for me leaving, I'm the highest ranked official here from my city. I can't leave. My supposed clearance was denied."

He let go of her and asked, somewhat accusingly, "Is that the only problem between us?"

"What do you mean?" she asked, confused.

"Are you enjoying your time here at the castle? Do you still want to leave?"

It took her a moment before she got what he was saying, and then she smiled. "You're jealous."

"Not jealous. I just want to make sure you still want to leave."

Now it was her turn to laugh. "You're so jealous, and, yes, I still want to leave. Are we going tonight?"

His face became serious as he traced one of his fingers along her cheek.

"No, Alissia. That's not the reason we're here," he said, somewhat sadly. "I needed to make sure you still wished to leave, and I wanted to tell you I'm getting a plan in place. But, no, I'm still working on it, and more of my people are on their way."

Her face now resembled his, as all her hope of leaving that night left her. Then the events of that day came to mind, and she said urgently, "But Ian knows about me being a power source. He figured it out today."

Luke's expression changed abruptly. "Alissia, what do you mean by power source, and what have you not told me?"

She knew the sudden look on Luke's face. He was mad. It took a moment before she remembered she had never told him about being a power source, and she had worn gloves during most of their time together.

She gave a weak smile and stammered, "Um, you know how I always wore gloves around you?" She noticed his jaw clench even tighter, and she swallowed before continuing. "Well, it was not just because I was cold. I . . . um . . . give more power to glow stones and other stones. Today at the pool, Ian saw the glow stone light up when I sat on it. I told him no one else knows about it, and he thinks it's our private, little secret now."

"What else have you not told me, Alissia?" he asked, between clenched teeth.

Alissia chewed on her bottom lip as she thought for a moment before answering, "I promise. The only other thing I haven't mentioned is I have night vision. Other than that, I think I told you everything."

His eyes turned to fury, but before he could speak, she grabbed ahold of both of his arms and said firmly, "Luke, we don't have much time. The guards are outside this door. I'm sorry. You're the one that said I shouldn't trust anyone. Remember? You were very convincing about that when we first met, and I listened to you."

"I didn't mean you couldn't trust me!"

She let go of his arms and said, weakly, "Well, I know that now."

He gave a sigh and ran one of his hands through his hair. "We'll save this conversation for later. You need to get back out there."

"But, Luke, how much longer? Ian isn't a fool, and I think he's not stupid when it comes to women. I can't keep pushing him away for long. Today I told him I was scared of him, and that should buy me some time. But, he's set on courting me."

Luke pulled her into his arms with more force than usual. "Ian isn't a fool, and he knows a lot when it comes to women. Are you attracted to him?"

As he searched her face, she realized it was fear he was feeling, and it surprised her. She looked into his eyes and said firmly, "Luke, I am not and will never be attracted to a lying, conniving, and manipulating womanizer. I'm not stupid. You don't have anything to worry about." She put her arms around him and added, "Please, don't ever think that."

He leaned down, and they shared another heated kiss before he pushed her away. "Go, before they become curious."

She put her hand on the latch and then turned around for one last look before opening the door and walking out.

One of the guards took a step towards the bathroom, and Alissia looked at Anika with wide eyes.

"Didn't you need to go also?" Alissia blurted out.

"Uh . . . oh, yes—I definitely need to," Anika stammered. She turned towards the guard and smiled awkwardly before adding, "Pardon me. Sorry."

As Alissia went to step aside, Anika clumsily bumped into her before opening the bathroom door and passing through.

Alissia stood in front of the door and gave the guards an uncomfortable smile. When she noticed herself nervously twiddling her thumbs, she began to walk slowly in the direction they were going, as if she was losing patience with waiting. The guards began to follow her, and she stopped several feet away. When her friend stepped out of the bathroom, Alissia started walking again. Anika had to run to catch up.

"Hey, I waited for *you*," Anika yelled out.

"I waited too," Alissia said, playfully.

The two women walked in silence for most of the way back to her suite, and Alissia turned Nadia away once there. The moment the door closed and the two of them were alone, Anika demanded, "What took you so long?"

"We had a lot to talk about. What took *you* so long?"

Anika glared back at her. "I thought he was going to kill me!"

Alissia started to laugh but stopped. "Why do you say that?"

"I think he thought I was a guard. He had a knife out. Alissia, do you know how scary that man looks?"

She knew Luke could look extremely terrifying when he wanted to.

"Oh, Anika, I'm so sorry. I didn't plan for you to go in there."

"Well, I did, and that was a first impression I'll never forget. I also learned he's working on a plan but doesn't really have one yet. So, what was so important that the two of you had to meet, and what did you talk about for so long?"

The look on Alissia's face must have given it away, and Anika's eyes got big.

"That was the reason?" she demanded, accusingly.

Alissia quickly stammered, "No, Anika, it's not like that. He wanted to talk about Ian. That's why he needed to see me."

"About Ian? What did he say?"

Alissia cleared her throat nervously before admitting, "He didn't have a lot to say about Ian. I think he was more worried I had changed my mind. He was making sure I still wanted to get out of here."

Anika looked confused for a moment before asking, "He thought you liked Ian?"

"I don't know. Something like that."

"He was jealous?"

"I wouldn't call it jealous," Alissia said defensively, knowing it was true. This was a conversation she did not want to have. Luke's feelings towards her were too private. She sat down on the sofa and said, "He's trying to get us out of here, and he had to be sure we still wanted to leave."

Anika sat down across from her. "He really cares about you, doesn't he? That's why he's trying to help all of us, not just you."

Alissia let out a frustrated sigh, already feeling guilty around Anika. "I don't know, and it's not as if any of that matters right now.

I have to stay focused on Ian. I messed up today, and now he knows too much. I wish I could pretend I was sick, but I'm sure the Dursts would send a doctor to me."

She shook her head and rolled her eyes. "He's like an octopus. Do y'all even have octopuses in this reality? Eight arms, lives in the sea?" Anika nodded, and Alissia added, "The man has hands everywhere, on my arm, in my hair, holding my hand . . . and I'm sure he's used to women giving him anything he wants. Oh, he's smooth. And you should see him in a bathing suit. Apparently, he does not sit behind a desk all day."

Alissia scrunched up her face in frustration. "In fact, what does the man do to have that many muscles? I thought he was a businessman. He looks like he could be a trained assassin like Luke."

Anika said, "He looks exactly like he's supposed to, Alissia. He comes from a wealthy family and either went to a private school, boarding school, or had a personal teacher. His family gave him the best education, and I'm sure he played team sports during his youth. If I had to guess, I'd say he's in the tenth division of swording and is also skilled in archery."

Alissia looked back at her friend in disbelief. "Does every man in this reality know how to play with weapons?"

Anika rolled her eyes and said, "Think about it. He comes from a merchant family. In his line of business, he does a lot of traveling. He comes from a powerful family, and I am very sure he knows how to defend himself. He does not sit around at a desk playing on one of those electricity boxes you told me about."

"It's a computer," Alissia said, somewhat defensively.

"Computer then. Even Grady still trains at the Eldership. It's what men do."

"What about Langley? Does he know how to use a sword?"

Anika said, "His training was much different than Grady and Ian's. He spent his youth working on the family ranch, and his mother schooled him at home. He had little time for divisional sports.

However, he got his skills from everyone on the ranch. They have their own contests and ways of doing things. Langley is highly talented in archery and fighting, not so much with a sword. He's also one of the best hunters I know."

"Great!" Alissia said. "So all the men in this reality are trained fighters, and all the women know how to knit and make pretty little things with their hands. No wonder the men think they can control everything."

Anika frowned back at her. "If Ian says he's courting you, then he won't try to take things too far. He'll want to do things properly. Just keep acting like the prestigious lady ambassador you are, and he'll have to respect you in that way."

Alissia responded, "In what way? What are the rules? Because we just met, and he's already kissing my hands and hugging on me. Not big kisses, but his lips are touching my body, and I don't want them to. What if he tries to kiss my mouth? I may sound silly, especially after what you know about me with Luke and Grady, but that's important to me, Anika. I don't want his mouth on me."

She did not want to say anything further, but she hoped her friend realized what she was trying to say. She had spent her entire life pushing men away. If and when she kissed a man or told him she loved him, she had to mean it.

She had spent most of her childhood not having control over her body. Her father had hit her and made her feel powerless and unloved. Then when she had gotten raped, she had not only felt guilt and shame, but also weak and powerless. Her body was hers to give when she chose to. No one would ever take that from her.

It also went against her moral beliefs. She was already struggling with the fact that she had kissed two men in the same day, and now they both seemed committed to her. Just today she had read words of love from Grady, and then practically attacked Luke in the bathroom. And that was after she had told herself to forget about Luke. There was no way she was adding another man to her life. It was complicated enough.

Anika said, reassuringly, "You don't sound silly, and I'm not mad at you about Luke. I talked to Langley about it, and we both realize your situation isn't normal. You were alone with Luke for weeks, and you went through a lot during that time. I can't even imagine what it must have been like with those two men. It would change me, and I'm sure it changed you in ways."

She let out a frustrated sigh and frowned before continuing. "I'm not saying I'm happy about it. Grady is important to me, and I hate watching him hurting like this. But, I understand how it could happen. I'm not judging you, and I don't think badly of you. I just ask that you handle Grady with care, no matter what happens. Alissia, he's not in a good emotional state. He could lose everything over this."

"You mean, over me?" Alissia said.

There was a moment of silence between them before Anika said, "As for Ian, you told him you were scared of him today and that he's moving too fast. Maybe he'll slow down, and we'll find a way out of here soon."

Alissia said, "What do you think would happen if I told him to stop courting me, that I don't want any of that right now?"

"I think Alrik would try to find another way to get at you, and it would probably be worse than Ian. Right now they're trying to gain your trust and pull you into their family. They're being nice. Do you really want that to change? It could be worse, much worse. Just play along for a while. Would you rather Alrik use force on you?"

After a pause, she added, "Oh, and don't forget that Ian now knows one of your secrets, and he promised he wouldn't tell anyone, not even his father."

"Do you think he'll tell Alrik?" Alissia asked.

Anika shrugged. "I don't know. That depends on Ian. Maybe you should try to get him to like you more than he likes his own father."

"How close is he to his dad?" Alissia asked.

"I don't know. I don't know much about Ian. What I do know is that you are a beautiful, powerful, and single woman, Alissia. You may not know how to fight with a sword, but you are not defenseless when it comes to one man."

Anika stood to her feet before adding, "There's an old women's saying in this reality that's been passed down throughout the ages, since before the Eldership. It goes like this: Win the man, win the kingdom." She began walking towards the door as she added, "And that is the advice I'll leave you with. Just be patient and act like the defenseless woman you believe men expect in this reality. However, I'll add that not all men expect us to be like that."

As Anika left, Alissia realized she must have offended her friend with the knitting comment. She closed her eyes in frustration.

Anika was right. Snubbing Ian was her last option. She would only do it if she had to. He was annoying, but, surely, she could keep him at a distance. She had been doing that with men all her life.

Chapter 11

Sleep did not come easy for Alissia that night. Thoughts of Luke teased her, and she longed to be with him again. The look in his eyes as he had asked about her feelings towards Ian haunted her. She had only seen him scared one other time, and that was when he had realized she had drugged him. His last words before falling asleep were that she needed him, and he now worried that she did not.

She hoped her words of reassurance had been enough for him. Although he was strong and seemed invincible, something about the way he looked at her those two times tugged at her heart.

Then there was Grady. No matter how hard she tried to forget about Luke, it was not working. Although she hated the thought of hurting Grady even more, her feelings for Luke were a problem they could not ignore.

As time went by, troubled sleep continued to stay with Alissia each night. She had heard that nightmares were the subconscious result of one's mind trying to solve unresolved problems. Her mind was consumed with more than enough of her share of unresolved problems.

She still woke up each morning feeling the presence of the Lamians in her head, and it shamed her that her dreams were either filled with gory images of death or heated images of her with Luke or Grady. She had even awakened one morning with the realization she had dreamed about Ian. She immediately tossed that image with the other creepy dreams her subconscious occasionally threw at her.

Although the assembly had cleared her calendar and made it a priority that she not be overcommitted socially, she still went to some social events, just not every day. She got to see Anika at least every other day. However, Ian courted her daily.

One day she even got to go to a temple at the edge of the castle with Anika and Langley. Although Grady had spent much time with her talking about their Creator, this was her first time going to a formal teaching to compare what she had already learned from her reality.

Since being in this reality, her life had spun out of control, and her mind was no longer at peace. Her thoughts were much darker than they needed to be. She also hoped that her visit to the temple would be a subtle reminder to Ian that she held certain beliefs when it came to dating.

Ian's hands always seemed to be touching a part of Alissia's body when they were together, but at the end of each day, she found relief in that he had not tried to kiss her. Her talk about being scared of him must have worked a little. Although she still considered him overly flirtatious, she felt that she could handle it.

In fact, a lot of their time together was spent with his parents or in public places. He took her out for dinner, to shows, or on walks in a garden during the day.

Alissia was in bed reading one night when she heard a small noise coming from the main room. Thinking it was Nadia, she got up from her bed and went to check it out. When she did not find anything, she decided it was just her imagination playing tricks on her. She walked back into her bedroom, only to find a small creature standing in the middle of the room.

Alissia jumped back and cried out in alarm. The tiny creature cocked its head to one side, as if studying her.

It was about a foot tall, covered in grey and black fur, with a round face, black nose, and big grey eyes. Its ears were small and pointed, and it was standing on two feet that resembled the paws of a raccoon.

The creature was adorable, and Alissia immediately knew it would not harm her. She was a Lamian, and all animals seemed to love her.

She walked back into the main room to see if the guards had heard her cry out. If so, they would most likely decide to check on her. After a moment of silence, she went back into the bedroom, locking the door behind her.

The small creature silently watched her, and Alissia thought she noticed intelligence behind those big, grey eyes. She tried to call out to it with her mind, but she immediately realized she could not. Like the creature that had bit her in the forest, she had no way to communicate with this animal.

She slowly walked up to it while saying softy, "It's okay. I won't hurt you."

The animal seemed to smile as it watched her. When Alissia sat down in front of it, the creature reached into its fur and pulled out a small piece of paper.

The first thing Alissia noticed was how different the paper was compared to what she had already seen from this reality. When she unfolded it, she noticed it was written in the old language, and her fingers began to shake in anticipation as she realized it had to be from the Lamians.

This is Mia. She is to help you. We cannot. She understands your words. We cannot communicate. Do not be angry.

Alissia's excitement left her, just as fast as it had come, and after reading the note twice, she crumpled it and held it in her fist. Anger and sadness filled her as she stared back at the tiny creature watching her.

She let out a small, frustrated laugh and said, "And how are you supposed to help me, Mia? I don't suppose you can get me and my friends out of here, can you?"

Mia responded by crawling into Alissia's lap and looking up at her. Alissia could not resist rubbing the creature's furry chest. When she heard a low, purring noise, she smiled.

"You are cute, but how can you help me?" she asked herself, out loud.

Mia put both of her tiny, raccoon-like hands onto Alissia's hand holding the note. She began to pry Alissia's fingers apart, and Alissia laughed before opening her hand.

"You want this?" she asked, holding out the crumpled piece of paper. She watched as the animal took the piece of paper and put it into her mouth. She then chewed and swallowed the note.

"Are you hungry?"

Mia just stared up at Alissia with her big, grey eyes.

"The note said you could understand me. Are you hungry?" When the creature did not respond, she got an idea and decided to ask the question again in the old language. She searched her mind for the proper words before asking again.

Mia responded by nodding her head, and Alissia grinned. "You do understand me," she said, in the old language. She was surprised at how easy the words came to her.

She stood to her feet and carried Mia into the main room, where a covered serving dish was filled with fresh pastries. She took the lid from the small platter and set it down before holding Mia up to choose one.

The small creature stared down at the pastries and reached out and touched one before changing her mind and choosing another.

She snatched the sweet bread from the dish, lifted it to her nose, and inhaled before taking a nibble from it.

Alissia laughed as Mia devoured the pastry. Once finished, Mia looked up expectantly, and Alissia held her up to the dish again and watched as her tiny fingers eagerly grabbed another one.

"I guess you were hungry. Do you think you'll want another one?"

Mia shook her head, and Alissia replaced the lid before walking back to the bedroom. She locked the door before setting Mia on the bed, and then she sat down and pulled the covers over her body.

After Mia finished the pastry, her tiny pink tongue began to lick her lips in search of remnants, and Alissia could not help but laugh.

"You are so adorable," she said.

Mia crawled under the covers and snuggled up close with her back against Alissia's chest. She purred softly as Alissia gently rubbed her fur.

"How are you supposed to help me?" Alissia whispered, thinking out loud.

The sound of purring lulled her into a deep sleep, and when she awoke the next morning, she found herself alone. The door to her bedroom was unlocked, and Mia was nowhere to be found. Alissia searched her chambers in confusion, and part of her began to wonder if the tiny creature had just been a dream. She searched her bed for traces of fur, but nothing could be found.

As she was finishing her breakfast, Nadia and Mela walked in.

"It's finished, and you're going to love it!" Mela said excitedly. She held up a garment bag and opened it to reveal the gown she had designed for Alissia to wear to the ball.

Within minutes, Alissia was standing in front of the long mirror in her walk-in closet. Nadia was sitting on the ottoman grinning with excitement, and Mela was fluffing out the bottom of the dress.

"Well, what do you think?" Mela asked, as she stood back for a better view.

The dress was the most beautiful thing Alissia had ever worn. It was long and black, with a heart-shaped top, and the bust was completely covered in sparkling gems. Alissia wondered if they were real diamonds as they shimmered in the light. The black bodice ended in a triangular shape in the front, and the lower portion of the dress was covered in layers of black and white tulle, giving it a smoky appearance.

Although the dress was accented with long, black gloves that ended above her elbows, Alissia did not like the idea of having her shoulders and top portion of her chest bare for Ian to be able to see or touch. She cleared her throat as she turned around to face the two women.

"Um, do you think we should cover all this up?" she asked, motioning to her bare skin.

Mela laughed and responded, "I've got something to help with that."

The designer eagerly pulled out a black, velvet box and opened it to reveal more diamonds than Alissia had ever seen. She stared at the necklace and matching earrings for a moment before asking, "Whose are those?"

"They're yours. I chose them especially for this dress," Mela answered. She picked up the necklace and set the box aside. She came up behind Alissia and pulled her hair to one side before placing the necklace around her neck.

When Mela reached down for the earrings, Alissia touched the necklace with her fingertips and asked, "Who is paying for all this?"

As Mela began to put the earring on Alissia, she said, "The Eldership. I was told you get the same allowance as a member of the assembly, which means you can afford the finest materials and all the extras that go along with them. In fact, I wasn't supposed to be your designer, but thankfully—well, not thankfully—Viviette got sick right before you got here. My boss was overworked and could not take another client, so she reluctantly put me in charge of your designs."

Mela finished with the last earring before stepping back and giving Alissia a grin.

"You, Lady Alissia, have done a lot for my career. People have been coming into the shop asking for your look, which means I'm getting a large following. They've had to hire more seamstresses to keep up with my designs, and I owe it all to you." She clapped her hands together and added, excitedly, "You are making me a famous designer."

Alissia stared back at Mela in surprise. "People are asking about the dresses I wear? They like them?"

"They love them," Mela answered.

Well, so much for my rebellion, thought Alissia.

Nadia stood to her feet and said, "She'll need matching hair clips."

Mela grinned and pulled out another box. As she and Nadia discussed how Alissia would wear her hair for the ball, Alissia stared at herself in the mirror. The dress was beautiful, too beautiful, and it showed too much. She cringed at the thought of Ian's fingers touching her back while they danced.

The thought of dancing with Ian immediately brought memories of Grady teaching her how to dance. Although it had only been a few months since those first nights in Pallen, the memories felt so distant. A sudden rush of sadness flooded through her, and she quickly excused herself and went to the bathing area.

After taking off the dress, Alissia put on a robe and removed her new jewelry. Her desire to be alone was great, so when she returned the items to Mela, she told the two women she needed to bathe. As soon as she was alone in her bedroom, she curled up on the bed and let the tears come.

She was tired of living a lie, and she was tired of having to smile at a man she could barely stand to be with. She had never been known for being fake, and she had always told it like it was, never worrying about what others thought of her. Now, she spent every day pretending to be something she was not, and it was beginning to feel like it was suffocating the life out of her.

She would gladly give up all the clothing, jewelry, expensive gifts, and everything else she had received since coming to the castle. Most of the women she had met already annoyed her, and she wished she could just walk away from everyone. Well, almost everyone, not her true friends.

She tried not to think about Luke and often had to distract her mind with a book when she was left alone. She had not seen him since their rendezvous in the bathroom, and over the past few days, she had been missing him more than she wanted to admit.

Thoughts of him filled her with emotions she had never experienced, and it bothered her that she could not control them. What she once thought of as arrogance and cockiness, she now considered cute and adorable. She often found herself smiling over the image of his smug grin or use of his pet name for her.

She remembered how he had shown up the day after Fang had killed her two kidnappers. Although she would never admit it to him, she knew she would have been lost without him.

Just thinking about his black, intense eyes and unruly hair filled her body with heat, and she often had to reign in her mind when memories of their self-defense classes came to mind. His body was lean and made with pure muscle. Although she had seen plenty of men like that at the gym, she had never felt a desire for any of them. However, her body greatly craved Luke.

He was fiercely intimidating, yet she now saw vulnerability in him she had never noticed before. His words of some people not being made for love haunted her. She had held onto that very same belief all her life. However, the thought of Luke believing that for himself caused her great pain.

Alissia forced herself to sit up, and she wiped the tears from her eyes. She told herself she did not have time for self-pity, and she needed to stay focused. With a fresh sense of determination, she began to get ready for the day.

Her private lunch with Morton's wife was canceled at the last minute, and Alissia was bothered by the sudden change in plans. Although she had met each of the assembly wives in private, some more than once, she had never had a moment alone with Felina. She was curious to hear what the woman had to say about being stuck in Pallen, or if she would even confide in Alissia.

Anika had mentioned that Morton was still vocally standing up to the assembly, but nothing had physically happened to him or his family. Although Alissia felt sorry for their situation, she was bothered by Morton's threatening words to Grady, and it was hard for her to like him.

She met Anika for a walk in one of the gardens after lunch, and she told her about the small creature that had visited. However, her friend had never heard of an animal matching that description.

Ian came to her that evening, and they had a private dinner before visiting with his parents in their suite. Alissia still had not met his sister and was beginning to get curious as to why she was never around.

Alrik seemed distracted that night, and Alissia wondered what was important enough to hold his attention with her around. As she was saying goodnight to Beula at the door, she noticed Ian and his father having a hushed conversation before Ian gave a curt nod and stepped away.

As the two of them were walking back to her suite, she asked, "Is something bothering your father?"

Ian was quiet for a moment before answering, "He's not happy with someone right now."

"Who?" she asked.

He smiled down at her and gave her hand a squeeze. "No one you should worry about, Alissia. The last thing you want to get involved in is politics." He gave her a wink and added, "You're too good for that."

Once she was alone for the night, Alissia began a Pilates workout in her bedroom, and it was not long before Mia entered the room.

Alissia immediately ended the workout and stared at the small creature curiously.

"Where have you been, little one?"

Mia responded by sitting down in front of Alissia. She then silently stared up at her.

"Can you at least show me how you're getting in here?" Alissia asked.

Mia stood to her feet, and Alissia followed her into the main room. Although Mia was too small to reach the handles of the French doors, she jumped up and caught them. She then turned the handles to open the doors before walking onto the veranda. Once outside, she pointed to the railing and smiled.

Alissia walked over to the railing and looked out in disbelief.

"You climbed up the castle wall?"

Mia grinned.

"I'm on the third floor. Doesn't that scare you?"

The creature shook her head.

"So, you're a climber? What else can you do?" When Mia did not say or do anything, Alissia asked, "Did you go back to the Lamians today?"

Mia shook her head.

Alissia thought for a moment before asking, "Have you been sleeping all day?"

The small creature shook her head again.

A cold chill went through Alissia, and she picked up Mia before walking back into her bedroom. She sat down in front of the fireplace with Mia in her lap and asked, "Have you been walking around the castle today?"

Mia nodded excitedly.

"And you've stayed hidden while doing this?"

Another nod came from Mia.

"All right, as long as you're safe. I guess you know what you're doing since the Lamians trust you and sent you to help me."

Even as she said the words, she knew she did not mean them, at least the part about Mia helping her. What could a tiny, adorable animal that resembled a walking cat and raccoon do for her? Her faith in the Lamians had lessened somewhat since meeting the creature they had chosen to send.

Remembering Fang, she asked, "I have a large, furry friend I call Fang. He's a wolf. Did you see him with the Lamians before you left?

The creature shook her head, and Alissia began to worry.

Mia abruptly stood up and began to tug on Alissia's fingers. After Alissia stood to her feet, she followed Mia into the main room. The creature pointed at the platter of pastries, and Alissia laughed.

"Ah, I see. You're hungry."

Mia chose two pastries before they walked back into the bedroom. Alissia locked the door and prepared for bed, and then the two of them crawled under the covers.

If anything, Mia helped Alissia fall asleep at night. She brought comfort and helped to ease the loneliness.

Chapter *12*

When the day of the ball arrived, Anika and Alissia spent most of the day at a very busy spa within the castle. Because of the handprints on her abdomen, Alissia refused to undress for a mud bath, and an exception was made for her to wear a bathing suit. Although she undressed for a massage, she made sure to keep her stomach covered the entire time.

Her soft skin that slightly shimmered as if covered in glittery body lotion intrigued the women at the spa, and Alissia received a lot of special attention from the workers. It seemed as if they all wanted to meet her, and their attention made Alissia slightly uncomfortable.

As she stood in front of the mirror that evening, she was amazed by her appearance. Nadia had pulled her wild curls onto her head, holding them loosely in place with twinkling hairpins. Curls fell down around her face, and her dark purple hair now sparkled with glitter.

Everything on her seemed to shimmer in the light. Her skin was natural, but the dress looked as if it were covered in glitter, and the jewels attached to the bust of the dress matched the long, diamond earrings and necklace she wore.

Since the ball was at the castle and she would not need to go outside, she did not need a cloak. However, Mela had designed a long, black wrap to go around Alissia's shoulders for the walk to the ballroom.

"You don't have to wear glasses at night, do you?" Mela asked as she and Nadia finished with the final touches. Nadia had taken extra care to apply sparkling eye shadow. Alissia noticed the two women were more excited about the ball than she was, although they were not even attending.

Alissia took off her glasses and let out a small sigh. "I don't have to, but I should. They look strange."

"No, they're beautiful. I would love to have eyes like you," responded Mela. She turned to Nadia and asked, "How much longer before her date arrives?"

"He should be here soon," Nadia answered.

"Then we timed it just right. I think she's perfect."

Alissia set her glasses aside and said, "Um, could you two give me a private moment? I'm a little nervous and would like to be alone to try to calm my nerves."

"Is there anything I can get you?" asked Nadia.

"No, I'm fine. I just need a quiet moment to myself."

Mela began to gather her bags, and Nadia helped her. When they finished collecting everything, Mela stood at the door and said, "You have nothing to fear tonight, Lady Alissia. You are beautiful, and Mr. Ian will be mesmerized by you, as will everyone else at the ball."

"Thank you, Mela. You have turned me into a princess tonight, and I appreciate all that you and Nadia have done for me."

The two women smiled before walking out of the room, and Alissia locked the bedroom door before rushing into the bathing room and collecting the sheath and knife she had rigged to go around her upper leg.

The dress was full of fluff and layers, and it took a bit of work to find her bare skin. She had to remove her long gloves before attaching the knife to her leg. She still did not know if she wore the knife for protection or the feeling of Luke being near her. All she knew was that it always brought comfort to her.

Once she was finished, she went to the mirror and put her gloves back on before staring at her reflection. Part of her wanted to wear her tinted glasses, but the idea of going without them excited her somewhat. Not only was she tired of hiding her eyes behind dark glasses, but also the idea of shocking everyone around her gave her a small sense of satisfaction.

Nadia had done an amazing job with her makeup, and although Alissia did not want Ian to find her attractive, she could not help but smile over her appearance. Until now, she had never had a custom-made dress from a designer or her hair and makeup professionally done, not to mention the diamonds.

Her hand went up to the jewels at her neck as thoughts of her mother and sister came to mind. She wondered if they would even recognize her if they were able to see her as she was now.

Her mind drifted to Grady coming to her room the night of the last ball. It felt like a lifetime since she had been both nervous and excited as he had stood behind her, the two of them staring at their reflection in the mirror. Just as her eyes began to tear up, a knock came at the door.

She quickly blinked back the tears and looked hard at herself in the mirror. She then told herself to get it together. She was not weak, and she did not have time for tears.

Once she opened the bedroom door, Nadia said, somewhat nervously, "My Lady, your escort has arrived."

Alissia walked into the main room to find Ian standing in front of the fireplace. His dark hair was slicked back, and he wore a black suit with a silver vest and white ascot. She could not help but wonder if he had known what color her dress would be or if it was just his luck that they matched.

He gave a smile that would have melted most women's hearts, but it had the opposite effect on her. This date was public and formal, and she dreaded every bit of it.

He met her in the middle of the room and gave an appraising look, smiling with his approval. With his eyebrows raised, he said, "No glasses tonight? I get the pleasure of gazing into your lovely eyes?"

His pleasure displeased her, and she suddenly regretted having made the decision to go without the matching, custom-made glasses Mela had chosen for the dress.

She forced a smile and answered, "It seems my designer and maiden talked me into going without them tonight."

"Well, I owe them much," he said while nodding at Nadia, who was standing alone in the corner of the room. The young woman smiled nervously back at him.

He pulled a little, black box from the inside of his suit pocket and held it out to Alissia. "I have a small gift for you."

She took the box from his hand and opened it to reveal a bracelet covered in shimmering diamonds. The sight of the jewels was enough to knock the breath from her. Memories of opening Grady's gift before the last ball flooded through her mind. Going to a ball with another man and wearing his jewels felt wrong to Alissia.

"You don't like it?" he asked.

Realizing her mistake, she smiled and stammered, "No, I love it. I just . . . I'm surprised. That's all. I thought you said it was a small gift. This is expensive."

He laughed and took the box from her hand. After pulling the bracelet out, he set the box on the table and turned his attention back to her. With an intense look in his eyes that made Alissia desperately want to look away, he said, "Money is nothing, Alissia. You are every-thing to me."

She followed his eyes to the bracelet in his hands and was sur-prised to find an inscription on the back. It read, *Only where the heart is can treasure be found. Alissia, you carry my heart. Ian.*

Instinctively, she gripped the wrap hanging over her shoulders and tightened it.

He then took hold of one of her hands and pulled it from her wrap. He gave it a small squeeze and lifted it to his lips for a light kiss. As he put the bracelet on over her long glove, he said soothingly, "I know we talked about not moving too fast, Alissia, but I can't stop my feelings for you." He glanced over at Nadia, and Alissia was certain he would have tried to kiss her if it were not for them being watched so closely.

It was against this reality's custom for a single woman to be in her chambers alone with a man. That knowledge filled Alissia with com-fort, and she suddenly became extremely grateful over the traditions of her new reality. Even tonight, Ian would not try to follow her into her suite alone, and she did not have to dread trying to get rid of him at the end of their date.

That small knowledge was enough to give her a reason to smile as she looked back at him. She silently told herself he was the type of man that had broken the hearts of many women, and she did not need to feel sorry for him. He was too experienced with his words, and he was too confident around her.

A fresh sense of resolve filled her as she reminded herself that she was not some lonely, gullible woman looking for a man to make her feel like a princess. His charms may work on other women, but her heart was untouchable. Well, almost. She knew Luke and Grady had both gotten through, where others had never before.

Although her heart had never been broken by a bad romance, she had witnessed many of her friends crying over men just like Ian. They had all been smooth talking and handsome, and they had all made promises they had never intended to keep. Alissia had always pitied other women for being so naïve when it came to trusting men with their hearts.

She would never give Ian the chance to make her feel powerless, and she refused to spend her entire evening in fear. She smiled up at him as she reminded herself of his disadvantage. He thought she was a weak and fragile woman. He had no idea of who she really was or what she was capable of doing. She would not be taken advantage of, and she would win this game she was certain he was playing with her.

Out of anger, she wanted to ask him if he only said those words because of his father or because she was a Lamian. Instead, she looked up at him and smiled.

"Thank you, Ian. It is lovely," she said smoothly.

Her words pleased him, and he said, "Shall we go now? I am ready to show you off to the world."

As the two of them strolled to the ballroom, he playfully flirted with her along the way. He often waved and spoke to the many other couples walking in the same direction.

The atmosphere around her was filled with laughter and excitement, and the thought of seeing Luke and Grady filled her with nervous anticipation. Even if she would not be able to spend time with them, she told herself she would be happy with only a glimpse.

As they neared the ballroom, Alissia could hear the music, and her mind traveled back to the dances she had frequently shared with Grady. Although she always felt guilt when she thought of him, memories of her time with him often made her smile. She would laugh whenever her mind turned to the fights she had constantly shared with Luke. Hating him seemed so foreign to her now.

Unlike the last ball, this one was inside. Ian still had to show the proper identification to get in, but once they walked through the large, wooden double doors, Alissia was drawn to the beauty of the décor.

The ballroom was enormous, with high ceilings and fancy chandeliers made of glow and heat stones. The upper level of the outer wall was made of glass, while the lower level held many French doors that led outside. Sconces filled with glow and heat stones were situated on the walls of the room. The marble-like floor was grey, with many glow stones set in place in the pattern of bella flowers.

A few couples were already on the dance floor in the middle of the room, while others were seated or standing at the many tables set up along the walls. A small orchestra was playing in a corner, with a bar situated nearby.

A server walked up to them, and Ian took two drinks from the tray.

"Do you need to stow your wrap?" he asked as he handed her one of the drinks.

"No, I'm fine."

He grinned and said, "From what I've seen of that dress, you have nothing to hide."

Alissia responded by taking a sip of her drink and was relieved when Ian's attention turned to a small group of people standing nearby. He took her by the hand and led her towards them.

She and Ian spent the next hour mingling as more people arrived at the ball. Unlike the last dance, all the women were overly complimentary to Alissia. She was now a woman with a title, and it seemed everyone she met wanted to befriend her. They all made comments on how beautiful she looked and how everyone was talking about her style in clothing. Some even commented on how they wished they had her eyes. She politely declined many lunches, and she tried to act shy. However, Anika was not by her side to help with the conversations, and the women were persistent when she tried to withdraw from them.

Ian seemed happy with showing her off to people, and he often brought attention to her. Although she forced herself to smile and laugh, she was soon annoyed by all the unwanted attention she was getting. It did not help that Grady was standing nearby talking to another group of people. She struggled with keeping her eyes off him and tried to physically turn her back to him so her eyes would not instinctively look his way.

"Hello, dear. You look lovely tonight, and I finally get to see your beautiful eyes," Beula said. She then gave Alissia a hug before Alrik pulled her into his arms also.

After he pulled away, he looked into her eyes and said, "Beautiful! My dear, you have beautiful eyes. Why do you choose to hide them each night?"

By now, Alissia was regretting her choice to not wear glasses. She did not like all the extra attention from everyone.

She smiled and answered politely, "They're different."

Beula responded, "Honey, different isn't always such a bad thing. You are a Lamian, and you should never be ashamed of that. You are a beautiful person, inside and out. There's no other woman I'd want to be by my son's side than you. We are all very blessed to know you."

Ian leaned down and kissed his mother's cheek.

"I agree, Mother."

He took Alissia by the hand and gave it a squeeze before bringing it up to his lips for a kiss. As he was lowering it, Beula took Alissia's hand from him and studied the bracelet on her wrist. She looked up expectantly at Ian, and he nodded.

"You did well, son."

He grinned in response.

"Have you seen your sister?" Alrik asked.

Ian shook his head, and although they continued to smile, Alissia felt a subtle shift in their mood. She was curious as to why she had still not met Emera, and part of her was eager to meet the mysterious sister. In Alissia's opinion, anyone that made the Dursts uncomfortable was worth meeting.

She and Ian talked to his parents for a long moment before he took her by the hand and led her towards the dance floor. They stopped at an empty table, and he pulled the wrap from her shoulders.

"You don't need that while we dance," he said, with a mischievous grin.

He then took her by the hand and led her onto the floor as a slow song began to play. He pulled her in close, and she felt his fingertips on her back, above the bodice of her dress.

"Ah, I finally have you in my arms, Alissia." He leaned down to catch a whiff of her perfumed body and added, "You smell so good."

Alissia closed her eyes and mentally scolded herself for spending the day at the spa. When she opened them again, she found herself staring into a familiar set of intense, dark eyes, and she felt her body stiffen.

Although Luke was standing with a small group of people near the edge of the dance floor, his attention was completely on her. She knew she should look away, but she could not bring herself to take her eyes from him.

Even while dressed in a formal, black suit with his hair pulled back, his appearance was fierce and intimidating compared to those around him.

Everything within her yearned for him at that moment, and she soon found herself forcing back threatening tears. Luke's attention went back to the people around him, and Ian turned their bodies so that she could no longer see Luke.

"Alissia?"

She closed her eyes and focused on her breathing.

"Alissia, is something wrong?"

Her eyes opened, and she forced her voice to sound calm, as she said, "No. Why?"

"You seem upset by something."

"I, um . . . I was just wondering if my people have dances like this. I can't remember anything, and it bothers me."

He gave her body a slight squeeze and said, "You know, some of the world's finest doctors live in Pallen, and they are available to you. I've been waiting for the right moment to talk to you about it, because I feared it would upset you." He paused before adding, "Alissia, I worry about you, and I want to help you get your memory back, if it's possible. I've already talked to some doctors about your memory loss, and they are willing to help."

Alissia had expected the Eldership to have her see a doctor when she first arrived, and she was surprised the subject had not been brought up before now.

"I don't want to take any medications," she said.

"Why don't we schedule time with a couple of doctors and see what they can do? In fact, you don't have to worry about it. I can take care of it for you, and I'll talk to Nadia about your schedule."

Before she could respond, the music transitioned into a fast song, and Ian began to swing her around the dance floor. She still remembered all the moves Grady had taught her, and she was relieved to be free of conversation for the first time since arriving at the ball. When the song stopped, she smiled to let Ian know she wanted to dance some more.

"Ah, I forgot how much energy you have," he said, laughing.

It was no surprise to find Ian was an exceptional dancer, and his fingers often found a way to playfully touch her body each time she passed by him. He enjoyed himself greatly, but after the third fast dance, he twirled her to the edge of the dance floor. Pulling her into his arms and breathing heavily, he said, "I need a drink, my love. I cannot keep up with you."

She laughed, and he took her by the hand and led her to the table where her wrap was located. After she sat down, he kissed her hand and said, "Wine for the lady?"

She nodded, and he left her to go to the bar on the opposite side of the dance floor.

Alone for the first time, Alissia began to look around the room, and she smiled to herself when she noticed Anika and Langley on the dance floor.

She was startled when an unfamiliar young woman abruptly plopped down on the chair across from her.

"So you're the Lamian everyone's talking about?"

Chapter *13*

"I don't see why people love these things so much," said the woman, while adjusting the top of her bodice. She scowled to herself and added, "Ugh! Can this dress get any more uncomfortable?"

After dropping her hands onto the table, she said, "You don't look like a Lamian. You're too tall for one thing, and since we don't have much time before we're interrupted, I'll just go ahead and say it. You're not a Lamian. So why are you here, and what do you want?"

Alissia stared at the girl in disbelief. She looked to be in her early twenties, maybe younger, and she spoke in a thick, unfamiliar accent. She had long, brown hair with natural honey-colored highlights. The front of it was loosely pulled back, leaving wavy tendrils to fall around her face.

Even with her fancy dress and jewels, she did not fully resemble a delicate woman from the Eldership. Her arms revealed muscles similar to Alissia's, she had short painted nails, and her skin was tan, yet they were in Pallen during the winter.

When Alissia did not respond, the girl leaned in closer and said in the old language, "You have put the Lamians in a lot of danger, and it is my job to find out why you have done this." She turned her head towards the bar, but too many people were in the way for it to be seen. Continuing in the old language, she added, "If you don't tell me what you are doing, I will have to make the decision on my own, and, while others would prefer you to live, your fate doesn't concern me in the least."

"Are you threatening me?" Alissia asked, in disbelief. Although she did not bother with the old language, she did use her fake accent.

"If that is how you see it. Why have you put the Lamians in danger?"

Alissia knew her time with the girl was limited, and her curiosity was more than piqued by the stranger's knowledge of the old language and of the Lamians.

"How do you know the Lamians?" she asked in return.

The girl frowned and said, "I asked you a question first. What are you doing here?"

"Maybe I don't want to be here," Alissia spat out. "Now how do you know about the Lamians?"

The girl ignored Alissia's question and responded, "If you don't want to be here, who do you trust?"

"No one."

The girl's scowl grew, and she leaned in closer. "Look, if you want help, I need to know if there is anyone we can use to get you out of here."

"And how do I know you're not trying to trick me?"

Before the girl could respond, they were interrupted by Anika's playful voice. "Alissia, I saw you on the dance floor, and you were having too much fun."

Alissia stood to her feet and accepted a hug from Anika before smiling up at Langley.

"Sit with me?" she asked.

"Where's your date?" Langley responded.

"Getting a drink. He'll be back soon."

Anika said, "Ooh, Alissia, I love the dress. Mela is amazing. Are those real diamonds?"

"I don't know," answered Alissia, staring down at her sparkly chest. She lifted her wrist and said with mocked joyfulness, "Look what Ian gave me." Anika's eyes got big, and she added, "There's even an inscription of love on the back."

"Wow!" was Anika's only response, her eyebrows raised.

When Alissia noticed Ian walking towards them, she quickly bent down and said to the girl still sitting at the table, "This is Anika. Whatever you have to say, you can say it to her."

Anika's eyebrows lifted questioningly, and Alissia said, "Talk to her about it."

Ian handed Alissia her drink before holding his hand out to Langley. "It's Langley, isn't it?"

"It is," Langley responded as they shook hands.

"I hear I should be thanking you for taking care of Alissia before she found her way to the Eldership."

Langley smiled politely. "I believe my wife wanted to spend the winter in Pallen."

Alissia became distracted when she noticed the strange, young woman get up from the table and slip into the crowd. Her eyes continued to scan the same area until Ian asked, "Isn't that right, Alissia?"

She looked up at him in confusion and said, "I'm sorry. I was daydreaming. What's right?"

"I was talking about how much you love to dance."

She looked over at Anika and smiled.

"You can thank Anika for that. She's the one that taught me."

He raised his eyebrows and said, "Really?"

She lied. "Yes, and she's a great teacher."

She pretended to distract herself by setting her drink down and putting her wrap over her shoulders.

The four of them talked for a moment before Morton and his wife walked over. Langley and Anika then politely excused themselves from the conversation.

"It's a shame you and my wife have not had a chance to get to know each other, Lady Alissia." Looking at Ian, he added, "It seems someone mistakenly removed your lunch date with Felina from your schedule. I want to personally invite you to have dinner or lunch with us later this week. Do you think you can have that arranged?"

Alissia's eyes went to Felina. Instead of a confident wife of an Eldership man, her face showed signs of worry and stress. Alissia could not help but feel sorry for the woman. She was used to being the wife of a prestigious and powerful man, yet suddenly she was stripped of everything. Not just her social status, her life was in danger.

Alissia smiled at Felina and said, "It would be my pleasure to join you, and I will have Nadia schedule something within the week."

"Hello, Morton. Felina, you look lovely as usual. Are you enjoying your evening?"

Felina answered Alrik with a silent nod.

"I've been telling Beula we should invite the two of you over for dinner soon," he said.

Beula added, "Or Felina and I can spend a day at the spa." Smiling up at her husband, she said, "There's more to life than food, dear."

"Ah, so there is," he said, giving his wife a playful grin.

Morton's face had turned red, and a look of fury was in his eyes. "Don't even pretend we're friends," he hissed, between clenched teeth.

Alrik nodded, "I understand we've had many disagreements lately, and we will probably never agree on certain things. However, I'm worried about you and your health, and I'm willing to try to ease some of the tension between us if you are."

"What do you mean, my health?" Morton asked, accusingly.

Alrik looked uncomfortable for a moment before saying, "Lord Gello told me about your conversation with Dr. Skelinty." When Morton went to speak, Alrik held up his hand and added, "Don't be upset. He only told me because he was worried. He suggested Grady step in and take your place so that you can rest."

"I will not be forced to step down," Morton said, angrily. The people around them began to turn around at the sound of his loud voice. "And I don't even know Dr. Skelinty. Is this your way of threatening me?"

"No threats, Morton. I've never threatened you," Alrik said.

"No, you get other people to do it for you."

Ian picked up Alissia's wine glass and gave it to her before taking her other hand. "Well, this is a conversation that does not involve me or Lady Alissia. Will you please excuse us?"

As he turned to leave, Morton said, "That's exactly who this conversation involves."

Ian shook his head and ignored the comment. He led Alissia away.

"What did he mean by that?" she asked.

He stopped walking and let go of her hand once they were halfway across the room. "My father and Morton disagree over many things. Only one of them has to do with you."

"Like what?"

"Morton is of the belief that you should be forced to go to Allure to meet the Elders."

"And what does your father believe?" she asked.

He thought for a moment before saying, "He believes you should have a choice." He took a sip of his wine. "Right now the Eldership is having internal disagreements on a lot of things, Alissia. It's been that way for a long time. I don't think you should worry anything about it. Let them fight among themselves. It has nothing to do with you."

His attention went to something over her shoulder, and Alissia turned around to find a man and woman walking towards them. She immediately guessed the young woman to be Ian's sister. She was very pretty, and her resemblance to Beula was strong. Although her long, black hair was pulled up into a complicated braid, silky, straight stands hung down around her face. She wore a long, burgundy dress that clung to her slender body, and it had a split up the side of one leg. She was taller than her petite mother, and she walked with an air of confidence.

"Brother," she said with a smile as she walked up to them, her accent noticeably stronger than the rest of her family.

"Emera."

She turned to Alissia and said, "So, you must be the Lady Alissia everyone is talking about."

Alissia gave a polite smile and nodded.

"It's a shame we have not met before now." She gave Ian a cool look and added, "I was beginning to believe my brother is embarrassed of me."

He smiled and said, "Emera, you know that is far from the truth."

She gave a snide laugh, and responded, "And what does our family know about truth, dear brother?"

His strained smile faded, and he said, "More than you are willing to give them credit for."

She turned to the man standing beside her and said, "I really could use another drink. Do you mind?"

Her date took her by the hand and kissed it before answering, "Of course not." He turned his attention to Ian and Alissia and said, "Pardon me." He then walked away.

Emera had a calculating look in her eyes as she watched the man walk away, and then she turned her attention back to Alissia.

"I have heard many delightful things about you, Lady Alissia. It seems my brother is not the only person enchanted by you. Even women can't seem to stop talking about you and your . . . uh . . . *unique* sense of style, and I admit that I was a bit skeptical until now. You are as beautiful as they say, if not more."

Although Alissia had received many compliments throughout the evening and was used to it by now, there was something about Emera that made her uncomfortable. However, her presence seemed to put a strain on Ian, and she was curious to know why.

She smiled back politely and responded, "Thank you, Emera. You are kind."

The young woman found humor in Alissia's words and said, "Oh, I wouldn't say that." She looked at Ian and added, "There are many that would disagree."

Ian did not respond, and Emera turned her attention back to Alissia.

"We should go to lunch this week and also do some shopping. If you don't mind, I would like to get to know the woman that has my brother's attention. Shall I set something up with your handmaid?"

"I would like that very much," Alissia answered, honestly. She was eager to learn more about this member of Alrik's family.

"Have you spoken with Father or Mother tonight?" Ian asked.

Emera responded coolly, "Speaking of Father, which do you think he would prefer the least, Grady Bolair or Luke Harrison?"

Alissia nearly choked on the sip of wine she had just taken. When she glanced up at Ian, she noticed his clenched teeth, and he seemed to be struggling with his calm façade.

He forced a smile onto his face and answered, somewhat warningly, "You already have a date."

"Oh, but he is such a bore, and he's beginning to get possessive. You of all people should know how annoying that can be, dear brother."

Before he could respond, Emera turned to Alissia and said, "Which do you prefer? You were with both of them, were you not?"

She smoothly hooked her arm into Alissia's and turned their bodies so they could see Grady standing with a group of people across the room.

Emera said, "Grady from Allure, and future elder. He's handsome and is one of Allure's most eligible bachelors, although I hear he's married to his career. That would be annoying."

She turned Alissia again, and Alissia's heart skipped a beat as she spotted Luke talking to a group of men.

Emera said, "Then there's Luke, dark and mysterious. Although, I hear he's married to his career also. Do you know people say he is a born killer?" She added, roguishly, "I can only imagine what he could do with his hands."

"Enough! You need to stop, now," Ian said, sternly.

Emera laughed and said, "Oh, but you know she's thought about it. What woman wouldn't?"

"I'm not a human woman," Alissia blurted out, pulling away from Emera.

Emera shook her head. "Oh, my dear, you are a woman, no matter what you tell yourself. And even the purest of women would have temptation, especially when it comes to those two delightful men."

To Ian she said, "I'm thinking Grady is my best choice."

He grabbed his sister by the arm and said warningly, "You need to stop playing games, little sister. It's time for you to get over it."

She glared back at him and said coldly, "I didn't start this game, remember? And besides, this is what you all wanted from me. You should be happy."

She pulled her arm free from her brother and smoothly walked away. Anger and confusion filled Alissia as she watched Emera walk up to Grady and put her hand on his arm to get his attention.

When Alissia looked up at Ian, he was glaring across the room, and she followed his eyes to find Alrik and Beula walking away from Morton and his wife. They were both laughing. However Morton and Felina did not share their enjoyment.

Her heart began to drum ferociously as a thought came to mind. Luke had already mentioned Grady being killed if he did anything wrong. Would this give Alrik a reason to kill him?

Her eyes instinctively went to Luke, and she found him staring at her. When their eyes met, she looked at him for a short moment before looking over at Grady and Emera. She looked back at Luke just as his head was turning back to her, and she was certain he had seen Emera with Grady.

He turned his attention back to the people he was with, and she looked up at Ian, almost dropping her wine glass when she met his stare. Although she quickly forced a calm look onto her face, she knew he had noticed her surprise from realizing he had been watching her.

His jaw twitched, and she thought she saw a flash of anger in his eyes. After a moment of silence, he took her by the hand and gave it a light squeeze.

"I am sorry about my sister. She is angry and bitter over something that happened many years ago, and she blames our father," he said.

He led Alissia to the back of the room, where they stopped at one of the doors leading to the garden. He then took the wine glass from her hand and pulled her wrap in tighter around her shoulders before opening one of the French doors. Her personal guards followed them as they stepped outside.

"Oh, wow! What are those?" she asked, in wonder.

The lawn was filled with white, tent-like pods covered in glowing, white bella flowers. Some were bigger than others and filled with multiple couples laughing as they talked. Others were small and meant to give a lone couple a bit of privacy, yet having been made of a sheer material, they were public enough for unwed couples to sit alone.

Flaming torches gave off heat and lit the way along each of the paths in the open garden. Ian chuckled lightly as he began to lead her towards one of the small, unoccupied pods.

"I love that about you, Alissia."

"What?" she asked, in confusion.

"You always seem amazed by everything around you. The things I've always taken for granted fill you with wonder, and I often wish I could see things through your eyes."

She said, "I guess that's a benefit from having no memories. Everything is new to me."

He held the sheer, curtained door to one side, and Alissia stepped through. She sat down on the cushioned bench in the pod, and although the walls looked flimsy and thin, the air was surprisingly warm. Two heat stones hung down from the ceiling to give off a small, red glow. The walls and ceiling seemed to shimmer from the light of the bella flowers covering the pod. It was both beautiful and romantic, not where she wanted to be alone with Ian.

Whether her anxiety came from their intimate setting or from the anger she had seen on his face earlier, she did not know. He seemed calm now, and there was no sign of his anger as he sat down beside her.

He took her by the hand and asked, "What are you thinking, my dear?"

Although the unwanted question made her heart beat even faster, she sounded calm as she responded, "I could ask you the same. You seemed upset earlier."

He nodded. "I was. Emera sometimes has that effect on people. She can be nice and perverse at the same time. I guess I wanted and still want to protect you from her."

"She's your sister. She can't be that bad."

"It's not that she's a bad person. She's not. She's just hurting right now, but she'll heal eventually."

"What happened to her?"

"She thought she was in love years ago, and she blames our father for the death of the boy. Father had nothing to do with it, but she refuses to believe that. In the end, his death was probably the best thing that could have happened to her."

"What do you mean?"

"He was not good for her. She was young at the time, and he took advantage of that." Ian gave her hand a squeeze before adding, "Alissia, I don't want you to get caught up in her pain. You should probably stay away from her. She's not stable right now, and I don't want to see you getting hurt."

His warning only made Alissia more curious about his sister. She said, reassuringly, "I won't get hurt now that I know what happened. In fact, it sounds like she could use a friend."

He shook his head and smiled, "I love that about you. You seem so innocent, and you try to see the best in people."

Alissia immediately thought, *Well that's a new one for the record!* His comment left her speechless, and she looked down to hide her amusement.

When he started to pull off her glove, she looked up at him in alarm. He laughed and said, "You can relax. I only want to feel your soft skin when I hold your hand." He set her glove aside and held her hand up to his. "So tiny," he said.

Every part of her body tensed up as she realized where the conversation was headed. He pulled her hand up to his lips and began to kiss each of her fingers. They were in the most romantic setting she had been in her entire life, and she was dressed to kill, thanks to Mela. With the right man, this could have been the perfect night, yet it was beginning to turn into a nightmare.

He lifted up her chin, and she found herself barely able to breathe as she met his gaze.

"Please don't be scared of me, Alissia," he said softly, and he began to lower his head to hers.

She turned just in time, and his lips met the side of her face. He tenderly kissed her cheek a few times before his lips began to travel the short distance to her mouth, and he placed his hand on the other side of her face.

"I'm not a human, Ian," she said, in desperation. When he turned her face towards him, she saw the strong yearning in his eyes, and everything within her told her to run. Although he was not forcing his body on hers like the night she had been raped, his unwanted desire caused her mind to panic, and she quickly stood to her feet.

In a hushed, yet frantic voice, she said, "You don't understand. I need to know who I am before I can commit to anyone. I don't even know what it means to be a Lamian."

He stared at her for a short moment, as if in thought.

"Alissia, are you in love with Grady or Luke?"

The question hit her like Pear Harbor, completely off guard. She felt her cheeks and ears inflame. "What?" she asked in mock disbelief. "Grady was a complete gentleman and treated me with nothing but respect."

She suddenly remembered the first time she'd kissed Grady, how she'd grabbed his neck and taken it like a cookie from a cookie jar. "I . . . I'm very grateful to him for all he has done for me, but our main concern was trying to find out what happened to me. He never once tried or spoke of anything else."

She felt the cool air bite at her flush, clammy skin and cleared her throat before continuing.

"As for Luke . . ." She faltered at his name. "He . . . he saved my life. But then he dragged me back to Pallen as fast as the horses would carry us. Do you know what it was like getting up before dawn every day and rarely stopping?" She made a facial expression showing her disgust as she added, "He even made me eat something called murdock root. Have you ever eaten murdock root?"

Ian shook his head, and she continued, "By the time I got back to Pallen, I was sore from riding a horse all day, I was starving, and I was exhausted."

"Do you think I don't respect you, because I want more?" he asked.

She sat back down next to him so that she did not have to speak as loud. The pod was made of thin material, and although it kept the heat in, it did nothing to muffle sounds. She could hear conversations from some of the other pods around her.

She thought about how to answer his question. In the real world, this would have been a perfect opportunity for her to say they should just be friends or that she never wanted to see him again. However, neither of those two options were a choice for her, especially since he knew about her ability to power stones. She just needed to buy more time.

She tried to sound sincere as she said, "Ian, I think you are an honorable man, and you seem to care about me a lot."

"I love you, Alissia. I know we've not known each other long, but I have never cared for anyone like this before. How about you? Do you think you could ever come to love me one day?"

Everything within Alissia screamed no. In an attempt to lighten the mood, she said playfully, "Well, you can be charming."

He smiled and looked down for a moment. Then he took her by the hand and looked hard into her eyes. "I will contact the best doctors Pallen has to offer, and we will learn more about who you are. Then, you will be mine one day, Lady Alissia."

Her smile faltered at his last statement, and she quickly looked down while she regained her composure. Unlike the excitement she had felt when Luke had spoken those same words to her, Ian's use of them caused her great pain, reminding her of a happier moment in time.

"Thank you for understanding," she said. She looked back up at him with a smile, forcing her pain aside.

As they walked back into the ballroom, she noticed Luke standing with a group of people near the doors. He glanced her way, and she immediately felt guilt over him seeing her walk in from the gardens with Ian. It did not help that Ian was holding her hand, as if she were his property.

By this time, she was mentally exhausted from everything that had happened in the few hours they had been at the ball. She still did not know anything about the strange girl that had asked too many questions and threatened her life, and she could not help but wonder if Anika had learned anything about her.

Alissia excused herself to go to the bathroom. As she was walking across the room, she noticed Emera dancing with one of the two men she had seen with Luke the night she and Ian had met him in the walkway. She wondered if Luke had sent one of his men to distract Emera from Grady.

When she returned, she found Ian talking alone with Luke, and she hesitated walking up to them. Ian soon noticed her and motioned for her to join them.

"I was just telling Luke how much you enjoyed his murdock root," Ian said, pleasantly.

Alissia pulled her wrap in tighter, and in an attempt to hide her shaking hands she did not let go of it. Appearing calm at that moment was her biggest struggle of the night, as each of her senses were directed at Luke.

Even in a suit, his presence was dominating. A memory flashed through her mind of one of the heated kisses they had shared in the bathroom, and she tried to push it away. Thinking this could be a test from Ian, she had to make an attempt to sound lighthearted as she smiled and responded, "I never want to eat murdock root again." She did not trust herself to say anything more.

Luke and Ian both laughed, and Ian put his arm around her and pulled her in close, possessively. She knew her body was tense, and she mentally demanded herself to get it together.

There was no sign of tension in Luke's voice as he said, "I believe it's an acquired taste, and I do apologize now, Lady Alissia, for all the discomforts you experienced while traveling with me. In my defense, I am accustomed to a certain lifestyle and spend most of my time traveling alone than with others, especially a lady such as yourself. My main concern was getting you back to Pallen safely, but I see now how hard that had to be for you. Please forgive me."

"No apologies are necessary. You saved my life. Thank you." She looked up at Ian and tried to sound playful as she added, "I would like to dance some more, if you are willing."

"Ah, it seems Lady Alissia has recovered from her travels, and she is filled with much energy. Pardon us as I try to keep up with her," Ian said.

Luke responded with a grin that made Alissia's heart flutter, and he nodded. "Good luck with that." He turned to Alissia and added, "I hope you enjoy the rest of your evening."

As he walked away, Alissia was surprised at the affect his departure had on her physically. It took all her strength to look away and force a smile onto her face as she peered up at Ian. "Ready?" she asked, trying to sound cheery.

They walked to an empty table, where he took her wrap and set it down. Once a new song began, they joined the other dancers on the floor. The first two songs were fast, and by the time Ian pulled her into his arms for a slow dance, her heart beat as if it was trying to escape from her chest. It took a moment before Ian spoke.

"Are you having fun?"

"I am," she answered.

"I should take you dancing more often. You would like that, wouldn't you?"

"I would, but do you enjoy dancing? It's not all about me."

"I enjoy spending time with you, Lady Alissia, and I enjoy seeing you smile. That is what makes me happy." He pulled her in tighter and added, "*You* make me happy."

"Have I made you happy tonight, or are you upset with me about earlier?"

He stopped dancing and placed his hand under her chin, tilting her face up so she would look into his eyes. He said, somberly, "No, I did not get upset with you, and I want you to always tell me how you feel. Alissia, I want you to know you can always be honest with me, and I never want you to think you have to do something for me that makes you feel uncomfortable."

She nodded, and he let go of her chin. He then pulled her back into his arms, and they began to sway to the music again.

He said, "I won't deny that I want to kiss you right now more than anything else, but I would never force myself on you. I will wait, and I will prove myself to you."

Alissia smiled up at him and said, "Thank you."

The next song was a formal slow dance, and she pretended to focus on the steps as they moved across the floor. Not wanting to talk to any more people, she kept Ian dancing for three more songs.

As they went to retrieve her wrap, Alissia happened to notice Emera leading Luke's companion outside, into the garden. Like Luke, the man had a dominating, military air to him, and Alissia was surprised by Emera's boldness. She was holding a glass of wine in one hand and pulling him along with the other. Although Alissia could only see his back, he seemed happy to be led by Emera. Emera turned around, and Alissia noticed the roguish look she gave to him as they reached the doors.

"Do you see why I'd rather you not spend time with my sister?"

Alissia smiled up at Ian and said, "Are you worried she'll want to drag me into the gardens also?"

Ian laughed as he helped to put her wrap over her shoulders, and they began to walk towards his parents. They were standing with another group of people not far away.

"Are you having fun, my dear?" Beula asked, as they walked up.

"I am."

"It seems Alissia loves to dance, and I will have to take her more often," said Ian.

Alrik said, "I had wanted to ask her for a dance, but your mother has kept me busy all evening talking to everyone. I've practically had to drag her to the dance floor more than once."

"I do love to talk," Beula said, with a laugh.

"Well I'll soon be walking Alissia back to her chambers," Ian said. "I just wanted to let you know Emera is still here and is outside in the gardens."

Beula gave Alissia a worried look and asked, "Have you met Emera?"

"I did."

"And how did that go, dear?" Beula asked.

"She was nice."

Ian shook his head and said, "That's not what I'd call it."

Alissia smiled and said reassuringly, "I understand, and it wasn't personal."

"Well, I hope she didn't say anything to hurt your feelings," Beula said.

"She didn't."

Ian bent down and kissed Beula on the cheek before saying, "Goodnight, Mother." He placed his hand on his father's arm and said, "I'll meet you for breakfast in the morning."

"All right, son," Alrik said. He bent down and kissed Alissia on the cheek before saying, "I'll see you soon."

Beula gave Alissia a hug before Ian took her by the hand. He began to lead her towards the exit; however, she soon found herself standing in front of Grady. He was talking with a small group of men when she and Ian walked up to him.

"Grady Bolair, I want to thank you for all you've done for Lady Alissia," Ian said. "She told me tonight how much you tried to help her, and I'm grateful to you for bringing her to Pallen safely."

Although Alissia's blood was rushing through her veins, she could not tell if it was because she was standing so close to Grady, or because of her confusion and anger towards Ian. As Ian wrapped his arm around her and pulled her body in close, she wondered if he was testing her or if he truly wanted to thank Grady.

Grady seemed calm and unaffected by her presence. He gave a curt nod and smiled.

"It's what I do. I only wish I could have saved her from being kidnapped in the first place." He turned his attention to her and said, "Lady Alissia, are you enjoying your time at the Eldership?"

She took his lead and said, "I love it here. Everyone's been so kind, and I should have believed you when you told me I could trust the Eldership. I never really did say thank you for all that you've done for me. I've been so busy since I've been here."

"That's no problem." He looked at Ian and said, "How long do you plan to stay in Pallen? Spring will soon be here. Where does your father have you going next?"

Ian looked down at Alissia and gave her a grin. When he looked back at Grady, he said, "We haven't talked about it much. I've been somewhat distracted lately by a beautiful woman, and I think a lot of my plans depend on her. I may be in Pallen for a while."

Grady smiled down at her, and with a nod, he said, "I see."

"Well, it's getting late," Ian said, as he let go of Alissia and held out his hand. Grady shook it and wished them the best before she and Ian headed for the door. However, a loud, feminine scream soon stopped them, and they both turned around.

A small crowd had surrounded someone, but there were too many people for her to see who it was. A man's voice yelled, "We need Dr. Skelinty. Now!"

Everyone moved out of the way as a man rushed into the midst of the crowd, and Alissia thought she glimpsed Felina crying before people covered her view.

The music stopped, and everyone in the room stared towards the commotion. Whispered conversations soon filled the air until a woman cried out, frantically, "No. No. He can't be dead!" She sobbed loudly before continuing, "He was healthy!"

The pain in her voice tore at Alissia's heart, and it took a moment before she realized Ian was saying something to her.

"Alissia?" She looked up at him, and he continued. "Let me walk you home."

She said, "But who is it?"

"Come," he said, leading her towards the door. "I'll tell you while we walk."

They walked in silence for a while before he said, "It was Morton. He's dead."

She had already suspected it was Morton, and she had been wondering how this would affect Grady.

"What happened?" she asked.

"I'm not sure, but I heard that he was diagnosed with gaulding this past week."

"What's gaulding?"

"It's a disease that attacks the heart and makes it swell."

Alissia thought for a moment before saying, "But he said he wasn't."

"True. But he also said he didn't want Grady to take his place. I don't think he wanted to give up his position."

"So Grady will be taking his place now?"

"I would think so. I'm not associated with the Eldership or familiar with all their rules, but I believe Grady is ranked high enough that he can take Morton's place here."

He lifted her hand up and gave it a kiss. "I wouldn't worry about matters of the Eldership unless it concerns you. I, myself, don't even bother with them."

"Really? Then why are you here?"

"I have trade business in this area. It's what I do for a living."

"So you travel a lot?"

"Just within the past few years. I haven't spent much time at home." He dropped her hand and put his arm around her shoulder. "However, that can easily change now that I've found a reason to stay in one place."

"What did Grady mean when he asked about where you were going next? Do you have plans to leave?" she asked, silently hoping he did.

"No, I'm not leaving any time soon. When I arrived in Pallen, I had planned to leave in the spring, but all that has changed."

"Why aren't you leaving?"

Alissia immediately regretted her question as he stopped walking and stared down at her. His full attention made her uncomfortable, and she bit down on her lower lip.

"*You* are the reason I have chosen not to leave, Alissia. My feelings for you grow with each day, and you are not someone I can walk away from. For you, I'm here to stay."

She forced a smile and was relieved when he turned and began to walk again. Once at her door, she said a quick goodnight before entering her suite. As with each night Ian walked her home, she was grateful for the presence of the guards at her door. If not for them, she often imagined Ian would have tried to give her a goodnight kiss.

Chapter 14

Alissia leaned with her back against the door and closed her eyes. She let out a sigh of relief, happy the night had finally come to an end.

"How was the ball?"

She opened her eyes to find Nadia sitting by the fireplace doing something resembling knitting. The woman placed her work in a bag before standing to her feet.

"You didn't have to wait for me, Nadia."

"Yes, I did. It's my job, and you need help getting all those pins from your hair. Shall I also help you get dressed for bed?"

"No, I can dress myself. However, if you will loosen the dress, I will change into my night clothes, and then you can undo my hair."

Alissia walked over to Nadia, and she removed her wrap and set it on the sofa before turning her back to the young woman. Once her dress was loosened, she held onto the front of it as she walked into the bedroom and closed the door. She then quickly changed out of the dress before putting on her long nightgown. She put on a robe to be sure her knife would remain concealed, and then she opened the door to the bedroom.

It did not take long for Nadia to carefully remove all the pins from Alissia's hair. The maiden then hung the dress and wrap in the closet before leaving for the night. Alissia made sure to let Nadia know she did not want to be disturbed in the morning. After all that had happened at the ball, she did not want to see anyone for a while.

Once alone, she washed her face and got ready for bed. As she was covering the glow stones in the room, Mia walked in.

"Hello, little one. I assume you've been roaming the castle. Aren't you afraid someone will see you?"

The creature grinned up at her as if that was not a problem to be concerned with.

Alissia was exhausted and not in the mood for talk. However, Mia was in the mood for food, and lots of it. After two pastries, the tiny fur ball devoured cookies, cake, and some raw root vegetables. Alissia wearily watched her furry little friend eat, and when she began to slowly lick each of her fingers, Alissia gave a mental scream.

"Finished?" she asked, with a forced smile.

Mia cocked her head and studied Alissia's face for a moment before walking towards the bedroom. The creature must have noticed her dark mood, because once they were in bed, she began to rub Alissia's hair soothingly. However, Mia's attempt to calm Alissia, along with the effect of the fireplace, did nothing to clear the crease in her forehead. Too much had happened that night.

She wondered about the young girl that had spoken as if she knew the Lamians, and she had also spoken of others. Alissia did not know if she should be happy the girl had mentioned helping her get out of her situation or if she should be worried the girl had mentioned killing her. Was she there to help, or was she a threat? She could have been planted by Alrik to find out how much Alissia actually knew.

Ian was getting too close, and she was beginning to feel more repulsed by his touch. Although Anika had warned her more than once that she needed to keep him entertained and on her good side, Alissia was beginning to wonder what would happen if she told him there would never be a chance between them. What would Alrik do then? Couldn't she just be a close friend to Alrik and Beula? Did she have to be his future daughter-in-law to keep Alrik satisfied? If she turned Ian away, would it put her friends' lives in danger, or just her own?

The fact that Ian knew one of her secrets and promised he had not told anyone, including Alrik, made her wonder if Ian was putting her before his father. She easily imagined him telling Alrik everything that happened between them, but a small part of her wanted to believe Ian was better than that.

She knew he was not naïve, and she did not believe it was a coincidence he had led her to Luke and Grady while at the ball. He had put his arm around her possessively, and she wondered if that was his subtle warning to both men.

The thought of Morton scared her, and she hoped that Anika would be able to tell her more about it in the morning, along with the details of the strange woman.

When she began to worry about having to see doctors, she quickly pushed those thoughts aside. She had known the day would come, and there was nothing she could do about it. She would have to find a way to deal with it when the time arrived.

She began to replay in her mind the conversations she had shared with Grady and Luke at the ball, and tears came to her eyes. Mia snuggled in closer and began to purr softly.

"I'm sorry," Alissia said, in the old language. "I'm just tired of living like this. I want my freedom back."

It did not take long before Mia's comforting touch and purring put Alissia to sleep. When she awoke the next morning, she was alone. She continued to lie in bed for a long moment, dreading the day ahead of her.

After doing some yoga, Alissia walked into the main room for breakfast. She was not in the mood to see anyone other than Anika that day, and during her bath, she decided she would pretend to be sick. She got dressed in comfortable clothing, picked out a book to read, and went back to her bed.

When Nadia came to her bedroom late that morning, Alissia said she did not feel well and told her to cancel everything scheduled for the day. Nadia became worried, and Alissia had to tell her sternly she did not need to see a doctor. She only needed a day of rest, and she did not want to be disturbed by anyone other than Anika. She then told Nadia to send word to Anika to come for a visit.

That afternoon, Nadia entered her bedroom with a large gift box, and Alissia was not surprised to learn it was from Ian. When Alissia asked about Anika, Nadia told her she had sent a messenger to Anika's rooms but had not heard anything in return.

The maiden left before Alissia opened the gift box to find a large collection of new books. They all looked interesting, and she would have chosen each of them for herself. She began to wonder if Nadia had anything to do with the selection of books he had chosen for her or if he had just picked out what was popular among other women. However, she could easily see Nadia telling Ian anything he wanted to know.

Alissia eventually got a message from Anika saying she would not be able to visit for a couple of days and for her to get well soon. In frustration, she asked Nadia if she had told Anika not to come. Her maiden seemed hurt by her accusation, and in the end, Alissia apologized for her foul mood and asked to be alone.

Although she was tempted to get dressed and march to Anika's rooms, she knew that would give Ian a reason to believe she was well enough to see him. She desperately wanted to talk to Anika. However, the events at the ball left her too tired to have to deal with pretenses.

In an attempt to distract her mind from everything, she spent the following day in bed reading. Once again, she had to reassure Nadia she was not overly sick. She just wanted some time to rest and be alone.

Ian sent her a card with a gift of various scented spa items, and she agreed to his arranging a private massage in her suite that evening. He also sent a note saying he had arranged for her to see a doctor the following afternoon. After the appointment, if she felt well enough, he would take her for a walk in one of the gardens before their dinner together.

The next morning she agreed to let Nadia fix her hair, and she got dressed for the day. Anika finally came to her suite for lunch.

"Are you finished now?" Anika asked, reclining on the sofa.

"No, I'm still mad." Alissia scowled. She was sitting in one of the chairs near the sofa, and her arms were crossed. "The ball was a nightmare, and I needed to talk to you."

"I know."

"That's all you've got to say?"

Anika smiled. "I'm sorry. I couldn't come though. I was too busy trying to find out more about Lita, the girl you introduced me to. I also spent some time with Grady. He's not in a good place right now, especially since Morton was murdered."

"How was he murdered?"

"He died of an enlarged heart. However, Luke told Langley there is a way to feign that type of death, but only a highly trained killer knows how, and only members of the league can get their hands on those types of ingredients legally."

"So the league killed Morton?" Alissia asked.

"Either that or another skilled killer; Alrik employs many as his own body guards here at the castle. They're just not supposed to have those ingredients. Either way, there is a high chance of it being murder, and some of the assembly members are in on it, along with a reputable doctor."

Anika let that sink in for a moment before continuing. "Morton's wife says he didn't go to see the doctor, but the doctor says Morton didn't tell his wife because he didn't want her to worry. Three of the assembly members have said Morton informed them of his condition, and they talked about letting Grady temporarily take his position."

"So what does this mean for Grady? Is this good or bad?"

For a moment, Alissia thought Anika was about to cry, but her friend feigned a smile and said, "Well, he'll be doing real work again. However, it's only for show. Look what happened to Morton for going against Alrik and the assembly. He'll go to their meetings and even be allowed to make some decisions, but he will also have to stand by and watch a lot of laws get broken."

Anika shrugged her shoulders and let out a sigh. "At least it will keep him busy, and he'll be distracted from you."

"Is that supposed to help?" Alissia asked, in frustration.

Anika said, matter-of-factly, "If you're going to end it with my cousin, it's best he stays busy and gets to do his other love, which is work. Alissia, I can't stand to see him lose both." Her voice cracked as she added, "It would destroy him."

Nadia walked in with their lunch, and after they were seated at the table and alone, Alissia said, "What about the girl?"

"Her name is Lita. I think we can trust her, and a plan might be coming together."

"She threatened me. Why do you trust her?"

"Alissia, we talked for a long time, and we didn't tell her anything until after she gave us some details. From what she says, there's another group of Lamians, and she is one of their protectors. When she and the others she works with heard about you, they immediately came to Pallen, and the night of the ball was her only chance to meet you."

"So she was there to meet me?"

Anika nodded while finishing off a bite of food. "Yes, and she knew she didn't have much time to talk to you. She also doesn't want to be seen with or near you. That's why she was hoping you had people you could trust."

In response to Alissia's frown, she added, somewhat triumphantly, "Anyways, Luke stopped by the stables last night and told Langley we did the right thing to give her his name. His people are still traveling, and he said that although he doesn't fully trust these people, he would take any help they can give in getting us out of here. He told them you would not leave without us." She paused before asking, "Is that true?"

Alissia responded as if the answer was obvious. "Why would I leave y'all?"

"Because it's a lot harder for all of us to leave than just you."

"So? It's not an option." In an attempt to change the subject, she asked, "So what do I need to do?"

Anika looked at her in disbelief. "And when would *you* be able to do anything? Out of all of us, you can't do anything. Guards surround you, Alissia, which is our biggest problem."

"So I'm just supposed to sit and wait while everyone else comes up with a plan? Maybe I can try to ditch the guards . . ."

"You're speaking in another language again, Alissia."

Alissia's eyes narrowed, and she said slowly, "Maybe I can get away from the guards, and—"

"And what?" Anika interrupted. "Honey, you can't go anywhere without your guards."

Alissia shook her head. "I can't believe you just called me honey, but you don't know what ditching someone means."

"Honey is sweet. A ditch is a hole on the side of the road. I simply don't get how a hole on the side of the road has anything to do with getting away from your guards, unless you plan on putting your guards in a ditch. However, I don't think you're that strong, even with your yoga."

Alissia watched Anika take a sip of chet. In defeat, she said, "What's the plan?"

"Well," her friend said, slowly. "I don't know."

"What do you mean, you don't know? I thought you said there was a plan."

Anika purposely put a bite of food in her mouth, and Alissia watched her chew it slowly. "Really?" she asked, sarcastically.

Once she had swallowed her food, Anika said, "I told you a plan was coming. I didn't say there was a plan. I mean, Luke just met her, and he's working with them on the details. All I know is that it will involve Langley at the stables."

Alissia scowled. "That's all you know?"

Anika copied her scowl and said, "That's all we've got. Langley. Horses. Stables. Escape." She grinned and added, "Oh, and a group of strangers that say they'll help us."

Chapter 15

"How are you feeling?" Ian asked, during their stroll to the doctor's office.

"I'm fine. Honestly, I wasn't even sick. I just wanted a day to stay in bed and read, and I guess I got greedy and took two days instead."

He took her by the hand and kissed it before saying, "Nonsense. We all need time to ourselves. I was just worried about you."

"Well, there's nothing to worry about, and thanks for the gifts. They were exactly what I needed."

"I thought you might like them. I missed you though," he said.

"So what's this doctor like? I've never been to one, or at least have memories of going to one."

He said, reassuringly, "You'll be fine. It may be uncomfortable, but that's all."

Alissia had fallen asleep the night before imagining what a doctor's office in this reality would be like. Without electricity or plastic, she was expecting it to be different. She also knew they used a lot of natural remedies, and she guessed he would know a lot about plants. She wished she had had time to ask Anika. However, they barely had enough time to discuss what had happened at the ball.

The doctor was located in a separate building outside the castle, and Ian told her that the man lived there also, which explained why it looked like a small cottage with a greenhouse attached to it. Once inside, she found herself in a pleasant living room being introduced to an elderly man named Dr. Welton. He was plump, had a wild mass of white hair, and wore a large pair of thick glasses.

Once all the introductions were made and the guards were finished looking around, he said, "Come then. Let's go to my office."

Leaving her guards in the living room, the doctor led Ian and her to a room off to the side, and once inside, she immediately regretted agreeing to see a doctor. She would have run if it were not for Ian blocking the doorway.

A reclining chair with hand and foot restraints were in the middle of the room. Many primitive-looking medical tools that looked more like torture implements were on a big table near the patient's chair, and dried herbs hung from the ceiling. Bookcases lined the walls, and they were filled with large, old books, various used candles, bottles of oils and other liquids, and clear jars. The jars held everything from crawling insects, slimy slugs, assorted internal body parts floating in liquid, and other things Alissia had never imagined she would find in a doctor's office.

A small elderly woman sat in a rocking chair in a dusty corner of the room. She was weaving something resembling lace with her shaky fingers, and she glanced up at Alissia before refocusing on her task.

The old man gave a cheery laugh and looked at Ian. "Oh, I see she's never been to a doctor's office." His face lit up, and he added, "Ah, but we don't know that, do we? She's lost her memories." Patting the medieval torture chair, he said, "Come, child. You'll be fine." He motioned toward the old woman and added, "This is my wife Gelda. She's deaf so she can't hear you. However, since you're a female, she will need to remain in the room."

Alissia shook her head violently and said, "I'll stand."

As if bribing a child, he said, "I'll give you a celium if you make this easy."

Alissia shook her head and said, "I don't even know what a celium is."

"I'll need your help with this one," the doctor said to Ian.

She spun around, and Ian put his hands up, as if in surrender. In a soothing voice, he said, "Alissia, I promise you can trust me."

Looking at the jars of slithering creatures, she said, "Why does he have crawling things and body parts in jars? "

"Well, dear," the doctor said. "Each of them has its purposes. However, I don't think you have to worry about any of that. We don't use them for an examination."

Ian said, "All he wants to do is take a look at you. We'll go from there." He took a step towards her and said, soothingly, "I'll be right at your side, and you'll be fine."

Alissia looked at the chair and said, "What about the restraints?"

Ian shook his head. "No restraints. That was never in the plan."

"I'll never speak to you again if you do," she warned, walking towards the patient's chair. He pulled up a chair and sat down next to her and took her by the hand.

"Remember, I said this would probably be uncomfortable."

The doctor clapped his hands together and said, "All right. We're ready. First, I want to check your reflexes." Noticing her shimmery skin, he picked up her hand and began to study it. In wonder, he said, "Is this your natural skin, or are you wearing something to make it glisten?"

"It's natural."

He began to rub the top of her hand and said, "It's so soft."

He then checked her reflexes and shoved a stick into her throat before he pulled out something resembling a stethoscope. Unlike the modern ones Alissia was used to seeing, this one looked more delicate, and she guessed animal parts were somehow involved in the making.

He placed it over her heart on top of her clothing, and Alissia immediately told herself she needed to thank Nadia for choosing a thin, high-necked dress. Otherwise, she would have endured the strange doctor putting his creepy hands under her clothing. That, and Ian would have been able to see more cleavage than she was comfortable with.

"Ah . . . uh . . . huh . . ." said the doctor.

"What?" Alissia asked.

"Your heartbeat is much faster than ours."

"How much faster?"

"Oh, quite a bit."

"Maybe that's because I'm scared right now," she said.

He lifted his hand and pulled the device from his ears before setting it on the table.

"No, it's unusually much faster than a regular heartbeat." He picked up what looked to be a medieval torture device and walked back to her.

"What's that?" she asked, ready to fight.

He laughed and looked at Ian. "Spirited little one, isn't she?"

Ian looked into her face and said, "I don't know."

Timid little Lamian. I'm a timid little Lamian. Don't hit the doctor. I won't hit the doctor. She mentally repeated those words as the old man took her dark glasses off and clamped the device onto her right eyelid before pulling it back. She immediately dropped Ian's hand and gripped both sides of the chair, her fingernails digging into the old leather.

I'm going to kill them! she mentally screamed.

The doctor held up a small, wooden rod with a glow stone attached to the end and held it up to her eye. The glowing light, along with the sunlight coming from the clear ceiling began to burn her eye, and she clenched her teeth tightly.

"Hmm . . . How is your vision at night?" the doctor asked.

Alissia's breathing began to get heavy as she tried to endure the light shining directly into her eye. It was not long before she let out a painful scream before knocking his hand aside. She heard the rod hit the floor as she sat up and put her hand on the tool at her eye and began to fumble with it.

Within seconds, she yelled, "Get it off! Y'all get this thing off me, Ian!"

Ian successfully removed it from her eye so that she could close it. Realizing she had just screamed out a demand in her southern accent, she slowly sunk back into the chair, praying Ian had not noticed.

"Well, then," came the doctor's voice from above her. "I guess I can understand that. Her eyes seem to be very sensitive to light."

Alissia clenched her mouth shut as a sarcastic reply came to mind. She felt something wiping the tears from the side of her face, and then her hand was gently pulled from where she was holding her eye.

"Let me help you," said Ian, soothingly. He held the cloth at her eye for a moment before asking, "Ready for you glasses?"

She nodded, and he helped her put them on. Then she opened her eyes and blinked repeatedly. It did not take long before her eye was back to normal, although she now had a mild headache. She turned her attention to the doctor, still standing at her side.

He cleared his throat and asked, "What is your vision like at night or in the dark?"

She tried hard to sound polite as she responded, "Dark. I can't see. Why?"

"Well, it seems your eyes seem to reflect light." He walked over to one of the shelves and began moving things around. When he turned back around, he was holding a jar filled with various eyeballs floating in a liquid.

He walked over and held the jar in front of her face. After he spun it around, he said, "Here it is. You see this eyeball right here?" He pointed at the eye, and Alissia shoved the jar away and began to gag.

"I'm done. I'm done, Ian," she said standing to her feet. At that moment, she did not care what Ian thought of her. A shy little Lamian would not stay in a room with a man holding a jar full of eyeballs.

Ian stood to his feet, and the doctor quickly set the jar aside before picking up a large needle attached to a glass vial.

"But I haven't had a chance to get a sample of your blood."

Alissia stormed out of the room, marched past her stunned guards, and bolted out the door. She had only gotten a few feet before Ian had caught up with her, and her guards were in their positions in front and behind her.

They walked in silence for a moment before Ian put her cape over her shoulders.

"Will you take a walk with me in one of the gardens?" he asked.

She nodded, and they continued in silence until they sat down on a bench within the nearest garden. The guards backed away so that they could still see Alissia, yet could not hear her conversation with Ian.

"I'm sorry," he said. When she did not respond, he continued with, "I guess I did not realize you would be upset. I now remember how intimidating a doctor's visit was for me the first few times I went as a child."

Alissia turned to him and said, "He had a jar full of eyeballs, Ian. That's not normal."

He nodded and said, "I guess if you've never seen them before." He let out a small laugh and said, "I used to enjoy it when the doctor would hold those up for me when I was a young boy."

Alissia frowned, and then she remembered she was supposed to be acting meek. However, she told herself she had a justifiable reason to be struggling with that at the moment.

"Do you forgive me?" he asked, while giving a look that should have melted her heart.

She reminded herself it would not matter soon, as she would be leaving. She only needed to play this game a little longer.

Turning to face him, she smiled and said, "I'm not angry. I'm fine."

Her sudden change seemed to confuse him, and he said, "Are you sure?"

She nodded. "I'm sure."

He smiled and relaxed his back against the bench before putting his arm around her and pulling her in closer.

After a moment of silence between them, he said, "Why do you think the doctor asked about your vision?"

Alissia felt herself swallow before she answered, "I don't know."

"Do you trust me, Alissia?"

"I'm trying to."

He let out a sigh and said, "I hope you know by now that you can trust me with anything. I've kept your secret about what you can do with a glow stone, even from my father."

He paused for a long moment as if in thought before turning their bodies so they were facing each other. Leaning in close, he studied her face as he said, "Alissia, I think I understand your fear and distrust of the Eldership, and of everyone. What if I told you I could take you away from all this and give you a private place away from people? A house in the mountains, on the beach, or in the country. You could have the best doctor, and I could ensure his confidence. I could take care of you, and you could have a private life. Would you be interested?"

She knew her face showed the confusion she felt. It took a moment before she responded with, "But what about the Eldership? And there's this threat of war people are talking about."

He said, "If there is to be war in this land, it will take time to prepare for it, and everyone is still trying to decide whose side they're on. You could leave with me this spring, and I could take you away from here before the war begins. Alissia, if you trust me, I can guarantee your safety, and I'm willing to give you anything you want."

"What do your parents say about this?"

A scowl came upon his face, and he leaned back and said, with disgust, "My father is too close to this war and the Eldership. His plans are not my plans, and when I say I would protect you, I also mean I would protect you from him. He's not the great man you think he is, Alissia."

Alissia's mind was churning, and Ian's words confused her. She had thought he was getting close to her because of his father. When she did not say anything, he took her by the hand and squeezed it.

"You don't have to give me an answer now. I want you to think about it." He began to rub his thumb around the top of her hand as he added, "I'm willing to give you everything I have to make you happy."

"But we haven't known each other that long," she said.

"Yes, but I've known others that have courted for less time than us, and they've spent the rest of their lives happily together. Alissia, we may not have the luxury of time if I am to get you away from here safely." He paused before adding, "I believe the Eldership and my father want to use you. You may love it here now, but things will change. I'm scared for your safety."

"Your father would hurt me?" she asked, hoping to sound naïve.

"He has hurt many."

"Why haven't you mentioned this before?"

He looked intently into her eyes and said, "I'm telling you now. The last thing I want you to do is worry, and I don't want you to be scared. I have all this under control. No one will hurt you if you leave with me this spring. Until then, don't speak of this to anyone. Don't even trust Nadia or your friend Anika. The Eldership has ears everywhere, but I have my own resources."

Chapter 16

an did not mention his plans for Alissia again as they finished their walk through the garden, nor during dinner, and she went to bed that night thinking about all the time she had spent with him. Although she still thought of him as a charmer and ladies' man, she began to wonder if he was truly as bad as she believed. Either he wanted to protect her from the Eldership, or he desired her for his own personal gain.

By the time she had fallen asleep, she decided she needed to get to know his sister to find out more about their family.

The next day Alissia told Anika everything that had happened. Her friend was amused by Alissia's experience with the doctor, and she explained that many of their medicines involve plants and animals.

She was also confused by Ian's words, as she had thought he was working with his father.

When Nadia came to her room that morning, Alissia told her to send an invitation to Emera for lunch that week. That afternoon Nadia told her it was scheduled for two days away, and Alissia wished it were sooner.

Over the next two days, she went out to dinner with Ian each evening. He told her his days were getting busier as he was preparing for the start of the heavy trade season. They had enjoyed a mild winter this year, and everyone expected an early start to spring.

She asked him more than once how he planned to continue to work with his father and help her to leave in the spring, and each time he would just smile and tell her not to worry about it and to trust him.

It bothered her that he would never talk about work or things of importance with her. She wondered if all men in this reality treated women that way, and then she reminded herself of how Langley and Grady had included Anika and her in making important decisions. Luke, however, usually made decisions for her, even if it was against her will.

When the time came for her to meet Emera, the guards escorted her to the restaurant, where she found the young woman already seated. After Alissia ordered her drink and the waitress left, Emera said, "So, my brother lets you eat with me. I'm honored."

"Who said he could stop me?" Alissia responded. As soon as the words left her mouth, she cringed. There was just something about the way Emera spoke that seemed to challenge Alissia. Although she was used to pretending to be shy and somewhat timid, no one else at the castle spoke to her the way Emera did. Her pride was not used to letting people talk to her that way, and she knew her tongue could easily get her into trouble around this woman. Beneath the table, she dug her fingernails into her hand in an attempt to remind herself to behave.

Emera smiled, as if pleased by Alissia's response. The young woman's eyes seemed to be studying her, and although it made Alissia somewhat nervous, she faked a nonchalant attitude as she said, offhandedly, "I was told you were recovering from your long journey and didn't feel well."

Emera took a sip from her drink and set it back down before saying, "It wasn't pleasant, but I guess I can't complain. At least I had my carriage and the use of an inn most nights. From what I hear, you had it much worse."

Alissia nodded and said, "What was so important you had to travel in the cold?"

"Haven't you heard? Almost everyone is traveling this way. We just happened to have been one of the first to get here."

"You mean, because of the talk of war?"

Emera nodded as the waitress set Alissia's drink on the table before pouring more chet into Emera's cup.

"Are you ready to order?" the waitress asked, looking expectantly from Alissia to Emera.

Alissia was too nervous to eat a large meal. Since she had eaten there before, she already knew what was on the menu. She said, "Yes. Emera, you can go first."

After Emera ordered her food, Alissia told the waitress what she wanted, and the woman left. Alissia then watched as Emera poured some honey into her drink and stirred it. She thought to herself how refined the young woman looked. Although she seemed to be younger than Alissia, Emera carried herself in a confident and elegant manner that was different than most others. However, her eyes seemed to look at everyone with distaste, and Alissia began to feel somewhat sorry for the woman. She did not look happy.

"My brother seems to enjoy your company, as I have never seen before, and I believe you've made him very happy."

Alissia shook her head and smiled. "I'm sure he was happy before he met me."

"You'd be surprised. Happiness is not something my family values."

"Then what is?"

Emera thought for a moment before answering, "Power. My father enjoys power."

"And your brother? What does he enjoy?"

"Depends on which brother. Aaron is the eldest. Then Ian, Kain, and I'm the youngest. Aaron and Kain are very much like my father, but Ian is different."

"How so?"

Emera grinned and said, "Ian and I don't make it a habit anymore to make our father proud. Truth be known, I go out of my way to cause him discomfort." She chuckled lightly at the look on Alissia's face and added, "You seem surprised. I guess Ian is more subtle than I am."

"What has he not told me?"

"My brother has his own reasons to be angry with our father, and I have mine." She paused, as if considering her words before she continued. "Ian spent his entire childhood trying to please Father, and he has worked much harder than my other two brothers, yet Father will never consider him to lead the company once he is no longer able. Instead, it will go to his eldest son, because Father holds to strict tradition.

"Aaron taunted Ian with this throughout his entire childhood. However, I've recently learned Ian has been doing more work for himself lately, and he's getting ready to leave Father's business." She paused and smiled before adding, "Ian tolerates things much better than I. Besides, I've been away for over six years. I could be wrong. Ian and father could be the best of friends by now. I don't know."

Alissia said, "Oh, I didn't know you've been gone. If you don't mind me asking, where have you been?"

"At school. This is my first time in Pallen since I was a small child, and I don't plan to stay long. I haven't seen my family much since I left for school, and I intend to keep this family reunion short." She blew on her drink and took another sip before continuing. "I do wish the best for you and my brother. He is my favorite of the family, and the only one I will miss. It would be nice if he could find someone to make him happy. He needs that."

The waitress brought their food, and both women began to eat their lunch salads. Alissia was still not used to the bitter taste of some of the winter greens, and she had to force herself to eat without picking through it.

Although she had dined with many women at the Eldership, the way Emera seemed to eat with perfect manners intimidated her somewhat, and she focused more than usual on how she ate.

Emera dabbed her napkin to her mouth before saying, "I've heard you've lost your memory. That's convenient."

"What do you mean?"

Emera lifted her drink and said, "Well, if I had secrets to keep, what better way than to lose them?"

Emera took a sip of her chet, and Alissia took a bite of her food, giving herself time to think of a response. Once she had swallowed, she wiped her mouth with the napkin and said, "I wish I knew what secrets I once had. I'm a bit lost without them."

Emera laughed.

"Well, they're your secrets, nonetheless, and you shouldn't have to give them up. I wish you the best with that." After she took another sip of her drink, she asked, "Do you love my brother?"

"We've not know each other very long."

"Yes, but you at least get an idea of whether you can fall in love with him by now. In my experience, it's something you can tell quite early on, maybe even on the first day."

Alissia thought she noticed a hint of sadness in the last part of Emera's statement, but she did not think it a good idea to mention it. Instead, she said, "Ian seems to be a gentleman, and he's been very kind to me."

"And that's a general statement," Emera said.

Alissia gave a polite smile and said, "I guess I don't fall in love easy, and I believe it takes time to get to know someone. However, your brother does show potential."

Emera grinned, and Alissia thought it to be the first sincere smile she had seen from the other woman.

"Ah, my brother has a challenge when it comes to you. He's probably not used to that. Serves him right."

"Where do you plan to go this spring?" Alissia asked.

"To start a new life. Somewhere far, far away."

"Do you plan to ever come back?"

Although Emera's eyes were on her, Alissia could tell her thoughts were somewhere else as she said, "No, I don't plan on returning."

"What does your family say about that?"

Emera's attention returned to Alissia as she answered, "I've only told Ian. He doesn't agree with my plans, but in the end, it's my choice to make, just as he has a choice to make right now when it comes to you."

Alissia hid her eagerness to learn more. She took a sip of her drink and said, calmly, "And what choice does Ian have to make when it comes to me?"

"Lady Alissia, my dear brother has to decide whether he loves you enough to fight for you." After a pause, she added, "And for your sake, I hope he does."

"What do you mean? Fight whom?"

Emera took another sip from her drink and wiped her mouth with her napkin before setting it down on the table. She gave Alissia a hard stare and said, "I, for one, do not believe you're what you pretend to be. I do, however, understand why you are playing this game. You are trapped and have no other choice, but don't take me for a fool, Lady Alissia. You are not so naïve, and you know the danger you are in. My advice to you is to fall in love with my brother and pray that he does the same. For love, many a man has died."

Emera rose to her feet before adding, "Now if you'll excuse me, I have done enough damage for one day. It has truly been a treat, and maybe we can do this again. I do wish you luck, Lady Alissia, and good day."

Before Alissia could respond, Emera walked away. Alissia looked down at her plate of half-eaten food and said to herself, "Well, that was interesting."

*****

While dining at another restaurant that evening with Ian, he asked, "How was your lunch with my sister?"

"Interesting."

He raised his eyebrows and said, "Should I be worried?"

"About what?"

"Honestly, my sister has become somewhat of an enigma, and depending on her mood, she could say anything." He paused before adding, "I'm hoping the flowers I sent to her this morning earned me a good report."

Alissia laughed.

"You sent your sister flowers? Were you worried?" she asked, playfully.

He grinned and said, "Yes, very much so."

"Hmm . . . What are some things your sister could have told me about you?"

He thought for a moment before answering, "That I'm madly in love with a beautiful woman and can barely concentrate on anything throughout the day, other than seeing her smile each night and hearing the sound of her voice."

"Somehow, I don't believe that is what you are worried your sister would say about you."

"Well, I will admit it's not the worst thing she would say about me."

Chapter 17

Another week went by without anything stressful happening. Alissia continued to spend her days socializing with Anika and the women of the Eldership. Mia came to her room each night, only to be gone when Alissia awoke in the morning. Ian stayed busy during the days preparing for the trade season, but he made time for Alissia each evening.

He and she had dinner with his parents one night, and on their walk to meet them, Ian reminded her not to speak of his plans for leaving. Although he acted his usual, polite self to his parents throughout dinner, Alissia thought she noticed a strain between him and his father that she had not noticed before. Alrik also asked her more questions than he normally did, and he seemed eager to help her with getting her memories back. By the end of dinner, she had agreed to meet with a different type of doctor, and Ian had told his father he would schedule the appointment.

As he walked her back to her rooms that night, he seemed bothered and somewhat distracted. He told her not to worry about anything. He was making arrangements for them to leave earlier than planned. Alissia had still not agreed to leave with him, but he seemed to have forgotten that small detail.

During Anika's afternoon visit the following day, Alissia shared with her friend how Ian and his father had acted over dinner. Once she was finished talking, Anika silently stared back at her with a grin.

"I don't see why any of this makes you happy," Alissia said.

Anika responded, mysteriously, "I think I have something to cheer you up."

"What, an escape?"

Anika sang, "Langley spoke with Luke last night."

Alissia tried to hide her excitement as she asked, "And?"

"You've been given a set of instructions."

"Are we leaving now?" Alissia asked, not bothering to hide her eagerness.

"No. Luke told Langley a plan is in place, and he needs to talk to you about it. However, he told Langley to make sure you didn't expect to leave that day."

"What day?"

"It seems you are going to take me to the spa. And not just any spa," Anika said, grinning. "You are to set up an appointment at DeFelio's. It's very secluded and pricey, and you're going to close it down for three hours."

"What do you mean?"

Anika's grin got even bigger, and she said, "We are going fleshing."

Alissia stared back at her friend with a blank expression.

Anika rolled her eyes and said, "We're going swimming without any clothes! Don't people go fleshing where you come from?"

"We call that skinny dipping."

Anika frowned and said, "Somehow, I don't believe skinny people are the only ones that swim without their clothes on."

"And like fleshing sounds any better? It sounds like you're fishing for people's skin or something. And why would I go fleshing?"

Anika laughed and said, "We aren't really going fleshing, silly. Since this is a public place, you're going to tell them you want privacy, and that is why you're reserving it for a few hours. The guards will search it before you arrive, and then when it's time to actually go in, you're going to tell them you want to go fleshing. You want complete privacy, and no one is allowed into the sauna section, not even the workers. That way we will be completely alone."

"I can do that?"

"Yes! You're Lady Alissia, and the Eldership will pay for everything."

Alissia asked, "Is it normal for people to go fleshing in this reality?"

"Not really, but you're a Lamian. You really don't have to be normal. Somehow, I don't believe the owners of DeFelio's are going to turn down your request. You'll be their most honored guest, and they'll be excited you're visiting their place. You can ask for anything you want, as long as it doesn't break a law."

Alissia hid her excitement and said, flatly, "And Luke's supposed to be there?"

"Yes."

"How?"

Anika shrugged her shoulders and said, "I don't know. He's with the league. I'm sure he's done plenty of things like this before."

"What does Grady say about it?"

Anika let out a breath and said, "We haven't told him, and Langley and I have decided not to tell him until all this is over." She paused before adding, "He has enough to worry about right now, and we don't want to add to it."

They sat in silence for a moment before Alissia said, "I'm sorry."

"We understand, Alissia. A lot has happened since . . ." Anika frowned and shook her head before continuing with, "Since you left

Pallen. We can't expect it to go back to the way it was. Right now I don't even know if I'll ever see my family again." Anika's lips began to tremble, and Alissia looked away, in an attempt at giving her friend some privacy.

Alissia wished she was better at comforting people, and she struggled for something to say. She had known since arriving at the castle that behind all Anika's laughter, there was a deep sense of fear and sadness over their situation. Although her friend always tried to be optimistic and encouraging, Alissia often saw the truth behind her façade of happiness.

"We'll get out of here. Remember, there's a plan now," Alissia said, trying to sound encouraging. Anika smiled weakly and nodded. "And now you can tell everyone you've lived in a castle. And not just any castle, but Pallen's castle. You have had the ultimate Pallen vacation."

Anika laughed, and Alissia said, "Tell me what all I'm supposed to do so we can go fleshing at the sauna."

*****

That evening Ian told Alissia he had arranged for another doctor to visit her on the following day. He told her the doctor would try to put her into a trance to help pull memories from her. Ian also explained that he would ensure all her words were kept private, even from his father. The way he reassured her he would take care of everything left her wondering what he intended to do.

Unlike the night before, he did not seem bothered or distracted. Instead, he was happy and confident, which is what Alissia was used to seeing from him. He worked his charm on those around him, and Alissia could not help but wonder what had changed since the night before.

The following afternoon Nadia prepared for Alissia's guests while Alissia sat on the sofa, anxiously awaiting their arrival. Although she did not know much about hypnosis, she had once heard a story from one of her colleagues. This woman had said her husband had been hypnotized at a show while on their honeymoon, and he had run around the room like a chicken and made a fool of himself.

Alissia worried she would tell all her secrets, and she had spent a restless night imagining the worst. Not even Mia's presence had been enough to lull her into a peaceful slumber.

When the knock came at her door, she rose from the sofa and stood in front of the fireplace, fixing a smile onto her face. Ian came to her side and kissed her lightly on her cheek before introducing her to Dr. Felixon and his female assistant, Shasta.

Shortly after the introductions and Nadia's departure from the room, Alissia lay comfortably on the sofa with a pillow beneath her head. Shasta watched from a seat in a far corner of the room, while Ian and the doctor sat in the chairs across from her.

In a soothing voice, Dr. Felixon said, "Lady Alissia, I want you to close your eyes and concentrate on my voice. I need for you to empty your mind of all your thoughts and let my voice guide you. Relax as you think about your favorite place . . ."

La, la, la, la. Find a bad place. Find a bad place. Remember all the times your sister would kick you under the kitchen table and yell out as if you had kicked her, and then you would get the spankin'. She would even bite her arm and tell Mom you had done it. Hah, that worked until she lost her front tooth, and Mom finally caught her. Served her right. La, la, la, la . . .

The doctor continued. "Clasp your hands together."

Alissia obeyed.

"Now, I want you to imagine that your hands are inside an iron lock. Around that iron lock is a thick chain, locking your hands in place . . ."

Alissia imagined herself running on a beach with her hands moving freely at her side. As the doctor continued to give out instructions, she remembered using her hands to fight with her father. They had been balled into tight fists and had given fierce punches with precise aim.

The doctor's voice changed into a gentle command as he said, "Now, open your eyes and try to pull your hands apart."

Alissia opened her eyes before pulling her hands apart. When she looked at the doctor, he was frowning.

"Lady Alissia, you have to want to do this for it to work. You have to allow yourself to surrender to my voice. If I am to reach into your subconscious, you must let everything go. Focus completely on what I tell you."

She gave an apologetic look and said, "I'll try again."

He nodded, and she closed her eyes and rested her hands onto her stomach.

After two more unsuccessful attempts, the doctor turned to Ian and said, "I am afraid there is nothing more I can do without the use of herbs. Unfortunately, some people's minds do not respond to therapy without them."

Ian looked at Alissia thoughtfully, and she sat up and put her feet onto the floor. After clearing her throat, she said politely, yet firmly, "I do not wish to use anything that will mess with my mind."

The doctor responded, "Lady Alissia, I believe your memories are still within our reach in the subconscious portion of your mind, and if you will only allow me to give you certain herbs, I can help you retrieve them."

"What exactly would the herbs do?" she asked, in an attempt to appear interested in his offer.

"They would put you into a semi-conscious state of mind. I would then be able to help you retrieve your memories while in that lower state of consciousness."

"And what are the risks? What are the chances my body would have a bad reaction to these herbs? Can you guarantee me they won't hurt me?"

The doctor answered, "As with any treatment, we won't know your body's reaction until we try, but, Lady Alissia, the chances are minimum. Many doctors use these herbs, and they rarely have negative consequences. I have no doubt that I can retrieve your memories if you agree to them."

Alissia turned to Ian and pretended to consider the herbs for a moment before asking him, "What do you think I should do?"

"I believe you should agree to them. The risks are minor, and you have a chance to get your memories back."

She turned to the doctor and said, "I will have to think about it, but I ask that you leave me with the names of the herbs you plan to use so I can do some research before I agree to them."

He nodded and said, "I can send a messenger with the information you will need to help make your decision."

Alissia stood to her feet and smiled. Ian and the doctor followed her lead in that the decision for the day was made. Although she had found a way to stall, both men did not seem bothered.

After the doctor and his assistant left her suite, Ian gave Alissia a quick kiss on the cheek and told her he had a meeting to attend. He reminded her of their plans for dinner and a symphony, and he said he would return soon.

During their dinner that evening, he asked if she trusted him, and she told him she was still trying. In reality, she still did not know what to think about him. Since he had given her the bracelet, she had made a point to wear it when she was around him, and her feelings toward him were no longer as vial. His willingness to defy his father when it came to her made it easier to think of him as a friend. If it were not for his insistence on courting her, she could easily find herself being comfortable around him. Although he still talked of love and his desire to protect her, he had not tried anything physical since the night of the ball, and that helped her to relax somewhat around him.

Chapter 18

Time passed by slowly over the next few days for Alissia. A messenger delivered the information she needed to study the herbs, but she kept herself busy with a full schedule. Not only did that help with her eagerness to see Luke, but it also gave her a legitimate excuse for not having a chance to read through what the doctor had sent.

Falling asleep at night was extremely difficult. She did not know when the last time she had anticipated something as much as she now did. No matter how much she fought against her imagination, thoughts of Luke consumed her mind. They filled her with excitement, and she found herself smiling throughout the day.

She awoke early on the morning she was to go to the spa, and she could barely get any breakfast into her anxious stomach. Although she normally would have just put on a bathing suit and wrap, she bathed and took special care in getting ready. She picked out her favorite scented oil and rubbed it into her skin. Unlike the day she had gone to the pool with Ian, she picked out a bathing suit and cover-up that most accentuated her body.

After Nadia finished braiding her hair, Alissia stared at her reflection in the mirror with a smile. She looked like a Greek goddess in the long, cream-colored toga, accented with a gold trim. It had a long split up one side, and she wore matching sandals. Her hair was in a simple braid, and it hung over one shoulder. She wore matching, gold earrings and upper-arm bracelets molded into the shape of snakes.

Beneath the toga, she wore a matching, cream-colored bathing suit dress. The sweetheart-shaped top was tight fitting, and it tied behind her neck. It was gathered at the sides and stitched to cause the material to have a loose appearance across her stomach, and it covered her bikini bottom, ending in small ruffles.

Nadia had gotten excited when Alissia told her she would not be wearing her dark glasses. The woman always seemed to take pride in Alissia's appearance, and this time Alissia did not argue with her handmaiden about wearing makeup just to go to a spa. Although it was only a small amount, it made a subtle change.

Even her glamorous appearance did not help to settle her nerves, and by the time Anika arrived at her chambers, Alissia was jittery with excitement. She reminded herself she had spent countless hours alone with Luke, and she was being ridiculous.

Guards surrounded her and Anika as they walked to the spa. It was not a short walk either. Alissia had never been to this part of the castle, and as they walked, Anika explained the spa was located on the lowest level, the same floor as the basement and dungeons. The spa was famous for its beauty and hot springs. She then told Alissia the reason Ian had not taken her there is because it was not considered proper for an unwed couple to go there together. It was considered too intimate of a place. Many married couples, however, spent time there for special occasions, such as honeymoons or anniversaries.

The lowest floor of the castle was chillier than the upper levels, and sconces containing glow stones provided all the light. The hallway leading to the spa was void of people, and once they arrived, the owners eagerly walked up to them. The husband and wife introduced themselves, and Alissia could sense the excitement her visit was causing. Guards had already searched the portion of the spa she and Anika would be using, and the owners assured her everything had been arranged according to Nadia's specifications when it came to food.

Alissia did not care what anyone thought of her as she reminded the staff and guards she and Anika would be fleshing, and no one was to enter the area during that time. She played the part of a noble woman and held her head high as she explained what she expected from the staff.

Two of her guards followed them as the owners led them down a stone hallway arranged with beautiful paintings and bella flowers along the walls. Alissia understood why couples chose this place for special occasions, as the ambiance was extremely private and romantic. Only an elite group of people could afford to pay for such an experience at this spa, and she could not help but wonder how Luke had gotten in or how he planned to get out.

Two of her guards were already standing outside the wooden double doors leading into the section of the spa reserved for her and Anika. They did not move from their posts as the male owner opened the door and motioned for her and Anika to walk through. Once inside, both she and Anika looked around in awe, and the owners beamed with pride from seeing their expressions.

Unlike the rest of the castle, they were now standing in a dimly lit, natural cavern with a large spring of water in the middle of the room. Although the walls of the cavern were covered in white bella flowers, both sides of the room had four large holes carved into the walls that were entrances into other rooms. At the back of the cavern, a wall of water flowed down from a ledge into another pool of water. A mist of steam seemed to fill the air, and the cavern was much warmer than the other areas beneath the castle floors.

Along each side of the pool of water were three large, crystal geodes. They appeared to be taller than Alissia, and she stood at five feet. The crystals that lined the inside walls of the geodes were blue in color, and a glow stone had been placed at the base of each of them, making the beautiful crystals glow brightly.

To the left of the double doors were three tables with thick partitions made from the cavern walls to separate them for privacy. The right side of the room had matching tables and partitions, and the owners led Alissia and Anika to the one with food set out for them. They were then shown what drinks were held inside the small bar carved into the wall at the end of their table.

During the tour, Alissia learned the first door on the left led into the men's bathroom, and the first door on the right led into the women's bathroom. Although the small bathrooms were decorated immaculately, the plumbing was much more primitive than Alissia had seen since being in this reality, but she understood how that had to do with the designers wanting to preserve the natural flooring and walls of the cavern.

The other three doors on each side of the room led into private saunas, and Alissia learned that only six couples at a time were scheduled for this area of the spa. Each couple had their own private table and sauna. Beyond this area of the spa, other rooms were available for massages and saunas, and they were normally reserved many weeks in advance. Because of Alissia's status, they had rescheduled all the guests that had booked for this morning and would be staying open later than usual to make up for the disruption in time.

When Alissia apologized for disrupting their schedule, the owners quickly dismissed her apology and told her they were honored to have her as a guest. They even told her they would be eager for her to visit again, and Alissia guessed they were being paid quite well for her visit.

Only one of the saunas was prepared for them, and Alissia and Anika followed them through the entrance, which was a hole carved into the cavern wall. They had to turn and walk a few steps around another wall that opened into a private, circular room with a stone alter set up in the middle. Two padded lounge chairs were in the room, and the walls were lined with sconces to give some light. The sound of music played softly from a small music box, and the female owner opened a case to show them where extra crystals were stored if they wanted to change the music.

A pot of floral-scented water hung down from the ceiling by a chain, and the husband poured a ladle of the water onto the stone alter. Fresh, scented steam filled the room before they walked out. As they walked back to the double doors, Alissia learned the fresh pools of water were filled with natural minerals from the nearby mountains. That is why the water had a strange, deep blue hue to it, and people came to swim in the water for the health benefits to their skin. A purifying flower could not survive in the water because of the healthy minerals, and the water purified itself. The heat came from stones strategically placed in the water.

Although Alissia was intrigued by her surroundings, she soon became impatient with the couple for lingering at the door talking about the history of the cavern. Under normal circumstances, she would have been much more polite, but she soon interrupted the conversation to remind them she wanted some time alone. She then repeated that no one was to come through the double doors without knocking first and then waiting for her or Anika to answer. She looked at the guards and reminded them sternly that she would be fleshing.

Once the doors were closed, she turned to find Anika laughing.

"What's so funny?"

"You. I don't believe you've ever talked liked that to your guards."

"I'm a shy Lamian, remember?"

"Not today, apparently."

Alissia walked past Anika and said, "You should go fleshing. It's good for your skin."

Anika removed her wrap but left her bathing suit on. She dipped one of her feet into the water and said, "Ooh, this is nice."

"I think I'm going to have a look around," Alissia said.

Anika gave a knowing grin and replied, "You do that."

Alissia started on the left side of the cavern and walked into the men's bathroom and the three saunas, but there was no sign of Luke anywhere. She then went to the two unused saunas on the right side of the room and began to worry when her search came up empty again. By the time she walked into the sauna with the fresh steam rising from the stone alter, she was anxiously chewing on her bottom lip. She stared at the steam for a moment, and her eyes began to tear up.

Although she understood how impossible it had to be for Luke to sneak in, she had been looking forward to this moment for days. All the excitement she had felt quickly turned into sadness and anger at the same time as she decided he had not been able to find a way in. Her temper led her imagination to thoughts of telling everyone it was her life, and she could do whatever she wanted. She was leaving the castle, and no one could stop her.

"Hello, Pixet," came Luke's voice, softly at her ear.

She felt his body at her back, and she closed her eyes and smiled. She did not dare turn around, fearing he would see how upset she had been. Instead, she forced her voice to sound calm as she said, "I didn't think you were coming."

He turned her around to face him before saying, "I told Langley I would be here. You doubted me too soon."

He was shirtless, and she found herself staring at his league tattoo. She took a step back and was caught by surprise by his choice of clothing, or lack thereof.

"You're wearing a skirt," she said, playfully.

Luke frowned and looked down. As he looked back up at her, he put his hands on his hips and said, defensively, "It's not a skirt. It's what all men wear to swim in."

He lifted up the black material to reveal a matching black Speedo that would have made Alissia blush if she could turn red. After dropping the mini-skirt, he asked, "What are you used to seeing men wear?"

The material was not much longer than his Speedo, and it had a slit on the right side. After seeing the Speedo, she was grateful for the extra coverage he wore, as she was used to seeing him in winter traveling clothes. His lack of clothing and the fact that every part of his lean physique appeared to be pure muscle was too distracting. Even in winter, his olive complexion made him look tan, and she wondered if he knew how attractive he truly was.

He must have misunderstood her silence, because he frowned and said again, "It's not a skirt."

She grinned at his defensiveness and said, "No, it's not a skirt. In fact, I've never seen you in anything other than your traveling or formal clothes. This is different."

His usual grin returned, and he said boldly, "You like it, don't you?"

She laughed out loud at his cockiness, and his grin changed.

"I've missed you, Pixet," he said with sadness, and Alissia's own feelings returned. He smiled again and said in his usual authoritative voice, "You should take that off. You're sweating."

Alissia became aware of the steam in the room, and she knew she needed to remove the toga before it became damp. She began to fumble with the clasp at her shoulder, and Luke stepped closer.

"Here, let me help you."

The moment his fingers touched the exposed skin of her shoulder, heat shot through her entire body. She began to focus on her troubled breathing, and as soon as she felt the toga loosen, she backed away, holding the dress in place.

"Thanks," she said.

His intense eyes stared into hers for a moment before he gave a nod and turned his head towards the door. Alissia pulled the dress down and stepped out of it. After giving it to him, he walked out of the room and put it on one of the hooks outside the door. She removed the arm bracelets and set them beside the music box.

"Now you're ready for a swim," he said, cheerily.

"I'm not going fleshing with you, if that is what you had in mind."

He laughed before saying, "No, that is truly not what I want."

"Really?" she asked, teasingly.

"Really. There's a difference between love and lust, remember?"

His reference to her words brought a flashback of the heated discussion they had shared in the cabin before Alissia had moved to the castle, and she looked up at him in surprise.

He walked over and took her by the hand. Leaning down, he whispered at her ear, "There's more between us than lust, Alissia."

Before she could respond, he led her out of the sauna room.

"You should properly introduce me to Anika. I think I scared her upon our first meeting."

Chapter 19

They found Anika soaking in the large pool, and she smiled when she noticed them walking towards her.

"There are loungers in the water," she said.

Luke and Alissia waded into the water, and Alissia climbed onto the stone lounger beside Anika. She lay back, and Luke picked up her hand and held it, as he remained standing at her side.

"Luke, this is Anika. Anika, this is Luke. I know you've already met, but I don't believe you've been properly introduced," Alissia said.

Anika responded, dryly, "Oh, we've met."

"I'm truly sorry I scared you, and I'm also sorry that you met me under such circumstances. I assure you there's more to me than what you saw that day," Luke said.

Alissia was surprised by Luke's apology. As he and Anika began to talk, Alissia realized this was their first time together in front of someone. This was also their first time together as a couple. Although she had spent countless hours with him alone, it had been nothing like this.

She observed how natural and relaxed he now seemed compared to what she had grown accustomed to. Gone was the controlled expression he had kept on his face. It was now replaced with a smile, and even his eyes seemed to radiate happiness at this moment. It was strange to see him like this.

"Isn't that right, Alissia?" Anika said.

Alissia looked at her friend and answered, "Yeah."

Anika laughed, and Alissia gave her a warning look. Although she had no idea what she had just agreed to, she did not want Luke to know his presence was distracting to her.

Luke said, "We do have a plan somewhat in place, and I'm confident it could work."

This sparked Alissia's interest, and she asked, "What's the plan, and when are we leaving?" As he opened his mouth to speak, she added, "And did you meet the girl from the ball? She threatened me, and I don't trust her."

She wondered what Luke found so amusing as she noticed one side of his mouth twitch.

He said, "The plan is complex, and I don't have an exact date on our departure. As for Lita and the others, I trust them enough to help us get out of Pallen, but that's all. Once we're out of Pallen, we have new problems."

"What do you mean?" she asked.

"Well, I have two of my men in Pallen now, but more of my people are on the way. As with everyone, we're all concerned with the threat of war. In my opinion, I don't believe anyone wants a civil war in the land, except for Pallen. The northern territories are unhappy, but after talking to Grady, I believe things can be fixed. It all depends on how the Elders in Allure respond to this new threat. Grady thinks this will force them to finally sit down and listen to the concerns of the northern territories.

"Alrik is having a hard time getting a following outside of Pallen. When he was hiding behind the assembly, Pallen was gaining the trust of many of the surrounding cities. However, people are now starting to realize he is in control of the assembly here. No matter what he's promising, people are not happy about the idea of leaving the Eldership to follow one man. He should have been more discreet with his power, but he got sloppy and had to speed up his plans when he found out about Alissia.

"I'm sure he already had a plan to get rid of Morton and his family. I'm guessing they would have had an unfortunate accident during their travel back to Allure. However, he can't discreetly get rid of Morton's family, Grady, Anika, and Langley."

Anika said, "I thought it was just Morton and his wife. Who else is here from his family?"

"Morton's daughter recently became a widow, and she traveled here with her parents. She also brought her young daughter. Since Morton's death, the women have not left their suite, and their guards from Allure never leave them."

"Are they safe?" Alissia asked.

"I believe they are. They're not a threat. Morton was becoming a problem for Alrik, and he found a convenient way to end that problem. He even got a doctor as one of the witnesses to help prove Morton died of a natural cause."

Alissia said, "Will they be able to travel back to Allure this spring?"

"I don't know. Alrik desperately needs more time to get more people on his side. Things are not going as he had hoped, and although he has not said anything openly in front of me, there is now talk that Ian will soon be marrying Alissia. In turn, she has given her loyalty to Pallen, and because of her, Pallen will control this land. He's assuring others he will have the support of the Lamians if it comes to a war."

Alissia said, "What? No one has said any of this to me, and I've been around the assembly wives. None of them have mentioned anything."

"They probably know nothing of it. Most of the men don't talk politics with their wives."

Alissia rolled her eyes and shook her head. "This reality treats women as if we're stupid."

Luke began to laugh, and Anika said, "Those women probably don't want to hear anything about it. As long as their husbands are members of the assembly, they're happy living in the castle with all the benefits."

Alissia frowned and splashed water onto Luke's chest. He stopped laughing and continued. "Anyways, I'm under the impression we don't have much time. I overheard the end of a heated discussion between Alrik and Ian last week. Alrik told Ian his time was up, and he was about to take care of it himself. I'm guessing he was talking about you, as I believe Ian is supposed to have your support by now."

Alissia said, "Ian told me he disagrees with his father, and he fears for my safety. He wants to get me out of here."

"That's what Langley has told me. He's also told me how madly in love you are with Ian," Luke teased.

Alissia looked at Anika and said, "Langley had better know how I feel about Ian."

"Oh, he knows exactly how you feel. It's not as if you don't tell me every time I see you," Anika said.

Alissia admitted, "He's not so bad as long as he doesn't try to kiss me. He's like a little puppy dog. He promises me he'll give me anything I want, and he's great when it comes to gifts."

"Hmm . . . we'll save that conversation for later," Luke said. "Ian's time is running out, and he's getting pressure from Alrik. We've almost gotten everything finalized and hope to leave within two weeks, which will be cutting it close. I've talked to some people and have convinced them to pretend to listen more to Alrik, so that may buy us more time and ease some of the pressure Alrik is feeling and giving Ian. I wish it could be sooner, but I don't fully trust everyone involved."

"What do you mean?" Alissia asked.

"Well, no one from my country knows the truth when it comes to you. They believe my goal is to try to prevent a civil war and to get you to the North, which, as you can see, will cause some trouble once we leave Pallen. I will have to handle things delicately.

"Then there's this other group of people that are concerned with protecting the Lamians at all cost. They already know that I know everything about you." Luke narrowed his eye at Alissia and added, "At least that's what I told them."

Alissia let out a sigh and said, "You don't believe me, do you? I told you that you know everything now. There aren't any more secrets."

"And you've not told me that before?" he asked, dryly.

"You're never going to forget that, are you?" When he continued to stare at her, she reminded him, "You're the one that told me not to trust anyone when we first met. I only did what you said."

"Anyways," he continued. "They believe I know everything about you, and I am pledged to protect you. They also know my men know nothing of this, so they understand the risks I am taking when it comes to you. However, I don't trust them with you. Their loyalty lies with protecting an unknown group of Lamians, not the ones you are searching for. They have already tried to persuade me into allowing them to take you back to their people, without me. They've also not trusted me with the location of their people, and right now we disagree with where you are to go after you leave Pallen."

He gave her hand a squeeze and added, "They may try to kidnap you the moment we get out of the city."

Anika said, "So we need them for the escape, but they are also another threat to Alissia?"

"Correct."

Alissia asked, in frustration, "Will I ever be able to just go where I want to go? Everybody wants to force me to go with them." She frowned at Luke and added, "Even you, or at least the old you."

"I was trying to protect you, Alissia," he said.

"That's not the only reason, and you know it, Luke."

He quickly scooped her up into his arms and excused himself to Anika before carrying Alissia away into deeper water. Once there, he arranged her body so that her feet were behind his back and her arms around his neck.

Being this close to him and the intense look he now gave her, made her heart flutter within her chest.

"I have given you my word, Alissia. I will help you find the Lamians that changed you, and I will protect you with my life. Do you believe me?"

His face was only inches away from hers, and he was gazing intensely into her eyes. Her eyes went to his lips, and memories flooded through her mind, giving her a longing to taste him.

"Yes."

As soon as the word left her mouth, his arms tightened around her body, as he pulled her in for a kiss. Power surged between the two of them as their tongues found each other, and her hands grabbed fistfuls of the unruly hair on his head.

It had been so long since she had been in his arms, and everything within her told her it was the right place to be. Passion soared between them, and then she suddenly felt herself being ripped away from his body. When she opened her eyes, she found him staring at her, and she thought she noticed a hint of sadness in his eyes.

"What?" she asked.

He shook his head and answered, "Nothing, Alissia." When he turned his head towards Anika, Alissia did the same. Her friend was still lounging where they had left her. Her eyes were now closed and her hands were clasped together on her stomach.

Luke carried Alissia back to the shallow water and set her down. He looked at Anika and said, "Please excuse us again, Anika. We're going to try the sauna."

Anika smiled and nodded, and once inside the sauna room, Luke reclined on one of the loungers. Alissia did the same on the other one.

Luke closed his eyes and asked casually, "So how are things going with Ian?"

"He's been busy lately so I only see him in the evenings, which is fine by me. In the beginning, he wanted to spend most of the day with me, and he was annoying. Lately, it's been easier. He hasn't tried to kiss me since the night of the ball."

"What happened at the ball?"

Alissia described all that had happened, and Luke admitted to sending one of his men over to distract Emera from Grady. She then told of her lunch with Emera, and as he listened, he held onto one of her hands, resting them upon his abdomen.

She told him everything that had happened to her since arriving at the Eldership. He asked questions and seemed to want to hear a lot of details, especially about Ian and her guards. He laughed when she talked about her visit to the doctor, and after a while, she realized she had done most of the talking. "So what about you? What's been going on since you've been here?"

He smiled and said, "Nothing as exciting as you. I spend my days trying to prevent a war, planning an escape for a beautiful woman and her friends, and I go to bed each night imagining when I'll finally be able to hold her in my arms again."

"I'm here now, and you're not holding me," she said, surprised by his words.

His smile faded, and he closed his eyes. After a moment of thought, he said, "I realize I have not given you a reason to want to be held by me. We did not meet under the best of circumstances, and I am aware our time together was not all that pleasant for you."

He looked for a moment as if he was struggling with what to say next, and then he continued. "I'm used to being alone, and you confused me."

Alissia was surprised by his sudden vulnerability, and it took her a moment to respond. "Well, you confuse me too."

He grinned, and then he stood to his feet and walked over to the music box. He looked through the various crystals before selecting one. When the music started, he turned around and held out his hand.

"You've never danced with me."

She laughed and said, "You want to dance?"

He pulled her to her feet and took her into his arms. The steam had lessened in the room, and she no longer found it too unpleasant to move. As they began to sway to the music, he smiled down at her.

"I've always had to watch you dance with others from across the room," he said.

He gave her a spin, and she grinned as he began to show her the dancing skills he had learned in his youth at the Eldership.

After a while, he pulled her body in close, and she responded by laying her head on his bare chest. She closed her eyes, and it was not long before all her cares were forgotten. Without even thinking about what she was doing, she smiled to herself, and then she turned her head and kissed his chest.

With her hand still in his, he lifted her face, and his lips came down to meet hers. Instead of the mad craving they normally shared between them, their kiss was slow and tender. His hand let go of hers and went to caress one side of her neck. She put both of her arms around his body, her hands holding tightly to his upper back.

She felt his other hand slowly move up her back until she could feel his fingertips on the back of her neck. When he pulled his mouth from hers and she looked into his eyes, all the defenses she had grown accustomed to seeing from him were gone. Everything within her wanted to ease the fear and uncertainty she thought she glimpsed in that moment, and her hands came up to pull him back down to her.

Her lips went to the bottom of his neck, and her tongue gently teased him as it made its way up to his mouth for another kiss. This time she took control, as one hand gripped his head and the other held onto the back of his shoulder. In that moment, she put everything she had into bringing him pleasure, and it was not long before he pulled away with a different look in his eyes.

He held her at arms' length and said huskily, "No, this isn't what I wanted."

She looked up at him in confusion and said, "I don't understand."

He let go of her and put some distance between them. A troubled look was on his face as he ran his hand through his hair and stared at her for a moment.

"Alissia, I want you to see there's more to us than physical attraction. That's not what I want from you." He let out a sigh before adding, "I know others are involved in this, and I don't want you to blame me and call this a mistake again. I need for you to see what it really is, and I need for you to realize what is truly going on between us."

A chime sounded as he finished his sentence, and she remembered it was a warning they only had thirty minutes left. She frowned in frustration and thought of how she should have reserved more time. Three hours was not long enough, and she should have demanded the whole day.

Luke said, "We don't have much time left." He walked back to her and picked up her braid. In an attempt to lighten the mood, he gave the braid a gentle tug and said, "You should have worn your hair like this while we were traveling. It would have made things much easier for me."

She rolled her eyes and said, "Yeah, I'm sure you would have loved dragging me around."

He grinned genuinely and dropped the braid. He then walked over to the lounge chair and sat down with his feet still on the floor. He patted the other chair in front of him, and she walked over and sat down to face him.

He picked up her hands and brought them to his lips for a quick kiss. After he lowered them back down, he let out a sigh and said, "All right, Pixet, we will soon be leaving Pallen, and that means you're about to leave the comforts of this castle. I hope you're ready to travel and haven't become too soft living here."

She went along with his change in subject and said, "I don't know. Can we kidnap one of the massage people to take with us?" He laughed, and she asked in a more serious tone, "Should I pack something? Do I need to do anything?"

"No, you don't need to do anything but wait and act normal. You can't pack, because that will get noticed. Your rooms are not private. What did you do with the knives I gave you?"

"They're hidden under various stones near the bath," she answered.

"Good. Just continue to deal with Ian, as you have been. He is actually helping our cause by keeping his father and the assembly from you, but his time is running out. Alrik is getting impatient so we'll need to leave soon before more is expected from you. Honestly, I'm surprised Ian has been able to keep you from them this long. His reputation with women precedes him, and they were eager to believe he could gain your trust and turn you into the perfect submissive bride."

Alissia scowled and said, "Yeah, the men in this reality seem to have a thing for believing they can control their women and that we yearn for their love and protection."

Luke laughed and said teasingly, "And that is how it should be."

Alissia responded by giving a dirty look, and he laughed even harder. Once he was done laughing, he said, "I'll miss you, Pixet, but we'll see each other again soon."

"Will Anika, Langley, and Grady be leaving with us?"

He nodded and said, "And Morton's family as well. They need protection also."

In that moment, Alissia was reminded of Luke's strong sense of duty to protect others, and she could not help but smile.

"What?" he asked, cocking his head to one side in confusion.

"Nothing," she answered. "Sometimes I'm reminded that you're a good man. That's all."

He frowned back at her and said, "Alissia, I know you have not seen the best from me, but . . ."

She pulled one of her hands from his and put her finger to his lips, silencing him.

"I don't need to see the best from you to know you are a good man, Luke. No matter how much you drive me crazy and keep me awake at night, it's you that I want to be with."

She noticed the momentary look of surprise on his face before he grinned. When she removed her finger from his lips, he said, smugly, "So I keep you awake at night? And you're crazy about me?"

She laughed at his usual cockiness. "I said you drive me crazy, which means you frustrate me."

He stood to his feet and pulled her up next to him. After they shared a tender kiss, his lips went to her ear. "Am I the one you want to be with, Alissia?" he whispered, his thumb stroking her neck.

Without hesitation, she answered, "Yes, Luke. It's you I want to be with. Is that what you want?"

He pulled her in for a hug and kissed the top of her head. "More than anything, Alissia."

A short moment later, he sighed and pulled away from her. Taking her by the hand, he said, "Soon. I promise we'll be together again soon. I'm working on it, Alissia."

Anika was already dressed and was by the table eating when they joined her.

"It's almost time to leave," Anika said, before taking a sip of her drink.

Luke said, "Yes, but we'll see each other again soon. It was a pleasure to meet you somewhat properly, Anika. I ask that you continue to stay close to Alissia, and tell Langley I hope to have news for him soon."

"Thank you, Luke. I understand you are doing a lot to get us out of here, and I hope we can be able to repay you one day," Anika said.

Luke shook his head and said, "Think nothing of it. I'm only doing my job as a member of the league. I only want to see you and your friends find safety, and justice be given to those involved in putting our land at risk. Now if you will excuse me, ladies, it is time I disappear and you get ready to leave."

Alissia did not try to hide the sadness she felt from being separated again. With a reassuring smile and squeeze to her hand, he said, "Soon. We'll be leaving soon." Leaning down, he placed a quick kiss on her forehead before whispering into her ear, "You keep me awake at night also." Then he turned to walk away.

"How will you get out of here?" Alissia asked.

He turned back around and gave a playful grin that made her smile.

"I'm with the league, Alissia. It's what I'm trained to do."

She and Anika watched as he walked to the unused sauna on the far right of the room. Once he was out of sight, Anika put her hand on Alissia's shoulder.

"You should get ready, and you might want to put a little water in your hair and on your face to make it look like you've been swimming."

Alissia nodded and walked over to the water flowing down from the ledge. She stood under it for a moment, letting the water soak her entire body. Then she picked up a nearby towel and patted her hair as she made her way towards the same sauna room she had just shared with Luke.

A smile slowly lit up her face as she put on the two arm bracelets. He cared for her, and not just a little either. He really cared for her. She now wished she had said more to reassure him of her feelings. He had seemed worried, but it was him she could not stop thinking about. He was the one she had longed to be with the night of the ball, and it was him she thought about each night as she fell asleep. And now she was certain he cared for her, and she wanted him to.

Thoughts of Grady came to mind, and she bit into her lower lip. Her decision was made, and she would have to tell him. The thought of hurting Grady even more tore at her heart, but she could not lie to him or herself.

Chapter 20

Once Alissia and Anika were alone in her chambers, they sat down in the chairs arranged near the fireplace. Although Anika remained silent, she looked expectantly at Alissia.

Alissia started the conversation with, "I've made up my mind, Anika, and I care a lot about Luke." She frowned and shook her head before adding, "I'm sorry. Grady is the last person I ever wanted to hurt, but I can't force myself into wanting him over Luke."

Anika looked troubled as she said, "After seeing the two of you together, I'm not surprised by your words."

"Are you mad?"

Anika shook her head and answered, "I told you Langley and I understand the situation. I don't believe you wanted it to happen. It just happened."

Alissia felt some relief from Anika's words. She said, "I still care for Grady a lot, and I dread the day that I tell him. Do you think he'll understand?"

Anika let out a long sigh and looked at the fireplace, as if in thought. Without looking at Alissia, she said, "I'm not going to lie. This is going to hurt him worst of all." She turned and gave Alissia a hard stare as she added, "Be careful with him, and even after you tell him, don't shove you feelings for Luke in his face."

*****

Over the next few days Alissia found it easy to be nice to Ian after learning how his father treated him during the day. If Ian was truly trying to protect her from Alrik, then she thought he at least deserved a little respect from her.

One morning she received a large bouquet of flowers from him. The card read:

My dear Lady Alissia,

I have a surprise awaiting you. Please be prepared for my arrival early this evening to escort you to a world full of wonder.

Love,

Ian

The card intrigued Alissia, and she made the mistake of asking Nadia what Ian meant by a world full of wonder. Although her handmaiden did not know the answer, she became greatly excited and insisted on dressing Alissia that afternoon.

The one thing Alissia was certain about in life was that she would never again look as beautiful as she did while living in this castle. With Nadia doing her hair and makeup each day and Mela's designer dresses, she looked nothing like her normal self. Once she left Pallen, she would go back to dressing herself, and that meant pulling her hair into a ponytail and wearing pants on most days.

By the time Nadia was finished with Alissia, she wore a semi-long dress with a tight corset. The top of the corset featured soft feathering, and the bottom portion of the dress hung down in shimmery layers below her knees. Deeply colored fabrics of blue, green, and purple were woven into the dress in a pattern that made Alissia resemble a butterfly.

Her arm gloves, boots, and even the hooded, soft, and velvety cloak were in the same pattern, and she looked as though she should have wings. Her hair was pulled up in a complicated mass of glittering pins, with loose curls hanging down. Along with the diamond bracelet Ian had given her, a simple necklace with a sparkling gem in the shape of a butterfly rested on her chest, and she wore matching earrings.

"I'm beginning to think you and Mela treat me like a doll," Alissia said, standing in front of the mirror.

Nadia laughed and said, "Lady Alissia, Mela is now a highly sought-out designer because of the inspiration she got from you, and your natural beauty has all the other handmaidens wishing they were me."

Alissia stepped away from the mirror and said, "I must have some privacy for a moment. Do you mind?"

As soon as Nadia left the room, Alissia went for her sheath and attached it to the upper part of her leg. She could not help but smile to herself at how Mela had gotten used to designing dresses with a lot of layering, which was different than the normal style, or was until Alissia came to the castle. Wearing a knife was the closest she could get to Luke for now, and it gave her another reason to smile.

When Ian arrived, she noticed his eyes subtly roam across her body in appreciation, and he smiled before holding out his arm for her.

"I don't believe anyone could ever tire of looking at your beauty, Lady Alissia," he said, as he began to lead her down the hall.

"You can thank Mela and Nadia for that," she responded. "Where are you taking me?"

He gave a mysterious smile and answered, "It's a surprise, and one I know you'll enjoy."

As they walked to the nearest castle entrance, she continued to try to pry the information from him, but he would not even agree to give a hint. Once outside, he helped her into an open carriage driven by a set of guards. She noticed another carriage behind and in front of them with more guards, and she asked him again where they were going.

He laughed as he covered their bodies with a thick blanket and pulled her hood over her head. Although spring was getting near, the night air was still quite chilly. He pulled her body into his and kissed the side of her forehead before saying, "Shh. I want you to look around and enjoy your surroundings. It's been a while since you've been away from the castle."

She gave him a mock frown before turning her head, but it was not long before she smiled to herself as she took in the beauty around her. The carriage soon entered a tunnel made of lattice and covered in blue and purple bella flowers. Long strands of the colored, glowing ivy hung down from above them, and Alissia looked up in amazement.

Ian reached up and stretched as far as he could and was able to touch the tip of one of the strands. It swung behind them as they continued to travel along the path, and he looked down and studied her face for a moment.

"You've never seen anything like this?" he asked.

She shook her head and continued to look around in amazement. He chuckled to himself before saying, "You are really going to enjoy what's coming next."

"I think you're mean for not telling me," she said, feigning a scowl.

Near the end of the tunnel, he said, "Close your eyes."

"Why?"

"Because it will be better if you wait for it. Hurry, close your eyes," he said, somewhat excitedly. She closed her eyes, and then she felt the blanket pulled from her body. "Don't open them yet. I'm going to put you in a position so you can see out in front of the carriage better."

He pulled her to her feet before lowering her knees onto the other bench. "Not yet. Keep your eyes closed," he said, softly into her ear. Although her eyes were closed, she could feel Ian's firm chest at her back, along with both of his arms reaching out at each side of her body. She felt his breath on her right ear as his hand gently moved a long strand of curls from her face.

"All right, look out in front of you," he said.

Alissia opened her eyes.

"Oh, my. It's beautiful."

The trail they were now traveling on was glowing bright blue, and it led to a building covered in blue bella flowers.

Ian was smiling as he watched her face. He said, "The path is filled with small glow stones and pebbles."

"What's there?" she asked, pointing at the building.

He grinned and shook his head, and she turned her attention back to the beauty in front of her. When they stopped, he jumped out of the carriage and helped her down. Alissia noticed that guards seemed to be everywhere, and they were watching her every move.

Ian took her by the hand and led her towards the door of the building. "Are you ready?"

"Yes! What is it?"

He opened the door, and Alissia walked past him.

The air around her immediately changed, as it was now warm and somewhat moist. It took her a long moment to take in her surroundings. The lighting coming from the bella flowers and glow stones was dim, and she could hear the sound of water, as if from a spring. Large aquariums were set up in the room, and she could see that they were filled with glowing, aquatic animals.

Ian took her cloak off and hung it on a coat rack, along with his. He then took her by the hand and led her towards an aquarium with variously colored, glowing crabs in it. They were larger than bowling balls, and she could not take her eyes off them. He then took her to another aquarium with variously colored eels in them.

They viewed several more aquariums filled with glowing aquatic animals before Ian began to remove her arm covers. It was only then that she realized she was getting warm.

"I'm sorry," she said.

He shook his head. "Don't be. I love to watch you when you're like this."

"Like what?"

"Happy."

She turned back to the aquarium and asked, "What determines the color they glow?"

"Age. The glowing comes from their bodies' response to the algae in the water. The longer they've lived, the more algae they've consumed over time, and the oldest are the bright white ones you see."

"And the youngest?"

"Those would be the dark purple ones."

A screeching sound, similar to a bird came from somewhere, and Alissia looked expectantly at Ian. He chuckled and said, "You'll see."

He led her around the room until she had seen all the aquariums. Then they passed through a thin curtain into a small room. Like the other room, it was dimly lit, but instead of being filled with different aquariums, it had a wall made of glass. Behind the glass wall was an ecosystem made for tiny, glowing tree frogs and insects. There was a small tree with water at its base.

"Would you like to hold one?" Ian asked.

The tiny frogs were adorable, and they intrigued Alissia. She nodded.

"What color?"

She watched the frogs for a moment before deciding upon the color blue, and Ian walked over to the glass wall. He bent down and unfastened a latch she had not noticed. He then reached in and fumbled around until he successfully caught a blue frog.

Alissia could not help but laugh at the amount of work it had taken him.

He closed the latch and turned his attention back to her. "All for you, My Lady," he said, with a charming grin.

He held out the tiny, blue frog, and Alissia took it from his hand. As the bonding process began to take over, she quickly pushed back the feeling and stopped the process.

Alissia stared down at the frog in her hand, and she could not believe how beautiful it was, glowing brightly from within. She touched one of its squishy feet, and it made a small sound, causing Ian and her to laugh. A short while later she gave it back to Ian, and he returned it to its home.

"Ready for more?" he asked, taking her by the hand.

"What kind of place is this?"

"It's usually a museum open to the public, but tonight it's just ours. It took a lot to convince the assembly into allowing you to come, but it was worth it."

They walked to a large set of double doors decorated with an elaborate carving of a tree. At the base of the tree was a pool of water filled with fish and other aquatic animals. Land animals and birds flying in the air were also carved into the doors, making them a work of art.

Alissia stared at the doors appreciatively for a moment before Ian said, "Are you ready?"

"There's more?"

A large grin filled his face, and he opened one of the doors. Alissia walked past him, and she immediately found herself in an ecosystem resembling a rainforest. There were trees covered in a variety of bella flowers she had not seen before. Brightly colored birds were resting among them. The ground was made of real grass and dirt, and unlike the rest of the building, the clear ceiling was extremely high above them.

She began to follow a narrow path lit by bella flowers. It ended into a clearing, where a large willow-type tree stood in the center of the clearing, and a small pond of water surrounded the base of the tree.

The flowers on the tree were glowing brightly in all different shades of color. It was unlike anything Alissia had ever seen before.

"It's a felion tree, and it's what's causing the animals to glow. Although they mostly grow in fresh water, some are able to survive at the base of a river, where it meets the ocean. And on those rare places, some of the salt-water animals living in the area begin to glow. However, it's toxic to most animals, and they avoid the area altogether."

He took her by the hand and led her to a bench near the water. A tall lamppost with a glow stone was situated behind the bench, giving them some extra lighting. She could see small, glowing fish swimming beneath the surface of the water, and tiny, glowing frogs and insects of various colors roamed freely near the water's edge.

As she sat down beside him, he said, "Felion trees do not grow naturally in this part of the land, and the people that work here have produced a small miracle in getting it to survive here."

He reached under the bench and lifted something wrapped in a small towel. "Here," he said, holding it out to her.

"What is it?"

"Open it."

She took it from his hands and unwrapped it to find a large jar filled with floating, green glitter. The jar glowed brightly in her hands, and it took her a moment before she realized it was not glitter she was seeing. It was tiny insects with wings, and they shimmered brightly, creating a beautiful, sparkling presentation before her eyes.

"They just hatched today," he said. "They need to be released into this environment, and you can be the one to do it. No rush, though. I know how women get lost when it comes to shiny, sparkly things."

"They're so pretty," she said. "You don't think they're beautiful?"

He let out a small laugh. "Yes, they are beautiful." His hand came up, and he trailed his fingers along one of her bare arms. "But, it's you, Alissia, and the beauty of your eyes that I get lost in."

She felt herself swallow nervously.

"How do I release the bugs?" she asked, lifting the jar up between them.

"Just open the container."

She used that as an excuse to stand to her feet, and she loosened the lid. However, before she opened it, she turned back to Ian.

"They aren't mean are they? I mean, do they bite or sting?"

"No," he answered, shaking his head.

Having played the part of being skittish, she turned back around and removed the lid from the jar, holding it far away from her body. It took a while before all the insects made their way out of the container, and once they flew away, they became too scattered to be seen. She did, however, notice a small bird suddenly swoop down, and she guessed it had seen them.

She sat back down and smiled at Ian.

"What happens if people drink the water," she asked, in attempt to make light conversation.

"Purifying flowers can't survive in the water, and humans get sick if they drink it."

A shrieking sound made Alissia jump, and she turned to find a large bird resembling a peacock, yet somewhat different, walking towards her. The bird stopped a few feet away and opened her large feathers to reveal her hidden beauty. Unlike a normal peacock, the tips of her feathers glowed subtly and twinkled in the night.

After a moment, Alissia began to wonder if the bird was showing normal behavior around her or if she was staring at Alissia because of her being a Lamian. The bird did not move but continued to stare at Alissia, as if expecting something, and Alissia mentally told the bird to walk away. As the bird closed her feathers and walked away, Alissia felt guilt over dismissing the expectant creature.

"That was odd behavior," Ian said.

Alissia responded lightheartedly, "Oh, I'm sure the bird is used to being around people. I guess it has just never seen a strange-looking Lamian before."

Ian quickly leaned down and kissed Alissia on her lips. Since she had been taken by surprise, it took a moment for her to pull away.

He grinned.

"You do not look strange, Alissia. Your beauty intoxicates me, and I lose myself in you every moment we are together. I go to sleep each night with memories of you tenderly caressing my mind, and I patiently await the day for your touch to my body."

Alissia instinctively looked around to make sure they were not alone, and she was relieved to see a couple of guards standing at a distance away. She could always use the excuse she did not like public displays of affection. She knew telling Ian that he scared her would not work anymore. She had used that excuse too many times.

Luke had told her they would be leaving soon, so she only had to keep pretending for a little while longer. In fact, tonight could be their last night alone like this, at least that's what she wanted to believe.

Not knowing how to respond, she smiled back at Ian as she picked up one of his hands. When she went to speak, a bird flew over him, and the romantic mood came to a sudden halt as bird droppings landed on his head.

"Oh, my," she said, trying to sound innocent, as the goop slowly began to travel onto the upper portion of his forehead.

He pulled his hand from hers, and as he touched his fingers to his head, his other hand grabbed the small towel. With a scowl on his face, he began to wipe at the mess.

Once finished, he gave a defeated smile and said, "I guess this means it's time to leave. I've made other arrangements for our dinner."

Chapter 21

*A*lissia did not have to wait long for Ian to get cleaned up while she went to the bathroom, and only a small portion of his hair was wet when they walked outside.

During their ride back towards the castle, Alissia pretended to be distracted by the beauty of the glowing path and tunnel. She then avoided Ian's attempts to lead their conversation into another intimate moment between them. She acted playful and lighthearted.

It did not take long before they were parked at one of the many places she had never been on the castle property. After he helped her out of the carriage, they walked along a trail filled with many glowing spectacles. Large, round stepping-stones with a white, glowing footprint on each of them led their way.

Glowing bella flowers wrapped around the trees like wild ivy, with strands hanging down from their branches. When Alissia asked Ian what would happen if the water containing the roots of the bella flowers ever froze, he told her these particular flowers would eventually go into hibernation. They would continue to glow and survive, but they would become extremely fragile. However, the entire water supply would have to be frozen for that to happen, and all the gardens in Pallen had caretakers. They make sure the water never goes below freezing temperatures by putting certain additives in the water.

He then explained how different types of bella flowers, much bigger and stronger than these, grew in colder climates and can even survive ice.

The path ended, and Alissia found herself staring out at a lake. White, domed tents were sitting on the water all around the edge of the lake. White bella flowers covered each of the sheer tents, and their lights twinkled in their reflection on the lake. A large tent sat in the middle of the lake, where a small band played soft background music. The entire scene looked like a small city of twinkling lights.

A man wearing formal clothing walked over to them, and Ian told him his name. They then followed the man to one of the many docks leading to a private tent. Lanterns containing glow stones were hanging down from rods attached along the railings on each side of the dock to light their way.

Once inside their tent, the man took their capes and set them on a coat rack. Although the tent was very similar to the one she and Ian had shared at the ball, this one was much bigger. It also had a wooden floor and floated on water.

A small dining table with a crème-colored tablecloth was set for two. A wooden cupboard and small work table was nearby with a wine rack attached to it. There was enough extra space for a couple to dance to the soft music playing in the background, and the glowing lights from the flowers and heat stones finished off the highly romantic setting.

The man pulled out a chair for Alissia to sit down at the small dining table. He then poured their wines with a side glass of water, and once Ian tasted the wine and confirmed his approval, the man went to a warming oven hidden within the cupboard. He removed two plates, and as he set one of them in front of Alissia, she realized she would be eating one of her favorite meals from this reality.

Ian had been watching her, and he smiled and asked, "I made the right choice?"

"Definitely!" she answered.

Once the waiter left, Alissia anxiously took a bite of her food. Although she had known since receiving the flowers that Ian had special plans for the evening, she now realized how much effort he had put into making all the arrangements. It was her belief that when a man went through this much trouble, it usually came with an expectation.

She knew Ian did not have a physical expectation. However, he expected a fast courtship to appease his father, although he also wanted to get her away from his father.

"Alissia, we have enough privacy here, and we can talk openly."

Her stomach tightened, and she forced another bite into her mouth.

He continued, "We have to leave Pallen in two days. I've discreetly made all the arrangements, and it has to be then. I'm beginning to fear for your safety, as my father and the assembly are under the impression it's time for you to become an active member of the Eldership. They feel they have given you enough time to get settled in, and they believe they have won you over with your living arrangements and lifestyle. I cannot keep them from you much longer. Alissia, I have actively fought against them in an attempt to give you more time, but there's nothing more I can do here."

When she did not respond, he said, "Although I have nothing to give you in Pallen, I have much to offer elsewhere. I am a man of great wealth and power, and I can give you almost anything you desire." He reached out and took hold of one of her hands. "Alissia, I love you, and even if you don't have the same feelings for me, I still want to take care of you, protect you, and honor you. I'm willing to give you all of me."

He let go of her hand and pulled a tiny box from his suit pocket.

"I have something for you," he said, holding it out to her.

Alissia stared at the box for a moment, and everything within her told her to run. She knew what was in it, and although most women would be excited at this moment, she was terrified and angry at the same time. She was scared of what she was about to say, and she was angry at being forced into a situation like this.

Men, love, rings, and anything romantic had never been for Alissia. Since being in this reality, she was continuously forced to have a male protector, and they all seemed eager to fall in love with her. It bothered her how she was collecting men at a fast rate, and Ian was yet another person she would have to hurt.

With shaky hands, she slowly took the box from his hand, and as she opened it, he said, "Alissia, will you marry me?"

She stared down at the elaborately handcrafted ring. It was filled with more diamonds than she had ever believed could fit on such a small piece of jewelry. She swallowed nervously before looking back up at him.

"I . . . uh . . . don't know what to say, Ian," she said, awkwardly.

"Alissia, I understand if you don't love me now, but I promise I will give you a life of happiness, if you will let me."

Although she had despised Ian when she had first met him, she now liked him as a person, and she did not want to hurt him.

She bit on her lower lip for a moment as she considered her words. Then she said, "Ian, I can't leave with you in two days."

The expression on his face changed into something she could not read, and although she searched his face, she could not tell if he was mad, sad, or confused by her words.

After a moment of silence, he said, "I'm sorry if this scares you, Alissia, but we have no other choice but to leave. *You* have no other choice, and I'm not saying this in force. If you don't leave, bad things will happen to you. Even if you don't want to marry me, I still stand by my promise to protect you. That means we leave."

He took the box from her hand and removed the ring from it. Placing it on her finger, he said, "Just wear the ring for now, so others will see it. It will make things better for you over the next couple of days and will appease many."

As she stared down at her finger, still in his hand, she quickly made the decision on how to handle the situation. She looked back up and gazed hard into his eyes. In a firm, yet gentle voice, she said, "Ian, I don't want to leave. I will wear this, but whatever happens to me here, I don't want to run, and I don't want you to have to run from others because of me. I care for you enough that I don't want that from you. You have a life, and it's a great one. I will not allow my problems to destroy you."

He said, determinedly, "You leaving with me will not destroy my life. I said I could not help you or give you much in Pallen. When we leave here, I will still have everything. My father has been so consumed with the Eldership over the last few years, that it's no longer him running the business."

He gave her hand a squeeze and added, "When I said we were leaving Pallen, don't think we will be spending the rest of our lives in fear and running from my father. That is not in the plan. You will have a beautiful home of your choice. I own businesses all over the land. We could travel, and I could show you things you've never seen before. When you want to settle, I can give you a house in the mountains, on a beach, in a city, wherever you choose. Alissia, I'm not offering you a life of fear. I'm promising you the life of any woman's dream. You can have anything with me, even the best doctors to help you with your memories, if that is something you are interested in. But, if you don't leave with me now, there's nothing I can do to protect you."

Well that didn't work, Alissia thought.

"Ian, I'm not leaving Pallen," she said, decisively.

He released her hand and sat back in his chair. After a moment of silence, he said, "Does this have anything to do with your friend named Anika? If so, I can still make arrangements to have her and her husband leave with us, and I could have them escorted safely back to Allure."

Alissia chewed on her bottom lip. Although she knew asking him if he could get Grady and Morton's family to safety was the wrong thing to do, it would make the situation a lot easier if they could all just leave in two days. She was certain Luke could find his own way out of Pallen.

There was nothing more she could say to Ian to protect his feelings. Instead, she looked into his eyes and shook her head. "I'm sorry, Ian. I can't leave with you, and it has nothing to do with Anika. She's a great friend, but she has nothing to do with me wanting to stay. The truth is you are better off without me, and that is all I will say. You are a great man, and you could probably have any woman you choose. I'm just not that woman."

She got up from the table and took the ring off her finger and held it out to him.

"I'm ready to go now. I'm sorry, Ian."

He stood to his feet, and he took the ring from her. In a resigned voice, he said imploringly, "Please, keep the ring for now. It will only help you."

As he put the ring back on her finger, he added, "I also ask that you don't talk to anyone about your answer, not even Nadia, and I say this for your own safety. Just accept it as a gift."

They did not speak as he helped her with her cape, and the silence continued as they walked back to the carriage. The walk back to her chambers felt like the longest walk she had ever taken with someone. Once at her door, he kissed her on the forehead in front of her guards. He then gave her hand a squeeze and said, "I'll see you soon."

Chapter 22

Nadia immediately noticed the ring, as if she had been looking for it. Alissia smiled weakly as her handmaiden took the pins from her hair and excitedly talked about elaborate weddings within the castle. By the time Nadia left for the night, Alissia was certain the woman would spread the news of her engagement, and it would not take long before everyone in the castle would be gossiping about the high-profile wedding.

After a hot bath, Alissia spread out on her bed and stared up at the bella flowers above her. She lifted her hand and looked at the ring.

"What has happened to me?" she asked herself.

A sudden movement at her feet announced the arrival of Mia, and Alissia put her hand down. She let out a small laugh as the tiny creature walked up her body. Her large eyes soon gazed down at Alissia from above, as if she were a cat sitting on her chest.

The intense look in Mia's eyes made her appear as if she were studying Alissia, and Alissia wished she knew what the creature was thinking. She soon sighed and began her nightly routine of a one-sided conversation in the old language.

"I'm engaged, Mia. Even after I said no more than once, I'm wearing an engagement ring for my own safety, it seems. Do you know this is the third engagement ring I've worn in the last few months, and yet I've never told any man that I love him? It seems I am a habitual fiancé. Men fall around me like flies, and I'm collecting them for my army."

A rumbling noise came from the creature, and her mouth opened to reveal many sharp and tiny teeth.

"Are you laughing?" Alissia said, in disbelief. "If that is what you are doing, it's not right. I'm trying to have a moment of self-pity, and you're ruining it."

The rumbling continued until the creature fell onto the bed.

"I'm glad you find this so funny. You do realize I've just snubbed someone that was trying to help me, and once we leave Pallen, I have to have another conversation like this again."

Alissia crawled under the covers and pulled some of the bella flowers from their water.

"I'm going to sleep so the Lamians that watch me, or whatever they do in the night, can get their laugh too."

She rolled over, and Mia joined her under the covers and snuggled against Alissia's chest. Although the creature was not able to communicate, her presence gave Alissia comfort each night.

A knock came from the maain door of the suite, and Alissia sat up in alarm. She looked at Mia in confusion for a moment, and the knock sounded again. Jumping from the bed, she grabbed her robe and put it on to conceal the knife hidden beneath her gown.

Mia disappeared under the bed, and as Alissia went to answer the door, she mentally prepared herself for an awkward visit from Ian. However, she was surprised when she found a strange man on the other side of the door.

He nudged her aside and entered the room, closing the door behind him. Alissia immediately knew something was wrong, because he was breaking an important custom by walking into her chambers alone. She wanted to believe Luke had sent him, but the expression on the man's face was anything but inviting.

"You need to get dressed quickly. Your presence is demanded elsewhere," he said.

"Demanded?" she asked, angrily. "Do you know how many rules you're breaking right now? I'm not going anywhere with you until you tell me who you are or what you're doing here."

"Luke sent me," he said, matter-of-factly.

"Luke?"

"Yes, now hurry. Dress in something to make it look as though you're visiting Ian."

Alissia rushed to her room and shut the door, locking it for privacy. She quickly found a warm, black dress that she could wear her traveling boots with, and her fingers were shaking with excitement as she added the knives to the boots.

Mia suddenly appeared before her, and Alissia whispered, "It's time, Mia. We're leaving tonight."

Mia shook her head, but Alissia turned to look at herself in the mirror. Her hair was wild with curls, but she did not have time to do anything with it. Instead, she went to the closet and grabbed a warm cloak with a hood. When she stared back at herself in the mirror, she decided she looked decent enough to walk the halls of the castle without drawing too much attention to herself. She quickly added some light blush and lip-gloss in case Nadia saw her. Her handmaiden was strict about Alissia's public appearances.

She threw on some arm warmers in case she would be traveling that night, and she grabbed a small purse and quickly filled it with three pairs of the sturdiest sunglasses she could find. Most of the ones she had acquired while at the castle were made of fine, delicate materials.

She took one last glance around the room to see if she would need anything else. She then ran back to the closet and found her old moneybag.

Although she left the bracelet Ian had given to her out of respect for him, she filled the moneybag with some of the jewels given to her by the Eldership. She chose the ones she thought to be the most expensive. She wanted to leave the engagement ring behind also, but she was certain its absence would get noticed if someone stopped her in the halls.

Once finished with the moneybag, she grinned to herself as she realized her unwanted time at the Eldership had given her enough jewels to take with her that she would never have to depend on anyone for financial support again. She could now even repay Grady all the money he had spent on her.

She put on expensive earrings, two more rings, and she hid some necklaces beneath her dress. She hid bracelets beneath both of her arm warmers, making sure to carry as much jewels as possible without being noticed. She even added some to her cloak's inside pockets, telling herself the jewels had been given to her, so she was not stealing.

As she walked towards the door, Mia determinedly shook her head.

Alissia whispered, "Mia, this is what we've been waiting for. Here, I can take you with me by hiding you under my cloak." She reached down to pick up the small creature.

"Ouch! You bit me!" she exclaimed, grabbing her throbbing hand.

An impatient knock came at the door, and Mia ran back under the bed. Alissia scowled towards the bed before unlocking the door and opening it.

"Who were you talking to?" the man demanded.

"No one. I hit my hand on something, and it hurt," she answered, rubbing her hand. She felt moisture on her fingertips, and she realized Mia had brought blood. Luckily, the arm warmer covered that part of her hand, and since it was black, it would hide the stain.

"I'm ready. What do I need to do?" she asked.

"Just act natural as you walk with me. I need you to smile and enjoy my company."

"What about the guards? How did you get in here?"

"We replaced them with our own. Don't worry, Lady Alissia. The plan is precise and well thought out. Now, we need to leave."

Alissia nodded and followed the man out of her suite. As she walked past the guards, she noticed she had never seen them before. Two more unknown guards walked behind them as an escort, and everything appeared normal to those she passed.

They walked for about twenty minutes in complete silence throughout the winding halls of the castle, and then they went to the lowest level, beneath the castle. The air became damp and cold, and the lighting was scarce. If it were not for her night vision, she would have found the environment even creepier than she already did.

The man led her along an underground maze, and she was relieved when they finally stopped at a small, open area in front of a wooden door, with a simple bench beside it.

Chapter 23

The man grinned down at Alissia and said, "Here we are, Lady Alissia. Let me get the door for you."

Alissia nodded, but there was something about the way he spoke that made her somewhat tense. When he opened the door, she cautiously looked into the room, and her heart immediately fell from her chest.

"Luke!" she cried out, running to the battered body chained to the wall. He was shirtless, and she could see he had been beaten badly. "Oh, my goodness, Luke. What happened?" Her trembling fingers touched his barely recognizable face, covered in gashes and bruises.

He opened his eyes slowly, but when he realized she was standing before him, he immediately began to fight against the chains.

"Stop!" she pleaded, fearing he would hurt himself even more. She began to tug at the rope around his mouth, but an eerily familiar voice soon stopped her.

"I would not do that if I were you, Alissia."

She turned around to face Ian. Although his voice was calm and he was still dressed in the fine clothing he had worn on their date, Alissia noticed a look on his face she had never seen before. His teeth were clenched, and she saw fury in his eyes.

"What are you doing, Ian? I thought you were against your father and the assembly. If you're mad at me, because I hurt you, then I'm sorry. Please don't take it out on Luke. He has nothing to do with this." When he did not respond, she added, "Ian, I know you, and this isn't you. You are so much better than this."

He calmly said, "I've been wondering which man had your attention. The night of the ball I guessed Luke over Grady, but I thought I still had a chance with you. I mean, no other woman has ever turned me down. Isn't that right, Gerald?"

The other man nodded, along with the two men dressed as guards.

"I showered you with attention and gifts. I know I'm not bad looking, Alissia, and I know how to talk to women. But none of that was good enough for you. I talked about my money and power, yet that didn't work either."

He let out a sigh and took a few steps towards her before adding, "I then got the idea to offer you protection. You seemed scared and fragile. I could protect you from everyone and everything." He added, incredulously, "Did you not hear all the promises I gave you tonight? Who would turn that down, Alissia? I even offered protection for your friend. But, no, that wasn't good enough either. And you know why? Because none of that matters to you, does it? There's nothing I can give you when your heart is set on something else."

She opened her mouth to speak, but he held up his hand and interrupted.

"Let me tell you a true story. There once was a young girl that had the world at her fingertips. She had beauty, wealth, people that loved her, and a promising future, yet she was willing to lose everything and give it all away because of love. Love does that to some people." Pointing his finger for emphasis, he added, "But, I saved her. You see, if you take the obsession away, it no longer becomes a problem. In fact, the young girl is now a very well-educated woman with a bright future ahead of her.

"My sister was willing to give up her place in our family to run away with a stable boy, and although I never doubted his love for her, they didn't belong together. They were both warned, yet they both were ready to destroy her life in the name of love."

He looked at Luke, and said, "He died a quick death. However, things will be different tonight." He paused as if in thought before adding, "This somehow seems more personal."

Alissia shook her head in disbelief. "You did that to you own sister?"

Ian smiled and said, "Yes, I did."

"You destroyed her!"

He shook his head and laughed. "No, Alissia. I did not destroy her, just like this won't destroy you."

Fear consumed Alissia, and she instinctively stood tall in front of Luke. She began to search the faces of the other three men in the room, hoping to find fear or doubt in at least one of their eyes.

They all laughed, and Ian said, "I believe she's got it."

"Ian, you don't want to be like your father, remember? You're better than him," she pleaded.

The grin immediately fell from his face, and he said, "Oh, you're right about that, Alissia. I am not like my father. I am better, and I'm smarter. Who do you think my sister blames for her loss? And to this day, my father still does not know how to repair their relationship. And who does she respect? Me.

"And while my father has been consumed with controlling the Eldership, who do you think has been traveling the land and running the business? Me. Whose name is now on most of the business titles and documentation, and who do the men respect the most?"

He sneered and added, "And how do you think this will end tonight? Let's think this through. Luke and you disappear together, never to be seen again. It seems you won his heart. My father can no longer promise the help of the Lamians or Lamian, whatever he's been hoping for. He has nothing to offer the other assemblies that are already skeptical of his plans, and he loses any support he has already won."

Taking a step closer, he said, "Oh, but there's more. He can't kill Grady, Morton's family, and all those innocent people from Allure. No one will support him if he goes that far, and honestly, I don't think he has the heart for that much bloodshed. In the end, my father will rot in a prison, if not sentenced to death." He paused before adding, thoughtfully, "I hope he'll be sentenced to death."

He turned to the other men, and they nodded their agreement. Then he looked back at Alissia and said, "Either way, since I'm the most aggressive with travel and have the best relationships within the company, I foresee most of the business going into my name. Although, it helps that I've already deceived my father into signing most of the needed documentation." He grinned and added, "I'm a patient man, and I've been working for this for a *very* long time, Alissia. I've already won, and my father will take the fall."

"So you plan to kill me also?"

He looked hurt by her question and said, "Oh, Alissia, why would I do that? You made a bad decision, and although there are unpleasant consequences and a lesson to be learned from it, I would never kill you. You do realize I intended to deliver on all those promises I gave you tonight. I even considered not ever being with another woman if we were to marry." He added, with emphasis, "I haven't been with a woman since arriving in Pallen. I took my courtship with you seriously, Alissia, and you should have done the same."

Alissia did not respond. She was too busy trying to come up with a way out of the situation. After a while, he gave a reassuring smile and said, "Let's just deal with this distraction you have right now. We'll get rid of Luke, you will leave Pallen tonight, and I will stay behind for a while to look distraught in front of everyone. I'll see you again soon, after you've had some time to think, and then we'll see what happens.

"Like I said, I'm a patient man, and I understand sorting through your feelings for Luke will take some time, especially after all we do to him. I'm sorry, but I want this memory to stay with you so you don't ever forget what happens when you make a wrong choice."

Memories of Luke telling her to think strategically and logically filled her mind. They had spent countless hours riding together with him describing dangerous scenarios, and she would have to find a way out of each of them. He would always tell her to force her emotions aside and assess the situation. Yet, even with three knives hidden on her body, she could not think of a way to save Luke.

She had seen Ian's muscled body, and realistically, there was no way she could physically fight off him and his three men.

"What's so important about me? I can't even remember where I come from," she asked, in an attempt to buy some more time. Determination rose up within her as she told herself Luke would not be killed without a fight from her, even if she died in the process. She quickly glanced over her shoulder to find him glaring wildly at Ian.

Ian exploded, "Enough!" He spoke through vise-like jaws, saliva frothing and spraying. "I've had it with your incessant lies!"

He breathed deeply, closing his eyes for a moment. Then he walked over to Alissia and pulled back the hood of her cloak. Leaning down, he whispered, "You've been keeping secrets from me, little one, but that ends tonight."

Alissia balled her hands into fists at her sides, mentally screaming Luke's words, *Remain logical, not emotional.*

As Ian unbuttoned her cloak, her fingernails painfully dug into her flesh. He tossed the cloak to one of his men, who set it aside. Then

Ian took her purse and opened it to find the glasses before giving it to the same man.

He smiled and said, as if nothing was wrong, "So this is what your hair looks like when Nadia is not around." He lifted his hand and picked up a cluster of curls. "I like it." Grabbing her by the head, he leaned down to kiss her, and she instinctively bit him. He ripped his lips from her teeth and backed away. Then he swiped at the blood trickling from his mouth before looking back at her with a satisfied grin.

"I knew it! I thought I noticed a fighter in you that day at the doctor's office. You've been playing the part of a delicate soul." He gave a sadistic grin and said, "I'm going to enjoy getting to know the real you, Alissia." His eyes roamed her entire body before he added, "It's going to make things a lot more interesting, don't you think?" Luke struggled fiercely behind her, and Ian laughed.

"If you kill Luke, I will never love you, and you're crazy if you think I will," Alissia warned.

"No, my dear. I've already tried to win your heart, but it was never available to me. You may never love me. However, one day you will accept me and what I have to offer you. Although you've made your choice against publicly marrying me, there are other options between a man and a woman. Being my mistress still has its benefits. I promise you'll enjoy all I plan to give you, and one day, maybe years from now, but one day, Luke will just be a memory of a life you weren't meant to live."

He turned to the three men and said, "Let's do this. I've waited long enough, and she'll be mine tonight." He turned back to Luke and added, "I'm curious to know what will happen when she gives her body to me. What do the stories say? Riches and power to those they favor?"

As Ian stepped away, one of the men went to grab Alissia, and she jerked away from him. Another man caught her from behind, pinning her arms at her side. She immediately began to throw her head back, but with his large size, she was only able to make contact with his chest. She stomped on his foot, but his boot deflated her blow.

She then tried the third thing Luke had taught her. She moved her body to one side and grabbed his manhood. Giving it a fierce pinch, twist, and pull, the man let go of her.

Before she could reach for one of her knives, the other two men grabbed each of her hands, and she aimed a kick at one of their groins. When her boot made contact, the man cursed and lifted his fist.

"Don't hit her!" Ian ordered.

A sudden pain shot through her arm as the other man pulled her arm up and behind her back. Alissia cried out as her body was slammed against the hard, stone wall.

Her aggressor laughed triumphantly and said, "She's a wild one, boss."

"So I see," Ian said, with amusement. "I like her even more now. She has fire in her, and those are the best kind."

The men laughed, and the man holding her arm lowered it slightly so the pain was less paralyzing. He grabbed a handful of hair from the back of her head and turned her around.

She glared at Ian in a full rage. By now, her hair was wild, her glasses were on the ground, and her breathing was ragged. At that moment, everything within her hated him.

After their amusement wore off, Ian nodded at the other two men and said, "Make it hurt. She needs to learn her place."

One of the men pulled out a long knife, while the other one punched Luke hard in the stomach. Alissia watched in terror as he repeatedly beat Luke with his fist. Once he stopped, he stepped aside.

The man with the knife cocked his head for a moment, as if in thought. Then he stepped up and began to slice at the league tattoo on Luke's chest.

Alissia gave a deathly scream as blood began to flow down Luke's body.

"No one can hear you, and no one's coming either," her assailant said, into her ear.

Tears rolled down her face as she silently watched the man slash at Luke's tattoo. All the while, Luke stared into her eyes. He said nothing, his jaw set and fists clenched. Even in pain, he refused to give his attackers the pleasure of seeing any weakness from him.

Alissia began to sob, and she mouthed, "I'm sorry."

Her words caused Luke to close his eyes.

The man with the knife stopped, and he stood back to admire the damage he had done. The tattoo was gone, replaced with gory slashes, and blood covered Luke's upper body.

"Stop! Please stop!" Alissia screamed, in her natural accent. "Ian, if you stop now, I'll give you everything you want tonight." Tears ran down her face. She looked at him and over-emphasized her southern accent as she pleaded, "I'll tell you everything now. I know where my people are, and it's true. I can give you power by giving you my body, Ian."

The men stopped and turned to Ian, and she continued to plead with him. "Tell these men to leave, Ian. I'll do anything you want. You've won. You have me."

Ian gave a nod, and her captor released her. She fell to the ground and tried to make herself appear small and vulnerable. She wiped at the tears on her face and said in a shaky voice, "I'll tell you everything, but please stop. Ian, please tell them to leave, and I'll tell you anything you want to know. Anything, Ian." She looked down and added, "I'll do anything."

Ian stared at her thoughtfully for a moment. "He has to die, Alissia. It's the only way to get him out of your mind."

Alissia closed her eyes, and in a resigned voice, she said, "I know, but he doesn't have to be tortured like this. Let me talk to you first, and then you can decide how to kill him."

She opened her eyes and stared up at him, sniffling.

He frowned before turning his attention to the man with the knife. "Give us some privacy. Leave it here, but don't make it fatal."

The man immediately stabbed Luke on his left side, leaving the knife there as he and the others walked towards the door.

As Ian ordered his men to close the door and not to enter until he opened it, Alissia quickly slipped a knife from her boot and hid it under her dress. She then looked up at Luke, who was staring down at her with a pained expression.

She did not think he had seen the knife, and she wished she could give him some reassurance. However, she did not even know how she was going to get past all four men. All she was concerned about at the moment was getting Luke down from the chains.

She looked down and closed her eyes, telling herself she was not too late. Luke would live. Then a sob left her throat as the reality of their situation forced its way into her mind.

"You know, it didn't have to be like this, Alissia," Ian said, soothingly. "If you would have listened to me and taken my offer, none of this would have happened. I never wanted any of this for you. For us."

At the sound of his voice, rage filled Alissia. It was the same rage she had felt each time she had beaten her father. It took all of her willpower to appear weak and helpless as she opened her eyes and slowly looked up at him.

"I didn't wake up without my memory," she said softly, hoping he would come closer. "My father is the chief of the Lamians, and I was betrothed to wed a man I did not like. He was not kind, and he was extremely cold to me. When I told my father how I felt, he would not listen."

Ian took a few steps towards her, and for a moment, she was tempted to throw the knife at him. However, if she missed or just wounded him, the other men would run back into the room once Ian called out to them. It had to be quick and quiet. She only had the advantage of surprise.

Her rage had stopped the tears, replacing her pain with an eerie calm. She looked up at Luke to give her a reason to cry. When the tears came, she let them come freely, hoping she looked defenseless and fragile, the opposite of how she now felt.

In a soft whimper, she continued with her story. "I ran away in the night, and I traveled for many days before being found. What I did was wrong, and my people won't ever accept me again. They will never allow me to go back."

She barely whispered the last sentence, and Ian had to come close to hear her words. He remained standing for a moment, staring down at her, as if in thought. Then he squatted in front of her.

She lifted her hand with the engagement ring. While staring at it, she said, "I actually went to bed tonight wondering if I had made a mistake when I told you no." She looked up at him and added, "Ian, if you had visited me tomorrow, you could have easily changed my mind. The more I thought about it, I realized you had the most to offer. Now I see you never loved me, and you only wanted something from me, just like everyone else."

With those words, he sat down in front of her, and she set her hands down at her side. He let out a sigh and said, "Alissia, did I let any of my men physically hurt you tonight?"

"No."

The conversation was going too slow for Alissia, and a sudden thought of Luke bleeding to death came to mind. Adrenaline raced within her as her fingertips touched the knife. She looked up at Luke and hoped Ian's eyes would follow hers.

"Do you love me, Ian?" she asked, her fingers wrapping around the knife. When she looked back at him, she found him watching her, and she realized he had never turned his head. She desperately hoped he had not seen the movement at her side, and then she told herself he did not even expect her to have a knife. To him, she was just another defenseless female.

He said, "I could ask the same of you, Alissia. What are your feelings towards me, especially now?"

"Confused, hurt, and angry," she answered. "But you've won." She paused before adding, "I'll give you anything you want, and I won't fight you, if you promise not to hurt me."

At those words, Luke began to struggle again, and Ian looked up at him.

Alissia immediately brought the knife up and slashed at his throat. Her fear of him being able to call for help pushed her to continuously slice away. As his body fell back, she jumped onto him and repeatedly stabbed him in the heart. She lost track of what she was doing, and once she came back to her senses, she was covered in blood. She dropped the knife and stood to her feet, stepping away from the mutilated body.

Chapter 24

She looked over at Luke, and they locked eyes for a moment. Then she ran to the door and slowly turned the bolt, all the while praying it would not make a sound.

When she tried to undo the shackles at Luke's feet, she found that her hands were too slick with blood. She let out an impatient sigh when she realized her dress was covered in blood also. She quickly wiped her hands on the back of Luke's pants. She then undid the shackles before retrieving a chair to stand on to reach the ones at his hands. She grabbed the other knife in her boot and cut the rope from his mouth.

"Luke, can you stand?"

He looked as if he was struggling to remain conscious, but he nod-ded slightly before shifting to hold his weight.

"All right, try not to fall. I'm going to undo you."

She undid the shackles from his wrists and hopped down from the chair.

"Let me help you," she said, seeing the pain in his eyes.

They walked a short distance before she helped him to the floor. Then she sat down beside his battered body. Blood was everywhere, and he still had a knife in his side. Tears began to take over as she realized she had been too late. She slowly pulled the knife from his body, and he opened his eyes and looked up at her. She could barely hear him speak as he said, "You should have let them finish me, Pixet. How are you going to get out of here?"

She wiped the tears from her eyes and said, "Who says I'm getting out of here?"

He smiled and lifted his hand to her face. "You're the most stubborn person I know." He cringed in pain, and she let out a short sob.

"I'm sorry, Luke. I should have done something sooner. I tried to think logically and not emotionally," she cried.

"This is not your fault. There was nothing you could have done, and I'm proud of you." She looked down at him in confusion, and he smiled somewhat before adding, "You remembered the moves I taught you."

She gave a short laugh and rolled her eyes.

He lowered his hand, and his eyes closed.

"Luke? Luke! I'm not ready for you to go. Please, Luke. Please don't die."

His eyes opened.

"Don't cry, Pixet. I'm going to die." His breath was ragged, and he winced in pain before adding, "Listen. We're in one of the dungeons below the castle, and I'm certain Ian's men don't have a key to the door. I need for you to stay in here and wait to be found. Don't speak or make a sound when the men begin to knock at the door."

He paused in pain before continuing. "I failed you, Pixet, and I'm sorry."

"You did not fail me, Luke. Please don't think that," she said, firmly.

He continued, "There's something I never told you. I fell in love with you, no matter how hard I tried not to, but I was never brave enough to tell you. I now wish I had told you sooner."

She wiped away more tears, and he said, "Hold me, Pixet. I want my last memories on this earth to be of your arms around me."

Alissia tried to be gentle as she lay down beside him.

"Luke?"

He turned his face towards her, and she positioned herself onto her elbow so that her face was above his. She could tell she did not have much longer with him.

"I love you, Luke." A tear fell from her eye and onto his bloody cheek as she moved a rogue strand of hair from his face. Then she tenderly put her hand on his chest, where his revered tattoo should have been but was now covered in blood and torn flesh. Carefully leaning down, she said, "This is what I want your last memory to be."

Her mouth slowly came down to his bloodied lips, and she lovingly kissed him. Although he did not respond immediately, his mouth soon parted, and he welcomed her touch.

The kiss was slow and tender, and she almost cried out in sadness as she felt his hand come up to her back. Pain of knowing this would be their last kiss filled her, and she poured all of herself into it. *I love you, Luke! I love you!* she screamed within her mind, hoping he would feel the love she wished she could pour into him.

A flash of heat suddenly overtook her body, and her mind became flooded in white light before she found herself in the body of a young boy. He was standing on a playground, and two other boys stood before him, taunting him. It was not the first time they had done this, and the young boy was filled with a rage that had grown over time, enough to make him lash out for the first time in his life. He struck both boys and was soon on top of one, punching him repeatedly in the face, until a man pulled him off the other boy. His rage immediately turned to shock, seeing how he had given one of his tormentors a bloody nose.

In an instant, Alissia found herself in a bed. She was still in the body of the same boy, and the room was completely dark. He was sad and confused, tears silently falling into his pillow. He did not understand why his parents had not wanted him and had left him at an orphanage. Trouble seemed to follow him wherever he went. He continuously disguised his sadness with anger, and he was quick tempered and ruthless. The other children were scared of him, and one day he overheard one of the adults talking about him, saying he had never had to deal with someone like the boy before. The boy was uncontrollable, and he disrupted the entire orphanage. The man wanted him gone.

The scenery suddenly changed, and the boy was a few years older. He was dressed in a uniform, and he was sprawled out on a different bed, looking up at the ceiling. All the other boys at the Eldership school had gone home for the holiday season, and he was the only one left behind. He imagined what it was like to have a family to go home to, and he wrestled with his pain and loneliness.

He studied hard, and he excelled in everything at the school. He held the highest grades, causing a lot of jealousy among his peers. They enjoyed taunting him and reminding him of where he came from. He took his anger and revenge out on them during their physical training. He was unbeatable when it came to his fighting skills.

Suddenly, he was a young teenager. Things were different now. His peers either feared him or respected him, and they often came to him for advice. He succeeded at everything he touched, and although he knew he should be happy by now, he felt like a fraud among everyone else around him. Only he knew the rage hidden deep within his soul, and it was a constant struggle to contain. He was bitter and angry, yet he hid behind the mask of a smile and forced laughter every day.

Time moved on, yet again, and he was an older teenager. He had been accepted into the elite division of the league, and his body was sore, bruised, and battered from intense training. His mind was tired from lack of sleep. As most of his peers failed and dropped out of the program, he endured the pain and continued on. Giving up was not an option. He would either succeed or die trying. Either way, he had nothing to lose.

Suddenly, he was standing over a dead body, yet he was still just a teenager. It had been his first official assignment, and the man had been his first kill. As he looked at the blood on his hands, he reminded himself he did not have time to dwell on what he had done. He still had to dispose of the body. He did not even know what the man's crime had been. No one had told him, yet he had obeyed the orders.

Years later, the boy was now a young man, and the body count had added up. He struggled daily with his conscience over the things he had seen and done. By now, he knew he only disposed of high degree criminals, but knowing this gave him little consolation. It was hard to justify what he did with what he read in the Book of the Creator.

Then Alissia was in the same body as he stared at his reflection in the mirror. It was Luke's face staring back at her. He was consumed with pain and rage. His friend and many people had died, savagely murdered. Men, women, and children—they were all dead.

Memories of their last night together consumed him. Everyone had been happy. There had been lots of food and wine. Laughter had filled the home. The two older couples whose children were grown had given their hard-earned advice to the young newlyweds expecting their first baby. Then there were the owners of the home and their four small children. No one could have imagined what would happen to those children.

His friend, another member of the league, had made one simple mistake, and that mistake had cost many people their lives. Luke's job had been the hardest. He was to clear the path for his friend. As he dealt with the guards and caused a distraction, his friend was supposed to assassinate one man, yet he failed. Only Luke made it out alive, and by the next morning, all the informants involved in the case had been slaughtered, including everyone within their families.

A flash of light, and Alissia found herself in another moment in time. Pain seared through her chest as she found herself sitting up in a chair. Luke was receiving the highest honor within the league, his tattoo. He did not flinch in front of the men around him, as this was a formal occasion and not just a tattoo. He had proven his worth and valor above and beyond to the league and Eldership.

Not only did he hunt down and assassinate the man responsible for all those deaths, he ruthlessly wiped out and destroyed the entire criminal organization with the help of the league. They had accepted his request to give him a team to command, and he had used that team wisely. He had made sure there would not be a replacement for the man he assassinated, as his team killed every possible threat of that happening.

He had learned the value of what he did for a living. It was his job to protect, and that meant threats to the people had to be stopped, at all cost. He also believed in the power of fear, and he wanted criminals to fear the league.

His continuous battle within himself had lessened. The Book of the Creator often talked about the battle between good and evil. Everyone in life had a part to play. His role was that of a protector.

He had learned from the mistake of his friend what one evil person was capable of doing. If his friend had been successful at assassinating his target, many lives would have been saved. Death is justifiable, at times.

Suddenly, Alissia was at a ball. She saw herself through Luke's eyes for the first time. She looked small and delicate standing next to Grady, but she was beautiful. At least, that was Luke's first thought. Intrigued by her differences, he watched her throughout the night. Some of the stories he had been told as a young boy while in the orphanage came to mind, and then he began to ponder over some of the books he had read.

She looked bored and uninterested in her surroundings, and then she turned, locking eyes with him. Alissia felt Luke's pulse quicken within his body. He reminded himself he had mastered a controlled façade long ago, and he dared not turn away. Instead, he gave a confident nod.

When she quickly turned her attention away, Luke smiled to himself. Then he noticed many others watching her. Was she a Lamian? Why else would she try to hide her eyes?

Alissia felt Luke's internal struggle as he watched her throughout the night. Before he had even met her, he decided that she needed his protection. Then she felt Luke's rage towards Alrik when her glasses were knocked from her face, confirming she needed his protection.

Time flashed, and she was in Luke's body as he stood in an alley, watching and waiting. When she watched herself step into the alley, she felt Luke's sense of urgency to get to her. He also knew others were watching, and he would have to time it just right.

Then she found herself in the cabin she and Luke had shared. He was watching her sleep and wondering what to do with her. She was a Lamian, and she was in danger. He could easily give her protection in the North.

Next, she was Luke as he was trying to fall asleep in the familiar tent they had shared. He was staring at Alissia's back, and he was confused and angry. The woman he was trying to protect despised him, and she was stubborn and difficult. In all his life, he had never been put in this situation, and he had never had one person frustrate him as much as she did.

Since meeting her, he now realized she was not a delicate creature. She was feisty, strong-willed, and cunning. She was also determined to go back to Pallen, not caring about the danger. He could not tell if it was because of her feelings for Grady or something else that drove her to disregard her own safety.

Time flashed again, and she was in Luke's body, riding bareback on a horse. Both fury and fear consumed him, and images of Alissia being tortured, raped, and drugged filled his thoughts. Lack of sleep pushed his mind and body to the extreme. When he was not imagining what all her kidnappers were doing to her, he was imagining, in great detail, the things he would do once he found her. Those images included tying her to her horse for the rest of their ride to his homeland. There were also the ones that scared him the most, him passionately losing himself with her body.

The image of her sleeping beneath a blanket appeared. Luke was now sitting by a fire watching her, and he was filled with relief. He had found her, and she was alive and safe. He also finally knew the truth of why she needed to travel back towards Pallen.

As he watched her sleep, something from within said he never wanted to leave her side. That sudden realization terrified him. He had never been attached to anyone, and as a young boy he had accepted that love was never meant for him.

Suddenly, happiness, among many other emotions, flooded through Alissia as she stared down into her own face. She was now in Luke's body after their first kiss, and as he stared down at her, he thought of how he never wanted to let her go.

Then he noticed it. She did not feel the same way, and pain ripped at his heart as he lifted his body from her.

Alissia then found herself on the same sofa as she realized she was reliving the moment she and Grady were in the kitchen together. Fear of losing Alissia to Grady filled Luke's thoughts, and he kept telling himself she did not want Grady. He desperately wanted to believe she would choose him over Grady. He knew the thought of losing her would be too much to bear.

Another flash of time, and she was staring at a wall in a dimly lit bedroom. Luke was having a hard time falling asleep. He was consumed with thoughts of Alissia, and he desperately wanted to see her. He knew Ian was known for charming women. What if Alissia fell for it?

Although her next bit of scenery was in the exact same location, the change in lighting and clothing told Alissia it was another night with different thoughts. Luke was in bed, and her words of love and lust being two different things was tormenting him. He knew he loved her, but she believed their attraction was only physical. He needed to prove to her it was love.

The cavernous walls of the sauna then surrounded her as she and Luke shared a passionate kiss. She felt his excitement, and then a sudden thought entered his mind. *There's a difference between love and lust.* An overwhelming sadness filled him as he realized he was failing at what he had come to do. Alissia needed to see and feel love, not lust.

An overwhelming and intense pain filled Alissia as she found herself witnessing the events of that very night. As Luke helplessly watched her in the room with Ian and the other men, he focused on Alissia, rather than the physical pain overtaking his body. His mind was consumed with the guilt of letting her down. The only person he had ever truly cared about, yet he could not save her. Knowing he was about to die was nothing compared to knowing he had not been able to protect the only person he truly loved.

The moment Alissia mouthed she was sorry, he realized she would blame herself for his death for the rest of her life. He closed his eyes, praying he would get a chance to tell her otherwise.

Darkness took over, and Alissia felt and saw nothing more.

Chapter 25

A stabbing pain shot through Alissia's hand, and she opened her eyes to find Mia staring down at her. Her head throbbed, and it took her a moment to sit up. The sight of Luke's bloodied body lying next to her immediately brought her back to reality, and with shaking hands, she turned his face towards her.

"Oh, my goodness! He's still warm. I don't think he's dead!"

She noticed a handprint branded into his chest, where his tattoo had once been, and she placed her hand on top of the print to find it matched perfectly.

She turned to Mia.

"I healed him?" she asked, in disbelief. "How can this be?" Mia just stared back at her, and Alissia demanded, in a whispered voice, "I can heal people?"

The small creature shook her head violently.

"But I did. He's breathing, Mia." She eagerly searched his body and realized all his wounds were now healed.

Alissia began to gently shake Luke's body, but nothing happened.

"Luke! Luke! Can you hear me?" she said, shaking his body even harder.

When he did not respond, Mia jumped onto his chest and grabbed both of his ears. She began to violently twist and pull them, and Luke's eyes shot open.

"Mia?" Alissia said, pulling the tiny fur ball away from his body. "When did you get so violent?"

"Alissia?"

Tears came to her eyes as she heard Luke speak her name. "You're alive," she said, her voice trembling with joy.

He looked confused as he slowly sat up.

"What did you do?" he asked.

"I don't know, but I'm sorry about your tattoo."

He looked down and touched the handprint. When he looked back at her, he smiled and said, "I like this better."

He leaned forward, and she met him halfway. As their lips touched, pain shot through Alissia's hand again.

"Ow!" said Alissia and Luke in unison, pulling away from each other.

Mia immediately jumped between them and grabbed both of their lips. The creature was small, but surprisingly powerful. She looked from Alissia's eyes to Luke's, and then she shook her head violently.

When she let go of them, Alissia looked down at her with a scowl.

"Mia! What is wrong with you?" She noticed blood coming from both her and Luke's hands. "You bit us? Stop biting!"

When she looked back at Luke, he was staring at her with a smile.

"What?" she asked.

"I've never heard you speak in that language."

He looked around the room, and his expression became serious. It took him a moment to stand to his feet, and Alissia did the same.

"Alissia, how long have we been down here?"

"I don't know"

"Ask your friend if she knows."

Alissia turned to Mia and asked, "Is it still the same night?"

Mia nodded.

"How late is it? Ugh! I mean, is it almost morning?"

Mia shook her head.

"Is it close to the middle of the night?"

Mia nodded.

To Luke, Alissia said, "It's close to the middle of the night."

"Good!"

He walked over to Ian's body and studied it for a moment.

Alissia slowly walked over, but she immediately turned her head away and began to gag from all the blood and gore.

"I really do need to teach you how to do a clean kill, Alissia."

Before she could respond, he walked over to her and added sternly, "Don't look at the body again. This is a memory you need to forget, and you need to always remember you did what you had to do."

He took her by the hand, and Mia began to make a rumbling noise.

"Are you growling now?" Alissia asked, incredulously. "Stop! We're not kissing."

She turned her attention back to Luke, who was studying Mia. He cocked his head to one side and said, "You know, I think your friend here could be a pixet."

"That's what you named me after? A tiny fur ball?" She put her hands on her hips and added, "It's because I'm petite, isn't it!"

He grinned and shook his head. "I don't think she likes me."

Alissia shrugged her shoulders and said, "Don't take it personal. I didn't like you when I first met you, either."

He dropped her hand and said, "Nice. Now look at the wall while I collect some knives and assess our situation. We have a very busy night ahead of us."

She began to stare at the wall, with her back to Ian's body. "How will this affect our escape?"

"Well, the good news is we leave tonight."

"And the bad?"

"The first half of the plan is no longer valid, and it would seem we will have to make it up as we go." After a pause, he added, "Also, I need you to tell me where we are exactly. I assume we're in one of the torture rooms under the castle, but I was hoping you could tell me exactly which one so I can plot our exit."

Alissia explained which entrance she had used to get to the lowest level, but after that all she remembered was a maze of walls and doors.

Luke surprised her with a quick peck on the cheek before saying, "Thanks, Pixet. That helps." He smiled down at Mia, who was growling again.

He went to a corner of the room, where a table was situated, and he collected all the knives that had been stripped from him.

His shirt was also there, along with his necklace and the ring attached to it. He put them on before walking over to her.

"How many knives did you bring?" he asked, still buttoning his shirt.

"Only three." She noticed his smirk as he looked down at the last button he was working on, and she added, "What?"

He looked back up at her and said, smugly, "Nothing. I just remembered your reaction when I gave them to you. That's all."

She crossed her arms and shook her head.

"You want me to say it, don't you?"

"Say what?" he asked, his grin even bigger than before.

"Well, I'm not going to say it."

He laughed. "You don't have to say it, Pixet. We both know I was right, and you were wrong." He replaced both of the knives in her boots. When he stood back up, he frowned and said, "Our biggest problem is how we look right now."

He was right. They both looked as though they had tried to wash themselves in blood.

"Maybe everyone is in bed right now," she said, hopefully.

"This castle never sleeps, and there are just as many servants at night as in the day. However, if we are where I believe we are, we are in luck. How did your friend get in here?"

When she asked Mia, the creature pointed up at a small opening in one of the upper walls. Alissia then realized there were many openings along the upper walls that she had never noticed before.

"Air vents," Luke said, answering her unspoken question. "It's how fresh air is circulated beneath the castle. If she crawled through there, it would be like traveling through a labyrinth of tunnels."

He picked up Alissia's cloak and purse and brought them to her. As she put the cloak on, he said, "If you keep your hood over your head, look down, and hide your hands, you really can't see as much blood. It's a good thing you wore black."

She took her purse from him and pulled the cloak over her head. He walked over to a chair and picked up Ian's suit jacket and tried it on.

"A bit loose, but it will do," he said. He took it off and set it back down. Pulling out a knife, he looked at Alissia. "Are you ready?"

She nodded.

"This should be easy. Stay here and let me take care of the three men," he said, walking towards the door.

Mia followed him, but he ignored her presence. He slowly turned the bolt, took a quick breath, and opened the door. He and Mia stepped through, and Alissia began to hear the sound of struggling. She even heard the sound of growling, and she laughed and shook her head at the thought of the tiny creature trying to help Luke.

A short moment later he returned but said nothing and acted as though he was deep in thought as he put on Ian's jacket. When he looked at Alissia, he casually said, "She's definitely a pixet."

"Why do you say that?" she responded, confused.

"Well," he began, as if struggling with the right words. He rubbed his hand through his messy hair, his fingers finding patches of blood. After rubbing his fingers across a dry spot on his pants, he looked back at Alissia and said, "She's very cute, wouldn't you say?"

Alissia nodded.

"It seems she also has a bit of a dark side to her," he added, somewhat hesitantly.

Alissia frowned as she walked towards the door. "Mia?" she asked, stepping out of the room.

Chapter 26

Alissia stopped short at the bloody scene before her, and when Luke pulled her back into the room after a short moment, she did not resist him.

"All right, you've seen what she's capable of doing. We can move on now," Luke said.

"That's what you named me after? That's what a pixet is?" she asked, incredulously.

As Luke gave her a weak grin, she thought about the scene outside the door. Mia almost looked cat-like while she had been licking blood from her fur. The tiny creature would have looked completely innocent and fragile, had it not been for the mauled body by her side.

The body seemed to be covered in bite and claw marks, especially the head. It was no longer even recognizable. The man looked as if a tiger, not a tiny ball of fur like Mia, had mauled him.

Luke's playful grin left him, and he brought his hand up to Alissia's face. "I didn't think I'd ever get to see you look at me like this again. I've missed you, Pixet."

"Pixet? Really? You're still gonna call me Pixet?"

He took a step closer, taking her by the hand and pulling her body into his. "Have I ever told you how attractive you are when you're angry?" he asked, softly, changing the mood between them. He leaned down, and she forgot about being annoyed with him. He gently kissed her bottom lip before she parted her lips slightly to let him in.

As their tongues touched, something strange and powerful began to sweep through her body, exhilaration like she had never known. Then a sharp pain stabbed into her thigh.

Alissia and Luke both cried out in alarm as they pulled away from each other. When Alissia lifted her dress, it revealed a deep gash, and purple blood was running down her leg.

"You bit me?" she angrily asked the small creature standing between them.

Luke bent down to look at Alissia's wound.

"She got you worse than me," he said.

"Probably because she knows I'll heal," Alissia answered, scowling down at Mia.

He stood back up and took her by the hand. "We should leave now."

Luke led them through the dark maze-like tunnels with a glow rock in his hand. When Alissia asked him if he knew where he was going, he showed her certain markings on the walls she had never noticed before. The markings were subtle, and you had to know what to look for to use them. Luke explained that most of the population within the castle did not even know about them, but all the servants did. They were like road signs for the workers throughout the castle, and they had to be trained how to use them, like knowing another language.

When Alissia asked how Luke knew how to use them, he reminded her he was with the league. He also said this was not his first time, nor the second, roaming beneath a castle.

The halls were empty, and when she asked him about it, he explained that Ian had chosen the best torture room for an escape. All torture rooms were near a group of dungeons, and there were a total of four groups of dungeons beneath the castle. You have to have high clearance to get anywhere near them. However, this group of dungeons had recently been evacuated for maintenance, and that meant they were in one of the few empty areas of the castle.

Luke went on to explain that Ian's plan had been perfect for getting Alissia out of the castle, because all the dungeons had their own private entrance. That meant they would not have to travel on any of the upper-level floors or use a public entrance.

When Luke put his finger to his lips, she guessed they were getting close to an entrance, and within seconds, they were standing at a group of stairs leading up to a trap door.

He stared up at the doors for a moment, as if in thought, and then he frowned and pulled out two of his knives. He then sheathed them again before leaning down and whispering into her ear, "I'd rather not have to kill any guards for doing their job tonight. Can you ask Mia if she can use one of the vents to get outside? Then she can distract them away from the door." He went to pull away, and then he lowered again and added, "You should also tell her not to kill them if she doesn't have to."

Alissia nodded and bent down to ask Mia. The creature wasted no time in disappearing, and they waited a few moments before Luke pulled out a knife. He set the glow stone down and covered it before creeping up the stairs. He then pulled a key from his pocket. After carefully unlocking the door, he slowly lifted it, just enough to peak out.

Alissia remembered that the moonlight had been dim that night, and she hoped that would work in their favor. After one of the longest minutes of her life, Luke began to motion for her.

Once she was by his side, he whispered, "Mia has them distracted, but they're not far. After I'm out, I want you to sneak out without being seen."

Alissia nodded and whispered, "Where did you get a key?"

"One of Ian's men."

"Don't forget I have night vision," she whispered.

He scowled down at her, and she realized he was still annoyed about her not telling him everything until recently. She pulled his head down and gave him a quick peck on his blood stained cheek. He then slowly opened the door and stepped out. Alissia quickly followed, and he shut the door behind her.

They ran for a long while before stopping at a group of trees.

"Where are we going?" Alissia asked, between breaths.

"To the public stables, Langley's stables. I have things prepared there."

"How much farther?"

"Not too far."

"Shouldn't we wait for Mia?"

He shook his head and answered, "We need to hurry, and something tells me she'll be able to find you. She tracked you earlier tonight, didn't she?"

"Yeah, but I don't know how."

"I have a feeling there's a lot you don't know about your little friend. Ready?"

Alissia nodded, and they set out again. This time on a path, making things easier.

As they got closer to the public stables, they noticed more guards in the area. Alissia's night vision and mind speak with animals helped them a lot, and they were able to get near the stables without being seen.

"I should have known you could see in the dark," Luke whispered, once they stopped. "I mean, it was obvious now that I think about it. You were traveling alone all through the night after you tried to kill me."

"Drugged you, Luke. If I had wanted to kill you, I would have. Remember, I warned you," she whispered back.

Although they were in a difficult situation, she had not felt this alive since arriving at the Eldership. Being with Luke, outside, and running filled her with adrenaline.

"We'll have to sneak in through the back entrance. There will be fewer guards that way," he whispered.

He took her by the hand, and they walked towards the back of the large building, stopping under a tree not far from the doors. Two guards were sitting by a fire, and Luke watched them for a moment.

"I can distract them with the animals," Alissia whispered, at his ear.

Luke grinned and nodded.

Alissia reached out with her mind and sought out the animals in the area. She chose a large dog, and it was not long before the dog was barking viscously at a distance away. When the two guards went to check it out, Alissia and Luke ran to the doors of the stables and slipped inside.

As soon as they were safe inside, they leaned with their backs against the doors and grinned excitedly at each other. The barn was very large and clean. Heat stones, placed strategically throughout the maze of stables, gave off a dim light.

"Now what?" she asked.

He took her by the hand and gave a playful wink. "Now we have a plan, although we're not on schedule."

He led her into the heart of the building and opened the door to a small bedroom. After pulling the cloth from a glow stone on a simple nightstand, a young boy swiftly sat up and pulled a knife from beneath his pillow.

Luke chuckled, and the boy set his knife aside.

"We leave tonight," Luke said. "Something happened."

Fear immediately replaced the boy's look of confusion as he noticed the blood covering them. He quickly pulled the covers from his body. Since he slept in his day clothes, he only needed to put on his boots. He then stowed his knife into one of them.

During this process, Luke said, "I need you to take Alissia with the blankets, and I'll go back to get the others."

"Alone?" the boy asked, and Alissia thought she noticed concern in his voice.

Luke seemed amused and answered, "You doubt my abilities?"

The boy quickly shook his head and said, "No, sir. I don't doubt you."

"I'll meet up with you once I secure the others, but don't forget all I've told you. I don't trust the people we're working with," Luke said. Before leading Alissia out of the room, he added, "Release the birds, quickly. I need everyone to be ready."

As Luke led Alissia through the maze of various stables and up a ladder to a hayloft, she asked, "What do you mean about the birds?"

"Devon is sending out birds right now to everyone so they'll know we're leaving tonight."

"Everyone? Are they carrying notes on them, and how do they know where to go?"

Her curiosity earned a grin from him, and he said, "The birds are gifts from the others that are helping with the escape. I've been told they have been trained by Lamians. Each of them knows where to go and have been in place for a while now in case of an emergency such as this. Everyone involved should awake to the sound of a bird pounding on their window, and they will immediately know what it means. Hopefully, they'll be ready, and my men will already be doing their jobs before I even get back to the castle."

He stopped at a large pile of hay and picked up a pitchfork before clearing a space in the hay.

"Did I have a bird, and how come I didn't know about them?"

Luke chuckled as he continued to move the hay.

"No, Alissia, you did not get a bird or know anything about them, because you were the most guarded person of all. I was going to personally come to you and relieve you of your guards." He set the pitchfork aside and looked up at her. "Does it bother you that you weren't informed?"

"A little. Everyone else seems to know about the plan but me."

"I assure you, the plan is a bit sketchy for now since it did not follow our timing, and no one knows what to fully expect. We have a plan in place to get you out of Pallen, but after that, there is no plan. And if it helps, none of the others know anything further than what to do once they see the birds. All they know is we're leaving the castle tonight, and they need to be ready and get into place. You're already ahead of them."

He squatted down and pulled away some boards to reveal a hidden storage area. He then pulled out a pack and held it out to Alissia. Once she took it from him, he pulled another one out and set it at his feet before lifting a medium-sized wooden box from the hole.

After putting the boards back into place and covering the hidden area with hay, he led her back down the ladder and into a small bathroom near the boy's bedroom. Although the bathroom did not have a bathing pool and was very simple, it did have a large work sink, and Luke quickly stripped from his upper clothing and began to wash the blood from his body.

It did not take long before Alissia cleared her throat and said, "I'll . . . um . . . wait outside." Before he had a chance to respond, she was standing outside the bathroom, with her back against the closed door.

After a moment, the young boy walked up and said, "I'm Devon." Looking closer at the blood in her hair, he asked, "Are you hurt?"

She shook her head and smiled at the boy as she stood up from the door. She remembered Anika telling her Luke had gotten Langley to hire the boy and that he was around twelve years old. He looked somewhat older.

"I've released the birds, and everyone should be getting ready by now, that's if no one is a heavy sleeper."

The bathroom door opened, and a freshly scrubbed Luke walked out with a new set of black clothing. He looked at Devon and said, "Everything ready?"

"Yes, sir. The birds have been released, and I'll wait to get the horses ready. Anything else I should do?"

"No, sounds like you have it all under control." Luke pulled out a few coins from his pocket and handed it to the boy. "You're going to earn this tonight," he said. He then gave the pack to Devon. "Hold onto this until I meet back up with you."

"Alissia, I need to speak with you alone before I leave," he said, walking back into the bathroom. She followed him, and he shut the door behind them.

"It will be a couple of hours before you can leave, so you should get cleaned up, as much as possible with this sink. Ask Devon for a bag to put our bloody clothes in. He will dispose of them in a manure pile. He knows the plan, although I'm sure you'll ask him what it is. Your job is to keep the dogs from attracting attention to you. I've told Devon that I've given you something to help cover your scent, so he won't think it odd if the dogs don't notice you. Do you think you can get the dogs at the gate to not do their job this morning? I've got two plans to get everyone off the grounds, and one of them involves sneaking people past the guards."

"What's the other?" she asked.

"That would involve the guards losing their consciousness. It really all depends on how things go this morning. We're not on the right time schedule, so I'll be doing a lot of improvising."

"I can get the dogs to ignore y'all," she said.

"Perfect." He added firmly, "Whatever you do, do not leave with anyone at the estate until I get there. No matter what they say to you, our agreement was that I would meet you there. I don't trust these people, and I've made it clear to them I will have them hunted down and killed by the league if they attempt anything. I will get there once I help to get everyone out of the castle, which should be not long after your arrival. We all need to clear the gates before they notice your disappearance and everything locks down."

"When do you think they'll find out I'm missing?"

"As soon as they notice guards aren't at their posts."

He opened the wooden box and pulled a blowgun and pouch from it. When he noticed her curious look, he grinned and set them back down. He then walked over and held her face in his hands.

Looking down at her, he said, "I told you I'm not a murderer, Alissia, and tonight I don't plan to kill any innocent guards of the Eldership unless I have to. There are other ways to achieve the same goal with less violence." He leaned in closer and added softly, "I need to leave now. All this will soon be over, and you'll be back at my side, where you belong."

He pushed her hair back and leaned down to whisper into her ear, "You are mine, Alissia, branded into my heart."

Alissia could feel her pulse rise, even before his mouth came down on hers. Their tongues met, and as he pulled her body in closer, the same sense of euphoria she had felt during their last kiss began to take over. All thoughts of where she was and their circumstances left her, replaced by a burning desire for Luke.

Although she noticed her body temperature rising, her passion was too strong to care. When Luke ripped their bodies apart, she cried out and opened her eyes, wanting more of him.

Luke held her at arms' length, and within an instant, his expression went from pure passion to terror as he looked into her face.

He immediately grabbed her hands and looked down at them. Beneath the red, dried blood covering her hands, she noticed purple streaks. The blood in her veins looked as if it was glowing within her body, and she knew her body temperature was much higher than normal.

"Alissia, are you all right?" he asked urgently, searching her eyes. "How do you feel?"

She turned to look at her reflection in the mirror and found that her face was also filled with purple color. Her eyes seemed to be glowing slightly. She shook her head in confusion and answered, "I feel great, or at least I did. In fact, when we kiss, it's amazing, but I don't think it's normal."

"No, something is very different. You are much more intoxicating than you should be. I could barely pull myself away from you just now."

He began to fumble with the button on her cloak.

"Luke, what are you doing?"

"I'm trying to see if we can get your body temperature down."

"You undressing me is supposed to lower my temperature right now?"

His fingers immediately stopped moving, and he lifted his hands up, as if in surrender. He took a few steps back and said, "Think about something—"

Before he could finish his sentence, the door to the bathroom abruptly opened and closed, startling Alissia, and her unbuttoned cloak fell to the floor. Mia took one look at Alissia before a low grumble began to come from her body.

Alissia had never seen the tiny creature bare her teeth until that moment, and it scared her. She immediately hid her fear with sarcasm and said in the old language, "Yes, we kissed. I guess you can see that, can't you?" When the creature glared back at her, she added, weakly, "If it helps any, I can now see why you don't want us kissing."

Alissia noticed that the color in her hands had begun to lessen, and she asked, "Will it go away? Am I all right?" Mia growled, and Alissia added, somewhat bothered, "Can Luke go now? He has others to save."

Mia moved from the door and motioned for Luke to pass.

"Will you be all right?" he asked.

"I'll be fine. Go."

Luke hesitated before he grabbed the box containing the blowgun, and then he turned back to Alissia. "We'll talk about this later. Until then, don't mention it to anyone. In fact, don't talk to anyone about anything that has happened tonight until we sort through this."

He went to open the door but turned back around and added, reassuringly, "Alissia, whatever this is, we'll get through it together. You do know that, don't you?"

She nodded and said, "Be safe."

He gave a cocky grin and raised his eyebrows. Then he was gone, closing the door behind him.

Chapter 27

Alissia sat down on a small bench and looked down at her hands. Seeing the blood caked under her nails, she stood back to her feet and began to undress. She wanted Ian's blood off her body as soon as possible.

Her arm gloves were still damp with blood, soaked in some places. Once her dress was removed, she looked down to find a lot of blood had soaked through to her body. She remembered Luke telling her she needed to learn how to do a clean kill, and she let out a small, sarcastic laugh. *Why do I even have to kill people? And how many more will there be?*

Feeling a chill, she reached out and powered the heating stone to its fullest.

"Well, at least that still works," she said to herself, seeing the stone begin to glow brightly. She looked over at Mia, curled up in a corner of the room, silently watching her.

After removing all her clothes and jewelry, she gave herself a sponge bath using the large sink and the soap sitting beside it. She then wrapped a towel around her body and looked at her face and hair in the mirror, frowning at the amount of blood still left. However, her color was back to normal, along with her body temperature.

She began to search the side pockets of the pack Luke had given her, and she found a small bottle of shampoo and mouth cleanser. She went back to the sink and scrubbed her hair and face before wrapping another towel onto her head. Then she swished some cleanser in her mouth.

She could not help but smile as she opened the pack to find new traveling clothes. She wondered if Luke had gotten someone else to shop for them or if he had done it himself. Either way, he had taken care of her. Although that would have bothered her before, she now took comfort in knowing he loved her and wanted to take care of her.

She got dressed and was able to make the blood on her boots less obvious, although not completely clean. Before packing all the jewelry she had been wearing, she cleaned the pieces that had gotten Ian's blood on them.

His engagement ring was the last piece of jewelry she cleaned, and as she scrubbed away the blood, she could not help but remember all the nice things about him. Although she had never loved him, she had just begun to think of him as someone she could at least call a friend.

She began to get angry with herself for allowing him to deceive her, and thoughts of Emera came to mind. She was Ian's sister, yet he had fooled her also. That knowledge did not lessen Alissia's anger. She deeply believed she should have known better.

She combed her hair and gave her head a hard shake, allowing her wild, wet curls to fall into place. Looking over at Mia, she said, "You should hide for a moment while I get a bag."

The tiny creature slowly got to her feet and stretched before disappearing behind a potted plant.

Alissia opened the door and stepped out. She found Devon sitting on his bed, as if he had been waiting for her. As soon as he saw her, he stood to his feet and said, "Do you need anything, My Lady?"

Her first instinct was to tell him to call her Alissia, but she knew that just because she was leaving the castle did not mean her façade was completely over. Luke would most likely refer to her as Lady Alissia in front of his men.

"I need a bag to put our bloody clothes in," she said.

He reached down and picked up a bag that looked to be made of old sackcloth, and then he stood to his feet. "Luke told me I need to dispose of them," he said.

"I can get them for you. They're a bit messy," she said, reaching for the bag.

"No, madam, I will take care of it for you."

As he walked past her, she did not know whether to feel bothered by having a young boy want to take care of her or happy the boys in this reality had such good manners. In the end, she rolled her eyes and decided to just go with it. The men in this reality seemed intent on taking care of women, which in a way was not such a bad thing. Although most of them seemed to think women could not take care of themselves, which bothered her greatly.

Alissia went to the bathroom to find Devon filling the bag with their stained clothing. She could sense his curiosity over the amount of blood, but he did not ask any questions. Once finished, he tied the bag in a knot and washed his hands.

"It will be a little while before we leave. You're welcome to try and get some rest in my bedroom. That's probably the safest place for you, in case someone decides to ride in early," he said.

"What exactly is the plan? Luke didn't have time to tell me."

"Luke talked one of the assembly members into giving the orphanage a wagonload of blankets and used clothing. I have the clearance papers to take it to the orphanage, and we leave before daylight. If the guards ask why so early, I'll explain that someone is relieving me of my duties this morning, but I am needed back as soon as possible. I'm only following orders."

He grinned and added, "You'll be hiding under a pile of blankets, and I'll add a cover over the back of the wagon also. The guards don't have a reason to search the wagon, and if they did, they would have to go deep to find you. Luke got a lot of materials to fill the wagon."

"You're not scared?" she asked. His show of confidence surprised her.

His grin got bigger, and he said, "No, madam. This is nothing compared to what I used to do while living on the streets."

"I thought you lived at the orphanage."

He shook his head, as if offended. "I've always taken care of myself, My Lady. You'd be surprised at what all I'm capable of," he said, with pride.

"I see." Having often thought those same words, she knew this was not a good time to ask about his past. Luke had chosen him and was confident in his capabilities. She should be too. The plan sounded solid.

"What about the others? How will they get off the grounds?" she asked.

He shrugged and said, "I don't know the details. Luke just said he didn't plan for things to be as easy for them." He picked up the bag and added, "But they do have three members of the league among them, and I wouldn't worry if I were you. If all goes well, they should be right behind us. He wants you to get past the guards before any of the alarms go off."

He walked towards the door, and she moved out of his way. Once outside the bathroom, he turned back around and added, "You should stay hidden in my room. I'll come get you once it's time."

"Devon?" she said, as he turned to walk away.

"Yes, My Lady?"

"Do you have something to write with, and does Emera Durst have any horses in this stable?"

"I do, and she is very fond of her horse and comes here often."

"Good. I would like to leave a note with her horse so she can find it."

Devon hesitantly said, "My Lady, Luke did not mention this in the plan."

"I am very aware of that, Devon," Alissia said, firmly. "However, something came up tonight that was not in Luke's plan, and I intend to do the right thing, or at least try. It won't have any effect on the plan."

"Yes, My Lady. I will bring you what you desire." He then turned and walked away.

Alissia shook her head in disbelief. She imagined Luke and Devon holding her down and putting the old restraints on her, and she had to remind herself that she and Luke were past that now. However, she could not help but think she was outnumbered when it came to Luke, now that he seemed to have a twelve-year-old minion.

Alissia pulled a new, black cloak from the pack. Unlike the elegant one she had been wearing earlier, this one was simple and made of a light material. It was not made for winter. She held it out in front of Mia, and the tiny fur ball allowed Alissia to pick her up, concealing her within the cloak. She then looked in the mirror to be certain it did not look as though she was trying to hide something.

As she stared at her reflection, she realized her black clothing matched Luke's, and she wondered if he loved the color out of necessity of sneaking around in the dark or if he just loved the color. He seemed to wear a lot of black, and her pack was filled with the same.

She checked her leggings and chuckled when she noticed the knife straps. Just as he had done before, he had bought her clothing that would conceal weapons.

Unlike the elegant clothing Anika had always chosen for her, Luke's choice of clothing gave her a mysterious and powerful appearance.

Just as she began to wonder if that was the way Luke saw her, her thoughts were interrupted by Devon.

"I placed some writing materials on my bed, and I'll take you to Emera's horse before we leave."

Alissia smiled and said, "Thank you, Devon."

Once he walked away, she retrieved her pack and went to his bedroom, shutting the door behind her. She put everything on the bed and began to sort through the pack, bundling her moneybag inside her clothing for extra security. She then wrapped the jewelry inside a shirt and arranged everything so the jewelry would not make any jingling sounds.

She set the pack aside and picked up the pencil and paper. After a long moment of thought, she wrote:

Dear Emera:

I am sorry to inform you, but your father is innocent of what you believe he has done. Ian confessed to me tonight that he was the one to dispose of the young man you loved, and he intended to do the same to me. I know you do not know me well, but I have no reason to lie to you. Ian had many secrets and fooled us both.

Lady Alissia

"Well, that's all I can do," she said to herself. She put the note in an envelope and wrote Emera's name on it. Looking down at the lump under her cloak, she got an idea.

"Mia!" she said in a low voice, not wanting to be heard by Devon. "Mia, I have an idea."

When Mia peeked out from under the cloak, Alissia held up the pencil and said, "If you can understand me, you can write."

Mia shook her head and disappeared back under the cloak.

Alissia got up and locked the bedroom door and sat back down on the bed. She took the risk of getting bit as she picked up Mia and set her down in front of her. Holding out the pencil, she said, "I have a lot of questions, and I need answers, Mia. I need you to do this for me."

Mia shook her head, and Alissia picked up the paper and set it down in front of Mia, along with the pencil.

"Now, what is happening when I kiss Luke?" she asked, firmly. Mia stared back up at her, and she asked again. "Why can't I kiss Luke?"

As Mia's tiny fingers wrapped around the pencil, an eager grin filled Alissia's face. She clasped her hands together as she eagerly watched Mia write something and then hold out the paper.

Alissia snatched the paper from her small friend, and the grin immediately fell from her face. Instead of finding writing, she found a mix of jumbled, ancient letters, but not in any order she recognized.

She grit her teeth in frustration and took a deep breath, closing her eyes. After a moment, she opened them and asked calmly, "Mia, can you write?"

The creature shook her head, and Alissia attempted to smile as she set the writing material on the nightstand. "That's all right," she said, to herself just as much as to Mia.

Mia crawled closer and rubbed her head on Alissia's arm. Alissia responded by scratching her on her neck.

"Do you know why I can't kiss Luke?" she asked.

Mia nodded.

"Will it kill me?"

Mia shook her head.

"Will it kill Luke?"

Mia looked up thoughtfully but did not give an answer.

"Mia, will it kill Luke?" she asked again, sternly.

The small creature looked up at Alissia defiantly, and Alissia shook her head in disbelief. "You're not going to answer my question, are you?"

Other than blinking, Mia did not move.

"That's cruel, Mia! I thought you were here to help!"

After a moment of staring at each other, Alissia said, "Can I heal people?"

The animal shook her head violently.

"Then how come I healed Luke? Answer that!"

Mia touched the eight-pointed star on Alissia's hand, and Alissia immediately became excited, hoping to finally learn something about the mysterious creature that had given her the mark.

"You know what this is? Did the Lamians send whatever did this to me?" After Mia shook her head, Alissia asked, "Is this a good thing?"

Mia nodded excitedly.

"So the Lamians had nothing to do with this, but it's a good thing?"

Mia continued to nod.

"Is this how I was able to save Luke?"

Mia nodded again.

"So I can heal people because of this," Alissia said, triumphantly.

Mia bared her teeth and slapped Alissia's hand, hard.

"Ow! Why are you suddenly so violent?" She pulled her hand away and said to herself, in English, "And this is what Luke thinks of me? *Pixet*, he calls me."

To Mia, she said, "So, it saved Luke, but there are consequences. Is that it?" Mia nodded, and Alissia asked, "Bad enough consequences that I should never do it again?"

Mia nodded excitedly.

"What if Anika is dying?"

Mia slapped Alissia's other hand and shook her head.

"What if Grady is dying?"

Mia growled and bared her sharp teeth.

"So I'm supposed to let them die, even if I can save them?"

Mia nodded.

Alissia thought for a long moment before asking, "Will Luke change like me now that I've healed him?"

The creature shrugged her shoulders.

"So you don't know what to expect. Is that what you're saying?"

Mia nodded.

"So now Luke needs to find the Lamians also?"

She nodded again.

Alissia let out a resigned sigh. "All right, I won't try to heal anyone again, and Luke and I will have to keep it a secret unless he begins to change. But, I don't see any reason for him not to change. I did to him what the Lamians did to me, didn't I?"

Mia shook her head.

"I did something different?" Alissia asked, confused.

A nod was her only answer.

"Great! So now I don't even know what I've done to Luke." A fearful thought came to mind, and she asked, anxiously, "I did heal him though? I mean, he's not going to fall down and die suddenly, is he? It's not temporary, is it?"

She thought she noticed a grin from Mia as the animal nodded.

"Then it was worth it, even if I can never kiss him again."

Chapter 28

Alissia had just fallen asleep when a knock came at the door. She jumped up from the bed, and as she put on her cloak and gloves, Mia swiftly climbed up her body. She situated herself above Alissia's left hip, where she skillfully clung to Alissia's fitted clothing with a surprising amount of muscle.

Alissia hefted the pack onto her back and grabbed the note she had written. She then made sure Mia was hidden beneath the cloak before she opened the door.

"It's time, My Lady. Did you finish your note?" the young boy said, with an unnerving sense of calm for what they were about to attempt.

"Yes."

He nodded before turning, and she followed him through a maze of stables before stopping in front of one.

"This is her horse, and I would not be surprised if she came for a ride today," he said, before opening the door. He walked into the stable first, as if for her protection, and Alissia followed.

Emera's horse was beautiful, and although Alissia did not know everything about horses, she could tell this one was worth a lot of money. He was black and sleek, and tight muscles filled his body. Alissia had to resist the urge to bond with him when he walked over to her.

"He usually doesn't respond to people so well," Devon said, watching Alissia pet the horse. "He's a beauty, isn't he?"

"I'm very impressed," she answered.

"I heard Emera trained him herself, and I can believe it. I've seen her with him, and I can tell she loves this horse."

"What's his name?" she asked.

"Anicetus. I don't know the meaning though."

Alissia knew the meaning. It meant "unconquerable" in the old language.

She looked around before deciding upon a small shelf in the corner of the stable. After gently pushing Anicetus away, she propped the envelope against a small bottle.

"Do you think she'll see it there?" she asked.

"I do."

Alissia then followed the boy through the maze of stables until they stopped at a wagon with two horses hitched to it. Devon had cleared a spot for her, and she settled down against the wooden wall of the wagon, directly behind his seat.

He placed blankets over her body before tying a large cover over the wagon, and once everything was secure, they were on their way.

It took a while before they reached a guards' post, and as they traveled, Alissia reached out with her mind to speak with any dogs they passed along the way. Although there were not many, she demanded each of them to remain silent that morning.

Alissia listened as Devon showed his papers to the guards and explained why he was leaving before dawn. She demanded the same silence from the guard dogs, and it was not long before they were traveling through the streets of Pallen.

They traveled for a long while, and Alissia began to get hot and uncomfortable from all the blankets and Mia's warm body attached to her side. When they finally stopped, it only took a moment before the cover was pulled back and her secret location was revealed.

She stood to her feet and quickly took in her new surroundings. Although it was still dark, daylight would soon be upon them. The wagon was parked inside the walls of a very large estate. The young woman she had met at the ball, along with two men she did not recognize, were standing beside the wagon.

"Get her inside, quickly!" demanded the eldest of the two men.

Alissia remained guarded as she allowed one of the men to help her out of the wagon, and then she was hurriedly rushed into a house. Unlike the main house on the property, this one was much smaller, and Alissia guessed it to be a guesthouse.

Devon remained close, and the expression on his face was hard and no longer at ease. It reminded her of how Luke would change his persona around those he considered a threat.

Once inside a sitting room, Devon was the first to speak.

"The wagon has to be taken to the orphanage. Here are the papers," he said, with a surprising amount of authority for a young boy.

The eldest told the young man and woman to deliver the wagon, and as the younger man took the papers from Devon's hands, he said, "Shouldn't he come with us?"

Devon immediately answered, firmly, "I will not be leaving Lady Alissia."

Alissia thought she noticed a look of surprise from the older man, but it was quickly dismissed as he said, "He stays. Hurry and get it done."

He turned to Alissia and said, "Hello, Lady Alissia. My name is Salvatore, and I'm in charge here. Do you need anything, maybe to drink or eat?"

Alissia shook her head.

"Very well. Let's go into my office. There is much we have to discuss. Your young guard is welcome to sit here and wait, and it should relieve his fears to know he can see the door from this room." He pointed to a closed door and added, "All of my people are away helping to transport the others, but they should be back shortly."

Devon went to object, but Alissia put her hand on his arm and said, with authority, "I'll be fine. You've gotten me here safely, and I thank you. Now I must do my part."

She could tell her words bothered the boy, but he remained silent as he nodded and watched her walk by.

Once inside the office, she took a seat in front of a large, well-crafted desk. Although Mia's grip on Alissia's clothing relaxed somewhat, the small creature's body stayed tense and alert.

As Salvatore went to close the door, the girl Alissia recognized from the ball abruptly stopped it with her body. She pried her way into the room, shutting the door behind her. Although she was still the same woman from the ball, she now looked and carried herself completely different. She wore tight, black pants, boots, and a white button-up shirt with a jacket over it. Her hair was pulled back into a messy braid, and she wore no makeup. A tribal ring tattoo was on her left, middle finger, where a ring had concealed it while at the ball.

The look was very different; however, it suited the young woman well, especially with the rage that now filled her eyes.

Alissia watched as the two of them shared a heated discussion in a foreign language, and although she could not understand their words, she sensed the girl was pleading with Salvatore. At first he seemed patient with her, but the conversation soon ended with him stopping her in midsentence, wherein he said something in a stern voice before opening the door.

The girl turned to Alissia and gave a look of fury before stomping out of the room.

Salvatore shut the door and sat down behind the desk. Alissia guessed him to be in his fifties, and like the young girl, his skin looked as though it was used to being in the sun. He had broad shoulders, and his hands showed signs of a man accustomed to labor. His brown hair was flecked with grey, and plenty of wrinkles were around his eyes. He wore a gold hoop in his right ear, and a black, tribal tattoo started at his left hand and trailed up his arm, concealing the rest of itself beneath his shirt. He wore a gold wedding band on the same hand.

"I apologize for my daughter's behavior. We seem to have differing opinions at this moment, and she is very much as fiery as her mother was." He leaned back in his seat before adding, "We weren't scheduled for your arrival this morning. Did something happen?"

Alissia answered, with her fake accent, "Someone tried to force me to leave Pallen last night, and I had no other choice." Not really wanting to talk about what had happened, she added, somewhat accusingly, "Your daughter has informed me that I am considered a threat to you and the Lamians."

He responded, "I apologize if she has given you the wrong impression of us. If there had been any other way to meet with you, I would have. Unfortunately, my young and single daughter had the best chance of attending an Eldership ball, although I feel she did not enjoy the formality of it all."

Alissia was tired of all the pretentious acting she had done while at the castle. She wanted the man before her to know from the beginning she was not a shy and defenseless woman.

"So am I a threat, and what do you want with me?" she asked, bluntly.

He stared at her thoughtfully before saying, "The Lamians went into hiding well over a thousand years ago, almost two. The captain that vowed his life to them was one of my ancestors, and since that time, most of my family and ancestors unknowingly have played a part in the lives of the Lamians. The legacy that captain left his family has turned into a major empire within this world. Almost all my relatives are wealthy, and they are powerful. However, very few of them know the truth behind their own wealth and power.

"You see, everything we have is from the Lamians. We deal in worldwide trade, specializing in trained animals, exotic plants, clothing, gems, and much more. The most amazing fact, however, is that we are the only suppliers of the jade stone, yet no one knows this piece of information, not even the suppliers themselves. Do you see what I'm saying?"

She said, "I understand that the Lamians have made your family extremely wealthy throughout the years."

"Yes, but do you understand the amount of secrecy and lies that wealth is built upon? Over a thousand years of secrecy and protection to the Lamians, where only a small portion of people in the bloodline know the truth. The others are just unknowing pawns to a service they do not even know they contribute to."

He gestured towards the wall, "For instance, the owners of this estate. They are clueless to my true reason for being here and consider themselves royalty compared to the men accompanying me. In their mind, we serve our purpose of delivering the goods that bring them wealth. They have no idea where we really get our animals or goods. They just know they buy them at a low price from us. Then they sell them for a large profit. It's a relationship that was established many years ago."

Alissia asked, "If the Lamians you protect truly want to be away from humans, why do they continue to have a relationship with your family? Why don't they just end it altogether?"

"We ensure they continue to keep their own private island, and no human goes near it, other than certain members of our family. That is our biggest benefit to them, although they do enjoy some of the goods we bring to them from humans.

"They also made a vow with my ancestors that they would continue to produce the jade for our people. We protect them, and they allow us to distribute jade throughout the world, building a world-wide empire that is built on the biggest secret within this world."

The only thing she knew about jade was that it was an extreme power source, the source behind her being brought into this reality. It was also illegal to own. Was he saying the Lamians were the ones that made jade? If so, that would help to explain one of the reasons she could charge a power stone.

She wanted to ask him more about the jade, but she knew that would let him know how little she actually knew about the Lamians. She was not ready to reveal any information just yet, so she decided she would have to pretend as if she completely understood what he was telling her.

"So the Lamians you protect live on an island?"

"They do, and they are eager to meet you."

She nodded and thought for a moment before responding, "Since people have learned about me, I have been kidnapped, held against my will, lied to countless times, and have learned more about humans than I would like to. Please forgive me when I say that I don't trust you."

"I understand. Yet, you are a human, or at least once was," he said.

"Yes, but I had more respect for the human race at one time, and that says a lot since I've never been a trusting person. I can see why the Lamians went into hiding, and I can see why they need to stay there."

"At least we agree on that. You understand how much of a threat you are to the Lamians. So I'm curious to know why you went out in public in the first place, and to an Eldership ball. As their protector, I need to know why you did that, and I also need to know what your intentions are."

Alissia looked down at her hands in thought. After a moment of silence between them, she looked up and said, "My intentions were never to harm the Lamians in any way. The ball was an unknowing and unwilling mistake. I want to trust you, but you understand I can't right now. I have a lot to think about, and I need to talk to the people I do trust. After that, we can talk some more."

"And who do you trust?"

"That would be Luke, Grady, Anika, and Langley. No one else."

"And you're sure you can trust them?"

She looked hard into his eyes and said, "I'm positive I can trust them, as can the Lamians. They have proven themselves in countless ways."

Salvatore let out a long sigh as he leaned back in his seat. He seemed to be in deep thought until a disturbance came from outside the door. He jumped to his feet, just as the door abruptly swung open.

Luke stood in the doorway, with a sword in his right hand, looking fierce, as she had ever seen him. He marched over to her and studied her face, and she gave a reassuring smile to let him know she was all right. Then she turned to find Grady staring at her from the doorway. He wore his sword on his belt, and she noticed some blood on his clothing that caused her to worry. The expression on his face was strained, and it saddened her to see him in such a way.

Luke turned around to face Salvatore, placing himself between him and Alissia. As he sheathed his sword, he said, "I'm guessing you're Salvatore. We have much to discuss."

"Ah, and you must be Luke Harrison. Your reputation precedes you, and I can see why. As you can see, Lady Alissia is safe, as agreed by my men. And yes, we have much to talk about; most importantly, I'm sure you're wanting to know how we'll be getting out of Pallen."

Alissia tried to push Luke from his position in front of her while Salvatore introduced himself to Grady. When he did not budge, she pinched him hard on his left wrist, and he looked down at her. She gave him a dirty look, and he finally moved to the side, letting her back into the conversation.

Salvatore motioned at two empty chairs arranged near the wall and said, "Please, have a seat. Both of you join us."

Luke pulled a chair up to sit on the left side of Alissia, and Grady situated the other one at her right side. As they sat down, Salvatore closed the door and sat back down at his desk. He studied the men's faces for a moment, and they did the same to him.

"Were there any problems in leaving the castle?" he asked.

Grady started with, "Just a minor setback—"

"That was taken care of appropriately," Luke finished, firmly.

An awkward silence filled the air for a short moment before Salvatore said, "I need to know who all you have brought to this estate, and we must come up with a story that will protect the owners. They know nothing about any of this, and it needs to remain that way. We have the use of this guesthouse, along with the large barn behind it. None of their servants or people are allowed near this area of the property while we're here.

"As far as they know, we are traders that do a large amount of business with them, and my people stay here often. None of this is uncommon for them, and they are completely unaware as to our true reason for being here. I tell you this, because I don't want them to face any repercussions with the Eldership. In fact, I want the location of this property to be wiped from everyone's memory once we leave."

Luke said, "I only have one of my men here. The other helped to escort an important family out of the city this morning. As for the man here, I have already told him we are paying you a large sum for your services in helping with the escape, and I can tell him that the owners of this estate are not involved. We are only dealing with you traders. The young boy that accompanied Alissia this morning is of my concern and not a problem."

Luke turned to Grady expectantly, and Grady said, "My cousin Anika and her husband Langley can be fully trusted, not only with the matter of the estate, but also with the Lamians. They know all the details when it comes to Alissia."

A wave of exhaustion suddenly came over Alissia, and her head began to throb. Although she had been extremely tired just moments before, it was nothing compared to how she now felt. The memory of losing consciousness came to mind, and she looked over at Luke.

She thought she noticed a subtle strained look on his face, and she became worried for him. She was surprised when he turned to her and said, in a concerned voice, "Are you all right, Alissia?"

She forced a smile onto her face, but the pain in her head had worsened to the point she desperately wanted to be alone. The fact that all three men were now staring at her made things worse.

"I'm fine," she lied.

He shook his head, and she thought she noticed him wince before he turned his attention back to Salvatore. Standing to his feet, he said, "I apologize, but I fear Lady Alissia may not be feeling well after the events of the night. I would like to escort her to where she will be staying." He held out his hand, and she accepted it, slowly standing to give Mia a chance to latch back onto her body.

Salvatore and Grady left their seats as well, and Luke added, "I would like to resume this conversation later this afternoon. Until then, I hope you don't mind if my man and the boy help your people when it comes to preparing food. Reece is a member of the league, and he will not allow any of us to eat the food unless he can assure its safety. You also understand he and the boy are not aware of Lady Alissia's true circumstances, so nothing is to be discussed in front of them."

"I understand," Salvatore said. "I'll escort you to the barn now, and you'll find it has large sleeping quarters and everything you'll need. Get some rest, and after I check on a few things, I can give you more details on how and when we'll be leaving the city."

Chapter 29

The barn was nothing like Alissia imagined it would be. Various bella flowers covered the outside, and the inside walls were filled with white bella flowers. It had a clear, tinted ceiling, and heat and glow stones hung down from the rafters.

It was large and housed many carriages of various styles. The center of the building was a spacious, open room with grass and dirt flooring. Hay bales were arranged all along the walls, and there were some hanging chairs made out of woven reeds. The chairs resembled oversized eggs hanging down from the rafters, and they were filled with comfy pillows.

A mix of wooden picnic tables and small iron tables were arranged on one side of the barn, near the sleeping quarters. The setting seemed to be the perfect place for a barn party, with an old, romantic ambiance. Although there were cobwebs in the corners of the ceiling and rafters, the barn was clean and very well taken care of.

Salvatore pointed to a set of double doors and explained that the horses were kept in a separate area of the barn. A loud roar came from behind the closed doors, causing Alissia to become curious, but the throbbing in her head kept her from reaching out with her mind.

The sleeping quarters consisted of one large room filled with bunk beds, and Grady carried her pack and set it down on one of the bottom bunks. He then set his belongings on the bunk beside hers.

Everyone seemed worried for her when she entered the barn, and after a quick stop to the bathroom, she desperately just wanted a place to rest. In the end, she chose one of the hanging chairs in a distant corner of the open room. Luke sat down in the one next it, and that's when Grady noticed Luke's unnatural demeanor. He looked at the two of them, knowing something was not right.

After glancing over his shoulder to make sure they would not be overhead, he stared hard into Alissia's eyes and asked, "What happened last night?" When she did not answer, he said, "Were the two of you poisoned?"

She gave a reassuring smile and said, "No, Grady. I'll be fine. I just need some rest. We didn't get any sleep last night, and I think our bodies are rebelling against us. That's all."

He looked at Luke and shook his head. "No, Alissia. Please talk to me. What has happened to the two of you?"

Luke answered for her.

"Leave her alone, Grady. She's had a hard night, and I need some rest also. You need to make sure no one believes we're weak. Reece doesn't know anything, and with him being with the league, I need for you to make sure it stays that way while I'm asleep. Take care of everything, and as far as everyone knows, we're just exhausted. Tell them I got hit over the head hard while I was with you, and Alissia is just tired and feeling sick."

Grady did not move but silently studied Alissia's face for a moment, and Luke said, harshly, "Go, before everyone else begins to think something."

"I'm fine. I just need some sleep, and then we'll talk," Alissia said, reassuringly.

When he went to take off her boots, she remembered the knives, and she caught his hands. "I'll get them. You should get back to the others so they don't worry."

He gave a worried frowned and nodded. "Get some rest, and then we'll talk."

As he walked away, she began to remove her boots, and Mia jumped from the chair and disappeared into one of the dark corners of the barn. Alissia arranged the boots on their side, concealing the knives. She then pulled up her feet and took off her cloak before settling into the pillows.

She had just covered herself with the cloak and was about to close her eyes when Luke asked, "How bad are you feeling?"

"I'm tired, and my head feels like it's been run over by a steamroller. What about you? You don't look well."

"The same. I'm exhausted, and I think my head feels as though it's been run over by the same steamroller."

She smiled. "Do you even know what a steamroller is?"

"I'm too tired to ask," he answered, and it was not long before they both fell into a deep sleep.

*****

When Alissia opened her eyes and sat up, the barn was dark, except for the glowing heat stones tind white bella flowers. She could see the stars shining through the clear ceiling, and she wondered what time it was. It was quiet, and Alissia guessed everyone to be asleep in the large room with the bunk beds.

She felt a chill and pulled her cloak up and around her.

"Alissia, come join me," came Luke's soft voice from the chair next to her.

She slowly stood to her feet and crossed the short distance between them, and then he pulled her into the large, hanging chair. Once she was comfortable, with her head and hand on his chest and her cloak over both of their bodies, she closed her eyes.

He brought his free hand up to hold hers, and they silently enjoyed each other's presence for a moment. Luke was the first to speak when he asked how she was feeling.

"Much better. My head doesn't hurt anymore," she answered. "And you?"

"I'm fine now, but I'm worried about the amount of time we spent sleeping. I will have to think of a reason." After a pause, he added, "I've got a lot of thinking to do."

"About what?"

"You're wanting to go the mountains to see the Lamians, yet if you travel there now, I'm afraid you'll lead people to them. You may need to travel in the opposite direction."

"Is this your way of trying to kidnap me again?"

"I never kidnapped you, Alissia. Besides, I don't think you should go to the North either."

"Then where?"

"I don't know yet. We need to see if we can trust Salvatore, and I also don't know what to tell Reece about you. I don't want to take you to another Eldership, but they are expecting me to. My only excuse for not having you leave the city with Morton's family is that you were brought here for safe keeping while we got the rest of the people out of the castle. You are a bigger priority to them than Morton's family, and I'm sure they are wondering why I didn't get you out of the city. My people will be upset with me when I don't deliver you to them."

"Can you tell them I refuse to go with you?"

"I'm a member of the league, Alissia. I'm not exactly supposed to take no for an answer."

"What have you told them so far?"

"I haven't spoken directly to anyone other than Reece and Jerrell. They left home right after I sent the first message, the night I first saw you at the ball. The others didn't leave until Jerrell sent a message that there was talk of a war. They just got here but didn't enter Pallen, and they've been waiting for me to get you out of the city. They want to make sure you're secure before they enter the war negotiations. I've been the representative for my people, but that's not my place now that others are available."

"What have you told them about me?" she asked.

"I haven't been able to send a detailed message since the two of us were traveling, and I've only sent out small, cryptic messages since being in Pallen. When we were traveling, I told them you were a Lamian, and we were on our way home. I also notified them of the bounty Alrik had put in place. I didn't send a message again until we were in Pallen, and it only warned them to stay out of the city.

"Some of my people, along with others all across the land, have traveled to the surrounding cities to get an idea of what everyone thinks about the possibility of a war."

"Do you think there will be a war?"

"I don't know. I don't believe many people want a war, but the Eldership is divided at this moment. The farther you get from the South, the more you'll find people supporting the idea of a war. They're tired of being taxed and seeing the South get most of the money.

"Although Pallen's assembly has assured a change if they were to lead the Eldership, most everyone knows Alrik is in control of Pallen, and they don't like the idea of one man being in charge. They support the idea of a change in leadership and war, but they don't believe Pallen to be the answer."

The two of them silently pondered their situation for a moment before Alissia said, "What are you going to tell your people when they ask why you turned around and traveled back to Pallen instead of continuing home?"

"I've already been asked that question by Jarrell and Reece and had to use my superiority to keep from answering it. I can't think of a single answer that will satisfy my people as to why I turned back and brought you to Pallen."

"Do you regret it?" she asked.

"Alissia, I knew the moment I made my decision what I was getting into, and I chose you. I don't regret that decision, nor will I ever. However, I had hoped to have the support of my people until you were safe. It's going to make things more difficult if we don't have anyone on our side, and everyone is against us."

He let go of her hand and pulled out the ring hanging from the chain around his neck. "Do you know why I wear this?" he asked, holding it up in front of her face.

"No."

"This is my seal for the Eldership. Whatever city I'm in, within the Eldership's control, I can use this seal, along with other documentation, for anything. It's one of the ways I pay large bills or extract money from a bank and gives me authority. It's my brand and goes with my signature. It makes my life a lot easier when I travel, and although I've been pulling money from my personal account and have money hidden in many places, I had liked to be able to use this as much as possible before officially leaving the Eldership and becoming a wanted man."

He put the ring back under his shirt and took hold of her hand again. "When we leave here, I won't be able to use it anymore, because it would be a way for people to track us. I have a large sum of money with me and am prepared for our finnancial concerns. However, you now need to understand that I will soon be a fugitive in this land."

Unlike the guilt she had felt towards Grady wanting to leave his career, she did not feel the same for Luke. She had seen his thoughts and been in his mind to know his career meant nothing compared to how he felt towards her. She knew that losing her would hurt him more than losing his current life within the Eldership.

She began to ponder if the same had been true for Grady. He had also been willing to leave his life behind for her. She then reminded herself Grady had more to lose than Luke. Not only did Grady have the perfect life ahead of him as a future elder, but he also had family. Luke was not giving up as much as Grady, and it was best that Grady go back to his life without her. She had made the right decision, even if it hurt Grady.

"What are you planning?" Luke asked.

"Nothing. Why?"

"I don't know. Usually when you're silent, I find that you're planning something."

She pulled her hand from his and said, accusingly, "Which reminds me. You named me after a pixet!"

He laughed and grabbed her hand again, kissing it before setting it back down on his abdomen. "I still believe the name fits you, and where is your little friend?"

"She's here somewhere. I bet if we attempted a kiss, she'd pop up out of thin air."

In a somber voice, he asked, "Alissia, did I hurt you when we kissed?"

"No, I asked Mia a few questions about it, and I learned a few things. It seems I'm not supposed to be able to heal people. The only reason I was able to heal you was because of what happened in the forest with that little fairy thingy. Apparently, the Lamians had nothing to do with it, but it's a good thing, not bad. Maybe that's why it glows when I heal animals. It's just another mystery I'll have to ask about when I finally get to meet the Lamians."

She chewed on her bottom lip worriedly before asking, "Luke, what if you turn like I did?"

"Then I turn," he said, matter-of-factly. Then he added, "Although, that wouldn't be good for you or the Lamians."

"What do you mean?"

"People know me. I'm not a Lamian. And if I start changing, they'll know you had something to do with it. Ian already thought something would happen if there was a physical connection between the two of you. We don't want others to have that same desire. How would we explain my change?"

Alissia let out a frustrated groan before saying, "I am so tired of all the lies and complicated stories."

He let go of her hand to put his arm around her and pulled her into an embrace. After kissing the top of her head, he said, "This will all be over once we get you to the Lamians."

"I thought we couldn't travel towards the mountains."

"Not directly, but we still can. It will just take a lot longer to get there. You know, lead people away from the mountains first."

"What about these people and the other Lamians?"

"What have you learned?" he asked.

She told him all that Salvatore had told her, and Luke thought for a moment before asking, "Do you want to meet these Lamians first?"

"Not really."

"I don't particularly want to either, but it may be our best option."

"How do we know he's being honest? What if there aren't another group of Lamians?" she asked.

"I didn't say to trust them. If we begin to think they're a risk, we would have to leave them."

"Is that what you think we should do?"

There was a pause before he said, "Alissia, I want you to find the Lamians as soon as possible, because there are too many unanswered questions. We don't know what's happening to you, and that worries me. I can't even kiss you without fearing I'm hurting you."

"I think I'll hurt you," Alissia said.

"Either way, we need some answers, and if I do begin to change, it may be best if we're traveling with others, at least until we know whether to trust them or not. Before making any decisions, we need to learn as much about them as we can. Ask questions when you talk to him, and I'll do the same."

"Do you think it's true that the Lamians make jade?" she asked.

"It would help to explain how you are able to charge stones."

A ball of fur abruptly pounced into the chair, and Mia's large eyes looked from Luke to Alissia.

The two of them slightly rearranged their bodies so that Luke was resting on his back, and Alissia was on her side, with her head on his chest. He took her by the hand again and placed it on his abdomen, with his on top.

In the old language, Alissia said, "We're just talking, Mia. No kissing."

The creature bared her sharp teeth, turned in a circle, and plopped down onto Luke's body, directly above their hands.

"I'm guessing we're safe," Luke said.

"She was the sweetest little thing when I lived at the castle. You bring out the worst in people, Luke."

He chuckled, and they lay in silence for a moment before Alissia asked, "How did Grady get blood on him? Did anything go wrong when y'all were leaving the castle?"

He let out a sigh and said, "You can say that. Grady had to use his sword. It was in self-defense, but that doesn't ease his conscience, especially since he knows many guards in Allure. This one was old enough to have his own family, and Grady recognized that immediately.

"I tried to help with his conscience by being the one to give the death blow, but I don't think it worked. In his eyes, he took the life, not me."

"You killed the guard?"

"The guard would have died either way," Luke said, unemotionally. "I gave him a quick death to stop his pain and to give Grady a reason to blame someone else for the death."

Alissia remembered Luke's struggle with his own conscience when she had shared his memories, and she asked, "What about you? How does it make you feel?"

"It's what I do, Alissia," he said. His tone let her know he did not want to talk about it.

"I want you to finish teaching me how to throw a knife," she said, changing the subject.

"Oh, so now you like my gifts?" he teased. "Wouldn't you rather me give you jewels to wear around your neck?"

"I have enough of them, thanks to the Eldership," she said. "Oh, and Ian."

"You brought some with you? Where?" he asked, sounding surprised.

She explained how she had filled her moneybag and had worn as much jewelry under her clothing as she could without being noticed.

His body shook with laughter as she finished telling him, and Mia looked up at them, not amused.

"I should have known," he said.

"What? It's mine, isn't it? They gave it to me," she said, defensively.

He gave her body a squeeze and said, "My little pixet. Yes, it's yours, and I doubt anyone will be bothered by it."

"Anyways," she said, ignoring his strange words of endearment. "If I had known how to throw a knife, things may have turned out differently last night. I had three knives, and there were four men. I was useless, and look what happened."

"Stop!" he said, firmly. "You will not blame yourself for last night. There was nothing you could have done differently against Ian and three hired killers, Alissia. You do understand that, don't you?"

"I just stood there and did nothing, and you almost died for it, Luke."

The hand behind her body went to her hair, and he began to rub her head with his fingertips. He said, "What could you have done differently?"

"I could have thrown a knife at three of them. I had three knives!"

"You still would have been left alone with one killer. That also takes a lot of skill and time to learn."

"I want that skill, Luke."

"And I will teach you, Alissia. It just takes time. You're already learning self-defense. Look what you did when they tried to grab you." He kissed her head, and his other hand left her hair and went back to holding her.

Her stomach rumbled, and she said, "I'm starving."

He nodded. "I am too. It probably took a lot of your body to heal me."

"I'm thinking it took a lot out of your body to almost die," she responded.

Mia abruptly stood to her feet and hid under the cloak, causing Luke and Alissia to look out in front of them. Just as they looked up, Grady walked out of the sleeping quarters and started walking towards them. Reece then walked out but turned towards the bathroom.

"Oh, no," Alissia said, sitting up hastily. She pulled her cloak from Luke's body.

"Maybe it's for the best he found out now, Alissia," Luke said.

"Not like this," she said, grabbing Mia and standing to her feet. "Not after all he's been through. It's wrong, Luke. He doesn't deserve it."

She walked over to her swinging chair and sat down, setting her cloak with Mia in it on the ground. As she began to put on her boots, Grady walked up. Although she knew he had seen her leave Luke's chair, she tried to give a calm smile, as if nothing was wrong.

"How are you feeling?" he asked.

"Normal again. Why didn't anyone wake us?"

"We tried, both of you."

Luke sat up and began to put on his boots. Once finished, he stood to his feet and said, "What did you tell everyone?"

"I told them you were hit over the head, but we both know that's not what happened," Grady said.

Luke scowled. "I've got enough to think about, Grady. What happened while I was out? Did you meet with Salvatore?"

"Reece and I met with him last night. It seems it will be a week before we can leave Pallen."

"Did you get the details?" Luke asked.

"Most of them. He said he would go over them with you today."

Luke gave a nod before leaving to meet Reece, who was now walking towards them.

As Grady sat down beside her in the chair, Alissia could not help but notice how much he seemed to have aged over the past two months. She could tell he had lost weight, and his usual confident eyes seemed to look tired. It killed her inside, knowing she would be hurting him even more.

"I was worried about you," he said.

She smiled and responded, "You know how much I like to sleep."

He nodded and gave a weary look at Reece and Luke's backs, as they were now walking towards the other end of the barn. Then he dug his boots into the ground and rotated the swinging chair in the opposite direction, giving them some privacy.

He immediately pulled her into his arms, and as he silently held her, Alissia closed her eyes, forcing back tears.

"I've missed you so much, Alissia," he said, his voice thick with emotion. She felt his entire body tremble, and she hated herself even more.

"I've missed you too," she said. She knew she needed to tell him about her feelings for Luke, but now did not seem like the right time. He was already filled with enough pain, and she could not bear to add to it.

He silently held her for a long moment, his hands getting lost in her hair. "What happened last night? Did you get hurt?"

Alissia scrunched up her face in thought and began to chew on her bottom lip, not wanting to talk about it. "Ian wanted me to leave with him, and he wouldn't take no for an answer."

"How did Luke get involved?"

"Ian and his men kidnapped him." Her stomach rumbled loudly, and she hoped it would give her an opportunity to change the subject. "I'm starving. Is there any food here?"

He let go of her and studied her face for a moment. "I guess you need to eat. There are some things that were set out for you and Luke last night. Are you sure you're feeling well?"

She knew he wanted to ask more questions, and he was holding back for her sake. She smiled and said, reassuringly, "I promise. I feel fine, except for being hungry. Is it okay if we talk about what happened later? I'm still trying to process a lot of it. Everything just happened so fast and unexpectedly, and I still don't know what we're going to tell Reece and Salvatore."

He tried to smile as he picked up her hand and began to rub his thumb along her palm. "We'll think of something."

Alissia stood to her feet and attempted to pull him up from the chair.

"Alissia," he said, not moving.

"Yes?"

"You know I love you, right?"

She looked into his troubled eyes, and knowing this would be the perfect time to reassure him of her love, she lifted her free hand up to his face and began to trace her fingertips tenderly along his cheek and forehead. As he closed his eyes and took in her touch, she said, "I've never doubted your love for me, Grady, and I never will."

A lump filled her throat, and she forced her pain aside, knowing he must be desperate to hear the words she had never spoken. *I'm sorry, Grady,* she thought to herself, before pulling her hand away.

"I really have to go the bathroom now," she said, trying again to pull him to his feet.

He stood to his feet, and they dropped hands before starting towards the other end of the barn.

"We can talk later," he said. "Reece and Devon are helping to cook breakfast, but you can eat some of what we have here. There's some leftover cake from last night. Reece doesn't want us eating any of their breads or cheese, because he only wants us to eat the food we help prepare. Anika, Langley, and Devon are going to spend the day baking with Salvatore's people so we'll have more food on stock."

Alissia nodded, and then she walked with him to the tables. She made a quick stop at the bathroom before joining him again. While she was eating a piece of cake and trying to enjoy a bitter-tasting chet for a drink, Anika and Langley walked out of the bedroom. They immediately came up to her and began to ask if she was feeling well, and it was obvious they were worried about her.

It was hard to feel comfortable around them while trying to avoid questions of what had happened to her and Luke. In the end, she wished out loud that she could get washed up, and Grady grinned.

"I have something to show you," he said, standing to his feet. "Are you finished with your cake?"

Alissia nodded, and Grady went to the bedroom and returned shortly with her pack. She got up from the table and followed him to a large door that he had to slide open.

"What do you think?" he asked, as they walked into the room.

The floor of this room was made of stone, set in place like bricks, and glow and heat rocks hung down from the rafters. White bella flowers grew along two of the walls, and the opposite wall from the door appeared to be another large, sliding door.

In the middle of the room was a bath with claw feet. Pedestals were situated around it with candles set on them, and a small cabinet holding towels and various bottles of bathing items was nearby. A standing mirror with a chair was in the corner of the room.

As Alissia walked up to the tub, she said, "This is just like the ones we have in my reality, except this one is bigger than a normal-sized one. Ours also has plumbing hooked up to them so they have a plug at the bottom and faucets at the top."

Grady set her pack in the chair and said, "This is a temporary bath. Since people rarely stay in this barn, they don't have a pool in place.

It would be too much for them to maintain. I'm sure they set this up, knowing we would be here."

He tested the temperature of the water before adding heating powder to it. Then he set a towel on one of the pedestals, and he lit the candles with a match.

"Need anything else?" he asked, standing in front of her.

She smiled and said, "You must think I'm crazy when it comes to baths. It's just that my reality's baths are not anything near as elaborate as the ones in this reality. We don't have exotic plants in our bathroom with a pool, glowing rocks, and water flowing down a wall." She walked over to the bath and added, "Although I miss a lot of things from my reality, I don't miss our electric lights and plain bathrooms."

He was watching her with a smile, and she lifted her hand to her hair, self-consciously. "What?"

He shook his head and said, "Nothing. I just remember the expression you always have when you see something new in this reality. I've missed it, and I can't wait to see it again."

Anika appeared at the door. She cleared her throat and said, "I'm sorry. Langley needs you, Grady."

Grady looked at Alissia and said, "You get cleaned up, and we'll talk more after breakfast."

Once he was out of the room, Anika shoved the door closed.

"Have you told him yet?" she asked.

Alissia gave a frustrated sigh. "Did it look like I've told him?"

Anika shook her head and said, "When are you going to tell him?"

"Soon. I just have to find the right moment."

Her friend scowled and said, "There is no right moment for this, Alissia."

"No, but it's definitely not going to be the first words I say to him, especially when he was nearly crying with me in his arms."

Anika frowned and said, softly, "Are you sure you've made your decision? Because once you do this, I don't want you playing with his heart."

Looking her friend firmly in the eyes, Alissia said, with certainty, "I'm positive."

"Okay. It's your decision, but once this is done, don't flaunt your relationship with Luke in front of him."

"I would never!" Alissia responded. As Anika turned to open the door, Alissia added, "Anika, hurting Grady is the last thing I want to do."

Anika did not respond, and Alissia soon found herself alone.

Chapter 30

Alissia took a long bath, dreading having to join everyone. She had too many secrets, and she was tired of all the lies. Her morning conversation with Luke got her to thinking about what he and Grady needed to tell the Eldership her reason for going to Pallen was.

Although Grady had led everyone to believe she had lost her memories and was a scared Lamian, that excuse would get Luke into trouble for not delivering her to the Northern Eldership. She needed to come up with something that would clear them both.

As she was getting dressed, an idea came to mind, and she began to ponder over all the details. By the time she walked out of the bathing room and set her pack on a bed, she began to feel excited that she might have found the perfect answer.

Everyone was eating breakfast, including Salvatore and his people, and he motioned for her to sit next to him. Luke and Grady were on the opposite side of the table.

"How are you feeling, my dear?" Salvatore asked.

"Much better. I just needed some sleep after what all happened the other night."

Lita walked over and roughly set a plate down in front of Alissia, revealing a tattoo of a dagger on the inside of her wrist.

When Alissia looked up, the young woman gave a forced smile before walking away. Salvatore began to pour some hot chet for Alissia, and she turned and asked, "Why doesn't your daughter like me?"

He smiled and set her drink down at the edge of her plate.

"She will enjoy your company soon enough. Right now, she's unhappy about the attention you have brought to the Lamians, and she sometimes has a hard time with her temper." He added, reassuringly, "She will soften up. Give her some time."

"Where is it you call home, Salvatore, if you don't mind me asking?" Luke said.

Salvatore answered, "I don't mind at all. Ask as many questions as you'd like. I'm from Taft."

"How do you feel about the pending war since you're not from our land?" Grady asked.

"Ah, but it does affect my trade. War is never a good thing. It makes it difficult trying to get through, and we have lost some of our own people at times due to wars in other lands."

As the men began to talk about the trading business, Alissia remembered a thought that had come to mind earlier, and she wanted to test it.

She looked at Luke and mentally commanded, *"Pick up your drink."*

When he set his fork down to pick up his drink, Alissia quickly looked away in surprise. Her heart began to pound as she realized she might be able to tell him what to do, just as with animals. Although it was not something she wanted to be able to do, she did want to know if it was a side effect to what had happened between them.

As she began to eat, she silently commanded, *"Get up and go to the bathroom."*

He immediately stood to his feet and excused himself before walking away.

Alissia knew this was a bad thing. Although a lot of women would love to be able to tell their boyfriends what to do, this went too far. If Luke knew, he would be furious, and she knew she was too honest of a person to try to hide it from him.

She pretended to be busy with eating as Grady asked Salvatore more questions about his trade business. By the time Luke sat back down, she was almost finished with her food. She picked up a pastry from her plate and took a bite, realizing it was delicious. She willed Luke to give her his pastry, and he picked it up, looked at it, and then took a bite before setting it back down.

"Where do you usually stay during the winter?" he asked Salvatore.

Alissia took another bite of her pastry and stared out in front of her in confusion. He had obeyed her first two commands but not the last one.

"Are you feeling well, Alissia?" Luke asked, in a concerned voice.

She realized all three of the men were now staring at her, and she quickly smiled and said, "I feel fine. I'm just easily distracted today."

Salvatore said, "You should get plenty of rest today. If you need anything at all, please let me know. If you're interested, I have a variety of herbs and spices from my land that can help you relax, if you would like to try them."

Alissia nodded, and Grady said, "Salvatore is not from our land, and you'll find that his food tiand spices are much different."

"I noticed a difference in the chet this morning," she said.

"Ah, we like ours strong and hearty," Salvatore said, proudly. He turned to Luke and asked, "Are we to meet this morning about the details?"

Luke gave a nod and said, "Yes. Let the others get started on baking, and we'll have more privacy. Would you like to meet here?"

"That will be fine," Salvatore answered.

Alissia turned her attention back to Luke and silently demanded, *"Give me your pastry!"*

He absentmindedly picked up his pastry and took another bite before setting it back down.

Lita and the two other women in Salvatore's group began to pick up the dishes and set them on a cart. When she came to Alissia, she did not even ask if Alissia was finished eating. Instead, she gave a dirty look as she picked up the plate before walking away.

Alissia stood up from the table and went to fetch her mouth cleanser from her pack. After a quick stop to the bathroom, she was ready to begin her day.

She found a seat at a small, iron table for two, and she watched as the others finished getting ready for the day. It did not take long before Anika, Langley, and Devon left to go help with the preparation of food.

When Alissia asked if she should go, Luke shook his head and told her she needed to stay for the meeting. Shortly thereafter, Grady walked over and sat down across from her.

"Feel better now that you've had a bath and eaten?"

"Much better."

He reached out and pushed a set of curls from her face. Gazing into her eyes, he asked, "How are you truly feeling?"

She thought for a moment before answering, "I'm a lot happier now that I know y'all are safe, and we'll soon be out of Pallen."

As she finished her sentence, thoughts abruptly began to flood through her mind.

Luke's lips were on her neck, gently teasing her as they traveled towards her mouth. His hand filled with her hair, and he pulled her head back and stared down into her eyes. The left side of his mouth curled into a grin.

"You are mine, Alissia," he said, his eyes searing into hers.

As his mouth came down on hers, she eagerly let him in and lost herself in his embrace. She felt his hand gripping the back of her neck, and she put her arms around him and pulled him in close.

"Alissia? Alissia, are you all right?"

Reality reclaimed control of her mind, and she looked into Grady's worried eyes. His hands were gripping hers tightly in the center of the table.

She tried to smile calmly as she pulled her hands from him and said, "I think I'm just feeling a little sick. You know, a little nauseous." As she stood to her feet, he did the same, and she added, "Maybe there was something in the food my body disagrees with."

Ignoring his response, she quickly turned and strode towards the bathroom. As she passed Luke sitting at a table with Reece, he glanced over at her, and she immediately looked away.

Once alone in the bathroom, with her back against the closed door, she took a long, shaky breath before asking, "What was that all about?"

The thought of Luke had been so powerful that it had completely taken over her reality. Everything had felt so real to her. She touched her lips with her fingers, still feeling his presence, as if they had just shared a heated kiss.

She closed her eyes and mentally commanded, *"Come knock on the door."*

It only took seconds before a knock came at the bathroom door.

"Yes?" she asked, trying to sound calm.

"Are you well?" came Luke's voice.

"I'm fine," she lied. "Go back and sit down. I'll be out in a moment." Then she mentally commanded, *"Knock on the door."*

He knocked again.

"I'm fine. You can go back now," she called out.

Only silence answered her, and she pulled her body from the door. She went to the mirror and studied her reflection to see if anything had changed. Once she was satisfied she still looked the same, she went to relieve herself and washed her hands.

She then told herself to get it together before she opened the door and walked out to find Reece, Luke, Grady, and Salvatore sitting on a group of chairs that had been arranged into a small circle.

As she walked up to them, Grady stood to his feet. "How are you feeling?"

She forced a smile and answered, "Much better."

"Are you sure?" he asked, worriedly.

She looked at each of the men watching her and said, reassuringly, "I'm fine." She then sat down on the empty chair between Salvatore and Reece. "Have I missed anything?"

Grady sat back down as Luke answered, "No, we're just getting started."

A loud, animal-like roar filled the air, and she remembered how she had heard the same sound when she had first walked into the barn. Once it finished, everyone looked at Salvatore expectantly, and he smiled and said, "I'd like to show you something after we're done with this discussion, if you don't mind, Lady Alissia."

"I don't mind," she answered.

He turned his attention back to the others and said, "Everything is ready for our departure. I have the proper paperwork to get out of the city."

"Are they not letting people out of the city?" she asked, in surprise.

Luke answered, "The city gates have been closed, and you have to complete a thorough search from the guards to get through the gates. Because Salvatore is a trader and we will be traveling in more than one carriage, it helps that he has the proper documentation showing he had already intended to leave the city on that date."

"What about the search dogs?" Reece asked.

Salvatore answered, "We'll be traveling with our own animals, and if the dogs bark, it will appear as if they're barking at them."

Luke added, assuredly, "We will be covering everyone's scent also, as extra precaution. However, I don't foresee the dogs being a problem."

"How will I go through without being noticed?" Alissia asked.

Salvatore said, "Our carriages have hidden compartments beneath them, and you'll be safe. We plan for Reece, Luke, and Grady to be hidden also. Devon, Langley, and Anika can easily pass as traders from our land, once we're finished with their disguise."

Alissia realized this was the perfect moment to act on the plan she had thought out during her bath. She cleared her throat nervously before saying, "I think it's time I was honest about something." She turned to Reece and then to Salvatore to let them know she was speaking directly to them.

"A lot of people have been wondering where I come from and why I've traveled to Pallen twice, and although Luke and Grady have been kind enough to guard my secret from everyone, I believe it's time the two of you knew the truth also."

When she glanced towards Luke and Grady, she found Grady sitting tall in his seat, staring at her expectantly. Luke, however, was leaning back in his seat with his arms crossed and his legs sprawled out in front of him. She thought she noticed a look of amusement on his face, and she turned her attention back to her plan.

"You see, I'm not even from this reality. The reason no one has ever seen a Lamian in almost two thousand years is because my people fled to another reality." She let her natural southern accent take over as she added, "I am from the United States of America, and people use electricity where I come from. We don't even have bella flowers."

By now, Grady's anxious stare had lessened, and he was studying her with an expression she could not read. Glancing at Luke, she thought she saw the side of his mouth twitch, and she turned her attention to Reece.

"When I met Luke, he was adamant that I return with him to the Northern Eldership. In fact, he did not take my no for an answer, and to this day, I compare his actions to kidnapping. However, I would like it known that in the end, he tried to help me. Once I told him the truth and how I was desperately trying to return home, he did the honorable thing, and I am very grateful for the services of the Northern Eldership."

She turned to Grady and added, "And Grady, I want to thank you for all the research you did for my people in the library and for your attempt in getting me back home to them." She tried to appear sad, and at that moment, she would have greatly welcomed tears in her eyes, but without a reason at that precise moment, her eyes were completely void of tears.

She looked down at her hands and said, "I understand now that I might never be able to return home, but I want to thank both of you for your attempts."

Salvatore said, "My dear, how were you to get back home?"

She looked up at him and answered, "My people sent me here, hoping we could return one day. I was to study this reality and then go back to them, but I had to be at a certain location within Pallen on a precise date. Luke tried to get me there, but when I was taken to the castle, I could not leave. I missed my opportunity."

"Is there no other time you can get back to your people?" Reece asked.

She thought for a moment before answering, "Maybe. The moon and stars have to be in a certain alignment for this to happen. I tell you all this now because I'm tired of all the deceit. There's no point in it anymore.

"The reason I told the Eldership I had lost my memory is because they expected things from me I couldn't give. I don't have any special powers or abilities. For some odd reason they believe I can help win a war in this land, yet I have no idea how I could do that. Over time my people have lost much of their history. They've freely dispersed themselves across different lands and have easily blended in with the humans, which is much easier to do in our reality.

"We aren't anything like our ancestors and have become very humanized over time. The idea of coming to this reality was an attempt to get our people back to nature and hopefully find some history from our ancestors so we could become what we once were, or at least try."

She looked at each of the men before adding, sternly, "I want each of you to understand that I am tired of being kidnapped, forced into going places I don't want to, and I'm tired of people trying to take advantage of me." She looked at Luke and said, "I don't care if the Northern Eldership can offer me protection. I don't want to be a part of any Eldership. The same goes for Allure," she said, turning to Grady. "I will not spend the rest of my life being controlled by leaders of this land, and I will kill myself before that happens. Have I made myself clear?" she asked, looking around at each of the Eldership men.

"I might have another chance at returning home. I just have to figure some things out, and it won't be in Pallen. I think I can get home another way, and that is what I want to pursue."

Luke asked, "And will your people not come searching for you?"

She shook her head and answered, "No, that won't happen. I was chosen because I had the least to lose among my people. I have no family that will worry over my return, and it was my honored duty to come to this land. I knew all the risks before I came. I was told how our ancestors were killed. It was agreed that if I failed to return, this land wasn't safe enough for any of my people to return. Their safety isn't worth the risk."

"You came from another reality?" Reece said, disbelievingly.

Both Luke and Grady nodded, and Grady said, "It's true. I know of this reality, and although we have no way of traveling there, the Eldership has a way of studying it. However, I can't talk about it outside the Eldership." He looked at Salvatore as he finished his last statement.

Luke added, "It's true, Reece. We can talk more about it later."

The assassin shrugged his shoulders and said, "I understand." Looking at Alissia, he asked, suspiciously, "And they chose a female over a male to do this job?"

Grady answered, "It would seem that in the other reality, women are not as limited in their duties. Lady Alissia has often reminded me of that."

She smiled at Reece and said, "Women are put in military positions and can even rule a land." She then looked at Luke and added, "Women are just as smart as men, if not smarter."

"So it would seem," he said, with a nod.

Chapter *31*

After the meeting was over and Alissia had learned most of the details regarding how they would be leaving Pallen, Salvatore asked if he could show her something. She agreed, and they walked towards a large set of sliding doors at the far end of the barn.

He pulled out a key to a lock on the door, and once inside, she found a massive animal similar to a lion. The main difference being that his fur was entirely black, and his face looked as if it had been smashed. He was pacing inside a large cage.

"His name is Shade," said Salvatore. "Would you like to pet him?"

Alissia grinned. She had never been this close to a lion or any other animal this fierce, and the thought of being able to pet him excited her.

Salvatore unlocked and opened the door of the cage. He then motioned for her to enter the cell before him, and without hesitating, she entered the cage and reached out to the large cat.

Shade almost knocked her down as he rubbed up against her body, like a cat begging for attention. However, this cat was almost as tall as her.

Alissia reached out and began to pet the thick layer of fur surrounding his face. She found it to be extremely soft, like the fur of a rabbit. It took a moment before she reached the much shorter fur along his body.

When the bond took control of her, she learned that Shade was used to walking around freely and was normally treated like a pet by Salvatore's people. He did not like being put in a cage, and it made him restless.

After the connection between her and the animal had broken, she looked up to find Salvatore watching her, as if he was studying her.

"I see you have an ability with animals," he said.

She immediately realized her mistake in thinking he knew certain things about her, and she said calmly, "I've always loved animals, and I've never been close to anything like this before. In fact, we don't have these where I come from. I was scared at first, but he seems friendly. How did you train him?"

He seemed to consider her words before answering, "The Lamians trained him, and he is one of many they have trained for us. We keep him around for our protection." He then added, "You didn't seem too scared of him when you walked into the cage."

She smiled and said, "I guess I trusted you when you opened the cage and motioned for me to enter. Was I wrong for doing that?"

He shook his head. "No, Lady Alissia. I'm sorry if I've made you uncomfortable. You seem to be full of surprises. Is it true you come from another reality, or was that all for Reece's benefit, as well as claiming to be a Lamian?"

She nodded. "I am from another reality, and I can tell you many things about it if you would like. As for claiming to be a true Lamian, I do not want humans to learn that the Lamians have the power to change someone." She looked hard into his eyes and added, "I am of the belief that humans need to know as little as possible about the Lamians."

He stepped out of the cage and responded, "I agree. And I would also very much like to hear about your homeland."

She gave Shade one last stroke along his back before joining Salvatore. As he locked the cage, he asked, "Is that where your Lamians are, the ones that changed you?"

"I believe that's what I said," she answered.

As they walked back into the open area of the barn, she found the other three men still sitting where she and Salvatore had left them. She silently commanded, *"Get up and go to the bathroom."*

She then watched as Luke got up from his seat and walked towards the bathroom.

Alissia sat back down beside Reece, and although he had never really spoken to her before, he now seemed full of questions. He and Salvatore quizzed her about her former reality, and she spent over two hours describing things they had never fathomed until now. In the end, they both decided their reality was much better, and they did not understand how people could destroy so much in the name of progress.

Alissia was happy she no longer had to talk in a fake accent, and she loved the idea of not having to pretend to be a helpless female anymore. She enjoyed telling Reece what women were capable of doing in her reality; although the idea of working alongside a female member of the league was not something he agreed with.

At least he was honest about his feelings. Grady denied having any thoughts of superiority; while Luke refused to say anything other than he was very happy the league was not filled with women. He also mentioned they could make traveling a nightmare.

Salvatore was hesitant to speak his true feelings, but in the end, he said women were made to be treated like delicate flowers, at least most of them. He then said his daughter, along with his dead wife, refused to be flowers, and they could easily break a man's arm, along with his heart.

By the time Anika and the others entered the barn carrying lunch, Alissia had gotten to know Reece and Salvatore somewhat better. The group of men had made her laugh, and she enjoyed talking to them, although she disagreed with a lot of their opinions when it came to women.

She sat with Anika and Langley while she ate, and they told her they had been getting to know some of Salvatore's people. He not only traveled with his daughter and son, but he also traveled with his two older nephews and their wives.

Lita did not join them in the kitchen, and both Anika and Langley had noticed her resentment towards them.

After the meal, Salvatore and his people left the barn, and Alissia excused herself to go to the bathroom. When she returned, she found Grady talking to Anika and Langley before they left to do more baking. Luke was sitting at a table with Devon and Reece.

She reached out with her mind and said, *"Train me to throw a knife."*

Luke got up and walked over to her.

"Would you like to have a knife throwing lesson now?" he asked.

She nodded and said, "Sure."

"I'll set everything up then."

As he walked away, Alissia stared at his back in confusion. Most of the time her mental commands worked, but not one hundred percent of the time.

She pushed her thoughts aside when she noticed Grady walking towards her. He stopped in front of her and asked, "So, when did you decide to tell people you weren't from this reality?"

"This morning while bathing. Was it a bad idea?"

"No, actually, it was a smart thing to do," he answered.

"At least now I can ditch the fake accent and talk normal again. I don't have to think about every little thing before I open my mouth, and most of all, I don't have to keep stopping myself from saying 'y'all' all the time."

He gave a small laugh and said, "Don't expect anyone to know what you're saying then."

"They never do, not even in my own reality, and I'm fine with that."

Grady glanced over his shoulder before saying, "Alissia, we should talk." He took her by the hand and led her into an empty stall. Once alone, he smiled nervously, and just like the first night she had met him, he seemed to be struggling with what to say.

"What's wrong, Grady?"

"Alissia, I understand we've not been together in two months, and things have been very difficult for you. I failed in protecting you."

"Grady, it was never your job to protect me," she interjected. "You can't feel guilty over something you had no control over. You didn't pull me into this reality, and nothing that has happened to me is your fault. Promise me you don't blame yourself."

He turned his face away from her, and she pleaded, "Grady, please. I already feel horrible for what I've put you and the others through. I ruined your lives."

His head shot back to her, and he said, "No, Alissia! I knew you blamed yourself, and I won't have that! I've told you we made our own decisions. I made the decision the moment I fell in love with you. No matter what happens, we can get through it together. I don't care about anything else but you, only you."

He took her face in his hands and gazed into her eyes. "We're together now," he said, softly. "Iand I'm not losing you again."

He doesn't deserve this. He doesn't deserve this, she thought to herself. Too many emotions filled Alissia, and she pulled her face from his grip and turned away.

"Are you ready?"

Alissia turned to find Luke standing at the door of the stall. He said, "Everything is almost ready. Reece is finishing now."

Greatly relieved by the distraction, she answered, "Oh, yeah. Thanks." Turning back to Grady she said, "I'm sorry, Grady. Luke, and maybe Reece, are about to give me a knife-throwing lesson. Can we finish this conversation afterwards?"

"A knife-throwing lesson?" Grady asked. He turned to Luke and demanded, "Since when is teaching Alissia to be a killer the right thing to do?"

Although Luke appeared calm, Alissia could feel anger coming from his body. It was not a feeling she would have normally felt. It was unnatural, seeping into her own body, and she was confused by it.

However, there was no sign of irritation in Luke's voice as he said, "Alissia has been placed in a position where it is in her best interest to learn to protect herself."

"By throwing knives, like a professional killer?" Grady asked, accusingly. "She's not a member of the league. She's not an assassin, Luke! Death has consequences, and she has a conscience!"

"She's not you either, Grady!" Luke snarled, no longer disguising his anger. He took a few steps towards Grady and added, "She's fully capable of dealing with the circumstances surrounding her. Some people don't have things given to them throughout their lives. She's a fighter, and you don't truly understand her if you think she'll sit back and spend the rest of her life watching others fight for her!"

Alissia had never seen the look of fury on Grady's face until that moment. Both of his hands curled into fists, and he took a few steps towards Luke.

"I know more about Alissia than you will *ever* understand," he said, through clenched teeth. "Yes, she's more than capable of dealing with her circumstances, but she shouldn't have to. She's been through enough!"

A sudden rage slammed hard into Alissia, and Luke stepped into the stall. "I agree," he snarled. "But we can't change her circumstances.

She needs to learn to protect herself, and if that means putting a knife through a man's heart, then so be it!" His lips curled up into an evil grin, and he added, "And don't you ever think you know *everything* about Alissia or that you're the only one that truly knows her, because you don't."

Grady's fist slammed hard into the side of Luke's face, and then he grabbed ahold of Luke and shoved him against the wall.

Luke licked the blood trickling from his mouth, and then he laughed.

"Enough!" Alissia said, forcing her way between them and pushing Grady back. "I'd like to speak for myself now since I know myself better than either of you."

Both men looked down at her, their eyes filled with fury. Luke's anger was unnaturally flowing through her own body, making it difficult for her to remain calm.

She placed her hand on Grady's chest and said, "I would like to learn how to protect myself better, and Luke has agreed to help me with that. This was my doing, Grady. Please understand, and don't be mad with me." When he did not respond, she continued, "Everyone is too emotional right now, including—"

"Is there a problem?"

Alissia turned to find Reece standing at the open door of the stall, and she immediately dropped her hand from Grady's chest and backed away.

Luke stepped up to his friend and said, "Everything's fine." He dabbed at his lip and added, casually, "Grady, here, believes Lady Alissia will be turned into an assassin if we give in to her request to learn how to throw a knife."

"He punched you?" Reece asked, incredulously.

Luke nodded and said, "It seems he's very passionate about Lady Alissia not having to experience the guilt of killing someone."

A knowing look came over Reece, and he replied, "Oh, I see." Turning to Grady, he said, "I understand why you would be scared of her having to live with the consequences of killing someone, but think of it this way; It won't hurt for her to learn how to defend herself." When Grady did not respond, Reece added, "If you want, we can give you lessons also."

Grady said nothing as he gave Alissia a quick glance before walking out of the stall, ignoring the two assassins as he passed by them.

As Alissia took a step to follow him, Luke said, "I'd let him calm down first."

She stopped in uncertainty, and Reece replied, "I agree. He looks upset."

She frowned but nodded before stepping out of the stall. She then silently watched as Grady walked out of the barn, and she guessed he was leaving to help with the baking. When she noticed the targets, she asked, "Where did y'all find all this?"

Reece responded, "Luke asked Salvatore where we could practice throwing our knives. It seems some of his men have an interest in archery. It would make sense, being they spend most of their time traveling with valuable items."

As she followed Luke and Reece to the center of the barn, Reece turned and said, "I can see why you want to learn how to protect yourself." He grinned before adding, "And since I'm one of the best throwers out there, I can understand why you would want to learn from me."

Luke laughed and said, "We both know who would win between us, and I'll be the one teaching Lady Alissia. We could use some of your knives though."

Reece glanced around before leaning down and pulling four knives from his boots. After setting them on the ground, he pulled a knife from each side of his hips, one from his upper leg, two knives from his upper arms, a larger knife from his back, and two small knives from each side of his upper chest. Once finished, twelve knives were in a pile at his feet.

While eagerly reaching into one of his pockets, he asked, "Shall we teach her about poison also?"

Luke chuckled and shook his head. "Only knives today."

Alissia stared at the two of them in disbelief. Reece seemed just a cocky as Luke, and she wondered if all the league members acted that way.

As Reece walked towards one of the hanging chairs, Luke began to pull his concealed knives from his body, and when he noticed Alissia reaching towards her boot, he quickly stopped her and whispered, "Keep yours hidden. I don't want anyone to know you carry a knife."

A few moments later, with Reece watching from the chair, Luke said, "Do you remember the grip I showed you?"

She picked up one of the knives and held it how he had shown her at the cabin.

"Good, girl," he said, approvingly.

Over the next four hours, Alissia was either throwing a knife or watching Luke and Reece throw one. Any time her wrist would begin to hurt, she would wait a moment for the pain to subside, and then she would begin again.

Although she had many things to be concerned about, she was determined to learn the skill of knife throwing, and she did not allow her mind to drift.

Salvatore and his people joined them for dinner in the barn, and Alissia took that time to do more tests with Luke. Although she sat with Grady, Anika, and Langley, she spent most of her time sending silent commands to Luke. He obeyed all of them without even looking her way, and by the time she had finished eating, she was certain she was able to control him. She also knew he would hate her for it, but she knew she would never keep that information from him. It would be wrong.

After the meal was over, Alissia got up to help clean, and Lita bumped shoulders with her, hard and maliciously. The young woman said something in a foreign language, and then she walked away before Alissia could respond.

Anger flared within Alissia. She had never been a person to be bullied, and it only took a moment of staring at Lita's back before she made the decision to confront her. Just as she took a step towards the woman, Luke stepped in front of her.

"Don't stoop to her level."

Alissia went to step around him, and he moved with her.

"Get out of my way, Luke. I just want to talk to her."

"The look in your eyes tells me you want to do more than talk. Am I wrong?"

She ignored him and tried to walk around him again.

"Oh, look. Here comes Grady. Maybe now is the perfect time for you to have a little talk with him." As Grady walked up, Luke said, "I believe Alissia was just looking for you."

Without waiting for a response, Luke walked away, and Grady said, "You want to talk?" He gave a confused look and added, "You look upset. Is something wrong? "

Alissia scowled at Luke's back before looking up at Grady. She shook her head and said, "It's nothing. I was just about to have a talk with Lita, and Luke doesn't think it's a good idea."

He nodded and said, "Walk with me?"

She took his lead, and the two of them strolled to one of the large swinging chairs on the opposite side of the barn. He sat down and patted the space beside him, and she joined him in the chair.

He was silent, and when she looked into his eyes, she could see the strain he was under. He had always seemed to know what to say and do around her, and she hated seeing him at a loss for words.

"Are you mad at me?" she asked.

"No, Alissia, I'm not angry," he said sadly.

She began, hesitantly, "Since being in this reality, I've had to depend on others for everything, and I can't stand it." She looked down at her hands in her lap and said, "It's not who I am, Grady, and I can't do it anymore. In fact, I have enough money and the means to pay back all the money you've spent on me, and more. I can—"

He let out a shaky breath and said, "Alissia, stop."

She looked up and saw the hurt in his eyes, and they silently stared at each other for a moment. A memory flashed before her eyes of their last night together. She remembered how happy he had been as she had trailed her fingers across his face. He had been filled with excitement that night, even talking about a surprise he had for her.

That memory seemed so long ago. She did not even feel like the same person anymore. She had lied and killed for survival. In another world or another life, she could have easily been happy with Grady, but not this one. Things were too complicated, and Grady deserved more. His life was perfect without her, and she wished he could see that.

"What are you thinking, Alissia?" he asked, softly.

She bit on her bottom lip and thought for a moment before answering, "I was just thinking about how perfect your life would be without me."

He shook his head and took both of her hands in his. As she looked into his eyes, she noticed how moist they had become.

"We've talked about this, Alissia. I love you, and I am nothing without you. Can't you see that? The Eldership means nothing to me anymore. For the past two months I've only thought of you, only you. I don't want anything else."

He paused before adding, "From the moment I saw you in the recordings all those years ago, I loved you. No other woman has ever touched my heart the way you have. I loved you before you even knew I existed, Alissia. No other woman could ever compare to you. They never have, and they never will."

He closed his eyes and let out a breath. Then he opened them and said, "Remember our last night together?"

She nodded.

"Remember that I said I had a surprise?" She nodded again, and he said, "I had made arrangements for us to be able to get married in secrecy within that week."

Alissia's heart stopped, and he said, "Tell me, Alissia. Would you have said yes that night? The night you were taken, would you have said yes when I officially proposed to you?"

Alissia looked down at her hands, held tightly in his. She fought the tears that threatened to come as she realized that was the night she had planned to tell him she loved him. That realization slammed hard into her, knowing she would have said yes to his proposal. If she had not run away, they would have gotten married that very week.

She then told herself if she had not run away that night, Alrik would have had Grady killed. Their marriage would have been short-lived, and she would have been a widow.

Images abruptly forced their way into her mind, and soon she was no longer in the barn with Grady.

She was outside, lying on her back on a blanket next to a large fire. It was night, and Luke was staring down at her while lying on his stomach and resting on his elbows.

"I love you, Alissia," he said. "Never forget that."

As he began to run his fingers through her hair, he smiled down at her. "Remember how I told you I would teach you the stars of this reality? I have so much I want to share with you. You are mine, Alissia, and I am yours."

His fingers began to trace the side of her face, and then he bent down and began to tease her with small kisses on her bottom lip. Her hand came up to find his hair—

"Alissia? Please, just answer that question," Grady pleaded.

Alissia blinked her eyes in confusion before looking out in front of her to find that Grady had turned the chair so they were now faced away from everyone else in the barn.

When she looked up at him, she did not know what to say. She did not even know what question he was asking. Her mind was playing tricks on her, and Luke's touch had felt too real.

As she searched for something to say, she pulled one of her hands free from his grip and placed it on top of his. She gave it a squeeze and let out a sigh before saying, "Grady, that's not an easy question to answer."

"It's not a hard one either," he said. He lifted her face and studied it, waiting for her answer.

She could barely breathe as she searched for the right words to say. His hand began to gently stroke the side of her face, and then it made its way to her neck. She could see the look in his eyes had changed.

Her body froze, as she mentally screamed, *This is wrong. This is wrong. This is so wrong.*

When his face began to lower, she placed her hand on his chest to stop him.

"Grady, I can't."

He stared down at her expectantly, and thinking hard over each word, she continued with, "I do love you. Honestly, I had never loved anyone before, and I didn't know how to tell you. Part of me wishes I had never left you that night." Her voice trembled, as she added, "I know I regret all the words I said in anger. I have relived that night so many times in my mind, and I hate that I hurt you. It was the last thing I ever wanted to do."

She paused before saying, "Then I realized that if I would have stayed, you probably would have been killed by Alrik's men."

"No, Alissia," he interrupted. "I had already made the decision we were to leave Pallen within days."

She shook her head and said, "You would have been killed, Grady. Death follows me wherever I go in this reality."

He reached up and wiped a tear that had escaped from her eye. She then rubbed both of her eyes and gave a sarcastic laugh.

"And I told you I wasn't the same person you had seen in those recordings, yet all I'm doing is crying now," she said, shaking her head.

She looked hard into his eyes and said, "Grady, you deserve so much better."

"No, Alissia," he said, firmly.

His mouth was on hers before she expected anything, and in a desperate attempt to show his feelings for her, he pulled her into his arms, determinedly. At first she was too stunned to do anything, and by the time she realized what was happening, he was in the middle of giving her a heated kiss.

"No. No. Oh, no, Grady," she said, pushing him away, gently, but firmly. "I can't."

She leapt from the chair and said, awkwardly, "I—I'm with Luke." As the words came from her mouth, she noticed Salvatore standing at the door leading to Shade's cage. From where he stood, she knew he had seen what had just happened between her and Grady. He immediately turned his head when she noticed him.

She then saw Luke walking towards them from the other side of the barn, and everything within her wanted to run. Dealing with Grady was one thing, but there was no way she could deal with Luke and Grady at the same time, not at that moment.

"I'm sorry," she said, looking down at Grady. Then she began to rush towards the sleeping quarters.

She shook her head at Luke and gave him a warning look when he started to veer towards her. The only thought in her mind was to get away. She needed to be alone, and the only place she knew she could lock herself away from everyone would be the bathing room.

She ignored Anika's cheery greeting when she walked into the bedroom, not trusting herself to speak. She quickly grabbed her pack, and as she made her way towards the bathing room, she silently prayed it would be empty.

Once inside, with her back against the locked door, she looked down at her shaky hands, and tears began to stream down her face.

Chapter 32

She did it. She broke the heart of the first man that had ever loved her, and she had loved him also. She still did, just in a different way. She thought over his words of how he had loved her before she had even entered this reality, and she hated herself for hurting him.

She turned her thoughts to Luke, and she knew in her heart she was making the right decision. She loved Luke, and he was her future. She just wished she did not have to hurt Grady in the process. He did not deserve having his entire world ripped apart because of her.

He needed to get back to Allure, as soon as possible. He also needed to become an Elder and fall in love with another woman.

She then remembered all the women she had met at the Eldership, and she cringed. Almost all of them had been shallow, and she could not think of a single one that would be good enough for Grady. She desperately hoped things were different in Allure.

Then there was Salvatore. There was no doubt in her mind he had witnessed what had happened between her and Grady. In his mind, he probably thought she was playing with Luke and Grady for her own pleasure. He already knew Luke had sworn himself to protect her, even against his own people. She had two powerful men at her side, both risking everything for her.

That would be questionable in her own reality, and this one was much more conservative. For a woman that had never spent much time around men, she now looked as if she was skilled in stringing them along.

And what if Luke decided he did not want anything to do with her once she told him how she could mentally control him at times? Would he resent her? He was not a man to be controlled, just as she would never allow herself to be controlled.

What if his body changed like hers? It was still too early to tell and could still happen. Something had happened. They could no longer kiss, and she had felt his anger earlier within her own body.

And what was happening with her mind? It had happened twice so far while talking to Grady. Her mind had pulled her into a place with Luke, as if it were real. Something was wrong.

Alissia got ready for bed, and she avoided everyone as she made her way to the solace of her big, swinging chair. Hours later, when everyone else seemed to be fast asleep, Mia climbed up and joined her, bringing some comfort to Alissia's tormented mind.

*****

"Some things will never change."

Alissia opened her eyes to find Anika staring down at her. She then shook her head and mumbled something incoherent.

Anika laughed and began to pull on Alissia's hand, and Alissia slowly sat up, realizing Mia was nowhere in sight.

"Have you ever woken with a smile on your face?" her friend asked.

Alissia responded with a scowl before she reached down and picked up a boot, being careful to conceal the knife. Once she finished putting on both of her boots, she stood to her feet. She turned to Anika and smacked her lips a few times before saying, "You're too perky in the morning, Anika. People like you scare me. What do you dream about at night, rainbows and unicorns?"

Anika laughed as she started to walk away, and Alissia followed her across the barn. After a quick trip to the bathroom, she stepped out to find Salvatore motioning for her to sit down next to him. Luke and Grady were already sitting across from him, and she dreaded having to face them.

"Sleep well?" Salvatore asked, as she sat down.

Alissia nodded and looked down at the bowl of warm oats waiting for her.

"You'll have to excuse Lady Alissia," Luke said. "Mornings are not her friend. Isn't that right, Grady?"

Grady looked at her and said, "I can remember a time she awoke with a smile."

Alissia remembered the morning she had woken up next to Grady on the sofa, and she nodded. Then she put a large bite of oats into her mouth and looked down at her bowl. She pretended to be preoccupied with stirring the oats for a moment before taking a sip of her drink.

As she set the drink on the table, she mentally commanded Luke to stop talking.

"I'm not your little pet, Alissia!"

Alissia immediately began to choke on her drink. Luke's voice had been loud and firm. It had also come from inside her head.

"Are you all right?" Salvatore asked, in a concerned voice.

Alissia nodded as she continued to cough, and he began to lightly pat her on the back.

"Oh, I'm sure she'll be all right. She's tougher than she looks," Luke continued, giving her a private wink from across the table.

She kicked his leg, hard, under the table, and he grinned even more when Grady winced from her lack of aim.

"Are you trying to fight with me?" she screamed in her mind. By now the coughing had stopped, and she turned to Salvatore and said, "I'm fine." She then looked at Grady and added, "I'm sorry. My foot slipped."

Grady nodded, his eyebrows raised.

"Why are you screaming at me?" came Luke's voice from within her head.

"How long have you known we could do this?" she mentally demanded.

Grady said, "How did you sleep, Alissia? Some of us were worried about you last night."

"Oh, please stop being nice to me," she thought.

"You want me to be mean?" Luke mentally asked.

"Get out of my head! Stop!" she mentally screamed. Meanwhile, she forced a smile across her face and said, "I slept well." She looked at Salvatore and added, "I adore those swinging chairs. They are extremely cozy and so much better than a bed."

"Ah, you like those?" he asked, grinning.

Alissia began to eat her food as fast as she possibly could without appearing rude.

"Want this?" Luke asked, mentally.

She looked up to find him holding his morning pastry while looking at her expectantly.

"No! Get out of my head!" she answered.

"Oh, so it's all right when you do it. At least I'm not ordering you around like some trained amoran," he thought, sarcastically.

Salvatore turned to her and said, "Lady Alissia, I imagine you would like some reading materials to take with you on our journey. I would be more than happy to show you to the library within the guesthouse this afternoon."

"I thought we haven't agreed to travel with him," she mentally said.

"We haven't," Luke answered. To Salvatore he said, "She needs to learn more about our reality. Do you have anything on plants, animals, or our natural resources?"

Grady said, "Lady Alissia studied a lot of those things during our time together. I gave her many books to read, as well as taught her how to dance and speak with my accent."

"Be nice, Luke! I swear. You better be nice to him."

"You realize he still thinks he has a chance with you, don't you?"

"Leave him alone, Luke. I'll take care of it," she thought.

She abruptly stood to her feet and smiled at the men staring back at her.

"That was delicious. I just realized I don't have my glasses on, and the sun is starting to get bright." She reached down and picked up her pastry, and then she motioned towards the sleeping quarters. "I'm just going to go get a pair. Y'all continue eating and enjoy."

She bolted before any of them had time to stand to their feet in a proper manner. Once alone on her bed, she found a pair of glasses in her pack and put them on. While nibbling on the pastry, she thought, *"Luke, can you hear me?"*

"Of course."

"You have a lot of explaining to do."

"I have explaining?" She could hear the sarcasm in his thoughts. *"You're the one that spent all day yesterday sending me mental commands. My only joy was to see your confusion when I didn't comply with all of them."*

"You did that on purpose?" Her temper began to rise, and she demanded, *"Do you have any idea how much thought I put into trying to figure out what has happened to us? It's not as if I want you to be my*

slave. I was trying to figure it out! You could have at least told me you can hear me speaking to you in your head."

"I think you enjoyed it," he thought.

She rolled her eyes and shook her head. Telling herself to be nice, she soothingly thought, *"Luke, I'm sorry if I offended you. It was never my intention. I'm just trying to find out what is happening to us."* When she did not hear anything back for a while, she thought, *"I'm sorry. I promise."*

Still nothing. After she finished eating her pastry, she thought loudly, *"Luke, did you even hear me?"*

"I did. I'm trying to have two conversations at once, Alissia. It's not as easy as it seems."

"Oh. How come I can't hear what you're thinking when you talk?"

He answered, *"I think the way this works is that you have to direct your thoughts towards me. That, and I can hear you when you feel panicked. When you're with Grady, your thoughts are slamming into me, as if they're everywhere."*

She began to chew on her bottom lip as she thought about all the things that had gone through her mind while she had been with Grady. *"You mean you hear all of my thoughts when I'm with Grady?"* she asked, cautiously.

"If 'oh, no. Please, no. This isn't right,' or 'I don't want this' is all you think when you're with him, then I don't understand what you ever had with him."

A sudden realization hit her, and she thought accusingly, *"Oh, my goodness! It was you! You did it!"*

"What have I done now, Alissia?"

"You made me think of you while I was with him. It was as if I was with you when I was really with him, and it confused me. You pig! I was trying to have a deep conversation with him, and you distracted me. Do you know what it's like trying to break up with someone for the first time in your life, while at the same time you're making out with someone else in your head?"

"I don't know how any of that would make you think I resemble a swine, and I don't understand half of what you just said. Thought. I mean, thought! And, besides, I didn't know if any of it would work. I was testing a theory."

"And you picked those two moments to test your theory?" she demanded.

"You seemed like you needed help, and besides, I didn't think it would work."

"How did you do it?"

He answered, *"I imagined doing things with you while directing my thoughts towards you."*

"Well, don't do it again when I'm with Grady. It's distracting."

"Well, maybe I didn't like some of your thoughts while you were with him. It was—"

"Was what? Finish your thought, Luke."

He answered, *"We're not thinking about this, and while we're at it, we need to train you to go to sleep at night. Your mind was everywhere last night, and you were restless. I felt every bit of it, and I was up almost all night. Alissia, too many people are trying to talk to me right now."*

Alissia immediately jumped to her feet and forced a smile onto her face before walking out of the room. She went to the bathroom and cleaned her teeth before pulling her hair up into a ponytail for the day.

When she walked out, Luke was still sitting at the table where she had left him, and she walked over and said, politely, "Excuse me, Luke. Can you help me set up the archery equipment? I want to get started with my practice."

He said, "Well, I believe it's already set up, but I need to give you some knives. I also need to watch you throw a few to help you get started."

He stood up from the table, and Grady and Salvatore nodded politely. Grady's eyes met Alissia's for a moment, and she struggled with her calm façade as she turned away.

"I feel that," Luke mentally said, as the two of them walked towards the archery equipment.

"Talk normal. It's freaky having you in my head. And what do you feel?" she asked.

"I never knew how emotional women were until now. When you're around Grady, you feel panic, especially when he kissed you . . ."

"You saw that?"

By now they were standing in the center of the barn, and he held a knife between them so it would appear as if they were talking about her lesson.

"I didn't see it. You screamed it into my head the moment it happened. I thought you were physically hurt and was coming to help you. Then you gave me an evil look as if I'd done something wrong. Minutes later, I felt an uncontrollable sadness, and I felt your mind racing all through the night."

He threw the knife and hit the target, before pulling another knife from his boot.

"Alissia, I don't think I've ever in my life experienced as many emotions in one day as I did yesterday. I am a man, and I'll admit that up until recently, females were not something I particularly knew or cared a lot about. I . . ."

"Do you regret it?"

"Regret what?" he asked.

"Us. Do you regret this?"

He glanced at the group of people before throwing the knife, hard and fast. After he let out a long sigh, he said, "I regret that we can't have a moment alone right now, and I'm beginning to wonder if I should even care about what Reece tells my people about us."

She could feel his frustration seeping into her body, as he added, "You should know better than to question whether I regret us,

Alissia. I'm sure you experienced certain things from my past, just as I did with you when you saved my life. And you should know how much I love you."

Her own fear immediately flooded through her as she realized what he was saying. "What do you mean you experienced things from my past? What did you see?"

"That's it." He swiftly grabbed her by the arm, and she could barely keep up with him as he practically dragged her into an empty stall.

"What are you doing? This does not look like we're having a casual conversation," she spat out, pulling her arm from his grip.

"I can tell Reece you were having a female moment of terror over your circumstances, and I was trying to calm you down."

She crossed her arms and said, sarcastically, "Really! That's all you can think of?"

"Not now, Alissia. I'll think of something to tell Reece, and I don't care what the others think about us. What matters now *is* us!"

He ran his hand through his dark, unruly hair and looked down at her with worry in his eyes. "Alissia, I love you, and I know you love me."

"What did you see, Luke? When I saved your life, what happened?"

He frowned and said, "I'm sure you saw things from my past too, emotional events in my life. We're even."

The realization of what he was saying slammed into her. She had never even considered that Luke had experienced the same thing that had happened to her during his healing. Not only did he know about her dark secrets, but he had also relived each of them, just as she had relived his.

Memories of the night her father had stabbed her came to mind, along with the night she had been raped while on a date. There was no doubt in her mind those were emotional events in her life.

He took a step towards her, and she backed away.

"The knife?" she asked.

He nodded.

"The date?"

He nodded again and took another step towards her.

She was aware of her own heavy breathing, and her hands balled into tight fists. She looked up at him and said warningly, "Don't pity me, Luke."

"Never," he said, soothingly.

She glanced to the side of him and told herself she had an opening, and then she jolted. Within the first step, he had her in his arms, and he pushed her body up against the stall. His hands grabbed hers, and he pressed them against the wall.

"Let go of me, Luke," she said, defiantly, while struggling in his embrace.

"No, Alissia. I can feel your panic, and you're not leaving me like this. I haven't done anything to you, and you're not going to push me away."

She looked around the stall hoping to find Mia, but they were completely alone.

"Please, Alissia, don't run from me."

The sadness she heard in his voice made her stop struggling, and she looked into his eyes. Neither spoke a word as they stared at each other, and after a while Alissia realized her breathing was back to normal. She no longer felt the need to flee Luke's presence.

He slowly released each of her hands. Then he pushed some stray curls from her face and pleaded, softly, "Promise me you'll never fear me again, Alissia. Never push me away or try to run from me again."

When she did not answer him, his voice cracked as he said, "Promise me, Alissia, you won't ever fear me like that again."

His fear now seeped into her body, and she realized he was scared of losing her. She had never meant to hurt him, and everything within her wanted to ease his fear and pain. She put her arms around him and rested her head on his chest.

"I'm sorry, Luke." She looked up at him and added, "I don't ever want to push you away. I love you."

They held each other tight for a long moment before she said, "I wonder where Mia is."

"I'm sure if we attempted a kiss, she would show herself," Luke said. Alissia laughed, and he pulled away and held her at arms' length. "This is new, but we'll get used to it, Alissia. Whatever is happening to us, we're in this together, and I will never regret any of it. I will never regret you."

She smiled up at him and nodded.

"Now, we should get back out there." As he turned away, he added, "I'll tell Reece you suddenly felt overwhelmed, and I had to endure trying to calm down an emotional female. I'm sure that will stop any of his questions."

Before she could respond, he stepped out of the stall.

"Really, Luke? You can't walk away from my voice anymore. I get the last word, and you better think of another excuse!" she mentally yelled.

When she stepped out of the stall, the first thing she noticed was Salvatore watching her. He was standing at the door leading to Shade, and she immediately wondered what all he had seen when he had walked past the stall she and Luke had been in. He smiled before disappearing through the door.

Alissia turned her head in the opposite direction and found Grady staring at her. He was sitting alone at one of the small iron tables.

Chapter 33

Alissia spent the morning throwing knives with Reece and Luke. Luke thought she was a quick learner, and she was happy when he decided to teach her another way to throw. After seeing Luke and Reece with their many skillful throwing techniques, she was eager to learn all of them. Luke seemed more than pleased by her excitement, and he assured her that he would teach them to her.

Grady watched them from a distance for the first hour, but then she turned around to find him gone. She guiltily hoped he had joined Anika and Langley at the guesthouse.

As everyone ate lunch together, she learned Grady had spent some time with Salvatore discussing the trade laws and regulations within the land. He seemed happy in front of everyone, but each time their eyes met, she saw the sadness in them.

After lunch, she went back to practicing with her knives, and Luke began to give Devon a knife-throwing lesson. Soon everyone in their group was sitting down watching her and Devon throw knives.

Everyone was lighthearted and joking until Lita stormed into the barn. Luke was sitting down in one of the swinging chairs, and she marched up to him and yelled, "Do you have any idea what you've done?"

Luke stood to his feet but said nothing, and Alissia threw her last knife and started walking towards them.

"What were you thinking? You're wanted all over Pallen for the murder of Ian Durst and the kidnapping of his future bride! Why didn't you tell my father what you've done? They have you responsible for the murder of five men!" she yelled, jabbing her finger into his chest.

Luke remained silent as she continued her verbal assault.

"And I thought a member of the league knew how to be discreet with their kills! Everyone is talking about how you savagely murdered two of the men! Ian's head was nearly decapitated! How did you think that would go with his father and the Eldership? What were you thinking?"

Salvatore tried to coax his daughter into silence.

"No, I will not be quiet!" she screamed, pulling her arm away from him. "It's time we knew the truth! He didn't just kill those men! He savagely mutilated them, and everyone is talking about it!"

She looked at Luke in disgust and spit in his face before saying something in a foreign language.

In a flash, Lita's body was slammed to the ground, and Alissia was sitting on top of her. A wild look was in Alissia's eyes as she fiercely gripped Lita's shirt collar with shaky hands. "You have no right talking about something you know nothing about," Alissia said, through clenched teeth. "I killed Ian Durst, and Luke didn't lay a hand on him or the other man they found like that. Luke almost lost his life that night but not before Ian threatened to rape me in front of him."

A fury Alissia had not experienced since the days of fighting her father raged within her, and it took her a moment to force herself off the woman's body. As she stood to her feet, she realized all eyes in the barn were on her. Anika had her hands over her mouth, and everyone seemed to be in shock from her words.

When Luke reached out for her, she pushed him away and darted off towards the bathing room. She slammed the door shut and locked it, collapsing to the ground.

As she stared down at her trembling hands, memories flooded into her mind. The night her father had tried to kill her, an uncontrollable rage had filled her, and after that night, he had never been able to hit her again. She had learned to be the aggressor, and she had been excellent at it, as she would always attack him first and without any mercy.

She remembered the fear in his eyes as she would knock him to the ground and beat him. It had made her feel powerful to put him down and give him the same pain he had given to her for so many years. However, one night he had laughed, blood flowing from his nose. He had looked into her eyes from the ground where he lay, and she would never forget the words he had spoken.

"You're just like me. We're the same, Alissia," he had said, laughing.

Tears filled Alissia's eyes, knowing it was true. Not only had her father been cruel, but his father had done the same to him also. It was in their blood. It was who they were.

For years she had felt that rage silently burning within her, and only she was aware of what she was capable of doing when it was triggered. Fear was nothing compared to her rage.

Since moving away from Georgia, the rage had left her. However, she had felt that same rage twice within the past few days, the first being when she had killed Ian and just now, when everything within her had wanted to hit Lita.

"Alissia, open the door," came Luke's soothing voice from within her head.

She did not answer.

"You promised you wouldn't push me away," he thought.

"I'm not pushing you away. I just want to be alone."

"Same thing, Alissia. You're shutting me out, and I can feel what you're feeling now. It's not true. None of it is true. You're not evil."

She closed her eyes and leaned her head against the door. Images of sitting on her father's chest as she hit him mercilessly over and over filled her mind. Although she had weighed nothing compared to him, he had never been a match for her once she allowed her rage to take over.

Rage was an amazing thing. It was powerful.

"Stop! Stop it, Alissia!" She heard a movement from behind the door. *"That's it. If you don't open this door, I will break it down to get to you. Do you hear me, Alissia? You know I'll do it."*

"Please, just give me some time alone, Luke."

"No, because you're not alone. Now, let me in."

Alissia stood to her feet and took a few deep breaths to calm down. When she noticed her hands no longer shaking, she opened the door, and Luke stepped into the room.

She allowed him to hold her, as he sat with his back against the door and her head on his chest. They said nothing, and his hand tenderly rubbed her head.

After a while, her breathing slowly returned to normal, and the memories of her father began to fade.

"You can be a pain sometimes," she said.

He chuckled and kissed her on the head. "Are you back now?" he asked.

"What do you mean?"

"Your mind took you to an unhealthy place."

"Luke," she began, hesitantly. "You don't see the things I'm thinking about, do you?"

"It depends on your emotional state. A strong feeling comes over me, and sometimes I get pieces of your thoughts."

"What do you think everyone thinks now?" she asked, in an attempt to change the subject.

"Does it matter?"

"I saw their faces, Luke. Everyone was staring at me."

"Yes, they were staring at you, but look at what all happened. They weren't staring at you as if you had done something wrong. We were all surprised from the moment Lita stomped into the barn and started screaming."

He positioned her body so that she was sitting up and facing him.

"Alissia, nobody is going to judge you or think you're evil. You did what you had to do, and they understand that. I mean, you told them what happened. They almost killed me, and Ian wanted to rape you. You defended us both." He frowned and added, "I'd be dead right now if it weren't for you."

"Yeah, but now we don't know what I've even done to you," she said.

"You saved me, and we're still together. That's all that matters, Alissia."

"And now you're a wanted man," she said.

He shrugged his shoulders. "You just told Reece what happened, and he'll tell my people. They'll know I'm not guilty of those things, and Grady knows also. He's with Allure. Alrik Durst may have Pallen under his control, but Pallen is only one city within this land."

"Can Alrik use any of this to benefit him?" she asked.

"Oh, I'm sure he'll try to find a way, and he'll use it. But I'm not worried about it, and neither should you. This changes nothing, Alissia. I had already suspected something like this would happen."

"What do I tell everyone when they ask about it?" she asked.

"Nothing. You shouldn't have to relive what happened, and they shouldn't expect you to. I'll explain what needs explaining, and no one needs to know about how you healed me. That needs to remain our secret."

"I know," she said, nodding her head. "Unless you begin to change."

"We'll deal with that if it happens."

She looked at the door and said, "What are you going to tell Reece about following me into the bathing room?"

He grinned and answered, "You know how you women get, fragile little things. I had to come in here and calm you down."

"You're evil."

His grin grew even bigger.

She stood to her feet, and he did the same.

"Are you ready?" he asked.

"Thank you," she said.

"For what?"

"For being here."

He kissed her on the cheek and said, "And where else would I want to be?"

A low growling noise came from above their heads, and they both looked up to find Mia staring down at them from the rafters.

"We are never truly alone, are we?" Luke said.

"It's kind of freaky, like a pet gone psycho." When she noticed Luke's confused expression, she let out a sigh and said, "Never mind. I forgot to speak proper."

He placed his hand on her back and kept it there as they walked towards their friends. Salvatore's people were no longer in the barn, and when Alissia walked up to everyone, Anika walked over and put her arms around her.

Alissia stood awkwardly with her arms down at her sides as she allowed Anika to embrace her.

"Why didn't you tell me?" Anika asked, pulling away.

Alissia looked at her friend for a moment and then turned her attention to everyone else. She forced calmness into her voice as she said, "A lot of horrible things happened the other night that I never really want to talk about. Ian was not the person most people believed him to be, not even his own sister. Luke and I barely got away from a very bad situation, and I did what I had to do."

She made sure to look into each of their eyes as she continued. "One of the reasons I want to learn how to throw a knife is because I've learned that people are determined to control and use me, and I truly need to learn how to defend myself much better."

Reece stood to his feet and said, cheerily, "Then I guess we should continue with your lessons."

As he began to walk towards the throwing knives, Alissia smiled. She did not detect any pity from him, and she welcomed the change in subject. She began to follow him, but Grady quickly caught up with her. She stopped to hear what he had to say, but when she noticed the hesitant look on his face, she said, "You want to talk in private?"

"I would like to."

She nodded, and they walked towards one of the empty stalls. Once inside, he said, "I understand why you don't want to talk about it, Alissia. I just wish you would talk to me again. What has happened that you feel the need to distance yourself from me? Is it Luke?"

She considered her words carefully before saying, "I am with Luke now, and Reece doesn't know anything about it. As for not talking to you, I'm sorry. I've been doing more thinking than talking."

She frowned and said, "Grady, I stabbed Ian to death, and now I'm trying to figure out what to do next. Luke says if I go to the mountains right now it would lead others that way." She shrugged her shoulders and added, "I've got a lot of thoughts, and I'm not really talking to anyone. I'm focusing on learning how to throw knives, and I'm trying to determine whether Salvatore is being honest. I'm not really thinking about my love life that much, except that I don't want to hurt you. That's the last thing I want to do, yet I see the pain in your eyes."

When he did not say anything in return, she asked, "What about you? What are you, Anika, and Langley planning to do?"

"What do you mean?" he asked.

"Well, what do y'all plan to do next? Don't you need to get back to Allure to talk to the Elders about the possibility of a war?"

He shook his head and said firmly, "I won't leave you with a group of people we don't know anything about."

"But, Grady—"

"No, Alissia, and I'm sure Anika and Langley will agree."

She knew from his tone there was nothing she could say to change his mind. Instead, she smiled and said, "Reece is waiting on me, and I need to go practice."

It took a few seconds before he nodded, and she walked out of the stall. Reece was in the process of throwing the knives when she walked over to him.

"Ready?" he asked.

"Yeah."

"Has Luke or anyone showed you how to use a knife at close range?"

She said, "Luke showed me some defense moves but not with a knife."

He grabbed her right wrist in a surprise attack, and she quickly faked a kick to his groin before her left hand came up and forced his hand from her wrist. She then faked a sideswipe to his throat.

"Nice!" Reece said.

"Watch it, Reece. I know from experience she has a deadly kick," Luke said, walking up to them.

Alissia crossed her arms and said, "Only to those who deserve it."

After the two assassins worked with her on a new throwing technique, Reece suggested he and Luke spar. Luke eagerly grinned in response, and Reece took off his upper clothing.

Luke took off his jacket, pulled his shirt out of his pants, and rolled up his sleeves.

"You're going to soil your shirt?" Reece asked.

Luke shrugged his shoulders and challenged, "You going to make me sweat?"

Alissia began to practice her knife throwing, but the sound of swords clashing immediately made her turn back around. The sight of two highly skilled assassins fighting with a sword was too much of a distraction for her, and she was soon sitting in one of the swinging chairs watching them.

Although Reece was fast and powerful, he was no match for Luke. It was not long before Luke was giving out advice with some of his swings.

Both men were drenched in sweat once they stopped, and Reece had a bloody nose from Luke's elbow. Apparently, sparring did not just mean with a sword.

As Reece walked towards the bathroom, Luke walked over to her. He was breathing heavy, and he ran his hand through his wild hair as he said, "I thought you were practicing."

"Y'all were too distracting."

"Ah, you were enjoying the sight, were you now?"

She rolled her eyes and groaned. "You are so cocky."

"That's a good thing?"

"You don't know what 'cocky' means, do you?"

"Alissia, we don't understand a lot of what you say. We just go along with it. And don't be surprised when everyone is giving you strange looks now that you've decided to start talking in your natural tongue."

"Everyone else is nice enough to go along with it," she said.

"Ah, but I'm cocky, remember?"

She laughed. "That's not a good thing."

He raised his eyebrows and held out his arms. "Want a sweaty hug?"

As he stepped towards her, she laughed and said, "Don't you dare come near me. I have a knife in my hand."

He stopped and challenged, "I'm sure I can take care of that little problem."

In a serious tone, she asked, "Luke, does it bother you that you can't take off your shirt in front of anyone now?"

He shrugged his shoulders and answered, matter-of-factly, "It's better than the other alternative, which was death. Besides, I like it. You've branded me, Alissia. I'm yours now."

Her pulse quickened, and she smiled up at him.

He sat down on a hay bale and said, "You need to continue practicing with the knives. Eventually, I want you to learn how to throw from a horse."

"What? While moving?"

"That's the plan."

"I can't throw from a horse."

"You can, and you will," he replied. "And you're also going to learn other weapons. You have so much to learn." He slapped his hands together and grinned. "Are you as excited as I am?"

She stared back at him blankly.

"Up! Up!" he said, motioning to the pile of knives.

She went back to her practice, and soon Luke and Reece were both giving her advice from their seats. When she noticed the two of them staring at something behind her, she turned to find Salvatore and Lita walking towards them. Although the young woman held a crossbow in her hand, Alissia noticed it was not loaded or at a readied position.

Lita walked up to Alissia and held out the weapon. "Here. Take it. It's yours. And I can teach you how to use it, if you'd like."

Alissia stammered, "Oh, thanks. I—I'd like that."

She took the weapon from Lita's hands, and the woman pulled a pack of arrows from her back and held it out.

"Thanks," Alissia said, taking it from her.

Lita nodded, and the two women stared awkwardly at each other for a moment before Lita gave a quick smile and turned. Without a word to anyone, she strolled out of the barn.

Salvatore, now sitting on one of the hay bales, said, "What Lita means to say is that she's sorry." He looked around at each of them before adding, "I apologize for my daughter's actions earlier. She is high-spirited and tempered, just like her mother. It just takes her time to warm up to people, but once she does, you'll find there's no one more loyal and dedicated than Lita."

Chapter 34

Alissia spent the rest of the afternoon learning how to shoot a crossbow. She sat with Anika for dinner and listened to her friend talk about cooking with exotic spices. Although Anika had heard of some of the dishes Salvatore's people prepared, she had never known how to cook the foreign meals and seemed eager to learn.

Alissia was grateful her friend did not mention what had happened earlier that day, and she was once again reminded how Anika always tried to look on the bright side of things.

When Alissia asked Langley if he would make it home in time to help his father on the ranch, he shrugged his shoulders and said his father could manage without him. He also said he would try to send a message to him if he had an opportunity after they left Pallen.

After dinner Salvatore asked Alissia to join him at the guesthouse, and she agreed. As he shut the door to his office and she found herself alone with him, she could not help but wonder why they did not need a female in the room. She rationalized it was because they were no longer in the palace. All formalities were gone. Either that, or it was because they were not courting. The customs of this reality sometimes confused her.

She was just happy he wanted to talk to her instead of Luke or Grady. To her, it meant he valued her opinion and thoughts, even if she was a female. Although she was grateful for each of the men in her life, she was determined she would have a say in where she would be going once they left Pallen.

"I would like to show you something," he said. He unlocked a leather box sitting on his desk. She had not noticed it the first time she had been in the room, and once open, it revealed an object wrapped in a soft cloth. He carefully lifted it from the thick padding inside the box.

"Maybe this will help you to trust me a little," he said.

He pulled the cloth away to reveal something resembling a small crystal ball. It was the size of his hands and attached to a simple, stone base. He turned it upside down and pulled something from it before setting it on the desk.

"Have you ever seen one of these?" he asked, holding up a small, crystal. Although it had a subtle purple tint to it, the crystal was clear. It was about an inch in length and in the shape of a columned rod with a dull point on one end.

As he held it out for her to take, she said, "What is it?"

"It's a jade."

Alissia took it from his hand and began to study it.

He said, "The Lamians always wear these around their necks, and it takes many years for them to fully charge one. You can tell by the color how much power is in the stone. This one is extremely weak and has lost its color. A powerful jade would nearly be black."

"They wear them as a necklace?"

"Yes, it absorbs their power over time. Do the Lamians you know not practice this custom?" he asked, sounding surprised.

"They didn't share many of their secrets with me," she said.

"And, yet, they transformed you, and you agreed to enter another reality for them?" he challenged.

Alissia held out the jade and said, "I am from another reality. Do you not believe me?"

Taking the jade from her hand, he answered, "Yes, I believe you are from another reality, but I can't help but wonder about the Lamians."

Alissia casually sat down in one of the chairs in front of the desk.

"You've been very kind to me, and I thank you. However, trust does not come easy or fast for me, and just like you, the protection of the Lamians is my number one priority."

"I understand," he said, replacing the jade in the base of the ball. "Maybe this will help." While covering the glow stones in the room, he added, "This will work best with less light. The jade is very low on power, and I don't even know if it has enough for a connection."

"What are you planning to do?" she asked, cautiously.

Finished with dimming the lights in the room, he sat down at his desk and said, "This is how we can communicate while traveling. It takes a lot of power from the jade. We don't even use this, except in the case of emergencies. Since learning about you, I've had to communicate more with the Lamians, and that is why I've nearly drained this jade. I'm hoping you'll at least be able to get an image so you'll see that I speak the truth."

He began to tinker with the ball, and from where Alissia was sitting, she could not see exactly what he was doing. Once he set the ball back on the desk, he motioned for her to come closer as he stared hard into it.

Alissia stood up and walked over to stand at his side, peering down at the ball. By now, it was glowing and pulsing.

"Hopefully, someone will be around on the other side to answer," he said.

They both stared into the ball for a moment before the pulsing stopped and a face appeared before them. The old man's face was pale and thin, and his straight hair was long and light lavender in color. He wore dark glasses, and although his lips moved as if he was talking, no sound came from the globe.

Salvatore said, "We don't have enough power for sound, and I don't know how much time is left. Let him see you, and try to talk so he'll realize we've lost the sound. I know he's been waiting, and if you want to see his eyes, take off your glasses to see if he'll do the same."

Alissia leaned down and said in the old language, "We can't hear you." She took off her glasses and pointed at her eyes. The man in the globe responded with a frown, but he followed her lead and took off his glasses as well.

His eyes seemed to glow, and Alissia stared into the globe and studied the Lamian staring back at her. He seemed to be studying her face as well, and the two of them stared at each other for a long moment before the globe began to glitch. The last image she saw was of his hand motioning for her to come.

"Well, that was interesting," she said, sitting back down and replacing her glasses.

Salvatore began to uncover the glow stones in the room.

"That was Falto, one of the ancients," he said.

"What do you mean?"

Sitting back down, he answered, "Lamians live to be well over three hundred years old, and Falto is in his three hundreds. He is considered one of the ancients, or leaders, of his people."

"Oh," she said. "Do they all wear sunglasses like me?"

He nodded and leaned back in his seat. "Yes, in fact, the Lamians are the ones that invented glasses here in our reality. As you can imagine, it was for survival purposes. Living on a sunny island was challenging for them in the beginning, and they had to start making their glasses darker. The sun is too bright for them on the beach, and they live in the forest. They can only meet our ships on the beach in the dark, early morning hours or late in the evening."

"What do they know about me?"

"They only know what we knew in the beginning; that a Lamian was in Pallen. Now that he has seen you, he probably could tell you are not a true Lamian."

"How?"

"Your eyes are not as bright as theirs, your skin is not as pale, and you're taller than they are. Although he could not see how tall you are, he most likely noticed your eyes. They don't glow as much."

"Have you ever seen anyone like me?"

"No, and I don't believe they have either. They are very private, and we have never even entered their living area. None of our conversations are personal. However, I do know they wear the jades around their necks, and I've heard many stories passed down from my ancestors."

She thought for a moment before asking, "What will they want to do with me?"

"They are a peaceful race so I would not worry about your safety. I assume they are curious as to how you came to be, and I am certain they will want to hear about another group of Lamians. It has always been our belief they were the only ones."

He leaned forward and his face became serious. "I do need to warn you that they will not allow us to transport all of your group to the island."

"What do you mean?"

"As I have stated, the Lamians are extremely private, and we have many rules we have to follow. You have three men, a young boy, and a female in your group. You will have to choose one person to accompany you to the island, and once there, I don't even know if that person will be allowed onto the island with you or told to stay on the boat."

He studied her for a moment before asking, "Do you know whom you will be choosing?"

An uncomfortable feeling came over Alissia, as she knew he had witnessed her intimate moments with both Grady and Luke. She quickly made the decision to clear up any confusion.

She said, "It occurs to me that you may have the wrong idea about me. I know you have seen me with Grady and Luke, and I would like for you to know it's not what you think. In fact, before coming to this reality, I'd never been interested in men or romance at all. However, Grady has done a lot to protect me and has cared for me dearly. I owe him a lot."

He leaned back in his chair as she continued. "I don't know if you are aware of the circumstances of how I traveled with Grady to Pallen, only to be kidnapped."

He nodded, and she said, "Well, through the kidnapping, I was deceived into believing Grady had done something, which he had not. Later I found out he was innocent. However, Luke protected me, and I spent a lot of time with him while traveling back to Pallen. Although we hated each other in the beginning, I admit that once we got to Pallen, we realized we enjoy each others company."

She struggled for the right words before adding, "We have feelings for each other."

Alissia had never talked about men or relationships with anyone other than her few words with Anika, and she hated having this conversation. However, Salvatore nodded as if he understood what she was saying, and the look on his face appeared friendly.

He asked, "And now you have a dilemma as to which one to choose?"

"I have made my choice," she answered.

He seemed to be in thought for a moment before saying, "Love is a strong emotion, and undoubtedly, you know by now that someone will be getting hurt. All that I can do to better the situation for you and the unlucky man is try to keep him busy and distracted during our journey. Although it will not ease his pain, it will help to keep his mind from dwelling on that pain. Do you wish to tell me which man needs that distraction?"

Alissia studied Salvatore's face. He was old enough to be her father, and at that moment she did not feel as if he was judging her. It appeared as if he was sincere about wanting to help, and if he was offering, she was eager to accept it.

She frowned and said, "I've chosen Luke, and he will be the one accompanying me to the island."

He nodded and asked, "What about the others? Being that they cannot accompany you on the boat, I have an offer."

She looked back at him expectantly, and he said, "I doubt your friends trust me enough to leave you. What if they travel to the coast with us, and once we arrive at the ship, I can have more of my people accompany them to Allure? Hopefully it will give everyone enough time to see that my intentions are exactly as I've told you."

When she did not respond, he added, "I don't have to have an answer now. You can think about it during our journey. My offer will not change, and during our travels, I will do my best to keep Grady distracted."

"And why would you do this?" she asked.

"Why wouldn't I?" He smiled and added, "It's nothing for me to extend kindness to a man with a mending heart, and I can easily arrange the schedule of some of my traders to escort your friends back to Allure. However, if I am not trusted by then, I am certain Grady can easily get an official Eldership escort from one of the other cities. However, that depends on how this threat of war goes, although I believe many still remain true to Allure."

He stood to his feet and said, "You have plenty of time to ponder over my words. Now, we should find you some books to read. Your friend Anika has already chosen some for herself. I've picked out a few that will teach you more about our reality, but I want you to choose as many as you like. We'll be traveling with wagons and will have plenty of space to carry them."

He began to put the globe away, and Alissia spent the next ten minutes choosing books. Once finished, Salvatore was determined to carry them to the barn for her, and she allowed him the "honor." As they walked into the sitting room, Lita left her seat and came up to them. "Do you mind if we talk in private?" she asked Alissia.

Alissia looked at Salvatore, and he gave a reassuring smile. When she nodded at Lita, the younger woman stepped into the office. Once inside with the door closed, Lita said, "I apologize for my actions earlier. My father has informed me that you are not of this reality, and you were not aware of the danger you put the Lamians in.

"Our people can spread the rumors of you not being from this reality and that will help to discourage others from searching for more Lamians.

"As for what I said about your friend Luke, I'm sorry for my temper. We didn't know the circumstances of that night, and I made the wrong assumptions. I'm sure it must have been hard on you to have to do what you did."

Lita looked at Alissia expectantly, and Alissia nodded. "That's fine. I understand." Although she was still angry, Lita's apology sounded sincere, and Alissia knew she would eventually forgive the woman. However, she did not foresee them being the best of friends any time soon.

As Lita put her hand on the doorknob, she added, "Maybe I can help you with your crossbow lessons while we travel."

Alissia smiled politely and said, "Yeah."

Chapter 35

As the week passed by, Anika, Langley, and Devon continued to help prepare meals for the journey, and Grady spent a lot of time at the guesthouse with Salvatore. Each day Alissia practiced knife throwing and the use of a crossbow. Luke and Reece added self-defense lessons that often involved her being slammed to the ground.

The two assassins kept busy by sparring and training Alissia. They rigged the target so that it moved across the barn on a rope. Although frustrated in the beginning, her aim was improving greatly, and she could now hit a slow moving target.

Luke reminded her to complain about muscle aches in front of Reece so he would not get suspicious of her healing, and Salvatore gave her some cream to rub into her muscles at night.

Mia remained out of sight, but Luke and Alissia often enjoyed testing her. Any moment they found themselves alone, they would taunt their hidden chaperone by attempting to steal small kisses. Each attempt always got noticed and allowed them to see Mia or listen to her growl from a hidden location in the barn.

Although Alissia did not go into details about what happened the night of the escape, she did share with her friends how Ian had admitted he was responsible for the death of Emera's boyfriend. She told them how he had planned for it to look as if she and Luke had run away together.

The day before they were to leave Pallen, excitement filled the air in anticipation of leaving the city. Langley and Anika spent most of their day at the guesthouse, getting their disguises in place, and by the end of the day, they were barely recognizable. Langley's face, arms, and hands were covered in black-inked tribal tattoos. He wore gold rings in his ears, and two on his hands. His hair was covered in a wrap, and his clothing was colorful. His usual friendly and inviting face now looked intimidating.

Anika was covered in brownish-red floral tattoos along her hands, arms, and face. Unlike her husband, hers were much more inviting and pretty. She wore a lot of gold jewelry that made tinkling sounds as she moved, and her long, auburn hair was pulled onto her head into a wild mess of dreadlocks, with a wrap around most of it. If that wasn't enough, she wore a long, brightly colored maternity dress, showing off a fake pregnant belly.

All the women in Salvatore's group now had the tattoos on their bodies, and even Devon had a few small tribal tattoos. Alissia learned the tattoos were temporary and would remain on their bodies for a few weeks. Anika informed her that she had learned that Salvatore and all the men traveling with him had a lot of permanent tattoos concealed beneath their winter clothing.

Salvatore and his people were not from this land, and their customs, along with their food, were much different. They dressed Anika and Langley to the extremes of their land when it came to the tattoos and hair. Although some of the guards spoke Salvatore's natural language, they hoped Anika, Langley, and Devon would not have to speak.

Later that night, Grady sat down with Alissia to talk. By now, she and he had learned how to have a conversation without discussing their relationship. She knew it was hard for him, and she hoped it helped that she and Luke never displayed any affection towards each other unless they were alone.

Grady stopped asking intimate questions. However, she often caught him watching her whenever they were in the same room, and she would respond with a smile.

As they talked on their last night in Pallen, he told her that Anika's pregnancy disguise was hard for her. Although she pretended to be happy, Anika had been trying to get pregnant since her first year of marriage. She had already visited doctors and taken remedies to help, but nothing had worked. Worry had recently begun to set in, and now she had to pretend to have a baby in her stomach.

Alissia made sure to spend time with her friend that night, in an attempt to distract her from sad thoughts. She never mentioned what Grady told her. She just tried to give Anika an extra reason to smile.

Everyone woke before daylight the next morning, and they ate a quick breakfast before getting into their places. There were a total of four carriages they would be traveling in. Salvatore and Devon drove Shade's carriage, which was a large, covered cage on wheels. Salvatore's nephew named Carlo and wife, Edda, drove the covered wagon filled with their traveling supplies. His other nephew named Romeo and wife, Bruna, drove the carriage filled with art from Pallen they planned to trade. Santo, Salvatore's son, and Langley drove a carriage with more traveling supplies.

Part of the floor of Santo's carriage could be pulled back, revealing a hidden compartment. Alissia and Luke, along with Mia concealed in Alissia's cloak, were squeezed into the hidden space. A rug was placed over the floor, and three chairs resembling beanbags made of leather were arranged on top of the rug. Anika and Lita sat in the chairs, and two large dogs rode with them.

Unlike the other women in the group, Lita did not wear a dress and remained in her usual pirate-like clothing. Her only jewelry was a necklace and earrings, and her hair was pulled back into her usual braid.

Alissia learned through Anika that the young girl had resisted the attempts of the other women to "turn her into a proper lady," something that had been unsuccessfully attempted by many over Lita's entire life.

Grady and Reece were wedged into a tight-fitting compartment beneath Shade's cage, where Shade paced the floor above them.

Alissia and Luke lay on their backs with Mia between them. Space was limited, and although there were some small air holes along the sides of the hidden compartment, it was dark and cramped. They held hands as they stared up at the thin towel hanging above them. It was there to protect their eyes by catching any dust or dirt that fell from the wood as they traveled.

Alissia said, worriedly, "I told Fang to follow the city gates and go to the mountains to find the Lamians, but Mia said she had not seen him."

He responded, "Mia could have left before he made his way to the mountains."

Alissia scowled in frustration. "I just wish I knew where he was."

He squeezed her hand and said, "We'll go to them one day, Alissia, and Fang will probably be there waiting for you."

Once the carriage began to move, noise filled the air, and things began to get uncomfortable. When they stopped at the gates of the city, Alissia reached out with her mind and controlled the dogs at the guards' post. She told Shade and the two dogs traveling with them to act somewhat aggressive. In the end, the guards did a mild search of the carriages before waving them through the gates.

Time went by slowly for Alissia over the next hour. Not only was it loud when the wagon moved, but she could feel every bump in the road. By the time they stopped and parked on the side of the road, Alissia was miserable and eager to leave the cramped, hidden compartment.

It did not take long before Reece and Grady joined her and Luke in the covered wagon. The two assassins shook hands, and then Reece pulled Alissia in for a tight hug. He said a quick goodbye to everyone, and then he mounted the horse Carlo had saddled for him. With a quick wave of his hand, he rode off to meet his people. He planned to tell them Luke was helping Alissia find a way back to her reality, where she belonged.

Soon Alissia, Luke, Grady, Anika, and Langley were sitting in the covered wagon as it lurched forward. Alissia and Grady could easily hide in the hidden compartment if they were stopped by guards on the road, and Luke assured everyone he could slip out of the wagon before the guards made their way to them.

Anika asked, "Are you sure you want to go to this island, Alissia? Do you trust them?"

"You said yourself you haven't seen anything to worry about," Alissia answered.

Anika said, "Yes, but we've been deceived more than once already."

"Yeah, but I saw one of the Lamians in the globe. Remember?"

Luke said, "I believe we've all thought about this, and we agree that Alissia needs to find the Lamians as soon as possible. Although these are not the same ones that changed her, they can still answer many of her questions, and we don't want to lead anyone towards the mountains. It's too much of a risk to go straight there. We just have to be cautious and continue to learn as much as we can about Salvatore and his people."

Grady nodded. "We'll be with you the whole way, Alissia. We've all agreed we won't leave you until we know you're safe and with the Lamians."

"That's right," said Langley. He looked hard into her eyes and gave a reassuring smile, "We're not leaving you."

Alissia forced a smile onto her face. However, her eyes soon met Luke's, and they shared a private, knowing look between them. He was the only one she had told of her conversation with Salvatore, and he knew she and he would be boarding the ship without the others. Luke agreed with her that it was best to wait until everyone got to know Salvatore better before she told them.

When Alissia had asked what he planned to do with Devon, Luke had told her that the boy would be staying with them until he no longer could. He believed Grady to be an honorable man and would help with the arrangements for the young boy once they had to separate.

She had been surprised by his answer when she had asked him why he did not just send the boy with Reece. Luke had shaken his head and said firmly, "I did not use the boy, just to send him away the first chance I got. He will stay with me until he no longer can."

Movement from the cloak in her lap caused her to look down, and she was surprised when Mia's head popped out from her hiding place.

"Oh, how adorable!" Anika said.

Mia immediately left her spot in the cloak and pranced over to Anika.

A grin filled her friend's face. "She likes me!"

"Either that or she wants to shred your face to pieces," Alissia said, sarcastically. Although she had not spoken in the old language, Mia glanced back at her and slightly bared her teeth before turning back around to readily accept Anika's attention.

Langley reached over and gave the tiny creature a long rub down her soft back, and it was not long before she was purring loudly in Anika's lap, as Langley and Anika both lavished attention on her.

"Why doesn't she do that for us?" Alissia mentally asked.

"Don't let it bother you, Pixet. She's harshest with those she loves. You get the honor of seeing her true self."

"Are you comparing me to her again?"

Luke's laughter filled her mind. *"I love you, Pixet."*

"You're never going to stop calling me that, are you?"

"Never!"

Unexpected Peril

Alissia Roswell: Book Three

Chapter 1

Alissia Roswell jumped from the covered wagon as soon as it came to a halt. It had been over three weeks since she and her friends had left Pallen with Salvatore and his people. Since guards along the road often unexpectedly stopped them, Alissia spent most of her time traveling in the covered wagon.

Each time they were stopped, she would hide in a hidden compartment, and she was certain she would have already been found if it were not for her ability to control the guards' dogs.

By now, Salvatore and his people knew about her power over animals. When they had first met Alissia, they had kept the lion-like animal named Shade and their two dogs in a cage and away from her, fearing she could use the animals against them. Now that they knew each other better and some trust had been established among her friends and Salvatore's group, the animals were allowed more freedom around Alissia.

Although Mia often showed herself to Alissia's friends and the animals, the tiny creature continued to stay hidden from young Devon and Salvatore's people. Luke and Alissia rarely ever had the pleasure of being alone together so the resourceful, little chaperone no longer resorted to growling or using her teeth on the couple. However, Alissia was no longer fooled by the fur ball's cute and innocent appearance. She had seen what Mia was truly capable of doing.

Alissia stopped in the midst of a stretch as she noticed a bare tree in the shape of a skull. The tree was only one of many standing above the unruly brush and weeds covering the long distance between the trail and thick woodland.

"It's eerie," Anika muttered, standing beside Alissia and gazing into the distance.

As the two women took in their surroundings, a cacophony of sounds, including bullfrogs and evening insects, could be heard from the direction of the unsettling trees. It reminded Alissia of the nights she had gone frog gigging and fishing as a child. However, she had never seen a row of tall, barren trees trimmed into the shape of human skulls.

"Somebody had to carve those trees," Alissia said, matter-of-factly. "They didn't just grow that way."

"No, they didn't, and that is why we don't leave the trail tonight," Salvatore said, as he and Luke walked up behind them. "We rest, and then we leave first thing in the morning. Alissia, it would help if you made sure Shade and the dogs understood this also. Otherwise, I will have to cage them."

Alissia nodded, and Anika did not try to hide her concern as she asked, "Are you sure this is safe?"

"I've traveled this way more than once," the older man said, reassuringly. "This trail is recorded on some of the earliest maps, and some people believe the stones beneath our feet were placed here before the land was settled. If so, the people that live in that bog have been here for a long time."

"How do you know it's a bog?" Anika asked.

He answered, "Look carefully around at the animals in the area and the trees, not to mention the sounds. We're also in the lowlands."

He stepped aside, giving Grady room to join them. While Luke and Salvatore had been driving the wagon Anika and Alissia had ridden, he had spent the day riding with Romeo. He and Luke had stopped hiding from the guards within the first week of their departure from Pallen. They now impersonated traders, even allowing their facial hair to grow out to help with their disguise.

Grady unconsciously lifted his hand and began to scratch at the unfamiliar hair on his face. Studying the strange landscaping in the distance, he said, "I've read about this place, but I never thought I'd actually see it."

"What have you read? Is it safe?" Alissia asked.

His hand left his face, and he answered, "Seems so, at least, if we don't go near the trees. There are numerous records of people going insane after they got too close."

"Insane?" Alissia asked, incredulously.

He chuckled and said, "The only people to lose their sanity are the ones curious enough to go near the trees—mainly researchers, teenage boys acting on a dare, and even hunters. Many warning signs are posted along the trail so people are aware of the danger."

"Most people don't even travel this way," Salvatore added. "They're too superstitious."

"Smart," Anika said.

Salvatore grinned. "Traders, such as myself, know this path is free of danger, as long as you abide by the rules."

"What rules?" asked Anika.

"Respect the ones that possibly built this path and trimmed those trees as a warning. It's obvious they don't want to be bothered." Salvatore clapped his hands together and turned to walk away before adding, "We leave at daylight. I don't think I need to add how imperative it is for you to stay close tonight. This trail is saving us a week of travel and is worth the discomfort."

Before walking away, he added reassuringly over his shoulder, "Besides, we have Shade and the dogs to warn us of any danger."

As Alissia stared at his back, she shook her head and said, under her breath, "So we're taking the fastest route, not the safest one. Where have I heard that before?"

Luke laughed as he placed his hand on her shoulder and gave it a playful squeeze. "Don't worry, Pixet. At least this time I don't have to worry about you trying to run away, getting yourself into trouble."

She scowled up at him, and he laughed even harder as he and Grady walked away to begin their evening chores.

"That's it!" Anika said, slapping her arm. "I've got to put on some insect lotion. They're horrible here."

Alissia gave a smug grin and said, "I wouldn't know."

Anika shook her head and frowned. "You could at least try to get them to refrain from biting everyone else."

"You know it's not like that," Alissia responded, as she watched Anika climb back into the wagon. "Insects are different than animals, and there's so many of them. I've found that they leave me alone so maybe I should leave them alone also."

By now, a routine had been established among everyone. Since there were so many of them and they slept inside the wagons, it did not take long before their chores were completed each night.

The women prepared their meals during the day as they traveled, and as soon as a fire was lit, a pot of food was placed over it. Although traveling with wagons meant they had to stay on heavily traveled or constructed paths, it was much more convenient and pleasant than traveling by horseback.

They had already encountered many rainy days, and the wagons ensured that their belongings were kept dry. They also held a large supply of food so that they did not need to stop in a village to buy more.

The weather was getting much warmer, and many wild berries, fruit, and edible plants grew along the trails.

Alissia learned that the horrible-tasting murdock root grew abundantly in the wild during the winter, and when she and Luke had traveled together, he had only stopped in villages for her sake. If he had been traveling alone, he could have easily lived off the land. Although he had seemed indifferent and uncaring to Alissia, she now knew he had subtly tried to make her less miserable during that time.

Since the night she had saved his life, their relationship had greatly changed. She had learned a lot from the bond she had shared with him, and there was no doubt of his love for her. She had experienced it from within his own body during their bonding process, or whatever it was that had happened between them.

Her worry over what she had done to him had lessened over time. Other than their ability to mind speak and feel heightened emotions between them, they had not noticed any more changes. His hair and eyes had not changed color, and she was hopeful that the Lamians would have an explanation for why they could not share a kiss.

She did not allow herself to believe she would never be able to be intimate with him, as those thoughts scared her too much. She had never loved anyone as she did Luke, and part of her desperately needed to believe that one day they would have all the answers to their questions, and they would finally be able to be together without fear and danger controlling their lives. Sometimes she even allowed herself to imagine a distant future with him, although she never allowed herself to go as far as thinking they could have children and live a normal life.

Everything about her future was uncertain, except for Luke. She knew he would never leave her side, and she found comfort in that.

"I love it when I catch you looking at me like that," came Luke's voice from within her head.

Alissia blinked and was brought back to her current task of stirring the pot of bean soup over the fire.

"I was just pondering whether I like this scruffy look of yours," she lied.

"Is that right?" She could hear the disbelief in his mental words. *"And by scruffy, I'm guessing that means hot?"*

She laughed out loud at his attempt to use one of the slang words she had taught him from her reality.

"What's so funny?" Anika asked, setting a box of dishes down near the fire.

"Oh, nothing," Alissia stammered. "I just had a strange thought. That's all."

Anika crossed her arms and frowned. Studying Alissia's face, she said, "You've been distracted a lot lately."

Alissia gave a lighthearted smile, in an attempt to hide her guilt. No one knew about what had truly happened between her and Luke the night of their escape, and since then, Alissia often got caught not paying attention to those around her.

Although she and Luke did not have many chances to be alone together, they spent a lot of time sharing mental conversations throughout the day. Some nights she even drifted to sleep with the sound of his voice in her head.

She knew her friend had a reason to be suspicious. Numerous times over the past three weeks, Alissia had rolled her eyes or laughed out loud during one of her mental conversations with Luke, only to realize Anika was watching her with a worried expression.

"Anika, I promise nothing is wrong. I just have a lot to think about. That's all." As she spoke the words, her eyes glanced past Anika to where Luke was tending to the horses. His back was now towards them.

Anika's eyes followed Alissia's, and she was smiling when she turned back around. "I see," she teased, before walking away to complete her next task.

"See what you made me do!" Alissia mentally said.

Luke's laughter filled her head. *"I can't help it you can't control yourself when it comes to me."*

"Anika's beginning to think I'm going crazy."

"Start closing your eyes, as if you're resting," he responded.

"Oh, that will work perfectly while I'm tending to the food."

After everyone had eaten and all the food had been put away, everyone sat around the fire to relax. The animals sat with them, and Alissia noticed how they continuously turned their heads towards the eerie woodlands, as if sensing some unseen danger in the darkness.

In an attempt to lighten the mood, Salvatore began to play music from his viola, and the others from his family soon joined in with other instruments. Shortly thereafter, Alissia found herself resting her back against Shade as she watched Anika and Langley dancing to the music.

Everyone in Salvatore's group played a musical instrument, and on the nights they camped in a private location and did not have to use extreme caution, they would entertain Alissia and her friends by the fire.

Alissia highly enjoyed the folk-like songs, much different than what she was used to hearing in her reality. Some of them were fast, and everyone would laugh as they stomped their feet or danced by the fire. Others were slow, with the men chanting along with the music. However, Alissia loved the ballads sung by Edda and Bruna the most. The wives of Salvatore's nephews pulled emotions from her she never thought she could feel just from hearing a song. It did not help that each of the sad ballads were based on true stories of love and death.

On this night, the music was fast and fun, in an attempt to lighten the mood of the eerie surroundings. Alissia grinned to herself as she watched Langley give Anika a twirl.

A set of legs stepped in front of her, along with an outstretched hand. "Will you dance with me?"

Alissia smiled up at Grady and accepted his hand. Although they had not shared a slow dance on nights such as this, they had enjoyed playful dancing more than once during their journey.

Luke was not jealous of Grady, and Grady had not said or done anything to make the situation more uncomfortable than it already was. She knew he was still struggling with the end of their relationship, which was one reason she and Luke refrained from open displays of affection. The fact that she and Luke could be intimate through their thoughts had many benefits and helped them to get through each day.

In the middle of the second dance, Grady abruptly stopped and said, "Do you mind if we talk? Alone?"

Alissia tried to hide her surprise with a lighthearted smile, and she answered, "Sure."

As she followed him to the wagon she spent most of her time in, she glanced back at Luke and met his curious gaze. *"It's nothing. He just wants to talk."*

Luke turned his eyes back to the musicians and did not respond, mentally or otherwise. Alissia forced a smile onto her face as she turned her attention back to Grady.

He helped her into the front of the wagon before hopping up beside her, and they sat down on the driver's bench.

"What's up?" Realizing she was talking in slang from her reality, she stammered, "I mean, is there something wrong?"

He looked down at his hands in his lap, and after a short moment, he lifted his head and smiled. "Nothing is wrong. I just wanted to wish you a happy birthday."

"It's my birthday?" Alissia said, completely surprised.

He nodded. "I didn't think you knew, especially with the differences in how our realities track time, but . . ." He cleared his throat, awkwardly. "But, when I watched the videos from your past, I remember what day you had visited the tree on your birthday."

Alissia did not know whether to be happy or sad at that moment. Life had been too crazy since she had entered this reality, and the thought of her birthday had never even crossed her mind.

She gave a weak smile and said, "Well, at least I now know what day to call my birthday. I guess that's a good thing since this is my new life and home."

He reached beneath the seat and pulled out a small, wooden box. It was handmade with intricate carvings.

As she took it from him, she said, "It's lovely. Thanks."

He chuckled. "You didn't open it, Alissia."

"Oh, I thought the box was the gift," she said, sheepishly.

He shook his head and said, "No, there's more. It's not much, as I didn't know what to get you that . . ." He frowned and paused before saying, "That would be acceptable with your new relationship status. Hopefully this will do." He tried to give a smile and added, "It's also one of the only things available on this journey. Luckily, Salvatore is a trader from a foreign land, and this is something he just happened to have with him."

Alissia slowly opened the box to find an assortment of small, brightly colored crystals. She picked out a red one and lifted it up to her face to get a better look.

"They're beautiful. Thank you, Grady."

He grinned and watched her for a moment before saying, "It's candy, Alissia. You're supposed to eat it."

Alissia gave a small laugh before placing the piece of candy into her mouth. Looking up at him, she said playfully, "You knew I wouldn't know what it was, didn't you?"

The foreign, sweet taste of the candy took her by surprise, and she began to rub her tongue around the small crystal. Although she had tasted many new things, some good and some bad, since being in this reality, a new flavor filled her mouth.

"Oh, my goodness, Grady. Have you tried one of these? It's like . . . I don't know. This is good, really good." She reached into the box and pulled out a green one. Ignoring his shake of the head, she forced a piece into his mouth.

"Am I right?" she asked, watching his face.

He nodded and said, cheerily, "They're supposed to be yours, Alissia. And, yes, I tried one when Salvatore first showed them to me. They're from his land, made with a unique blend of spices." He turned his head away as he added, "I thought you would like them."

She recognized the hurt he was trying to hide. Not wanting there to be an awkward silence between them, she tried to sound happy as she said, "You always know what I like." She paused, struggling with what else to say. "You spoiled me, Grady."

As soon as the words left her mouth, she regretted them. He turned back to face her and said, softly, "But that's not what you want, is it, Alissia?"

She bit on her lower lip as she looked down and replaced the lid to the box of candy. When she looked back up, she said, "I will always love you, Grady. Unfortunately, my life is too complicated, and . . ." She stopped, remembering the last time she had told him he deserved better.

"I'm complicated, Grady. My new life is full of questions and all about survival. I'm sorry."

He abruptly stood to his feet and hopped from the carriage.

"Come. It's your birthday."

She accepted his outstretched hand and let him help her down, and when they began walking towards the fire, the music changed. Everyone stood to their feet and began to sing a birthday song in her honor.

She smiled awkwardly and then accepted a friendly hug from Anika.

"I didn't know it was your birthday today," Anika said, before pulling away.

"Neither did I."

Langley gave her a hearty embrace, with Alissia's arms trapped at her sides. Once he released her, he said, "So how old are you now?"

"I'm twenty-nine."

He glanced towards Grady, now standing near the fire with a thoughtful look on his face. "Grady didn't mention it was your birthday," he said, in a low voice. "I guess he wanted to share this moment alone with you."

The music stopped, and Salvatore walked over. He gave her a warm smile and said, "I hope you've had a pleasant birthday, Alissia. Since Grady informed me, I have taken time to ponder over a gift for you. The one I have chosen is something I do not have with me but will be able to acquire once we enter the port city."

Alissia gave an uncomfortable smile and said, "Don't worry about it."

"No worries, my dear. It is both an honor and pleasure to share this moment with you."

Salvatore's son Santo, along with his nephews Carlo and Romeo joined them.

"Edda and Bruna have something for you also," Romeo said.

Over the past three weeks, Alissia had learned that Romeo and his older brother were complete opposites. Carlo did not talk much, whereas Romeo had a playful personality and spent a lot of his time joking around with his younger cousin Santo. His wife, Bruna, was very pretty and shy, and she and Edda were cousins and seemed to be best friends also.

Alissia often found herself somewhat envious of the family bond among Salvatore's group. It was obvious they all enjoyed each other's company. Even Lita's occasional temperamental remarks did not seem to bother them.

There was something among them she had never seen or experienced for herself, and although she was happy for them, she often found herself wishing things had been different in her own life. They reminded her of the one thing she would never have.

"So is it a bad thing if I ask how old you are?" Romeo inquired.

Carlo said, disapprovingly, "You don't ask women that."

"Don't tell me you're not curious to know how old she is. She could be over a hundred," said Romeo.

"True," said Santo, grinning at Carlo's frown.

"Guys," Alissia interjected. "I'm only twenty-nine. Do I look a hundred?"

"You really don't know much about your future, do you?" Romeo said.

Alissia felt Salvatore's hand on her back. He said, "I expect you will age differently now, although I'm not certain."

Alissia shrugged her shoulders. "I don't know if anything is for certain when it comes to me."

"She's an enigma," said Santo.

"Really, Santo?" Carlo scowled.

Alissia could not help but laugh at Carlo's disapproval of his younger brother and cousin.

Romeo said, smugly, "See. She doesn't mind."

Lita stepped into the circle. "Here. Happy birthday," she said, holding out a closed fist.

Alissia held out her hand, and Lita dropped the small gift she was holding. "I make them," she said, somewhat awkwardly.

"Thank you, Lita. It's very pretty."

Alissia stared down at the three-chord wrap bracelet. It was made of woven material, tie-dyed in various shades of pinks, purples, and blues. A hand-carved, wooden button was used for the clasp. "Did you make the button, too?"

Lita nodded.

"Wow! Thank you," Alissia said, impressed.

"Aw, you did something nice, Sis."

Lita's elbow immediately went into her older brother's stomach, knocking the breath from him.

"I make them all the time," she said, as if it were nothing.

"We have something for you also," Edda said, excitedly. She and Bruna both stepped into the circle now around Alissia. They each held something behind their backs.

Alissia placed the bracelet in her back pocket and said, "Y'all didn't have to give me anything."

"But we want to," Edda answered. Bruna nodded in agreement. She then turned to Edda, urging her to go first.

Edda grinned and held out an old leather bag. "You have to look inside to find the gift."

Alissia took the bag and opened it to find one of Edda's knitted projects. When she pulled it out, she realized it was a grey, thick sweater. It was an open-front style, and she immediately noticed the amount of detail in it.

"Oh, it's beautiful," exclaimed Anika.

Edda grinned proudly. "I grabbed one of my smallest ones. Try it on to see if it fits," she said, taking the bag from Alissia.

As she began to put her arms in the sweater, Alissia said, "You made this?"

"I sell them, and I can teach you." She motioned towards Bruna and added, "We can teach both of you."

The sweater was thick and warm, and although Alissia would not need it any time soon, she loved it. She wondered how much time it had taken her new friend to make it.

"There's more," Edda said, reaching into the bag.

It took a moment for Alissia to realize what it was Edda was holding out to her. The knitted, black hat was big, much too big for Alissia's head.

Edda and Bruna both laughed at the confusion on her face.

"Here, let me show you how to wear it," Edda said, passing the old bag to her husband. "It fits like this."

The woman placed the hat on Alissia's head and pulled her hair up into it. Once finished, it not only held her hair, but it loosely covered her ears and the top portion of her forehead.

Bruna held out a mirror, and Alissia took it from her. As she stared at her reflection, Edda said, "See, it's supposed to fit like that. You can also wear your hair down with it. It's tight enough at the edges, either way."

Alissia grinned at Edda. "I love it."

"I know you won't need to wear it for a while, but they will definitely keep you warm next winter. I mean . . ." Edda glanced at Salvatore before adding, "Unless you're on the island. You won't need it, if you stay on the island."

Alissia shrugged her shoulders and said, "You never know. I may have other places to be." She passed the mirror to Edda and began to take off the sweater. "It's definitely warm."

Once she had taken off the sweater and hat, Anika took them from her, and Bruna held out another used leather bag. "Sorry. I didn't have anything else to put them in," she said.

"That's fine. Thank you, Bruna," Alissia said, taking the bag from her. She then opened it to find a knitted pair of leggings and long boot socks.

"They will keep you warm next winter, and you can wear the leggings under your pants or with a dress," Bruna said.

Alissia grinned. "I love them. In fact, all of this would be very expensive where I come from, and I have never owned anything like this before." To both the women, she added, "I really love and appreciate the gifts."

Edda said, "We can teach you." She looked at Anika and added, "Both of you, if you would like."

Anika nodded excitedly and said, "I know how to do the simple stitches, but I'm not near as talented as the two of you."

"I would love to learn how to make something, although we probably should start out with something small," Alissia said, causing the two women to laugh.

A short while later, everyone began to say goodnight and Alissia glanced towards Luke to find him sitting alone. He was staring into the fire, and she thought she sensed a bit of anger coming from him.

She asked Anika to carry her gifts to the carriage they shared with Langley, and as everyone began to get ready for bed, Alissia walked over to Luke. She stepped in front of him and began to study his face.

"Are you angry?" she asked.

"No."

"Are you sure, because I think I can sense it?"

He glanced towards Grady before standing to his feet and saying, "I'm not angry, Alissia. I'm just a little bothered that I was not informed it was your birthday."

"I didn't know either."

"Someone knew," he said, looking at Grady, who was now crawling into his bedding in a corner of Shade's barred carriage.

He then looked back at Alissia and gave a determined shake of his head. "No problem," he said, smiling. He picked up Alissia's hand and added, "We will have many years to celebrate together."

He pulled her body in close and lifted her feet off the ground. She gave an involuntary laugh when he playfully nuzzled her neck. After setting her back down, he gave her a kiss on the cheek and said, "Happy birthday, Alissia." He grinned playfully and gave her a wink before walking away.

She stared at his back for a moment before realizing she was being watched, and then her eyes met Grady's. After giving a quick smile, she turned away.

"You did that on purpose, Luke."

"Did what?"

"You knew he was watching."

"Can I not give you an innocent kiss without being accused of anything?"

As Alissia began to walk towards the carriage she slept in, she rolled her eyes and thought, *"You're not innocent, Luke, and you know it!"*

She heard the smugness in his tone as he said, *"I gave you the only gift I had on such short notice. What else was I to do? Maybe if Grady had not kept it to himself . . ."*

Alissia began to get ready for bed, and it was not long before she was wrapped snugly in her blanket. While Anika and Langley slept in a corner closest to the front of the carriage, Alissia curled up at the opposite corner, near the closed, back flaps.

The air smelled strongly of the lungona plant they used to keep insects away. The leaves of the plant simmered in a small container set on top of a tiny cooking stone.

"Are you sure we're safe?" Anika whispered to her husband.

Not wanting to eavesdrop on their conversation, Alissia began a mental conversation with Luke.

"Are you sure we're safe?"

"As long as no one enters the forest, we should be safe, Alissia. People have been traveling this way for many years, and nothing has happened on the trail. We also have Shade and the dogs, and I'm taking the first watch of the night. We should be fine, so you should get some sleep."

Mia crawled under Alissia's blanket and snuggled up next to her. The tiny creature did not seem worried about their surroundings, which also gave Alissia some reassurance.

"I would help distract you tonight, but I need to stay focused while on watch," Luke mentally said.

Alissia grinned to herself and decided to send a quick thought of her own to him. She began to imagine they were standing together on a beach under a full moon. *She wrapped her arms around his neck before pulling him down for a heated kiss.*

She then abruptly ended her thoughts and began to laugh to herself.

"Nice visual, Alissia. Now get some sleep before I get too distracted. You've given me enough to think about for the night."

"Goodnight, Luke," she thought, happily. She then pulled Mia in close and drifted off into a peaceful slumber, thanks to Luke.

*****

"She's waking up!"

The unfamiliar voice was raspy and in the old language. Alissia let out a small moan before noticing that the sound of bullfrogs and night insects was much louder than it should be. Her head felt foggy, and she struggled to open her eyes as she realized she was in a boat. She could feel the water's movement beneath the hard surface under her back, and she recognized the sound of paddling.

A hand immediately covered her eyes, and something was placed at her nose, causing her to cough from its stench.

"Shh . . . Rest now, little one. It's not time for you to wake."

Suddenly, it became impossible to keep her eyes open, and Alissia's mind drifted off into darkness.

Dear Reader,

Thank you for choosing the Alissia Roswell Series, and I hope you are enjoying her adventure. The third book in the series will be filled with more creatures and an intriguing landscape, and I hope you will continue on in her journey.

Writing a novel is a passion that takes an immense amount of time and effort, and I ask that you consider leaving a review on Goodreads or Amazon for the books in this series. It is the biggest way you can show your support, especially for a new author such as myself.

If you would like to receive insights into the next book, you might want to subscribe to my newsletter. I have only sent out three in the last six months, so I assure you there will be no spam. However, you will be the first to see the cover reveal and read the first two chapters of the next novel.

You can sign up for my newsletter at my blog and keep up with me at the following locations:

www.tiannaholley.com
www.facebook.com/authortiannaholley
www.google.com/+TiannaHolley
twitter.com/holley_tianna
www.tiannaholley.tumblr.com
www.goodreads.com/author/show/7140745.Tianna_Holley

Thank you for your support,

Tianna Holley

Writer of passionate, fantasy romance without the guilt.